D0064868

TERRIBLE ANGEL

"There is only one way to appease a ghost. You must do the thing it asks you. The ghosts of a nation sometimes ask very big things and they must be appeased, whatever the cost."

—PATRICK PEARSE
CHRISTMAS DAY 1915

TERRIBLE ANGEL

A NOVEL OF MICHAEL COLLINS IN NEW YORK

DERMOT MCEVOY

THE LYONS PRESS
Guilford, Connecticut
An Imprint of The Globe Pequot Press

10 9 8 7 6 5 4 3 2 1

Printed in the United States of America

Library of Congress Cataloging-in-Publication Data

McEvoy, Dermot.
  Terrible angel : a novel of Michael Collins in New York / Dermot McEvoy.
        p. cm.
  ISBN 1-58574-742-4 (Hardcover : alk. paper)
  1. Collins, Michael, 1890-1922--Fiction. 2. New York (N.Y.) --Fiction.
  3. Revolutionaries--Fiction. I. Title.
  PS3613.C43 T47 2002
  813'.54--dc21
                                        2002010342

DEDICATION

This book is dedicated to the memory of six people who have touched my heart and soul over the years.

Simone McGuire, my gentle, sweet lover whom God took from us too soon. I always called her an angel and now she is.

Joe Flaherty, one of the great writing talents who knew the American Irish inside out—and joyfully tortured them on the pages of the *Village Voice* in the 1970s. He was my friend, hero, mentor, and the funniest man I've ever known. He showed us how to live and, courageously, showed us how to die. I think I miss Joe more each day. I know, somewhere up there, he's working on a celestial Daily Double right now.

Gil Unger, my longtime conspirator-in-cholesterol at the Palm Restaurant on Second Avenue, whose joie de vivre still inspires me to this day.

My first cousin, Kathleen (Kay) Bartley O'Neill of Great Western Square, Phibsborough, Dublin. Kay was always ready with a strong cup of tea, a bed when you were in need, and good craic in the kitchen with the rest of the family on a Saturday afternoon.

And for my parents, Mary Kavanagh and Dermot McEvoy—who worked hard in America, but never forgot Ireland in their hearts.

ACKNOWLEDGMENTS

I want to thank all on this page who were always encouraging and never seemed to tire—I guess—of the antics of Michael Collins as they daily took to the page.

Tom Dillon for his help on the Village Vanguard scene and for sharing the wise counsel of his late father who always believed that "a child is never a tragedy."

Neil Granger for being Neil Granger. *Semper Fi,* friend.

Sinéad and Phil Cane, who prove every day that the Irish and British can get along, a special thank you for your superb intelligence work.

John Mellor, for always being there, be it in New York or New Orleans.

Brian Unger and his daughter Holly, who were there that day in Rincon, Puerto Rico when the first words were written.

Gerry Bartley and Father Vince Bartley, my first cousins who are more like brothers to me, for their help in so many areas.

John McDonagh, teacher and bartender extraordinaire, for his help on the Gaelic dialogues.

Eamon Delaney for always being ready to fill in a piece of the Dublin puzzle.

Julie Gold and Larry Kirwan, two immense song-writing talents, who went out of their way to help me track down permissions to their work.

John Hamill for always having the right contact at the right time.

Dennis Duggan for his wise counsel.

John O'Neil for his invaluable computer contribution.

A special thank you to Pete Hamill and Frank McCourt, two old Lion's Head regulars, who took time out of their hectic lives to read and comment on my manuscript.

Christy Nolan, my gentle Dublin friend, for being a fan and always offering encouragement, especially when things seemed the bleakest.

Terry Golway, for sharing many an e-mail conspiracy with me.

I also want to offer my utmost appreciation to those who helped shape the manuscript:

Kate Thompson for her expert and insightful copyediting.

Tom McCarthy, my editor at the Lyons Press, whose advice I treasure and who I hope to work with for many years to come.

Joanie Leinwoll, whose encouragement, common sense and line-editing expertise will always be appreciated.

Tania Grossinger, whose advice helped this book immeasurably and also supplied the plot for another Collins book.

Michael Coffey, whose friendship I value the most on this earth, and whose advice and encouragement kept me going.

And lastly, Yvonne Nolan, my wonderful straight-talking Dublin friend, without whose incredible line-editing this book would never have seen the light of day.

IN AN OLD COURT-YARD,
SEEN FROM A LANE-WAY,
DOWN BY THE LIFFEY,
SOMEWHERE IN DUBLIN,
WHITENED WITH STONE-DUST
DWELLS AN ITALIAN;
AND HE MAKES ANGELS. . . .

WHAT DOES THE POOR DUSTY,
DUBLIN ITALIAN
KNOW OF THE GRANDEUR
OF HIS GREAT NATION?
GRIM CIVILISERS,
LAW-GIVERS, ROAD-MAKERS,
FOUNDERS OF CITIES,
DREAMERS OF ANGELS. . . .

I AM A LOVER
OF BEAUTY AND SPLENDOUR,
LOVER OF SWIFTNESS,
LOVER OF BRIGHTNESS,
LOVER OF SUNLIGHT
AND THE DELIGHTFUL
MOVEMENT OF WATER,
STARVING IN DUBLIN
FOR BEAUTY AND BRIGHTNESS,
STARVING FOR GLADNESS:

GOD SEND AN ANGEL!
NOT A MERE FIGMENT
FROM CHILDHOOD REMEMBERED,
GOD, BUT A FAR-FLASHING
TERRIBLE CREATURE,
AN AWFUL TOMB-SHATTERING
BURNING IDEA
OF BEAUTY AND SPLENDOUR,
A WINGED RESURRECTOR,
ONE WITH A MESSAGE
TO MAKE THE ANNOUNCEMENT:

NOT IN HIS DEATH
BUT IN CHRIST'S RESURRECTION
LIETH SALVATION.

—From "Angels" by Oliver St. John Gogarty

A Fenian's Who's Who

For those not conversant in the history of the Troubles (1916-1923), I thought a thumbnail sketch of some of the Fenian hierarchy might be appropriate. A "Fenian," by the way, is an elite—albeit usually unsuccessful—Irish revolutionary. It is a highly regarded term when used by nationalists and an epithet when employed by Unionists.

Kevin Barry—eighteen-year-old Dublin medical student who was captured by the British after an IRA ambush. He was hung by the neck in Mountjoy Gaol on 1 November 1920 and buried on the premises. In 2001 his remains were removed to Glasnevin Cemetery, where he was given a full state funeral as the *Taoiseach* (prime minister), Bertie Ahern, stood by. The rebel song dedicated to his memory is known to millions.

Sir Roger Casement—knighted because of his humanitarian deeds as a British consul in Africa, Casement remains the most enigmatic and interesting of the 1916 men. His job for the Rising was to land guns off the coast of County Kerry, and he failed miserably. There is still fervid debate today over the legitimacy of his "Black Diaries," which the British cited as proof that he was a homosexual and a pervert—and which were also used by the British to quiet the dissent that was beginning to swell against his execution. He was the last of the 1916 rebels to be murdered. Hung by the neck, Pentonville Prison, London, 3 August 1916. His remains were returned to Ireland in 1965, and he was buried in Glasnevin Cemetery with full military honors.

Thomas Clarke—although seldom credited historically, Clarke was the brains behind the Rising. He spent considerable time in New York—between serving time in British dungeons—and was the only naturalized United States citizen to be shot by the British. His wife, Kathleen—who gave Collins his first job and cover after the Rising—would become the first woman Lord Mayor of Dublin. He was executed, Kilmainham Gaol, 3 May 1916.

James Connolly—Jim Larkin's successor at the Irish Transport and General Workers Union, Connolly was a devout socialist. His Citizen Army joined with the Irish Volunteers to fight the British on Easter Monday. He was so severely wounded in the leg in the GPO that gangrene set in and the British were forced to seat him in a chair for execution, which they did, in Kilmainham Gaol on 12 May 1916.

Eamon DeValera—born in New York City in 1882, his mother sent him back to Ireland to be raised by his uncle. He was the only 1916 commandant not shot by the British, primarily because of his American citizenship. He spent most of the crucial years during the War for Independence in the United States raising money. Seeing the political dangers of negotiating the Treaty, he sent Collins to London in his stead. He turned against both the Treaty and Collins, prompting the Irish Civil War of 1922-23. Later turned to the ballot box and for almost four decades was either *Taoiseach* or President of Ireland. Died in Dublin in 1975.

John Devoy—an incorrigible Fenian. After serving time for his part in the Rising of 1867, immigrated to New York, where he was joined by such rebels as Clarke and Rossa. He made his living as the editor of the *Gaelic American*. As daring as Collins himself, he organized the voyage of the *Catalpa* that rescued Fenians from an Australian penal colony in 1876. He was Collins's moneyman in America and came to hate Eamon DeValera. Died in 1928 and is buried next to Jeremiah O'Donovan Rossa in the appropriately named Republican Plot in Glasnevin Cemetery.

Oliver St. John Gogarty—doctor, poet, writer, politician, wit, he served as Joyce's avatar for Buck Mulligan in *Ulysses*. In the tense days of August 1922 he had the emotionally gruesome task of embalming two of his friends, Arthur Griffith and Michael Collins. He was a close personal friend of W. B. Yeats and later went on to become an Irish senator. He once said of DeValera: "Every time he contradicts himself, he's right!" Died in New York City in 1957.

Arthur Griffith—a professional newspaper man, he founded *Sinn Fein* in 1905. A signee of the Treaty that established the Irish State, he became president when DeValera defected. Died at the age of fifty of a cerebral hemorrhage on 12 August 1922. Churchill, in admiration, referred to him as "this quiet little man of great heart and great purpose."

Seán Heuston—perhaps the most obscure of the 1916 rebels. He commanded a small group of men who held the Mendicity Institution against overwhelming odds for two days on the Liffey at Usher's Island, blocking the British advance on the Four Courts. Dublin's Heuston Railroad Station would be renamed in his honor. Executed, Kilmainham Gaol, 8 May 1916.

Seán Lemass—participated in the Easter Rising at the age of sixteen and through luck was released to his parents. He was one of Collins's gunmen in the assassination of the British Secret Service in Dublin on 21 November 1920, of which he was not proud. He often put off questions about his participation with the words, "Firing squads don't have reunions." Went on to become one of Eamon DeValera's trusted ministers, working the economic side. In 1936 he founded Aer Lingus. He finally became *Taoiseach*, in 1959 and began to turn DeValera's bankrupt Irish economy around. He was also the first to make peace overtures to Northern Ireland and became the first *Taoiseach* to visit the North in 1965. Died in Dublin in 1971.

Seán MacBride—a longtime agitator, he even traveled to South Africa to fight against the British in the Boer War. Husband of Maud Gonne, which made him a natural antagonist of W. B. Yeats, Gonne's romantic pursuer. Father of Seán MacBride, who would win the Nobel Peace Prize in 1974. Executed, Kilmainham Gaol, 5 May 1916.

Seán MacDiarmada—(John McDermott) Thomas Clarke's right-hand man. A master organizer, he is credited with reviving the Irish Republican Brotherhood in Ireland just before the Rising. Many were drawn to the movement because of his charismatic personality. Executed, Kilmainham Gaol, 12 May 1916.

Thomas MacDonagh—poet, writer, and professor, he was in command of Jacob's Biscuit Factory during Easter Week. Executed, Kilmainham Gaol, 3 May 1916.

Terence MacSwiney—the Lord Mayor of Cork who starved himself to death in a British prison in October 1920. His example would be followed by many nationalists, including Bobby Sands in 1981.

Pádraic Pearse—the "President" of the Provisional Republic, Pearse was a schoolmaster and poet. His father was English, mother Irish. Ironically, his full name was Patrick Henry Pearse. Did he ever hear the words of the American patriot Patrick Henry—"Give me liberty or give me death!"? He wrote *Poblacht Na h Eireann,* the declaration of independence posted around Dublin on Easter Monday. His previous claim to fame was as the orator at the Glasnevin grave of the old Fenian Jeremiah O'Donovan Rossa in August 1915: ". . . the fools, the fools, the fools!—they have left us our Fenian dead, and while Ireland holds these graves, Ireland unfree shall never be at peace." Executed, Kilmainham Gaol, 3 May 1916.

Joseph Mary Plunkett—son of a Papal Count, Plunkett was one of the most mysterious leaders. He traveled clandestinely in Europe trying to raise interest in the Irish cause. Dying of tuberculosis at the time of the Rising, he married Grace Gifford in his prison cell the night before his death. Executed, Kilmainham Gaol, 4 May 1916.

PROLOGUE

The English first came to Ireland in the personage of Strongbow in the year 1170. Strongbow would be followed by Henry II, King John, and a host of others. Their aim was twofold: to conquer the Catholic natives and to exploit the island economically. By 1652 these goals had become reality as Oliver Cromwell drove Catholics from their lands and scattered them to the west with the Cromwellian admonition, "To hell or Connaught!" Soon the plantation of Scottish Protestants into Ulster took place and the penal laws were effected, making Catholics basic nonentities in their own country.

The American and French Revolutions were to have a galvanizing effect on certain educated Presbyterian nationalists. Men like Theobold Wolfe Tone and Lord Edward Fitzgerald would copy the ideals of their American and French counterparts and establish the United Irishmen as the first modern Irish revolutionary movement. But pike was no answer to cannon, and the Rising of 1798 ended in brutal defeat.

In 1840 the devastation of the potato famine began. There is no real way to calculate how many died. There are only two revealing statistics. In 1840 the population of the island stood at eight million. By 1850 the population had died to four million. How many perished and how many escaped to America is still subject to debate.

What is debated today is whether famine was used as a brutal economic tool against the Catholic natives. Was there ever really a famine in Ireland? Farm animals and food were regularly exported from the island during this period. Economic times for the British gentry were good; the only famine was on the impoverished indigents who died for the want of their staple, the potato.

In the United States the Irish Republican Brotherhood (IRB) was formed in 1858. After the American Civil War these "Fenians" returned to Ireland and were thoroughly routed by the British in 1867. But unlike other revolutionary movements, the Fenians would not die. In North America they invaded Canada several times, seeking to "liberate" it from British hegemony. In Ireland they reinvented themselves as the "Invincibles" in the 1880s and began another terrorist campaign. They agitated for land reform, and this crusade was adopted by Charles Stewart Parnell and his Land League. Parnell, the head of the Irish delegation at Westminster, fought for Home Rule for Ireland, making both the Protestant gentry and the Catholic Church uneasy and, in a way, allies. Parnell succumbed to scandal because of his affair with a married woman, Kitty O'Shea. Her husband, Captain O'Shea, brought suit, and the court returned a verdict against Parnell and Mrs. O'Shea on November 17, 1890. Parnell would be dead within the year.

Exactly one month and one day prior to this judgment, on October 16, 1890, Michael Collins—without a pedigree—was born in Woodfield, the family farm near Clonakilty, County Cork. At the age of sixteen he secured a position in the British civil service in London, working in the postal system. In January 1916 he returned to Ireland as a member of the radical IRB and fought as a staff captain in the General Post Office (GPO) during the Easter Rising. Imprisoned in Wales, "The Big Fellow," as he was nicknamed, went about building an intelligence network, which upon his return to Dublin in December 1916 was put into effect. With the help of friendly Special Branch detectives inside Dublin Castle, the citadel of British power in Ireland, he was able to read top-secret documents before they reached the British.

Collins invented, trained, and supplied the guerrilla IRA, but one of his greatest triumphs was as Minister of Finance. With that cabinet portfolio he was able to bankroll the new state by hiding vast amounts of money collected for the National Loan (mostly from the United States) in banks right under the nose of the British. The British tried to find the money with the help of bank examiners, whom Collins promptly had assassinated. Soon the British were having trouble attracting bank examiners to work in Dublin, which Collins duly noted. So did the British. They put a ten-thousand-pound bounty on his head.

Collins's greatest coup was as Director of Intelligence of the IRA. On November 21, 1920, which became known as "Bloody Sunday," Collins's personal squad—nicknamed the Twelve Apostles—assassinated the entire British Secret Service in Dublin.

The following July a truce was declared and Collins—at the behest of Eamon DeValera—went to London to negotiate the peace treaty with Prime Minister David Lloyd George and Winston Churchill. On December 6, 1921 Collins signed the treaty that separated Ireland into the Irish Free State and Northern Ireland by declaring: "I may have signed my actual death warrant." DeValera went against the treaty, but the Irish people voted for it. A civil war ensued with DeValera's antitreaty forces on one side, while Collins and Arthur Griffith led the Free State. Atrocities were committed by both sides. On August 12, 1922 President Griffith died of a stroke, and Collins became head of state at the age of thirty-one. Ten days later Collins was assassinated by rebel forces at Beal na mBlath, County Cork.

With the ascent of Eamon DeValera's political star in the 1930s, the memory of Michael Collins and his marvelous deeds faded from Irish memory for nearly four decades. Not unlike a deposed commissar under Stalin, Michael Collins was forgotten in the country he had founded. It was not until the fiftieth anniversary of his death in 1972 and the publication of Margery Forester's *Michael Collins— the Lost Leader* that interest in Collins, the revolutionary and politician, was rekindled. DeValera's death in 1975 further cleared the air, and Tim Pat Coogan's twin biographies *Michael Collins: The Man Who Made Ireland* and *DeValera: Long Fellow, Long Shadow* did much to reevaluate, refurbish, and restore the reputation of Collins in the eyes of the Irish people. The reinstatement was completed with Neil Jordan's pacan of a film, *Michael Collins,* which starred Liam Neeson as The Big Fellow himself.

There is no historical evidence of Michael Collins having ever visited New York City.

That is, while he was alive . . .

1. | BEAL NA MBLATH
COUNTY CORK, IRELAND

"My God, I love this country," said General Michael Collins as he plopped down into the back seat of his Leyland open tourer staff-car, "even if this fookin' weather is killing me." Collins was suffering from a massive head cold, and his chest was filled with muck. "Here it is the harvest and I'm already wearing a winter overcoat," he said to General Emmet Dalton. "I'm all worn out."

Dalton knew what Collins meant. With the death of President Arthur Griffith only ten days ago and the Civil War still raging, Collins, the Chairman of the Provisional Government and Commander-in-Chief of the Irish Free State Army, had the weight of the world on his broad shoulders. He had come to Cork to rally the troops, assuage the rebels, and perhaps have a conciliatory chat with Eamon DeValera.

"God, Emmet," said Collins, "I wish I could meet with the Chief."

"Chief," Dalton spit out, "my arse. You're the fucking Chief now. DeValera has left you—and Ireland—high and dry." Collins did not reply because he knew it was the truth.

"Let's get going," Collins finally said. "It's getting late."

"Yes," replied Dalton. "I want to be out of here by dark. I don't trust this place."

"But these are my people, Emmet," said Collins. "What could happen to me in my own county?" Dalton gave him a look. "Come on, Emmet, stop worrying. Sure we even have two of the Twelve Apostles with us," said Collins of Joe Dolan and Seán O'Connell, two of the men from his personal squad, veteran shooters from Bloody Sunday.

"We're off, then," said Dalton tersely, and the small convoy began making its way through the Cork countryside.

At times heavy overgrowth choked the dirt road, nearly reducing it to a cow path and slowing the convoy's progress. The road took a steep drop into a mini-ravine and Collins looked up for the late-afternoon sun, which stubbornly refused to break through the overcast. The sloping hills and their boulders looked ever more gray and intimidating.

Collins looked on down the road and saw an ass and cart far ahead of them. There was something about an ass and cart that always delighted Collins, reminding him of his humble beginnings. "Will you look at that, now," said Collins with a smile. "Isn't that something! Sure he's moving faster than we are. I don't think we'll catch up to your man. Where are we now, Emmet?"

"Beal na mBlath," said Dalton as he juggled the oversized map in his lap.

"Beal na mBlath," said Collins, playing with his rather inept Irish-language skills. "The gap of the flowers. How lovely."

"The *mouth* of the flowers," snapped Dalton. He wondered what had overcome his hard-driving boss, the only man standing between Ireland and total chaos. Was he going soft?

Suddenly, shots rang out from above. Dalton knew instantly that they were in the eye of a perfect ambush. "Drive like hell!" he screamed to the driver.

"Fuck that," said Collins. And in the worst snap decision in the history of Ireland, he leapt from the staff-car and said, "We'll fight!"

The shots were coming fast from above. The machine gun in the accompanying armored car was silent.

"What the fuck's going on?" said Collins as he drew his pistol and fired away. He looked at the armored car and said to Dalton, "Cover me. I've got to get that machine gun going."

He leapt from behind the touring car, stood up, and fired his revolver before pivoting and beginning a sprint for the silent armored car. The last thing Michael Collins felt was like the full impact of a sledgehammer behind his right ear.

"Oh, my God," cried Seán O'Connell. "Mick, Mick, my God, Mick!"

Collins was facedown, blood gushing from his head. O'Connell cupped his motionless friend in his arms and knew there was only one thing to do. Before the soul escaped the body. Say a Perfect Act of Contrition.

He put his mouth to Collins's blood-soaked ear and intoned: "Oh my God! I am heartily sorry for having offended Thee, and I detest all my sins, because I dread the loss of heaven and the pains of hell . . ."

2. | THE KINGDOM OF HEAVEN

". . . But most of all because they offend Thee, my God, Who art all-good, and deserving of all my love," spoke Michael Collins. "I firmly resolve, with the help of Thy grace to confess my sins, to do penance, and to amend my life."

He was joined by a chorus with the final "Amen" that startled him into awareness. Collins opened his eyes for the first time in seventy years and looked into the face of his mother, who was cupping his head just as Seán O'Connell had. "Mammy," Collins said as his eyes grew huge with a lovely shock.

"Mícheál," said Marianne Collins, the *"Me-haul"* of the Irish further startling Collins. "You're still are my handsome baby," she said as she kissed him. Collins sat up from his mother's lap and saw his father as he remembered him—old and dignified.

"Daddy," cried Collins as he hugged the old man.

"Mickey," said Michael Collins Senior to his youngest son, whom he had fathered at age seventy-five. "And how is my favorite *garsún?* I was so happy and proud when you were born, son, for a child is never a tragedy."

"Oh, Daddy," said a weeping Collins, "why did you leave me? Why did you die? I missed you so much."

"I had to, son," said the senior Collins in the thick West Cork accent that made his English almost incomprehensible to the innocent ear. "For it was God's will."

Collins shook his head and then with the enthusiasm of a small boy said, "Remember, Daddy, when we would walk in the woods and you would tell me the stories of the Fine-men?"

"It was the *Fenians,* Mickey," said the old man with a proud smile, "and they were fine men!"

"And we would sit under the big tree and you would tell me stories of the faeries and their forts. And when I wouldn't believe you, you laughed and hugged me and rubbed the stubble of your beard against my cheek until it hurt."

"Did it, son?"

"Yes, Daddy, it hurt, but I loved it because you were my daddy." Then Collins the boy grew silent, and he bowed his head. "But then you died and what was I to do? I had no daddy and I missed you so much."

Mr. and Mrs. Michael Collins were silent, feeling the pain of their six-year-old son. He was dead and they were dead, but a child's pain remained.

"Come," said Marianne Collins as she took a handkerchief from the bodice of her dress. She put a finger inside the hankie, wetted it with her tongue, and rubbed a dirt smudge off her son's forehead. Just like when he was a child, he could feel his skin turn red in cleanliness. "There," said the mother, satisfied, "at least your penny-ha'penny face is clean now."

"And you, Mammy. You sent me to England. Why? I didn't want to leave you and Ireland."

"*Mícheál,*" she said, "there was no future for you in Ireland. You had to get out."

"And the first year I was away," said Collins, "you died."

"I didn't want to die, *Mícheál.*"

"And I couldn't come home from London to you when you died. No money and my mammy dead. You shouldn't have sent me away."

"Mickey," said his father, "you had to leave. Ireland's a poor country. She leaves few scraps for her dogs and even less for her people." Even in heaven, it was impossible to escape the Celtic diaspora. A century had passed, and a family was still in pain.

"Michael," said Tom Clarke, the old Fenian and instigator of the 1916 Uprising, as he put his hand on Collins. "Your mammy and daddy were right. If they hadn't sent you to England, there would be no Ireland today. By sending you away they gave Ireland a future."

Collins looked at Clarke and shook his head petulantly like the child he once was. "No!" he shouted as he stamped his foot.

Then he came out of it. He blinked his large blue eyes and looked about.

What was going on?

He looked around and discovered he was standing in fog. Not cold and damp like a London fog, but warm and comfortable. Part of it was so thick you could serve it up in a dollop, yet other parts were ethereal, somehow revealing the mystery within. He turned back to his parents just as they were absorbed by the heavenly fog. He reached out to them, but they were gone—as if God were taking them away from him for a second time.

Collins remembered the thunderous bang on his head and felt behind his right ear, touching his hair and scalp, but everything felt fine. He looked down at himself and saw his general's uniform. Someone had taken his greatcoat, and his tunic was open.

"How are you, son?" asked Tom Clarke. Collins looked around. Next to Clarke were other 1916 revolutionaries: Seán MacDiarmada, Pádraic Pearse, James Connolly, and Joseph Mary Plunkett, all as he remembered them—only all their maladies were gone.

MacDiarmada was without his walking stick—and his polio.

Connolly was standing, showing no leg wound from the GPO. And Plunkett—so sick at the end that Collins had to dress him and practically carry him out of the GPO—showed no tubercular scars on his neck. Pearse still had his cast eye and Clarke his glasses, but they were always like that. And, of course, there were no signs of the Kilmainham bullets or their quicklime graves.

"What's going on?" said Collins, startled. "You're all dead!"

"It's all right, Michael," consoled Tom Clarke as he took Collins by the arm and hugged him. "You are, too."

Suddenly it hit Collins. "Where am I?" he asked Clarke.

"You're in heaven, Michael. Here, we call it the Kingdom of God. This is heaven's reception room," said Clarke as he gestured at the fog, "a sort of triage for souls."

"Where have I been?" said Collins.

"Michael," said Clarke, "you've been in purgatory."

"Purgatory? But I don't remember." Collins looked around again. "Where's Dev?" he asked.

"DeValera," said Clarke, "isn't here." No one else spoke a word. It was beginning to sink in.

"How did *I* make it, then?" asked Collins.

Clarke laughed. "You can thank Seán O'Connell," said Clarke, "for that Perfect Act of Contrition. That gave you a chance, and Mr. Pearse here is a pretty good solicitor to have on your side. Both theologically and politically, he convinced the Lord that you belong."

But it had not been that easy. Clarke had always had a bond with his young charges like MacDiarmada, Pearse, and Plunkett. He was like the Fenian Pied Piper, always proselytizing, always eyeing the great prize. Clarke had been aware of Collins since 1914 when he was still in London. Then, he had used him to shadow Casement in America. When Collins arrived in Dublin in 1916 they had spent many hours

together at Clarke's tobacconist shop across the street from the Parnell Monument. What had cemented their bond were the actions of
Captain Lee-Wilson. When the rebels had been marched out of the
GPO and garrisoned next to the Rotunda Maternity Hospital, Lee-
Wilson had delighted in tormenting and humiliating Clarke. With
perverted panache he had stripped Clarke naked, right in the middle
of Rutland Square. Collins was furious. He looked at a young British
soldier who was averting his eyes, too shocked to look anymore at
the embarrassment. "What's his name, Tommy?" Collins had asked.
The soldier caught Collins's London accent. "Captain Lee-Wilson,
mate," had come the reply. Collins nodded. That night he hugged
the naked Clarke to keep him warm. Days later Clarke would die
before the firing squad, but Lee-Wilson's name was burnt into
Collins's soul.

It had taken years, but finally the word had come from Wexford
that Lee-Wilson was a Deputy Inspector for the Royal Irish Constabulary. "We'll let the boys of Wexford take care of this one, lads,"
Collins had told the Squad.

And in heaven, where he was being joined daily by the newly
rebel dead, Tom Clarke couldn't help but relish Lee-Wilson's bloody
assassination. "You take pleasure in tragedy, Thomas," Michael the
Archangel had chided him.

"No, I delight in justice!" Clarke had responded stridently. But
the Archangel would not be drawn into the debate.

Clarke and the Archangel did not speak again until the day
Collins died. No Collins, and Clarke demanded to know why. "The
Lord is taking Michael Collins under advisement," said the
Archangel cryptically. "He has been consigned to purgatory."

Clarke began to protest, but the Archangel raised his huge hand.
"Let Michael's soul rest, Thomas," he had told Clarke. "The Lord
knows what is best for your friend." Clarke, a small man with a

droopy mustache and a sometimes bewildered smile, looked sadder than the Archangel had ever seen him.

Pearse had battered the Archangel and the Lord with polemics on Irish history, supplying the reasons why Collins did what he did. The Archangel paid scant attention to them, but he remembered Tom Clarke's sad eyes.

Years later, the Archangel had approached Clarke. "Michael Collins will have to prove himself on earth once again if he is to become part of the Kingdom of Heaven, so sayeth the Lord."

"When?" asked Clarke excitedly.

"Not yet," said the Archangel, "the time is not right."

But every time their eyes met, the Archangel was forced to think one name: Michael Collins.

In August 1971 the British began internment in Northern Ireland. "When?" asked Clarke of the Archangel. The Archangel bowed his great head and softly said, "The time is still not right, Thomas."

When Bobby Sands and the other hunger strikers died in 1981 Clarke went to the Archangel, but before he could say a word he was told, "The time is too volatile, Thomas. Introducing Collins into that situation would only be folly."

When the Martin Twomey situation presented itself Clarke did not hesitate. "The time is right," said Clarke adamantly, and this time the Archangel agreed.

"So Pearse convinced the Lord that I belong?" said Collins.

"Yes, God was particularly troubled by the events of Bloody Sunday, 1920," said Clarke.

"They had it coming," spat Collins defiantly. "For they were the scum of the earth. By their destruction the very air of Ireland was made sweeter." Collins turned abruptly and went face to face with Clarke. The mentor had become the student. "My conscience is clear. There is no crime in detecting and destroying in wartime the spy and the informer. They have destroyed without trial. I have paid them back in their own coin."

"Indeed," said Clarke uncomfortably, "but we've been having discussions with the Lord about that and argued extraordinary circumstances on your part."

"We reminded God," spoke up Pearse, "that the British managed to murder two million Irish men, women, and children during the famine without the aid of one gas chamber!"

Collins looked blankly at Pearse. "Pádraic, what's a gas chamber?"

"It's a device," began Pearse in his best schoolmaster style, "used to kill large numbers of human beings with lethal gas. Just like the Nazis did in World War II to the Jews."

"World War II?" said Collins. "Another Great War? What year is it?"

"It is the year of Our Lord 1992, Michael," said Clarke.

"My God," said Collins, "seventy years in Purgatory! Thank God I'm in Heaven."

"Well, Michael," said Clarke, nervously clearing his throat, "you're not in yet."

"What?"

"You're on probation."

"Probation?"

"Probation," said Clarke. "As I said, I've been talking to the Lord about the struggle, and with the help of Mr. Pearse here He's beginning to see our side of it a little better. He feels very bad about Black '47 and He realized that we were forced to take extreme measures to, shall we say, equalize the situation."

"Like Bloody Sunday?"

"Like Bloody Sunday," said Tom Clarke. "He didn't believe you had to shoot all those British Secret Service agents, but Churchill helped you out."

"Winston," said Collins, smiling. "You could always make a deal with Winston."

"And some say he hoodwinked you," said Connolly in his sharp Edinburgh burr. Collins looked at Connolly, and his face blushed a bright red. He had been stung by the rebel he admired the most.

"Jim," cut in MacDiarmada, who immediately saw Collins's torment, and Connolly spoke no more after looking at those blazing black Fenian eyes.

Thank God for the Irish Republican Brotherhood, thought Collins.

"You also had a little help from another Michael," said Clarke. Collins looked confused. "Michael, the Archangel," continued Clarke. "He took a very special interest in your case. He believed in you, Mick, and he took your case directly to the Lord. Without the Archangel's intercession your soul would have been lost. The Lord listens to few, Mick, but He listens to the Archangel. It is said, Mick, that the Archangel's ability to fight evil is so powerful that he can even reach down into hell to retrieve a soul. In your case, he reached into purgatory. You two have a lot in common. The Archangel—like yourself—is a warrior who fights the battle of the faithful."

Collins stood silent, stunned with humility—which was not his natural state.

"Anyway, with the continuing troubles in the North, the Lord has reviewed your case and has put you on probation."

"More troubles in the North?" said Collins. "If I had lived . . ." His voice trailed off.

"When will it all end?" said Plunkett, sadly shaking his head.

"When Cromwell gets out of Hell!" returned Collins, who startled himself with his own vehemence. The others stared at Collins and realized how the British had found their match in this man.

"I know, Mick," Plunkett tried to soothe him "But at least we have the Republic."

"A Republic?" said Collins.

"A truncated Free State," spat Connolly, still crotchety. "I gave my life for a truncated Free State, and all they do is rename Amiens Street railway station after me!"

"Pearse got Westland Row," said MacDiarmada, laughing. "You should have gotten the Number 19 tram to Glasnevin Cemetery named after you, Mick." They all laughed except Clarke.

"Stop it," he commanded. "We're dealing with Michael's immortal soul here."

"Probation," said Collins. Then, out of the corner of his eye Collins saw a solitary figure approaching. He was one of those men who not only was naturally alone, but also had an air of desolation about him. He was immaculately tailored in diplomatic pinstripes, and his beard was exquisitely groomed. Dark, basset-hound sad eyes receded behind the hirsute cheekbones. He was an extraordinarily handsome man. Only MacDiarmada was as good looking. MacDiarmada had black-Irish features, but this man was saturnine. As he approached, Collins finally recognized him. "Sir Roger?" asked Collins.

"Michael," said Sir Roger Casement, "it's been a long time."

"New York, 1914," said Collins.

"A long time," said Casement. He did not greet the other patriots with handshakes or hellos, only with a nod. Tom Clarke turned his back on Sir Roger. Only MacDiarmada stepped forward and touched Casement's arm in greeting before going back to Clarke. Although Casement had converted to Catholicism just before he faced the gibbet, he was still considered a suspicious Protestant by this bunch of dead rebels.

"I'm sorry," said Collins.

"About what?" said Casement.

"Your diaries," said Collins.

"It's alright, Michael," said Casement, "the British tricked you."

Collins nodded. He was referring to the "Black Diaries," which the British cited as proof that Casement was a deviate. "A homosexual deviate!" the official had literally spat at Collins in the autumn of 1921 when he was in London negotiating the treaty and had examined Sir Roger's diaries. It came out *homo-says-u-all,* the way the British public school boys liked to roll it around in their mouths before they finally spat it out. Collins wiped the spittle off his forehead with a handkerchief and almost laughed at the fervor and the verbal gyrations of the glorified clerk from the Home Office.

"A deviate," said Collins, playing with the man.

"A homo-says-u-all de-v-ate!" the man repeated with even more vehemence.

"Whatever," said Collins, keeping a straight face and wondering what all the fuss was about; not knowing he had given comfort to the enemy. Collins knew what Casement was, and what did it matter?

"They didn't trick you often, but they tricked you this time." Casement smiled. "It doesn't matter."

"Yes, it does," said Collins stridently.

"No it doesn't. Nothing matters anymore," replied Casement.

"You're wrong, *Sir* Roger," said Clarke.

"I see where Mr. Clarke is speaking to me today," said Casement. Collins looked around. Plunkett was looking down at his feet in embarrassment. Connolly was looking at the sky. Pearse looked at Clarke and MacDiarmada, hoping they'd do something to lift the pall that Casement's arrival had cast.

It's heaven all right, thought Collins. Irish heaven. Everybody hates each other here. The grudges remain.

"Yes, *Sir* Roger," said Clarke, "I am talking to you today. The struggle continues. Right now it is the struggle for Michael's soul that is important."

"You know, Mr. Clarke," said Casement, "I never wanted that knighthood. In fact, the British revoked it before they hung me."

Clarke looked straight at Casement, still not trusting him after all these years. "You let us down," he said quietly, referring to the disaster at Banna Strand.

Casement shrugged. *"Fe ghlas ag Gallaibh."* Clarke did not understand him, but he had been zinged by the lone, erstwhile Protestant rebel.

"Imprisoned by the foreign enemy," said Pearse, who'd taught Irish to James Joyce. Clarke reluctantly nodded, and MacDiarmada gave a sly smile.

"Imprisoned by the foreign enemy," said Clarke finally. "Indeed you were, *Mr.* Casement. Indeed you were." The remark had broken the tension.

"Anyway," said Casement with some amusement, "I heard Seán talking about Glasnevin, and I thought I'd see what all the excitement was about. You know, Michael, we're not far from each other."

"Far from each other?" asked Collins.

"In Glasnevin," said Sir Roger. "We're buried only a quick walk apart."

Collins nodded. "So you finally made it home."

"I did indeed," said Casement with a sad smile. "Home at last." He shook Collins's hand. "I'll see you when you come back, Michael," said Casement. "We'll have a chat then."

"I'll look forward to that, Sir Roger," said Collins.

"God be with you, Michael," Casement said as he took his leave, exchanging nods with the other dead rebels. Clarke stepped back, allowing Casement an exit.

"Probation," said Clarke, returning to the subject at hand. "The Lord wants one more good earthly deed out of you before you're in. You know, it's just like the IRB up here—once in, never out."

"This is your last call, Mick," said MacDiarmada, the ex-Belfast publican who knew a few things about last calls.

Collins smiled. "What do I have to do?"

14

Clarke smiled back. It was the same Collins—driven and precise. "There's an innocent lad from Belfast in a New York prison. If you don't get him out by October 15 he's going back to stand trial in Britain for murder. And, as you know, the Irish in Britain don't win those kind of trials."

"I can do that," said Collins. "Sure, didn't I get Dev out of Lincoln Gaol in England?"

"You did indeed," said Clarke, "but this time it's all up to you. You'll have little support staff in place. You'll be in New York. It will be very difficult."

"I'll do what I have to do," said a defiant Collins.

"Ah, one other thing," said Clarke. "No violence. No killing. No maiming."

"No go!" shouted Collins.

With Collins's shout a brilliant light appeared in the sky and a wind whirled clouds down to his feet and out of nowhere there he was—at least twelve feet tall, immaculately tailored in white, with brilliant emerald-green wings. In his right hand he brandished an enormous gold sword.

"Why are you defying me, Michael Collins?" he demanded.

Collins stuttered, "My Lord!"

"I am not your Lord. There is only one Lord thy God."

"Then who are you?" asked Collins as Tom Clarke jabbed him in the ribs with his elbow.

"I am Michael, the Archangel. Why is my namesake defying me?"

"I wasn't."

"Don't lie to me," said the Archangel. "I said no violence. That is enough. You have maimed enough in your day."

"Then why did you stick your neck out for me?" shot back Collins.

"Because you are a good man who believes in justice, Michael Collins, and good men, even in heaven, are sometimes hard to find."

"You expect me to get this poor chap out of a New York prison without using force? You're not being realistic."

"Use your head, Michael Collins. You were always the smartest Fenian, the most innovative. There is no need for violence. I'll protect you."

"You'll protect me?" said Collins, dubious.

"If you trust in me, you need not fear, for I will protect you," said the Archangel.

"So why don't you just get this lad out by yourself? Why do you need me?"

"I don't need you, Michael Collins. But I need your soul." The Archangel's eyes were riveted on Collins, fierce as lasers. "Remember the words of St. Augustine: 'Good men are of greater value than bad angels.'" There was silence. "Those are the Lord's rules," said the Archangel. "You either play by them—or my old friend Lucifer can have you!"

"I'll play them as they lay," said a subdued Collins, and the Archangel nodded.

"Well then, son, God bless you," said Tom Clarke as Michael Collins evaporated before their very eyes.

3. | Dublin Airport

Ernie Fahey was getting nervous. They had assured him back in the Bronx that this Collins fellow he was to meet and take back to America would be on time. The flight would be leaving for New York in less than two hours and so far, no Mr. Collins.

Ernie went to the information desk. "I'd like to page Michael Collins," he said. At that very moment Michael Collins materialized on the departure floor at Dublin Airport. He stood there in the uniform he had died in—stained on the right shoulder, front and back, by his own dried blood—and passersby pointedly avoided him. "Someone call the Guards," one said.

"Michael Collins. Paging passenger Michael Collins on Aer Lingus Flight 105 to New York. Please make yourself known at the information desk."

Jaysus, thought Collins, they're already looking for me. I'm a wanted man!

Ernie Fahey kept scanning the floor for his man. He was looking for a man who matched the passport photo in his pocket. "Jesus," said Fahey aloud, "that must be him." He was looking at a country bumpkin out of another time who he was supposed to take back to New York for a big job.

"Collins?" Fahey asked as he touched Michael on the shoulder. Collins almost leapt in place as he spun around.

"Yes?" said Collins menacingly.

"I'm Ernie Fahey from New York. I'm here to take you to America."

"Good to meet you, Ernie," said Collins, relieved. "I've never been to an aerodrome this big before. It's quite intimidating."

Fahey suddenly noticed the blood on the tunic. "My God, Collins," he said, shocked. "What happened to you?"

Collins looked down at his front, saw the earthly blood, and didn't know what to say. "I had an accident," he finally uttered.

"Collins," said Fahey, "we've got to get you some new clothes. You're a mess. You look like you've slept in these for years."

"Seventy," said Collins.

"Seventy what?" asked Fahey.

"Seventy years," said Collins.

"Yeah, sure," said Fahey who was now quite sure that this country bumpkin was also a nut. "Come along," he said as he headed for the only men's haberdashery shop in the airport.

As they walked into the shop the lone clerk became distressed at the sight of the bloodied Collins. Fahey looked at the clerk, spread his hands apart, and said two words: "The works." He started opening up Collins's tunic and was pulling it off before Collins knew what was happening. "These your grandfather's clothes, Collins?" asked Fahey.

"No, they're mine. Specially tailored," Collins replied.

"Yeah, sure," said Fahey as he pushed Collins into a changing room. "Everything off!" Fahey commanded. "What is it, jockey or boxer?"

Collins thought for a second. He was no fookin' jockey. "Boxer," he yelled out. Soon shorts, shirts, socks, and shoes were flying back and forth for fit. Then Collins stood in new boxers in the middle of the shop looking for a suit.

"Here's a nice one," said Ernie looking at the price tag of one hundred pounds.

"No, Ernie," said Collins, "I like this one better." The tag said four hundred pounds. Fuck it, thought Fahey. It was all expense account money, anyway.

Collins stood in front of him, immaculate in the top half of a conservative dark blue three-piece suit, adjusting his French cuffs. Seventy years of purgatory, and he was still a fashion plate.

"Pygmalion," said Fahey sarcastically.

"Shaw," said Collins. It meant nothing to Ernie Fahey. "You know, I knew Shaw," said Collins.

"I'm sure you did," said Fahey as he pulled out his American Express card.

"I did," said Collins. "Sure I had dinner with him only three days before Beal na mBlath."

"What's Beal na mBlath?" asked Fahey. The store clerk, with Collins's trousers in hand, looked on, dazed, as if the sound of the enigmatically poetic *Beal na mBlath* had slapped him into another time frame.

"I think," said Collins still standing without his trousers and deep in thought, "I think I died at Beal na mBlath."

"Jesus," said the clerk as he handed the trousers to Collins, and their eyes met.

"How much?" said Fahey, a rebel in need of a history lesson.

"Six hundred and twenty-seven pounds in Irish *punts*," said the salesman, his eyes still bolted on Collins.

"What's that?" said Collins as the clerk absently took the American Express card.

"A credit card," replied Fahey.

"How does it work?"

Both the salesman and Fahey looked at each other. "Where are you from, Collins?"

"West Cork."

"That explains it," said Fahey. He quickly signed the charge and took Collins in tow. "Let's go get a drink." As the two of them left the shop in pursuit of the nearest bar, the salesman made the Sign of the Cross.

In the airport bar Collins found a table in back, and Fahey returned with two pints of Guinness. *"Sláinte,"* they intoned together, and soon the brown milk was flowing down Collins's throat for the first time since that fatal day at Beal na mBlath.

"Here's the deal," said Fahey, handing Collins two passports. "You'll use the American one going into New York, the Irish one coming back home. Got it?"

Collins nodded as he looked at the passports, both using an old photo taken at Christmas 1916. He looked at his date of birth, October 16, 1960. He was still thirty-one.

"Here's your Aer Lingus ticket. We're in first class so we can chat."

"What's this air boats, air fleet?" said Collins, translating *Aer Lingus* literally from the Irish.

"Aer Lingus?" said Fahey. "Sure it's Ireland's national airline. Here's your carry-on. You're an American on a business trip. Got it?" Fahey and Collins gulped their drinks and headed toward the check-in gate.

They waited on line together. "Next!" came the command from the beautiful ticket taker.

"We're together," said Ernie Fahey, presenting his ticket. Collins mimicked him.

"Can I see your passport for I.D.?" the ticket taker said. Collins saw Fahey present his blue American passport and followed suit.

"Michael Collins," said the Aer Lingus clerk. "I read about you in school. You were something!" she joked.

"I was?" said Collins smiling, delighted to know someone of the present generation had made a connection to his name.

"Enjoy your flight. Boarding in thirty minutes. Passport control at Shannon."

They stepped forward and headed toward the plane. "Little hussy," said Fahey to the amusement of Collins.

"Fine-looking lass," said Collins.

"Saints preserve us," said Fahey.

Soon they were in the departure lounge, looking out at the huge Aer Lingus Boeing-747.

"My God," said Collins, "it's gigantic." He admired the shamrock on the tail, then looked at its nose. "*St. Patrick,*" he said.

"God bless us, we'll be safe on that one," laughed Fahey as they boarded, heading left toward first class.

Collins sat down and watched Fahey strap himself in. He held the ends of his seat belt in the air, bewildered. "What do I do with this yoke?"

"Jesus," said Fahey in exasperation. He took the seat belt and secured it around Collins's waist, then pulled the strap to trap Collins in the seat. Collins looked out the window and saw the old landing tower surrounded by the newer buildings. The nose of the jet turned west, and Collins felt the surge of the four engines begin to hurtle the 747 down the runway, then the lift, shooting them clear past the Ballymun flats. The whine of the hydraulic system and the retracting landing gear startled Collins.

"It's all right," said Fahey to his right, "it's only the wheels coming up." Collins nodded and relaxed. It was a beautiful day, and Ireland was never greener. Collins thought of the tricolor he had seen on the rear of the fuselage, looked at the fertile land below, and felt pride.

4. | SHANNON AIRPORT, COUNTY CLARE

"How long have you've been in Ireland, Mr. Collins?" asked the American customs agent at Shannon Passport Control.

"Just twenty-four hours," said Collins. "A quick business trip."

"And what is your business, Mr. Collins?"

"I'm in the travel business," ad-libbed Collins. "I move people between New York and Ireland."

"Enjoy your flight," the customs agent said as he stamped Collins's American passport.

Minutes later their plane was heading down the Shannon runway, shooting toward the cliffs of Clare. This time the retracting landing gear did not disturb Collins. He was adapting to his new life.

"God knows when I'll see Ireland again," said Fahey as he watched the coast retreating behind him.

"I'll be back as soon as I can," said Collins confidently. "Let's get down to business."

In hushed tones Fahey explained the problem and the mission. Martin Twomey, a Belfast father of five, was caught up in a British sweep of the "usual suspects." Although he had no contacts with the IRA, he was imprisoned. In fact, his Belfast roots were tenuous. He had moved there from his native County Kerry when a cousin of his wife had secured a position for him at a local factory. Sentenced under the Special Powers Act, Twomey found himself sitting in the Maze prison. While Twomey was being transferred from the prison for a court appearance, the IRA had tried to break out another prisoner. During the shootout—in which two MI5 security agents, riding shotgun for the Royal Ulster Constabulary, were shot dead— the IRA man and Twomey were sprung.

"MI5," said Collins. "British domestic intelligence. I've dealt with them before. Cute 'hoors. Like their friends in 'G' Division, Dublin Metropolitan Police."

Fahey just shrugged. He explained how breaking out Twomey was a great publicity coup for the IRA in the nationalist neighbor-hoods of Belfast and Derry. Twomey, through no effort of his own, became a folk hero. For his own protection he was shipped off to New York and its anonymity.

"What happened then?" asked Collins.

"We got him a job at a bar on Third Avenue, Paddy Dolan's," said Fahey. "Everything was going fine until one day in 1989 a couple of FBI agents strolled in, ordered a couple of pints, and slapped the government bracelets on him."

Fahey went on to explain that by using O'Dwyer & Bernstien, civil rights lawyer Paul O'Dwyer's law firm, he had managed to delay Twomey's extradition until now. Even pleas from Amnesty International and the Irish government, both of which felt the Twomey case was a blatant miscarriage of justice, fell on deaf ears— both American and British.

"He's a bit of a hapless eejit, isn't he?" said Collins.

"Who?"

"Twomey." Fahey looked at Collins and saw he didn't suffer fools. Period. "He's not doing anything, gets locked up, then gets sprung by mistake, then gets arrested *again*. This man is a hazard to himself!"

"Well," said Fahey, a bit stunned by Collins's bluntness, but somewhat in agreement, "maybe, but he's become a symbol."

"So what's the rush in getting him out?" asked Collins.

"There's an American presidential election in about a month," said Fahey. "According to the polls President Bush is going to lose. The guy he's running against, Bill Clinton, is playing for the Irish vote. Plus he hates the British prime minister, John Major, because of some dirty tricks Major played on him in the campaign at the behest of Bush."

"In other words," cut in Collins, "if the British don't get him out by the election, he isn't going."

"Exactly," said Fahey. "And that would be fine with us if he just stayed here, but our intelligence has learned that he's going out on October 15. If we don't spring him he's going back to London to stand trial for the murder of those two MI5 men. And you know Twomey is not going to win that one. Under British law you're innocent until proven Irish."

Collins gave Fahey a knowing look. "Why would the American government conspire with the British to do this?" asked Collins.

"It's called the 'Special Relationship,'" said Fahey. "Goes back to World War II, when the Yanks saved the Brits' bacon for the second time." Thanks to Mr. Pearse, Collins knew about World War II and he nodded. "The Brits wink. The Americans wink. The Irish get fucked."

Collins nodded again. "What's your story?"

Fahey was taken aback. "I'm executive director of the Northern Ireland Relief Fund," he finally said.

"A front organization?" asked Collins.

"Well," began Fahey, not knowing exactly what to say.

"A front," said Collins.

"A front," Fahey finally admitted. "We get the money to the Belfast boys so they—"

Collins raised his hand. "I don't want to hear anything else."

"But—" insisted Fahey.

"The less I know," said Collins, "the safer it is for you." By sheer instinct, Collins still knew how to play espionage. "And yourself?" asked Collins. Fahey didn't know what to say. "What do you *really* do?"

"I'm. . ." said Fahey, looking for the right words, "I'm a business-man on Wall Street." He paused for a second, then continued, "I was recently voted one of the top one hundred Irish-American businessmen by *Irish America* magazine," he said proudly.

Collins, who as Minister of Finance had dealt with many a recalcitrant Irish businessman, was not impressed. "An Irish business-man," said Collins, "is a mick with *his* hand in *your* pocket!"

Fahey was speechless, and they both sat in silence for minutes. "What are they holding him on, a murder charge?" Collins finally asked.

"No," said Fahey, "illegally entering the country."

"Where is Twomey right now?"

"He's in a federal lockup for illegal immigrants at 201 Varick Street in Greenwich Village," said Fahey.

"Ah, Greenwich Village," said Collins. "Knew it well."

"You did?" said Fahey.

"Yes, I remember it like it was yesterday. Arrived on the *Lusitania* in 1914. Pier 54, Cunard Line, bottom of West 14th Street. Came over with Casement, you know. Tom Clarke didn't trust Casement, and neither did John Devoy over in New York, so they sent me to baby-sit Sir Roger. Had me disguised as a priest, no less."

"1914?" said Fahey.

"Indeed," said Collins truthfully. "The last summer the *Lusitania* would see."

Fahey was silent. This fellow Collins mystified him. One moment he was all business, the next he was ranting on about Roger Casement and the *Lusitania*. Where did they find them? thought Fahey.

"Who's your man in the Village?" asked Collins.

"Tom Butler," said Fahey. "You'll be staying with him."

"When do we land?" asked Collins.

"We should be in JFK at three-thirty," said Fahey.

"What's JFK?" asked Collins.

"John F. Kennedy International Airport," replied Fahey. Collins shrugged his shoulders. "The only Irish-Catholic president in the history of the United States. He was so young when they assassinated him," said Fahey. "A great loss."

"Tell me about it," snapped Collins. He wondered if this JFK fellow had gone to purgatory or straight to Heaven when they blew *his* brains out.

"The Republicans still claim Kennedy stole that election in 1960," said Fahey.

Collins smiled at the thought of another Irish politician, even an American one, stealing an election. "There's an old Fenian saying," he said softly. "Vote early. Vote often."

5. | THE LION'S HEAD SALOON
GREENWICH VILLAGE, NEW YORK CITY

The Lion's Head was located at 59 Christopher Street. As soon as Michael Collins stepped into the place, he felt right at home. With all its shiny wood and dim light it epitomized the perfect bar—one that combined the best aspects of the womb and the coffin, as one of its former patrons, the late Joe Flaherty, had often commented.

"Tom Butler," said Fahey, "meet Michael Collins."

Butler was behind the bar, working the noon to eight P.M. shift. At six feet two inches and 275 pounds, he was an impressive figure—especially with his gleaming bald head. He had enormous lips that could give the brightest of smiles or purse mockingly in disgust or anger. His round head made him look like the Man in the Moon if the Man in the Moon were a Celt. In fact, he looked like an enormous Irish Telly Savalas. He supported his right arm with his left hand and when Collins stuck out his hand to shake, Butler awkwardly offered his left hand, backward in a handshake.

"What can I get you lads?" asked Butler.

"Ah, nothing for me, Tom," said Fahey. "It's been a long forty-eight hours. I just want to get home to the Bronx. I'm beginning to miss the wife and children."

"So you're over that nineteen-year-old secretary down at the job," said Butler.

"Hush!" said Fahey in a low voice as if Butler were giving away a state secret. Butler beamed, and Collins smiled. "I have to go," said Fahey. "You know where you can reach me."

"Thanks for the help, Ernie," said Collins. "I'll be in touch."

"I'm at your disposal," said Fahey as he turned and walked out the door.

"And yourself," said Butler.

"Do you have Irish whiskey?"

"Does the Pope give Benediction?" said Butler as he limped down the bar, dragging his right leg, and grabbed a bottle of Black Bush for Collins.

"Bushmills?" said Collins, still suspicious of the Protestant brew.

"They're all owned by the same French distillery nowadays," said Butler. "Good luck, Michael."

"Call me Mick," said Collins.

"And you can call me Sugar," said Butler, his immense gut revealing the riddle.

Butler eyed Collins. "I feel like I know you from somewhere," said Butler.

"Been out of circulation for a while," Collins replied as he looked Butler straight in the eye.

"I get off at eight," said Butler. "Why don't you have a drink and wait for me?"

"That would be grand," said Collins as he settled into a seat at the end of the bar beneath the front window. On the walls were book jackets. "Where did all the books come from?" asked Collins.

"Written by the regulars," replied Butler.

"Any good ones?" asked Collins.

"Sure. The Hamill boys, Pete and Denis. Joe Flaherty, the guy who wrote *Chez Joey,* was a great writer and friend. Died in 1983.

Dick Walton, David Markson, Paul Schiffman, Vince Patrick, Tania Grossinger, Bob Ward, Joel Oppenheimer. All good writers. And that Michael Coffey is a hell of a poet," said Sugar pointing at the jacket near the bathroom bulkhead.

"Irish and Jews," said Collins.

"Jews and Irish," said Butler. "Lost tribe we are, so they say."

Collins smiled and then noticed the fingers of his right hand. They were stained a brownish orange from nicotine. He had forgotten; he was a smoker. He looked down the bar, but hardly anyone else was smoking. "Do you have any fags?" asked Collins.

"Fags?" said Butler.

"You know," said Collins gesticulating with his hand in a sweeping manner, "fags, you know, cigarettes."

"Ah, cigarettes," said Butler, "right over there in the machine. Here, let me give you the change." Butler gave him three dollars in quarters. Collins walked over to the machine and just looked at it. He peeked over his shoulder to Butler for help.

"What's the matter?" asked Butler.

"What do I do with these shillings?"

Butler frowned, then smiled. "Put them in that slot on the upper right."

Collins nodded, then slid the coins into the cigarette machine. He looked at the selections, saw no Woodbines, and settled on a pack of Lucky Strikes. Why not? Collins said to himself.

Shillings, thought Butler. They haven't used shillings in Ireland since they went to the decimal system twenty years ago. What, exactly, was going on?

"Thanks for the fags, Sugar," said Collins as he returned to the bar.

"Mick, you better be careful with that fag stuff around here." Collins shrugged his shoulders. "You know, they're gay." Collins shook his head, and Butler could see he wasn't getting it. "Queer."

"Quare?"

"Homosexual."

"Jaysus," said Collins, "here too!"

Butler smiled. "Enjoy your fag," he said.

A woman from the other end of the bar walked to Collins's end. Butler shook his head.

"You have a nice accent," she said, "where are you from?"

"Ireland," said Collins.

"You know who you look like?" she asked.

"No," said Collins suspiciously.

"You look like that Irish actor, Liam Neeson."

"I don't know who he is," replied Collins.

"Well," continued the slightly tipsy woman, "Liam Neeson is supposed to have a *schlong* on him about this long," she said as she held her hands about a foot apart.

Collins nodded. "What's a *schlong?*" he asked. Butler cleared his voice and lowered his eyes. Collins nodded. "Oh," said Collins, "I see."

"My name's Gail," the woman said. "What do they call you?"

"The Big Fellow," said Collins as he finished his whiskey and headed to the men's room.

"I thought you'd never get rid of her after that comment about 'The Big Fellow,'" said a laughing Tom Butler to Michael Collins as they sat down in the back room of the Lion's Head.

"Ah, she was only looking for a toss, but I'm here on business, not pleasure," said Collins as he lit another Lucky. "I won't be shaggin' anything in New York this time."

The back room of the Head was just as comfortable as the bar. Three rows of shiny wood tables were handled by the sexiest waitresses in the Village. On the brick walls were pictures of boats on the high seas and posters from the Broadway plays of Lanford Wilson,

the Pulitzer Prize-winning regular. Collins was facing the twin windows in the front, and from his position he noticed he could check
every female anatomy from the waist down. He didn't want to be
distracted by the temptation. He then looked up and saw a poster
for a play at the Abbey Theater about *The Invincibles*—the wild
Fenians of the 1880s—and knew there would be no distraction from
the window.

"First, Tom," said Collins, "can I ask you a personal question?"

"Sure," said Butler.

"What's wrong with your arm and leg?"

Butler grimaced. "Stroke," he said.

"Jaysus," said Collins, "how do you drag yourself up and down a
bar all day?"

"It ain't easy," said Sugar as he readjusted his dead right hand on
the table in front of him. Collins could see he was uneasy about the
subject, and he got right down to business.

"What's your connection to the organization, Sugar?"

Tom Butler was beginning to see that Collins didn't beat around
the bush. He wanted answers, and he wanted them now.

"I don't belong to any organization," laughed Butler. "My old
man was in the IRA back in Roscommon. Killed a couple of Black
and Tans right after the truce so they didn't escape justice, if you
know what I mean. Had to leave the country in 1922. Came here
and opened The River Shannon bar in Washington Heights. A lot of
the old comrades used to come around, and the old man would do a
favor occasionally. When Dad died they'd ask me once in a while for
a favor. I believe in this one. I'll help you all I can." He looked down
at his crippled hand. "As you can see, I have nothing to lose."

"I'll have to get inside that prison," said Collins.

Butler whistled. "That doesn't sound easy, Mick."

"Okay, Sugar, I've got an idea. It worked for me the last time I
was in New York and the Village."

"You were here before?" asked Butler.

"1914," said Collins.

"I see," said Butler, looking hard at the man on the other side of the table, a man almost thirty years his junior.

"Do you know a priest, by any chance?" asked Collins.

"I do," said Butler, "Father Bill O'Donnell. He works out of St. Bernard's on 14th Street. A great guy, a man's man."

"Grand," said Collins. "I want you to get in touch with Ernie Fahey and tell him to get his intelligence officer down here for a meeting tomorrow night at eight o'clock. See if you can get Father O'Donnell to attend also."

"Where you want to meet? At my apartment?" asked Butler.

"No. Out in the open where everybody can see. If you look like you're not doing anything wrong, people think you're not doing anything wrong. You get my drift?"

"I see," said Butler. "Here in the dining room tomorrow at eight o'clock. No problem."

"I also will need a Luger," said Collins.

Butler was getting uncomfortable. "A gun?"

"Yes," said Collins. "I took a liking to the Luger 9mm. Had this German sailor who used to bring a few with him to Dublin every trip he made. A good, sound gun."

Sugar shook his head. "Maybe you should ask Ernie about that."

The words were no sooner out of Sugar's mouth than the Archangel appeared behind Butler. Collins turned white. He looked around the room at the other diners to see if they had seen what he had seen. Obviously, they hadn't. Collins looked up at the Archangel again and felt small in his presence. Those eyes, those fookin' eyes, thought Collins. It was as if Collins were pinned to his chair by the Archangel's eyes. For the first time in a long time, Collins felt fear. He began to hyperventilate and his face flushed. He wanted to get out of there, but he was frozen in his chair. He didn't know what the

Archangel might do next. Then like that, it was over as a sudden calmness engulfed him. Collins was dazed, for he didn't know what to make of the situation.

"On second thought, Tom, I don't think I'll need a gun for this job. Not right now, at least." Collins looked up to see the Archangel nod his immense head and as quickly as he had appeared, he was gone.

"Jeez, Mick," said Butler, "you look like you've seen a ghost."

"Not quite."

"My God!" exclaimed Butler excitedly. "Jesus!"

"What?"

"My hand," said Butler, "I can move it!" And for the first time in seven years Tom Butler picked up a glass with his right hand. He held it up in the air, turning it with his now mobile wrist and letting the light shine through the water. He started to laugh. First there was a giggle which rapidly turned into a guffaw. People turned to look at him. "Mick," said Butler excitedly, "what the fuck's going on?"

"It's a sign," said Collins, timidly.

"A sign from what?" said Butler.

"From above."

"Jesus," said Butler again, doubtful, but happy with the limited movement he was beginning to feel in his right side.

"All right," said Collins suddenly as if trying to put the episode behind him. "I want to get the ball rolling early tomorrow morning and take a look at that prison with you." But Butler was not paying attention to him. He was still surveying the light through his raised water glass. "Sugar," said Collins, "did you hear me?"

"Yes, yes," Butler replied impatiently, then he laughed again. "Yes, I'll take care of it. What are you up to tonight?"

"Bed."

"Bed my ass," replied Butler, "Let's celebrate my hand! How about a little jazz up at the Village Vanguard?"

"Jazz," said Collins, somewhat lost. "Isn't that Negro music?"

"Well, yeah, I guess," said Butler, laughing at the rather anachronistic description.

"It was just beginning in London when I was negotiating the treaty there in 1921. A lot of the black lads came over from Paris."

Butler looked at him hard for a minute and finally said, "Tommy Flanagan's over at the Vanguard tonight."

"An Irish lad?" said Collins.

"One of the best," replied Sugar.

6. | TOM BUTLER'S APARTMENT
125 CHRISTOPHER STREET

Tom Butler was an insomniac. He slept in short bursts. Forty minutes here, nineteen minutes there. To him, a good night's sleep was keeping his eyes closed, faking sleep for two hours. This strange night after they had returned from the Vanguard he had given his bed to Collins and launched himself on the couch. He could hear the Spanish street boy below, on horny Christopher Street, laughing as he rubbed his crotch against the gringo's hips in a doggie dry hump. *"Coo-loh!"* laughed the Spanish street boy.

Butler looked into his room where Collins lay asleep on the bed, fully dressed except for his jacket. Collins's right hand rested across his vested chest, almost under his left armpit. It would have been perfect if he was wearing a shoulder holster, but he wasn't. Collins did not snore. There was only the imperceptible small rise and fall of his massive chest. Butler shook his head, and Angus, Butler's cairn terrier, raised his head, then cocked it, as if asking instructions from his master.

The dog had taken to Collins. Usually when someone came into the house, Angus was in a snit-frenzy. Jumping up and down, barking, outraged that his territory had been invaded. But when Collins had entered the apartment, Angus came right up to him and stood by his leg. "Good boy," said Collins as he petted Angus. The dog rubbed his side on the cuff of Collins's trousers. He followed Collins wherever he went in the apartment.

"You've found a friend," said Butler.

"I have," said Collins. Butler nodded as Collins went into the bathroom and closed the door. Angus sat outside, waiting. Now, Collins was asleep and the dog stood guard.

"What do ya think, Angus?" asked Butler, and Angus rested his chin whiskers on his paws, as if nodding. "Yeah, you're right," said Butler, who then went back to his couch and hoped for an hour of sleep. But he couldn't sleep. He got up and went over to his old armchair, which looked down the short hall to his bedroom. Angus lifted his head off the floor and watched Butler's movements, then again rested his chin on the cool wood floor of the bedroom.

Angus always made Butler think of his father, for he had inherited the dog when the old man died. Butler shook his head. His father hadn't died. He had been murdered in his Washington Heights apartment, which was above his bar, The River Shannon. Frightened to death in his own bed by some prick of a junkie looking for an old black-and-white television set to fence for drugs. The thief had come into the bedroom at two o'clock in the morning. The junkie was so doped up that he fell into the bedroom from the fire escape and woke Butler's father. The dog barked, and old Mr. Butler tried to get out of the bed, but he never made it. He fell back in the bed, dead from a heart attack. The last thing he heard was Angus's bark as he skewered the junkie's ankle. The dog ripped into it like it was a knob of prime rib, and the junkie struggled to get back out the window but couldn't free his leg from Angus's terrier teeth. "Fucking *perro*," said the junkie in Spanish. The neighborhood was changing, but Mr. Butler would not change with it. He still had his old Irish customers on Social Security and he welcomed the new

Spanish ones, the Puerto Ricans and the Dominicans. "Not our kind," said old Murphy. "They drink more Guinness than you do, and I don't have to wait for Social Security to arrive on the third of the month to get paid, either," replied Mr. Butler. The junkie finally extracted himself from Angus's jaws and fled up the fire escape and across the roof, hopping buildings as he headed in the direction of the George Washington Bridge, out there, illuminated like a diamond necklace against the night.

Angus barked, but Mr. Butler did not reply. Angus cocked his head. He could see his master's bare belly, but there was no sound out of Mr. Butler. He barked, then leaped for the bed, falling short, then leaped two more times until he caught the blanket and pulled himself up to his master. He stood right by his master's ear and barked and barked and barked, but his master would not talk to him. Finally, he rested his wheaten chin on Mr. Butler's forehead, trying to warm his master from the cold January air coming in the open window.

The bartender from The River Shannon found Mr. Butler the next afternoon. Angus had growled at him, and he called Tom Butler. Tommy Butler took one look at his father and called the funeral home. He saw the dried blood on the floor by the window, put Angus on a leash, and walked downtown to New York-Presbyterian Hospital on 168th Street. With Angus leading the way he looked in every cubicle in the emergency room.

"Sir," said the head nurse, "you can't do that. Why, you can't bring a dog into this hospital. We're sterile here."

"I'm sure you are," said Butler as he and Angus finished checking every patient in the ward. "Any dog bites last night or this morning?" he asked. The nurse started to protest, but Butler gave her a look that was terrifying. "Some junkie frightened my father to death last night," he said.

The nurse nodded and went to the front desk. She took a clipboard and flipped the pages on it. "Manny Rojas," she said, "438 West 179th Street."

"Thank you," said Butler, and he and Angus walked out of New York-Presbyterian Hospital. There was no Manny Rojas at 438 West 179th Street, but that did not deter Butler. He put the word out on the street he wanted Manny and he wanted him bad. Then he waited in his father's apartment for Manny Rojas to show up. It was not unusual for junkies to come back for one more hit. Manny knew there was still a black-and-white television set in old Mr. Butler's apartment, which was now empty, except for Tom Butler, Angus, and a double-barrel shotgun. Butler sat in his father's favorite easy chair every night for two weeks from six P.M. to six A.M., waiting for Manny Rojas to come back for that black-and-white TV. Waiting for him to step into the dark, empty apartment, waiting for him to take both barrels full on. Manny was lucky—he never went back. And with the word out on the street about Butler looking for him, he shook down his family and friends and jumped the next American Airlines flight for San Juan. Tommy Butler took Angus down to the Village, and the two of them got along famously. Tommy loved food, and Angus loved scraps. They were a match made in heaven.

Butler opened his eyes. "Angus," he said, "come here." The dog lifted his head, looked up at Collins in the bed, then again rested his chin on his paws. Butler felt his right arm. He could now flex his fingers into a fist. He looked up at a portrait on the wall and wondered. "Angus," he called one more time and this time the dog nodded his head. Butler nodded back and thought of a man he had never met, Manny Rojas, and for the first time that night drifted off into a fitful sleep.

"Rise and shine," said Michael Collins as he pulled the blanket off a snoring Tom Butler.

"Jesus," said Butler, "what time is it?"

"Six A.M., Mr. Butler." They had been at the Vanguard until three A.M. talking to Tommy Flanagan, the barman Tom Dillon, and their friend, banker "New York John" Mellor. "Jaysus," Collins had said, "I'm all Tom-ed out!"

"Go away," pleaded Butler.

"Come on," said Collins, "let's get going."

Butler went to physically lift his right leg off the couch and soon discovered he didn't need to. "Jesus," said Butler, "my leg's getting better too!"

"How's the arm?" said Collins.

"Better than last night. The leg's stiff, but it's a part of me again. It's not a dead weight stuck to my body. I can't explain it."

Collins could, but he wasn't talking.

"What's this?" asked Collins as Butler sat upright on the couch wearing only a T-shirt and boxer shorts.

"Television," said Butler.

"How does it work?" asked Collins. Butler pressed the button on his remote control and CNN appeared.

"My God," said Collins. "Moving pictures."

"I want you to know," said Democratic presidential candidate Bill Clinton, pursing his trademark lip, "that I feel your pain."

"Jaysus," said Collins, ever the professional politician, "he's awful!"

Butler laughed. "You think he's bad, wait till you see the other guy!"

At that moment President George Herbert Walker Bush came on the screen waving his arms and in his best Greenwich, Connecticut-Texas Republican whine declared: "Bunch of bozos. Ozone men! Want to do things that would not be prudent."

"Who is this fucking Presbyterian?" said Collins, immediately making a mental *mea culpa* to his heroes, the United Irishmen of 1798.

"That's the president of the United States," said Butler, "the man who's going to send Martin Twomey to England to rot in prison!"

Butler stood up from the couch, walked over, and turned on the light. Above the TV, on the wall, was a portrait of Michael Collins painted by Leo Whelan in 1922.

"It's you, isn't it?" asked Butler.

Collins eyed the portrait for a moment. "Yes, it is." Butler just stared at him. "Don't be afraid, Tom. I won't hurt you. I'm not really a ghost," said Collins.

"You're an angel, as far as I'm concerned," said Butler. "I've been a captive inside this body for seven years, you show up, and within hours I have movement in my right side. It's a miracle—and it's also fucking weird!" Collins cleared his throat, not knowing what to say. "My father was spiritual," continued Butler. "He gave that portrait to me just two weeks before he died. He said I might need it some-day. He loved you, you know. A lot of people loved you for what you did for Ireland. If it wasn't for you, there would be no Republic of Ireland today."

"Their prayers must have helped me get out of purgatory," said Collins.

"Why are you really here?" asked Butler.

"To save my soul," replied Collins. "I have to perform one more good earthly deed to get into Heaven. I've been assigned to save Martin Twomey, an innocent man, from a terrible fate. It's my last chance. Will you help me, Tom?"

"I will indeed," said Butler softly.

"You father was a good man," said Collins.

"You knew him?" asked Butler incredulously.

"Not really, but I know he had to leave Ireland because of me. He was following my orders when he plugged those two thugs. I guess you could say the reason you were born an American is because your father helped me take care of a little unfinished business." Collins cleared his throat. "I can't use any violence this time, Tom. Direct orders from the top." Collins smiled. "But they didn't say I couldn't hire an enforcer. Will you be my enforcer, Tom?"

"I will," said Butler as he slapped his two ham-sized hands together playfully, almost like a kid with a new toy. "I haven't had a good rumble in a good while," he said, smiling. "You still want a gun?"

"I was told not to be violent, Tom," said Collins, "but nobody said anything about a little healthy coercion." Collins, having trouble breaking old habits and feeling guilty, looked around for the Archangel, but there was no appearance this time. "No, Tom," said Collins. "I don't think we'll need a gun this time. Turn it off," he said of the television. "Let's get moving. It's getting light. I want to see that fookin' prison."

"I have a question," said Butler. "What's it like?"

"What?"

"Purgatory," said Butler.

"It's like nothing," said Collins, describing his purgatory fugue. "The only way I can describe it is that it's like going around the moon in a daze. You see the brightness, then you swing around the backside of the moon and it's dark, then back to the light. It's like swinging between the light of Heaven and the darkness of Hell. Your soul is in the balance, and you don't know if you're going to the light—or to the darkness."

A chill came over Thomas Butler. "Like going around the moon?" he said.

"Exactly," said Collins.

"In 1969 America put two men on the moon," said Butler.

"Get out!" said a truly startled Collins.

"While the two guys walked on the moon, another astronaut sat in the capsule going around the moon waiting for them."

"Sounds like a lonely job," said Collins.

"That astronaut's name was Michael Collins," said Butler.

The two men looked at each other in silence, which was broken by a screeching terrier howl from Angus directed upward, as if toward the moon. Not another word was spoken between them as they dressed, then headed out the door to the Federal Building at 201 Varick Street.

7. | Li-Lac Chocolates
120 Christopher Street

Tommy Butler was pressing his sixty-year-old nose against the window of Li-Lac Chocolates, looking at all the Halloween candies and doing his best impression of an eight-year-old boy.

"Can I a buy you a lollipop, son?" said Michael Collins to his new friend.

"I can't help myself," said the man known as Sugar. "I have an addictive personality. I love food, women, opera, booze, baseball, Willie Nelson, and—especially—sweets."

Sugar knocked on the window, and a middle-aged woman answered the door. "Mr. Butler," she said in a thick Eastern European voice, "how are you?"

"Fine, Sophie," said the Sugar. "Can I get a pound of that broken milk chocolate?"

"Ah, Mr. Butler, it's too early!"

"Sophie," said Butler, "I haven't had breakfast yet."

"Mr. Butler," said Sophie as she poked Butler's enormous gut, "you should go on a diet!"

Butler laughed. "This is my friend, Michael Collins from Ireland."

"Hello, Sophie," said Collins, "how are you this fine morning?"

"Fine, Mr. Collins," said Sophie. "The Irish, they are everywhere!"

"Yes," said Collins beaming, "it does seem this way in this very fine city!"

"God bless America," said Sophie.

"God bless America," echoed Michael Collins.

Sophie went inside and returned with a white bag full of broken milk chocolate. "Make this last three days," she admonished Tommy Butler.

"Thank you, Sophie," said Butler as he handed her a ten-dollar bill.

"No, no," she said, but Butler would not be dissuaded.

"God bless you, Sophie," said Butler as he tore the top off the bag and slid a small chunk of the chocolate into his mouth.

"Mr. Butler," said Sophie, "you're walking much better today."

"I know," said Butler, beaming. "I found a new doctor!" Butler nodded toward Collins.

"Oh, God bless you, sir," said Sophie, and then she closed Li-Lac's front door behind her.

"Want to take the car?" Butler asked Collins, pointing out his old Buick Park Avenue, parked right in front of Li-Lac. "Rides like a tank and takes more gas then a 747."

"Why not," said Collins. "When in America . . ."

"We have alternate-side-of-the-street parking here," said Butler. "I have to move the car every couple of days or they'll tow me." Collins nodded. "I used to think the street was cheaper than a garage, but I've changed my mind. Every time I park here for 'free' I end up buying twenty-eight bucks' worth of chocolate in Li-Lac's. I think the garage is cheaper."

Butler wheeled the big sedan out onto Hudson Street, then drove east on 10th Street past the Sixth Precinct. He turned right on Bleecker, then right again when he got to Seventh Avenue.

He reached over and turned on the radio to WINS. "You give us twenty minutes," said the announcer, "we'll give you the world."

"What's that?" asked Collins.

"A radio," said Butler. Collins looked at the dashboard like he was mesmerized. Collins shook his head and looked at Butler, totally astounded. Butler smiled and finally said, "It's a wireless."

"A Marconi?"

"An advanced model," said Butler.

"My God," said Collins, shaking his head. New York 1992 certainly was different from Dublin 1922.

Butler pulled the car up in front of Walker's Luncheonette—"Finest Food & Drink's"—on Downing and Varick Streets.

"Very fookin' funny," snarled Collins to Butler.

"What?" said Butler in genuine innocence.

"Downing Street? Why don't you just bring me to Number 10. I'm sure Winston and Lloyd George will be waiting for me!"

Butler doubled over in laughter. "You know, Mick, there is a Number 10 Downing Street down the block on Sixth Avenue. It's a dry cleaners!"

Collins smiled back, but the coincidences were beginning to annoy him. He looked up at 201 Varick, and his heart sank.

"I think I'll go for a walk. I want to take a look at this place." He pulled out his pack of Luckys. "Do you have a match?"

Butler pressed the dashboard cigarette lighter in, then pulled it out and lit Collins's cigarette.

Collins inhaled the smoke, "Do you have any other miracles in that cupboard?" he asked as he exited the car. He looked at the imposing structure known as 201 Varick Street. It went up eleven stories and sat on one solid city block. It was surrounded by Houston and King Streets north and south and backed up in the west by Hudson Street. "Shite," whispered Collins. He walked across Varick

Street to the main entrance, which sat under two flagpoles flying American flags. He looked in the doorway, which led up to a tall desk—built for intimidation—behind which sat a uniformed officer. Collins started walking down to the corner of King Street, where the Village Station post office was located. Another fookin' post office, Collins said to himself. He looked across at Downing Street, a block away, and looked at the street sign to see he was on King Street. Downing Street and King Street and another bloody post office. He surmised that St. Michael the Archangel had a hell of a sense of humor.

He crossed King Street and looked up at the windows, all of them sealed shut. Nothing going in—or coming out. Impenetrable, thought Collins. He crossed Hudson Street and stood outside the Saatchi & Saatchi Building; he observed that the United States Department of State had a passport services office at the back of the building. He then crossed Houston to the back of the old public school and looked at the truck bays and the Department of Veterans Affairs office entrance. He retreated to Butler's car.

"What do you think?" Butler asked Collins.

"Lincoln Gaol, it's not," said Collins as he shook his head.

"Can you get him out?" asked Sugar.

"I don't know," said Collins. "I have to get into that place."

They sat in silence for a moment while Collins thought. "Did you call Ernie Fahey yet about that meeting tonight?"

"Not yet," said Butler.

"Well, let's find a phone," said Collins.

Butler slid his hand into his jacket pocket and took out a phone, flipped it open, pulled up the antenna, and started to dial.

"What's that?" asked Collins.

"A cell phone," said Butler. He smiled at the unbelieving Collins, then pressed the buttons to summon Ernie Fahey. Ernie answered, and Butler handed the phone to Collins.

"Ernie," snapped Collins.

"Jesus," said Ernie. "It's not even seven o'clock yet."

"Rise and shine," said Collins tersely. "We don't have much time."

"Where are you calling from?"

"I'm on the cell phone," said Collins, as if he used one all the time. "Tonight at eight, I want to meet you and your intelligence officer down at the Lion's Head. Tommy will also get that priest, who's going to get me into that prison."

"I don't know if Detective Quinney can make it," said Fahey.

"Tell him to make it. The clock is ticking." He looked at the phone and hit the off button, then pushed the antenna in with the palm of his hand. He snapped the lid closed.

"Nice work," said Butler.

"Can you call your Father O'Donnell and get him over to the Head tonight?" asked Collins.

"After Pappy's finished mass," said Butler. "What'll I tell him?"

"Pappy?"

Butler laughed. "We affectionately call O'Donnell 'Pappy' because he's a combination of *Padre* and *Daddy* to all of us at the Head."

"I see," said Collins. "Then tell Pappy to find another Roman collar. That's how I'm going to get into that building."

"Want some coffee?" asked Butler.

"A little Bewley's in the morning would be grand," said Collins.

"I also want to go meet Gino, my OTB runner, so he can make a bet later for me. So I'll be a few minutes."

"What's OTB?"

"Off-track betting," said Butler. Collins gave him a blank stare. "You know, a turf accountant?" Collins nodded his head. "There's a horse in the seventh race at Belmont, Fenian Laugh, that my man says can-do. You interested?"

"Put a fiver on his nose for me," said Michael Collins with a Fenian laugh of his own.

—

Butler returned to the car with the hot coffee. "What's this *Hews-ton* Street, Tom," asked Collins. "Named after Houston, Texas?"

Butler laughed. "It's *House-ton* Street, Mick. It was named after some Dutch guy who went to the Constitutional Convention in 1780-something. I've also heard it's from an old Dutch word that was around long before anyone ever thought of fucking Texas. Remember the Dutch were here before the Brits."

"So ould Sam Houston never made it to Greenwich Village?" asked Collins.

"No," said Butler. He heard Collins sigh, as if in pain. "You alright?"

"Yes," said Collins, disconcerted by the realization that *Houston* also reminded him of another of his friends, Seán Heuston, who had made the wall in Kilmainham. "Ah, God bless young Seán Heuston," said Collins, too softly for Butler to hear.

"As I said when I was a soldier in Texas in the 1950s," said Butler unaware of Collins's pain, "'if there was a back door to the Alamo, Texas would still be part of Mexico!'"

"Nice war, that," said Collins, still shaking his head about Seán Heuston, yet amused by Butler's assault on the state of Texas.

"Huh?" said Butler.

"The Mexican War," said Collins. "Just a land grab. Take it from the Mexicans, then bring in slaves to work the land. An excellent exercise in Anglo-Saxon racism."

"Who told you that?" asked Butler.

"Vladimir Lenin," said Collins.

"You knew Lenin!" exclaimed Butler.

"Yes," said Collins. "I met him at an economics conference in London before the Great War. Interesting lad."

Collins and Lenin in the same room, thought Butler. What a scene!

"And don't forget the *San Patricios,*" said Butler, referring to the Irish-Catholics who deserted the American army to fight on the Mexican side.

"You know your stuff," said Collins, "the *San Patricios*—the first Fenians!"

"I don't know if they did it for the sake of liberty. Those Latin women with those brown, round bottoms—the Irish go for that, you know," said Butler.

"I've heard," said Collins, laughing. "Our lads were all over South America in the nineteenth century. Who was it? Bernardo O'Higgins down in Chile? And don't forget Ned Kelly, Australia's own Rapparee. God, the lads could travel."

The hour moved toward nine A.M. and the rush-hour crowds were beginning to emerge from the Houston Street station of the Seventh Avenue subway. Collins just sat and watched, then shook his head.

"I don't know, Tom. I don't know if I can get your man out of there. It's so bloody fortified!" said Collins.

Butler didn't say a word. He reached across Collins and pulled a CD out of the glove compartment, opened it, and slid it into the CD player.

"What's that?" asked Collins.

"A compact disc player. In your day, a gramophone," replied Butler as a haunting female Gaelic voice emerged:

Mo chara is mo lao thul
Is asiling tri neallaibh
Do deineadh areir dom
IgCorcaigh go deanach

At leaba im aonar

Collins turned white as his inconsequential Irish became perfect:

My friend and my calf
A vision in dream
Was revealed to me last night
In Cork, a late hour,
In my solitary bed

Then the booming voice of Larry Kirwan and the soul-piercing percussions of the Black 47 band proclaimed:

Back on the streets of Dublin when we fought the Black and Tans
You were there beside us, a towerin' mighty man
And God help the informer or the hated English spy

Butler looked at Collins, who was staring straight ahead, goose bumps on his forehead.

By Jaysus, Mick, you'd crucify them without the blinkin' of an eye
Still you had a heart as soft as the early-mornin' dew
Every widow, whore, and orphan could always turn to you

The voice went higher, more strident:

Hey, big fellah . . . where the hell are you now
When we need you the most
Hey, big fellah . . . c'mon
"Tabhair dom do lamh"

Collins sat staring ahead as Kirwan sang the last lines:

And though we had to shoot you down in golden Beal na mBlath
I always knew that Ireland lost her greatest son of all

Butler turned the CD player off. He stuck out his hand and said, *"Tabhair dom do lamh,"* which, although he knew no Irish, he somehow knew meant "Give me your hand." Collins took Butler's hand and shook it, staring right in Butler's eyes. "You can do it," said Butler. "Only you can get that lad out."

"My God," said Collins, "that was about me!"

Butler laughed. "Larry Kirwan calls it 'The Big Fellah.'"

"Larry Kirwan," said Michael Collins. "His band's a bit loud, isn't it?"

"It's Irish rap, reggae, or whatever you want to call it. Smoke a few shamrocks and it really sounds good!" Butler laughed.

"Shamrocks?" asked Collins.

"Dope. Marijuana. The smoke and the hope of the great unwashed. Nevertheless, you can see how this new generation loves you. DeValera and his cronies are long gone. The people know the truth about you now. No more lies. Leave it to Black 47 to tell the truth."

"Black 47?" said Collins.

"Kirwan's band," said Butler. "Named after guess what?"

"I know," said Collins. "I know." There was a moment of silence. "Tom, I can't fail this time. Last time it was Kevin Barry, and I couldn't get him out of Mountjoy Gaol. I fucked up! Then they hung the lad. I can't fail again." Collins went silent.

There was an uneasy hush as Butler absorbed the morbid history lesson of a patriot, Kevin Barry, he had known only in a song. Finally, Collins spoke. "Tommy, would you call Father O'Donnell now? I'll need him at that meeting tonight." Butler reached for the cell phone as Michael Collins sat in silence, thinking how to get Martin Twomey out of 201 Varick Street, as he still mourned for

Kevin Barry.

———

Michael Collins watched as the truck with the hot-dog carts arrived just before eleven A.M. and planted its cargo on the corner of Downing and Houston. Butler saw the word *Sabrett,* and his stomach began to growl. Lunchtime was approaching.

"Let's get out and take a walk, Tom," said Collins.

"Hold on, Mick," said Butler. "I can't leave the car here. They'll tow me. Let me bring it around to Hudson Street." Butler turned the key in the ignition and expertly swung the car across Varick through the Holland Tunnel-bound traffic, scooted to King, made a right on Hudson, and planted the car near the corner of Hudson and St. Luke's Place, opposite the Little League baseball field.

As they emerged from the car Collins surveyed the field and said, "Last time I was here, Tommy, this was a cemetery."

"You weren't really here before, were you?" asked Butler.

"It's the truth," said Collins. "In 1914 with Casement. John Devoy here in New York didn't trust anyone with a 'Sir' in front of his name, and ould Tom Clarke back in Dublin felt the same way, so they pulled me out of London for the job. I traveled as Father Michael Collins. I made a hell of a priest!"

"I bet you did," said Butler.

"We arrived on the *Lusitania* down on 14th Street. I dropped Sir Roger off at Devoy's newspaper downtown, and then I came up here. Come on," said Collins as he started walking east along St. Luke's Place.

Butler, who was now walking with just the trace of a limp, stopped in front of Number 6. "Home of James J. 'Jimmy' Walker, the mayor of the City of New York during the Roaring '20s," said Butler.

"One of our lads?" asked Collins.

"You could say that," said Butler laughing. "A bit of a rogue." Collins gave Butler a curious look. "It was said that funds were missing. Mayor Walker was forced to take an extended sabbatical."

Collins smiled. "So he *was* one of our lads!" They continued walking east past the Hudson Park Branch of the New York Public Library. "It looks a bit different," said Collins. "The library and this street weren't here," he said referring to Seventh Avenue South as they crossed to where St. Luke's Place became Leroy Street.

"You have a good memory, Mick," said Butler. "This street was put in about 1916 when they were building the Seventh Avenue subway. Long time ago."

"Ah, the Underground, 1916. Not so long ago for me, Tom," said Collins. "I was pretty busy in 1916, too."

Butler thought, then smiled. Collins stopped in front of Number 20 Leroy Street. "This is where I stayed," he said. It was one of five Federal-style houses in a row that dated from the 1830s, and one of the few that had remained unaltered through the years. Unlike the others that had been built upon, it still retained its short windows on the top story—the old servants' sleeping quarters. "It was a rooming house then," said Collins. "Mostly seamen. Sure there was nothing in this neighborhood then but seamen and Italians."

"The seamen are gone," said Butler laughing, "but the Italians remain."

"When I was living here," said Collins as he sat on the building's stoop, "I was introduced to a fellow named Thorne, who was a steward on the *Lusitania*. Turns out he was a German agent working for Franz von Papen, the military attaché for the German Embassy in Washington. Devoy and von Papen did a lot of work together."

"Von Papen," said Butler. "Hitler's bagman in Austria before World War II?"

"Sugar," said Collins, "you'll have to forgive my ignorance. I take it that this Hitler fellow is the one with the gas chambers that Pearse was telling me about."

"Patrick Pearse?" said Butler, his eyes opening wide in amazement.

"Yes," said Collins, finding amusement in the unlikely scenario. "I had a chat with the Provisional President before I came down here." Butler shook his head. "Anyway, I met in this very building with von Papen, his agent Thorne, Casement, and Devoy and talked about the Germans supplying arms for the Rising. I was always suspicious of the Germans. No one does anything for the Irish for nothing. And it was nothing they did, too. Bunch of old guns off Banna Strand with Sir Roger. Casement and Thorne were always going off by themselves together. I heard that Thorne was locked in the brig of the *Lusitania* when she went down."

"But Mick," said Butler as he seated himself beside Collins on the stoop of Number 20, "did he also go down on Casement?"

"What?"

"You know," said Butler, making a gesture at his groin.

Collins glared at Butler. "Now don't be starting with that nonsense," he said.

"But I read you said the Black Diaries were in Sir Roger's handwriting," said Butler. "That they were legitimate."

Collins's *faux pas* continued to haunt him. "And maybe I shouldn't have," he said with agitation in his voice. "I was working on the treaty in London when I saw them. They *looked* like they were in Sir Roger's handwriting, but how could I be sure? The British are meticulous. You know they would use only the most expert forger." Collins paused. "And they tried the same shite on Parnell, trying to connect him to the Invincibles. I shouldn't have helped them out—even if it was true." Collins was getting angrier by the second. "You will not get anything from the British Government," he said, his face flushed, "unless you approach them with a bullock's tail in one hand and a landlord's head in the other!" Butler started laughing. "And what's so funny?" demanded Collins.

"With sentiments like those," said Butler, "we could run you for office right here in New York. I even have your slogan: 'Rent Control, The Way It Oughta Be!'"

Collins caught himself and joined Butler in laughter. "I take it they don't like landlords here in New York either," he said. Then the smile left his face and he became dead serious again. "But fuck 'em," he said. "The British are preoccupied with buggery. Probably because of all the cold showers they took with each other in public school. They're despicable, and they'll try anything." Then Collins shook his head. "I sometimes think of that picture of a smiling Sir Roger up there with those golden-haired German sailors in the conning tower of the U-19 and wonder. Even Devoy thought he was a little 'high-strung,' as he liked to say. But Sir Roger was a sound man. An amateur in many ways, but a real idealist." Collins looked at Butler. "I sometimes have trouble with idealists."

Butler shook his head. *"The ghost of Roger Casement / Is beating on the door."*

"What's that?" said Collins.

"William *Butler* Yeats."

"Friend of Dr. Ollie Gogarty's," said Collins, smiling at this Butler. "Met him when I used the good doctor's home in Ely Place, off Stephen's Green, as a safe house." He shook his head and laughed. "Gogarty always used to introduce Yeats as 'The Archpoet.'" Collins smiled. He was up to his arse in archpoets and archangels. "Yeats claimed he was in the IRB since his London days, but he certainly wasn't one of those types to go out with Vinny Byrne on a mission."

"Who's Vinny Byrne?" asked Butler.

"My head shooter in the Twelve Apostles," he said. "Anyway, Gogarty used to delight in tormenting Yeats. He was always asking me questions about Seán MacBride in front of Yeats. I hardly knew MacBride, but that didn't stop Gogarty. 'Silly Willie,' he used to tease him. Apparently Mrs. MacBride wouldn't give old Willie the time of day."

"A drunken, vainglorious lout," Butler laughed. "That's what Yeats thought of Seán MacBride."

Collins grunted. "Yeats was up in the fookin' clouds if you ask me with his bloody faeries and all, but the good Dr. Oliver seemed to like him enough. *The ghost of Roger Casement / Is beating on the door,"* Collins slowly repeated the refrain to himself as he stood up and gently felt the doorknob of Number 20 that Casement himself had actually touched in 1914. Collins shook his head in exorcism as a chill ran down his spine.

"You're like a walking history lesson," said Butler. "Casement, Clarke, von Papen, Devoy, Yeats, Gogarty." Butler didn't have the heart to tell Collins that Gogarty had, in fact, embalmed him. "You don't think of Fenians in Greenwich Village."

"Fenians everywhere!" said Collins as he fanned his left hand in front of him in an arc. "Devoy lived two blocks from here. On Barrow Street. Everywhere!"

Collins laughed, and Butler shook his head and said, "I hear. Come on, let's get something to eat." At the corner of Leroy and Bleecker they turned left and walked up the street past Faicco's Pork Shop. Butler waved to a balding man standing in front of Zito's bread shop. "How's it goin', Charlie?" said Butler as Charlie Zito waved back. They halted in front of John's Pizzeria. "Do you like pizza?" asked Butler.

"Like it?" said Collins, "I've never even heard of it."

They entered the shop and took a booth along the far wall. They were the first in for lunch. "What'll it be, gents?" said the young Italian waiter.

"Let's have a large pie," said Butler, his lips moistening in anticipation, "with sausage, meatballs, lots of garlic, and a few strips of anchovy for good measure. Bring a couple of beers, too."

"What's this pizza?" said Collins.

"Ah, it's only tomato sauce and cheese on bread, but the way they do it here, with their coal-fired ovens, it's a feast. The best in New York." Collins shook his head as two young women entered. They looked like NYU kids to Butler.

"I hope this pizza stuff is better than these paintings," said Collins as he pointed out the mural above him and the one on the opposite wall.

"Yeah," said Butler laughing, "they're pretty bad, but that's part of the charm of this place. They've been here almost sixty years, and it's part of the atmosphere. John's wouldn't be John's without these lousy paintings! And, of course, no slices!"

Two mugs of beer arrived, and Butler took a big gulp, got up, and headed toward the front. "They also have one of the best juke-boxes in the city—second to the Lion's Head, of course," said Butler over his shoulder as he quickly slid toward the jukebox, once again enjoying his newfound dexterity. One of the NYU girls got up and joined him.

"You know the Lion's Head?" asked the girl, pulling her brown hair from her face.

"Know it? I'm a barman there," said Sugar, never one to shy away from a beautiful girl with an easy question.

"So the box here isn't better than the Head's," she said coyly.

"No, not quite," Butler said as he looked at the girl, gulped, and adjusted his glasses so he could read the tunes. "Ah, here's a good one." He dropped four quarters into the slot and played G-86, the great Glenn Miller instrumental, "American Patrol." As the tune heated up, Butler turned to the girl and without saying a word whirled her around, flung her out on the breakaway, and pulled her back. "My God," she said, "what's that?"

"Why," said Butler, "that's the Lindy Hop."

The other girl—a blonde—found Collins and before he knew it she had pulled him out of the booth. "Come on, handsome, let's dance!" Collins stood there in his three-piece suit as the girl imitated Butler's moves and circled Collins. "Oh, you're hopeless," she finally said to Collins, who laughed and watched as the girl joined her friend and surrounded Butler, who despite his size had the dexterity of a ballet dancer and the quickness of an NFL middle linebacker.

"American Patrol" stopped, and the waiter handed a pizza box to Butler's dancing partner. "That will be $14.15," he said.

"You're leaving?" said Butler.

"Yeah," said the blonde, "we got to get back to the dorm. We promised our roommates a John's Pizza."

"Well, come over to the Lion's Head sometimes and ask for me. My name's Sugar."

"Sugar, eh," said the blonde. "And what's your friend's name?"

"They call him The Big Fellow," said Butler laughing as Collins grimaced.

"Oooh!" said the blonde as they headed toward the door. "See you at the Lion's Head."

"Jaysus, Sugar," said Collins, "we're here to work, for God's sake. I can't get over how brazen American girls are. Remember, there's an innocent man rotting in a jail not five blocks from here."

"I know, Mick, maybe you should just call it just 'Brazen Head,'" said Butler, almost giddy, still out of breath and laughing. "But you've given me my body back. It was so great to be able to dance again. How can I ever repay you?"

"Let's get Twomey out," said Collins. "That's the only thing." Collins thought of Number 20 Leroy and Casement and 201 Varick and Twomey. *The ghost of Roger Casement* was beginning to bang on Collins's conscience.

8. |

At eight P.M. the ship's clock of the Lion's Head struck eight bells, and Tommy Butler snapped up the bridge of the bar and allowed his relief to replace him.

"Moving good, Sugar," said Father Bill O'Donnell.

"Feel like a million, Pappy. Never felt better," said Butler as he jabbed a finger into O'Donnell's own awesome gut.

"Ah, you'd be knowing, squire," said the priest as the front door opened and Collins blew in, his intensity and energy filling the room.

"Mick," said Butler, "this is Father Bill O'Donnell."

"Nice to meet you, Father," said Collins as he eyed the priest, who was dressed in civilian clothes. O'Donnell was a man almost as big as Butler himself, but pear shaped, with a handsome—despite his fifty-nine years—baby face. Collins took O'Donnell's hand to shake it. He turned the priest's hand to examine the fingernails. There was dirt impressed into the cuticles, which pleased Collins. He looked straight at O'Donnell, who had a surprised, embarrassed look on his face.

"I was painting the bathroom in the rectory this afternoon," he said in explanation.

Collins smiled. "Busy hands are happy hands," he said as he released the priest from his grip.

It was an old trick of Collins's. Back in London in his early days in the IRB he had been youthfully anticlerical, going so far as to shock a local *Sinn Fein* club by suggesting a radical remedy to the Church's antinationalism: "Exterminate them." He could laugh about it now, but to the eighteen-year-old Michael Collins everything tended to be black and white. He still smarted at the Church's betrayal of Parnell. And although maturity had assuaged his anticlerical feelings, suspicion still stood guard at the back of his mind. Collins had gotten in the habit of looking at priests' hands during this period of his life. Country priests had dirt-soiled hands, toughened by their hardscrabble life. City priests, London priests, had the soft hands of the lazy—beautiful, shiny nails that reflected no inner holiness but rather the easy comfort bought by the largesse of their hardworking parishioners. Even as his anticlericalism had abated, his interest in priests' hands had not diminished. Collins was interested in priests who were willing to get their hands a little dirty—literally—in the interest of liberty.

"Sugar has told me a lot about you. I'll get right to the point—can you get me into that prison?"

"Mick," said O'Donnell, "I've already made an appointment for tomorrow morning at ten-thirty. I've been in to see Twomey many times, and there shouldn't be anything suspicious about me bringing another priest."

"So you know your man Twomey," said Collins.

"He was my parishioner before he was your prisoner and cause," said O'Donnell, sizing up Collins in his own way.

"Touché," said Collins with a smile. "So you're the chaplain down there?"

"The de facto chaplain at least," said O'Donnell. "With two parishes stretching from 14th Street to the south Village, I guess I just took it over."

"Keeping an eye on the lads?" added Collins.

"The lads are Mexicans, Haitians, and Chinese—all enjoying the hospitality of the Immigration and Naturalization Service. Twomey's the only mick in the place, Mick." O'Donnell laughed at how many "micks" he could get in one sentence.

Collins turned serious. "Father, what's your estimation of getting Twomey out of there, either by force or some Fenian magic?"

"Zero," said O'Donnell as he snuffed out the butt of a Camel cigarette and immediately lit another. "There is no Fenian magic for this place," he said sucking in the new smoke. "It's solid. But take your own look and decide."

"I will," said Collins. "I'll come by the rectory tomorrow morning and borrow a Roman collar."

"I'll be waiting for you," said O'Donnell.

"Sound man, the Father here," said Collins to Butler.

"The best," said Butler. "Would you like a drink?"

"I'm here to work," said Collins, "not partake in a hooley." Just then Ernie Fahey and Detective Quentin Quinney entered the bar.

"Mick," said Fahey, "I want you to meet Quentin Quinney." Collins looked Quinney up and down. "I don't know what we'd do without this man, Mick," added Fahey.

Without missing a beat, Quinney pulled out his wallet and flashed his detective's shield at Collins.

"Jaysus, Mary, and Joseph," whistled Collins in a low voice, "will you put that thing away! Do you want to tell the world?" Quinney, looking like a child disciplined in church, did as he was told.

Quinney was about five feet six inches and weighed all of 135 pounds. Maybe the badge made him feel bigger, Collins surmised. Quinney was cut out of the James Cagney mold—short, but tough. Like Collins, he wore an impeccably tailored three-piece suit, his khaki, almost matching his stale complexion. The humidity of the

Indian summer day had matted his blond hair to his head. As he rocked back and forth on his heels, his jaw pulverized a piece of chewing gum.

Collins decided to calm him by taking his hand and looking him directly in the eye. Maybe he was just nervous over the meeting. "I've heard very good things about you, Quinney," he said as he shook his hand, mindful to put his left hand on top of Quinney's right hand, cupping him, as they used to say back in Dublin.

"Thanks," said Quinney, still intense. Fahey then introduced Quinney to Butler and O'Donnell. "Alright," Collins finally said slapping his hands together, "shall we adjourn to the back room for a discussion?"

"You guys want a drink? What are you drinking, Mick?" asked Butler.

"Sherry," said Collins, finally relenting to Butler.

Quinney snickered.

"Excuse me?" said Collins.

"Oh," said Quinney with a nervous laugh, "Ernie here told me you were a pretty tough guy, and I've got to admit I don't know too many tough guys who drink sherry."

"Well," said Collins, "maybe I'm not so tough." Collins looked Quinney squarely in the eye and said, "I only drink sherry when I'm working. It makes drinkers feel comfortable with you and, besides, you don't get drunk from sherry." There was something strangely disquieting about Quinney, but Collins wasn't sure what it was.

"I see," said Detective Quinney as Collins led them into the back room to the round table.

When they were seated Collins pulled out a Lucky and lit it. "Excuse me, sir," said a middle-aged woman from far across the room, "but if you're trying to kill yourself don't try and take me along, too!"

"Madam," said Collins curtly—now solidly in his business mode—"I know it's none of your business, but I'm already dead. Thank you."

"Well," said she, "I never."

"And I'm sure she hasn't," laughed Butler.

Collins turned immediately to Quinney. "Detective," said Collins, "tell me about yourself."

"I'm assigned to the NYPD's intelligence unit. We collect intelligence on terrorist groups, the A-rabs and the like, and keep a close eye on them."

As soon as he heard the word *terrorist,* Collins's heart sank. Arabs, my arse, he thought.

"We also keep an eye on the Mau Maus," said Quinney, laughing, "and other people of color from County Kenya who might want to cause trouble."

Collins looked at Sugar, who shook his head. "Now why," said Collins, the ultimate troublemaker, "would they want to cause trouble?"

"You know how they are, the colors," said Quinney.

"I'm sorry, I don't," said Collins truthfully.

"They're always wanting more. More control, more welfare, more rights, more something."

"Sound like the lads in Belfast to me," said Tommy Butler, an expert at inserting the needle. Collins smiled.

"That's different," spat Quinney. "You know what I mean."

"Alright. Alright," said Collins calmly. "We're not here to argue American politics. We're here to see if we can get this chap Twomey out of 201 Varick."

"He's going out on Thursday, like it or not," said Quinney. "How are you planning on getting your hands on him?"

"I don't know yet," said Collins as he played with his pack of Lucky Strikes on the table in front of him. "I was hoping maybe you could enlighten me."

"Best way would be at the prison," said Quinney. "They'll take him by van to Kennedy Airport. If you could snatch him as they are bringing him out you may have a chance."

"How do you propose I snatch him, as you say?" asked Collins.

"Well," said Quinney, "you could hijack the van before it gets to JFK, preferably close to the prison."

Collins folded his arms across his chest and said nothing. He did not like Quinney's plan—too many holes, too loose, too dangerous. "What's the airline?" he finally asked.

"British Airways," said Quinney.

"Where did you get your information?" asked Collins.

"As a courtesy the INS, that's the Immigration and Naturalization Service—"

"I know," interrupted Collins.

"Well," continued Quinney, a bit surprised, "the State Department and the British Foreign Office always coordinate moving prisoners with NYPD. The word from State came down last week. They want Martin Twomey out of here, pronto."

"Who did you deal with on the British side?" asked Collins.

"I don't deal with anyone," said Quinney. "We go through channels. The British contact the State Department, State contacts INS, and INS contacts us to provide security to the airport and at the airport."

"So you don't know anyone, is that it?" asked Collins.

"That's it," said Quinney.

"How did you get involved with the organization?" asked Collins.

"Ernie here is an old friend of mine, and when he asked for some intelligence help I thought it was only natural."

"Natural?" said Collins.

"Sure," said Quinney. "The cause goes way back with my family."

"It does?" asked Collins. "How so?"

"My paternal grandfather—named Rory Quinney—was in the GPO in 1916," said Quinney.

"No, he wasn't," said Collins evenly, his eyes almost pinning Quinney to his chair.

Quinney was taken aback. "How do *you* know?" he challenged.

"I know because *I* was there!" said Collins. "There were no Quinneys in the GPO in 1916."

"Well," said Quinney, in verbal retreat, looking at Collins oddly, "that's what I was told."

Quinney had been taken aback. He tried not to show any reaction. The story about his grandfather had always elicited a smile, a nod, or a wink, but this was the first time it had been flat-out plummeted as an untruth. It was only supposed to be a colorful story, but to Collins, Quinney thought, it was reality. Who would question such a story? And why?

"Aw," said O'Donnell, signaling the waitress for another vodka and lighting another Camel, "if everyone who claimed they were in the GPO in 1916 were really there, it would have been a very busy place."

"Yeah," said Butler, "if you listen to the old-timers they were all patriots—yeah, sure, well after the fact."

"Indeed," added Ernie Fahey.

Collins still knew that Grandfather Quinney wasn't in the GPO, but he let it drop.

"Detective," said Collins, "I want you to do me a favor."

"Anything," said Quinney.

"I want to know the name of the man in charge of the British side of the operation on this side of the Atlantic. And I want that name by this time tomorrow."

"I don't know if I can do that," said Quinney.

"What?" said Collins. "We're dealing with fookin' murderers here, man."

Quinney knew he was dealing with murderers, too, but he wasn't sure which side they were on. He was quiet. Collins cleared his throat. "I'm thinking," Quinney finally said.

"Don't hurt yourself," counseled Butler.

Quinney glared at Butler. "Okay, I'll try," said Quinney.

"Don't try. Get that fookin' name for me," demanded Collins. "You're in intelligence. If you can't get one fookin' name for me what good are you?"

"What do you want it for?" asked Quinney.

"I want to send his wife fookin' roses," said Collins in a voice barely above a whisper. "What do you think I want it for? I want to get Twomey out, and the British might want to help me. They've been cooperative in the past!"

Quinney was silent as Collins just stared at him. Something wasn't right.

"*Shiucrá,*" said Collins in Irish to Sugar, "*ní maith liom an fear seo.*" Collins waved the back of his hand at Butler in disgust.

Butler, whose Irish consisted of saying "*Sláinte!*" before downing his drink, knew exactly what Collins had said: "I don't like this man."

He was shocked, but before he could think he blurted out, "*Mise leat féin*"—"I'm with you."

"*Tá rua micheart anseo, bá cheart duim bherth auama leis,*" said Collins.

"Something's wrong here," Butler heard Collins say. "We should be careful with him."

"What's going on here?" demanded Quinney, his face red.

"Yes," said Fahey, "why all the Gaelic?"

"They're like a couple of wise spics," said an agitated Quinney, "always yapping away in spic talk."

Collins looked at Quinney with surprise. He didn't know what a spic was, but he figured it wasn't a compliment.

"Couple of spics, eh?" said Butler as he eyed Quinney, a man used to being in control who was now powerless, except for his revolver. "Keep them on the table, Detective," commanded Butler. "You know what I mean." Deliberately, Quinney placed his hands, palms down, in front of himself.

"Quentin," said Fahey. "Calm down."

"Cool off," said O'Donnell, "both of you."

"For fuck's sake, stop it!" commanded Collins. "I'll have no infighting. This is not a democracy. I'm the boss-man, the dictator. Is that understood?" Everyone settled back in their chairs and calm was restored. Collins wasn't used to such disturbances; he could always count on the Twelve Apostles, his personal assassination squad. Americans, he surmised, always had to ask questions and have answers before they did anything.

"Okay, here's the plan," said Collins as he turned to Quinney, who was sitting with a repentant look on his face, his hands flat on the table in full view of Butler. "Detective, you'll get me the name of the British agent in charge of this operation by eight tomorrow night. We'll meet here and plan the escape." Collins pushed away his untouched sherry. "Gentlemen, we are down to three days to come up with a plan and execute it precisely. We don't have time for this disruptive shite and debate. I'll see you all here tomorrow night."

The words *shite* and *debate* hung heavy in the air for a moment. Spics, thought Collins. Spics and micks, he amended. Then Michael Collins stood up, jammed his hands deep into his coat pockets, and walked out the emergency fire exit of the Lion's Head.

It was almost midnight and the crowd was beginning to thin out when Collins reentered the Lion's Head, a Macy's shopping bag in hand. He went to the end of the bar and sat at the "point" chair, which gave him a perfect view of who was coming in or going out of the front door of the Head.

"Hi," said the bartender. "What'll it be?"

Collins looked up, caught off guard by the female voice. "A Black Bush," he said with surprise in his voice.

"On the rocks?"

"Neat."

"Cool," she replied. Collins grunted. He reached into his pocket and threw some crumpled bills on the bar. The bartender put Collins's drink in front of him and pushed the money back toward him. "Sugar says Michael Collins's money is no good here."

Collins looked at her. "You know my name?"

The bartender brushed her long brown hair from her face and smiled. "The Village. It's a small place." She paused. "The Lion's Head is smaller."

Collins shook his head. He didn't know if he was annoyed that people knew him or happy he had some support. He looked down the bar, which seemed to have quieted at the mention of his name. "That's grand," he said as he sipped his whiskey and watched the bartender in the tight jeans promenade to the south end of the bar. For the first time since his return to Earth he felt movement in his groin. "Ah, Jaysus," he said softly as he shook his head, almost in fright.

Well, that was one thing that hadn't changed, the way women bewildered him both sexually and emotionally. Only here in America it was worse. In Ireland, Church firmly in ascendancy, there was not much hope of a shag or even a touch before marriage. London was different—it always had been to him—but Dublin, with an arch-bishop seemingly under every bed, was a lost cause sexually. It seemed that Dublin women had invented the word *modesty*. Shin-high boots, petticoats, skirts to the ground, blouses so bulky it was impossible to tell what was under them. Even his fiancée, Kitty Kiernan, was like that. Always sending different messages, confusing him. Hot on the letter page in London, sometimes cold to the touch in Dublin. Not much skin there, but still the lure of a marriage that would never happen. Women weren't necessarily the cause of insanity in men, Collins knew, but they were certainly carriers.

The only skin to be seen in Collins's day was in Monto, Dublin's red-light district. He'd be there on business, and the ladies would have the flirts: "Hiya, Mick, how about a free one for the cause? You can Up My Republic anytime!" Collins couldn't help but smile, then move on. The revolution was the best thing that ever happened to the girls because of the presence of the British Army—paying customers every one. So in an indirect way, Collins was like the head pimp because, without him, there would be no British Army to keep the girls happy. He smiled at the inane thought. Whatever they were, one thing was for sure, the girls were not informers. They kept their mouths shut, in a manner of speaking, and their ears open. There was good information to be had out of Monto. British spies telling their secrets in the flesh bed only to die in their own bed because your woman knew what was important. She would take their money, but she was still an Irishwoman.

But now, here in New York, it was hard to not be distracted. Like this afternoon at John's Pizza. Two beautiful young girls in tight jeans, bare midriffs, and no brassieres. Collins actually tried looking away from them to avoid temptation, but he couldn't. It was their nipples that Collins couldn't avoiding staring at. Nipples drove Collins daft. It seemed that New York was the land of swaggering nipples—hard, erect, and in your face.

"Since you know my name," said Collins when she returned, "would it be impolite to ask yours?"

"Naomi," she said extending her hand, "Naomi Ottinger."

"Hello, Naomi, please call me Mick," said Collins as his eyes sat transfixed on her bare navel, peeking out from the top of her jeans.

His eyes moved up and caught her nipples, big as plump raspberries, all at once made happy by the chill of the air-conditioning.

"Will do, Mick," she said as she picked up the bottle of Black Bush and poured herself a drink, then leaned over the bar-bridge and went face to face with Collins, breaking his fixation. "You frightened Sugar, you know. He was worried about you, the way you rushed out like that."

"I was at the Empire State Building," said Collins, stridently trying not speak into her chest.

"Oh," she said, leaning back and surveying Collins. A Celtic King Kong if I ever saw one, she thought. Collins didn't know it, but there are two things American women always check out on men when their clothes are on: their eyes and their shoes. Collins's shoes had a black spit-shine you could see yourself in, and his eyes were blue, clear, permeating, and highly intelligent. Blue eyes and brown hair. There was Viking blood in there somewhere. Butler had called him The Big Fellow. "God, he's gorgeous," she whispered, absently.

"What's that?" said Collins, keeping eye contact. "I didn't hear you."

"Oh, nothing," Naomi said. "You were saying, you went to visit the Empire State Building?"

"Yes, it wasn't here the last time I was in New York, so I wanted to see it. It's nice, but I like the Woolworth Building better."

"I love the lobby there," said Naomi. "I think the Woolworth Building has the most beautiful lobby of any building in this city. All the tiles and those high cathedral ceilings. The best," she said shaking her head in certainty.

"The city has grown."

"By leaps and bounds," said Naomi laughing. "New stuff every day. Too *much* new stuff, if you ask me. Real estate industry is ruining this city. If they haven't co-opped it, they've malled it." She snapped her head in affirmation of her own statement.

"Indeed," said Collins. He was beginning to warm to her spunk.

"Hey, Naomi," said the always self-important Black Stanley—who insisted he was a "Negro" but was called "Black" by the Head's regulars simply to annoy him—from down the bar, "get that pretty little ass of yours over here and get me a drink!"

"Stanley," said Naomi reaching over and tapping the drunk on his arm, "it's time to go home." Black Stanley was a media celebrity who spent his Sunday mornings on the talk-show circuit pontificating about personal responsibility and integrity. Black Stanley's own personal responsibility and integrity tended to cease with the fifth martini.

"Oh, Naomi," said Black Stanley as his hand reached out in search of a breast, "I think I love you."

Collins knew a fraud when he saw one. Collins intercepted the hand before it touched Naomi's pouting breast, looked Black Stanley in the eye, and said one word, "Go!" Black Stanley, one of the most renowned gasbags in the Village, took one look at Collins, did not say a word, threw a twelve-dollar tip on the bar, and bolted for the door. Collins returned to his seat.

"You didn't have to do that," said Naomi with an edge in her voice. "I can handle people, and I can handle this job."

"I'm sure you can," said Collins, showing a smile. Naomi noticed that Collins had a small gap between his two front teeth. She hadn't noticed it before, because Collins rarely gave a full smile. He was the kind of man, she surmised, who did not smile easily. Naomi turned and walked down the bar, and Collins, surveying her backside, shook his head. Soon she was back.

"Sugar was afraid you'd get lost."

"Sugar," said Collins, "is always afraid I'll get lost. I walked up to 34th Street to see the Empire State then I went to Macy's to get some shirts, ties, and underwear. I was beginning to get a wee bit gamey, as they say."

Yeah, gamey, Naomi said to herself.

"Also got meself a cheap watch," he said as he plucked a pocket watch from his vest. "How do you like my fob?"

I like your fob just fine, thought Naomi, then caught herself and said, "What?"

"The chain for my pocket watch?"

"Oh," said Naomi, "it's fine, very nice." The last time she had seen a pocket watch on a man was in an old Sherlock Holmes movie.

"I won't be here long," said Collins, "but I'm a stickler for time. Anyway, Sugar lent me his credit card. Credit cards are wonderful things, Naomi."

"Tell me about it," she said, "I'm up to my neck in hock with them."

Collins laughed. "Yeah, I bet they can be a terrible temptation, but Sugar'll be paying the bill, not me." Both of them chuckled. "Then I took the Underground back down here. I like the Underground. It's so noisy I can think."

"Underground? Oh, you mean the subway."

"Yeah, well, they called it the Underground in London where I used to live. Where'd Butler go?"

"Oh," said Naomi, "he went over to the Vanguard to catch the early set with Tom Dillon. Said he was going right home after that."

"Is anyone sitting here?" asked a young woman who was impeccably dressed in a black business suit. She had exquisite high cheekbones and extremely long black hair, parted in the middle. Skin like cream. A Celtic beauty.

"No, not a'tall," said Collins, gesturing for her to take the barstool next to him. "So it's the Vanguard for Sugar tonight," continued Collins to Naomi. "Maybe I'll join him."

"What'll it be?" asked Naomi as she unsuccessfully tried to open a bottle of beer on the opener under the bar. Never taking her eye off Collins's new bar mate, she finally popped the bottle-top on the fifth try.

"Oh, I don't know," the woman said softly. She looked at Collins. "How's the Irish whiskey around here?"

"It'll rush the heart," he said.

"I could use a rush," the stranger said. "By the way, my name's Patricia."

"I'm Mick Collins," he said looking intently into her eyes. There was, as they like to say, a pregnant pause.

"And I'm your bartender," Naomi finally said testily, breaking the bond. "What'll it be?"

"Black Bush?" said Collins.

"That fits me fine," said Patricia as she crossed her legs, showing thigh, then turned to Collins. "Long in the country?" she asked as Naomi placed the whiskey before her.

Collins nodded his head and finished his whiskey. Patricia held a cigarette in air, waiting for Collins to light it, but he would not bite. No matter how beautiful she was, he didn't like questions from strangers. As Naomi nosily clicked a pink Bic lighter to ignite Patricia's cigarette, Collins pulled out a five-dollar bill and threw it on the bar for a tip. Patricia blew blue smoke his way. "Will you be here tomorrow, Naomi?" he asked.

Naomi plucked the five bucks off the bar and tucked it into Collins's suit jacket pocket. "I sure will, Mick, and your money is still no good here." Collins shrugged, picked up his Macy's shopping bag, and headed for the door. "Hey, Mickey," Naomi called after him. Collins turned around. Nobody ever called him Mickey, except for his father. "See you tomorrow, Big Fellow?"

Collins nodded. "Fair enough, tomorrow. *Slán agat,*" he said and walked out the door, leaving the lady in black in a camouflage of ghostly smoke.

Collins walked up Seventh Avenue to the Village Vanguard. On the sidewalk people, mostly Japanese tourists, were queuing up for the next set. Collins opened the door and walked down the steep steps, which looked like they were leading to a cave. "I'm with Tom Dillon," he said to the doorman at the bottom, then slid around to the right and the bar. Dillon waved him to a seat next to Butler at the end of the bar and he sat down against the large mural, right under the ample belly and boobs of Lady Jazz.

"How are you, Mick?" said "New York John" Mellor, familiar Greenwich Village *bon vivant*.

"Grand, John, and how are you today?"

"Oh, I'm fighting a hangover the size of a small European country, but other than that I'm fine."

Collins laughed. "That country be Ireland?"

"And its milk be whiskey," said Mellor. "And I'm buying."

Dillon slid his hand under the black Village Vanguard T-shirt that was hanging above the cash register and removed a bottle of twelve-year-old Jameson's. "My own private cache," he said, doing his best Donal Donnelly imitation from John Huston's *The Dead,* and began pouring for Butler, Mellor, and Collins.

Collins turned to Butler. "Sugar," he said, "where's my money?"

"Money from what?"

"Fenian Laugh. You said he was a can-do horse. Where'd he finish?"

The color left Butler's face. "There was a spill. He had to be destroyed."

"My God," said Collins, shaking his head. He didn't like the omen. The night was turning solemn.

Tommy Flanagan was about to do his final number. "Ladies and gentlemen," said Flanagan, seated at the opened-top piano, a gentle man with a gentle voice. "It's a pleasure being with you here tonight at the Village Vanguard—the jazz museum of New York, of the world. Here's to my old boss, Ella Fitzgerald; it's called 'Lady Be Good.'" He played the slow version, catching the attention of the audience to such a degree that they could not take their eyes off Flanagan's cocoa-colored bald head and white goatee, which were prominently highlighted by the rich red curtain behind him.

As Flanagan played his beautifully gentle music, the four Irishmen at the bar clinked glasses just as the phone began to ring. "Village Vanguard," said Dillon, who then listened for a moment. "Hold on." He motioned for Collins to come around, which Collins did by going back out the way he came in and swinging by the portrait of King Oliver. Dillon motioned for him to come behind the tiny bar, something that Dillon never allowed, except for Wynton Marsalis. "It's Naomi," he said to Collins. "There's a problem."

"Yes, Naomi," said Collins. "What's wrong?"

Naomi hesitated. "Something's not kosher."

"Kosher," said Collins, "what's kosher?"

"Mick," said Naomi exasperated, "as soon as you left your *pal* Patricia got on the pay phone and called someone named Quinney, and your name was mentioned."

Collins turned white. "Thank you, Naomi," he said. "You've done me a tremendous favor. I owe you one." He hung up the phone and gestured for Butler to follow him into the Vanguard's old kitchen, which hadn't cooked a hamburger in over twenty years but was once home to the celebrated Village eccentric Joe Gould.

"Fookin' eejit!" cursed Collins so loudly that he could be heard by Tommy Flanagan in the front of the Vanguard.

The force of Collins's curse shocked Butler. "Mick, what's wrong?"

"I'm a fookin' eejit," Collins repeated.

"Why?" said Sugar.

"I fooked it up, Tom. I can't believe how I fooked it up!"

"Fucked what up?" said a confused Butler, who was still holding his glass of whiskey.

"The whole, fookin' operation," said Collins, as he sat down on the desk, blocking Butler's view of the picture of his old friend, Dexter Gordon.

"How so?"

"That fookin' Quinney!" said Collins suddenly standing in the middle of the deserted kitchen, his right fist punching at the air.

"Slow down," said Butler. "How did you screw up?"

"I should never have allowed Quinney to meet you lads. I must have been in purgatory too long. You should never allow principals to know each other. Never break the cell! If Quinney is an informer, he knows everyone!"

"But Ernie said he was alright," said Butler.

"What the fuck does Ernie know?" said Collins. "He's up in the Bronx playing revolutionary. Whatever you think about the British, always remember they are fookin' cunning. Never under-estimate them."

"What are you going to do?"

"I have to find out about Quinney. Good ould QQ. What's his game? Why should he be interested in helping us? There's nothing in this for him. Nothing except losing his fookin' pension. He's not right. I've got to find out about him. We're all in jeopardy."

Collins went silent. He looked at Butler, whose moon-face lit up in an ear-to-ear grin. "I have just the man," said Sugar.

"You have?" said Collins.

"Yes. Earl Holder. Detective First Grade, NYPD. Retired. IAD."

"IAD?"

"Internal Affairs Division," said Butler.

"What is it?"

"They police the police."

Collins let out a breath. "We'll be having lunch with Detective Holder tomorrow, right, Tom?"

"Right you are, General," said Tom Butler, leading the way back to the bar.

Collins leaned against the round cushion on the bar edge, threw back his head, and downed the Jameson's. Out of the corner of his eye he could see himself in the mirror in front of him reflected in the mirror behind him. He could see one, two, three Michael Collinses tossing back whiskey. He thought if he could stoop a little bit lower he might be able to see an infinity of Michael Collinses. He smiled at the dreadful thought. Dillon refilled his shot glass, and he listened to Flanagan's soft touch on the piano keys in his tribute to Ella. Collins turned to look at Flanagan, who was bent over the keyboard like an old Asian wise man or a Talmudic scholar, trying to find God between the black and white ivories. The genteel piece calmed Collins, and he joined the others in applause.

Flanagan looked up and nodded. He leaned forward and spoke into the microphone, "Thank you, thank you." He cleared his voice and said, "Did anyone hear a ruckus back there in the kitchen before?" Collins blushed. "If there was a ruckus," said Flanagan, "must have something to do with my old friend Collins from Ireland." Collins squirmed in his seat. "Now Ireland"—he pronounced it *I-er-land*—"is a beautiful country, and I have performed there, in Dublin town, many times. And there are some beautiful tunes I've heard there. And I think I'd like to play one for my friend from County Cork. It's called 'Danny Boy.'"

Accompanied by his bass player and drummer, Flanagan played a haunting "Danny Boy," so slow and melancholy that it was almost a dirge. Collins could hear Butler down the bar in a whisper: *Oh Danny Boy, the pipes, the pipes are calling . . .* " Tears came to Collins's eyes. Must be the whiskey, he thought because he did not think of himself as sentimental. *"Oh, come ye back,"* continued Butler, *"when summer's in the meadow . . ."* Collins shot Butler a look that made him stop. Dillon poured Collins another Jameson, and Collins thought about youthful summers with his sisters and brothers in the meadows of West Cork, so carefree and loving.

Or were Flanagan and Butler hinting at another summer, that cold summer day at Beal na mBlath? "*Oh, come ye back,*" Collins spoke aloud so all could hear him, "*when summer's in the meadow.*" But it was now October, and Collins knew he would never see Ireland in summertime again.

9. | TOM BUTLER'S APARTMENT

"So," said Tommy Butler as he stretched in his undershirt and shorts, "what's the agenda for today? I'm off all day."

"I think I'll go to mass over at St. Bernard's before I hook up with Father O'Donnell," said Mick Collins.

"You know how to get there?" asked Butler.

Collins looked at Butler with disdain. "Back in 1914—" began Collins.

"I know," cut in Butler smiling, "I know. But all I'm asking is, do you know your way around the Village?"

"Sugar," said Collins, "Greenwich Village is just like Dublin. Twisted streets, running at all angles. Nooks and crannies. Like Dublin, it's perfect if you're running a revolution and you know where you're going. You're the cat, not the mouse. If I can get around Dublin, I can certainly get around this place."

"Just don't get lost," said Butler.

"Don't worry about me, Sugar," said Collins, "just find your man Earl Holder and set up a meeting." Butler nodded. "Give me the cell phone." Butler handed it over. "Get hold of Earl, set up an appointment this afternoon in the Lion's Head for the three of us, then call me on the cell phone."

"Will do," said Butler.

Collins slapped him on the back and headed for the street. He proceeded east on Christopher Street past the Lucille Lortel Theatre and McNulty's Coffees. At Bleecker Street he swung left and north. Across the street he noticed a shop selling what they called "Vintage Clothing." The sign said everything was ten dollars. "Thank God," said Collins. One thing about America that completely baffled Collins was that hardly anyone wore hats. In Dublin hats were a necessity because of the constant rain, but here in New York the only hats he ever saw were those baseball caps, which, for some reason, everyone wore backward. He needed a trilby or a homburg, and he needed one bad.

The shop was closed, but there was a woman inside doing inventory. Collins rapped on the front window. "We're closed," she said through the door.

"I know, but do you have any old hats?" asked Collins.

"Hats?"

"Yes, maybe an old trilby?"

"A what?"

"A homburg?" Collins tried again.

The woman's face brightened as she opened the door. "I've had one for over a year that no one wants. Want to try it on?"

"Yes, indeed," he said and entered the store. She presented him with a black homburg that fit like it was made for him. He looked at himself in a mirror, then took it off and played with it, looking for the perfect shape. He put it back on and snapped the front lip down. "Perfect!" he said. "How much?"

"Everything is ten dollars."

"Then we have a deal," said Collins, handing her a ten-dollar bill. "Now I don't feel so naked!"

He crossed the street and was passing Kim's Video at the corner of West 10th Street when he saw a store on the other side of the street, CONDOMania. I wonder what that is? he thought but decided to keep going. Next to CONDOMania was the "Bleeker St. Mini-Mart." So "mini," thought Collins, that they couldn't afford the *c* in Bleecker. He passed a psychic shop that promised a peek at the future, and Collins knew that that was the last thing he needed on this bright morning. He then came upon a line of antiques shops stacked together like dominoes. This area of the Village reminded him of London's Soho at the beginning of the First World War, a bit bohemian, populated by people with an atypical view of life in general.

He was about to cross 11th Street when something caught his eye. He stopped and turned. Staring back at him was a photograph of himself on the cover of a book. He stuck his nose against the window of the Biography Bookshop and read the title: *Michael Collins: The Man Who Made Ireland* by Tim Pat Coogan. He recognized the picture. It was a profile shot of him, probably taken while politicking for the treaty in front of the Bank of Ireland in College Green in 1922. He looked at the book, fascinated, his mouth open.

"Pssst," a voice said, "hey you, you Collins?" Collins looked about but there was no one near him, only people across the street, rushing to work.

"Hey, Collins," the voice said again, seemingly coming out of the ground. Collins craned his neck and saw a black nose poking out from the doorway of the closed bookshop.

"You Collins?" the old black woman asked.

"I am."

"You should be dead by now. That's an old picture."

Collins smiled. "What if I told you I *am* dead," he said.

"I believe you. I believe *everything* people tell me nowadays. Everything."

The woman had a beat-up old A&P shopping cart filled with her worldly possessions. She also had a huge blue recycling bag that bulged with empty soda cans.

Collins walked up to her. "What are you doing here?" he asked.

"I live here, Collins. Haven't you ever seen a homeless person before?"

"Homeless?" said Collins.

"Homeless, Collins. That be two words: *home* and *less*. That's without a home, Collins. Homeless. Got it?"

"You don't have anyplace to live?"

"That's it, Collins. I live here in this doorway. Every night after they close I come back. When they open at noon I go to the park and look for cans. Got it?"

Collins nodded. "Why do you look for cans?"

"Because I get a nickel deposit for them."

"A nickel deposit?"

"Collins. That be five cents. One-twentieth of a dollar, got it? I give the man at D'Agostino's one can and he give me five cents."

"That's your job?" asked Collins.

"That's it, Collins," she said. He nodded in response. "You pretty famous, aren't you?"

"I'm not sure," he replied.

"Well, they wrote a book about you, you must be famous," she insisted.

"I don't know," he honestly replied.

"Collins, you're famous and I'm hungry. Can you help me out?" Collins stared at her. "Breakfast, Collins. Breakfast."

Collins, seemingly mesmerized by her, asked the obvious. "You want money for breakfast?"

"That's it, Collins. I want you to grease my palm with moo-lah, the green stuff with the pictures of the dead presidents on it."

Collins reached into his pocket and gave her one of Butler's twenty-dollar bills. "Is that enough?" he asked.

"Twenty! Collins you must be famous—or you crazy!" Collins smiled. "Thank you, Collins," she said as she got up from the bare ground. Without warning, she gave him a kiss on the cheek. "I can eat today, thank you." She immediately went back to the ground and curled up toward the doorway. "Have a good day, Collins."

Collins smiled. "You have a good day, too," he said as he looked at the book one more time. "I'll see you later." He began to walk away, toward the children's playground at Bank Street and Eighth Avenue, then turned back toward his new friend. "What's your name?"

"Sadie, Collins."

"I'll see you later, Sadie."

"Yeah, sure, Collins," said Sadie without hope.

Collins looked at the people rushing to work, attaché cases swinging, as they made their way to Wall Street and the money. He wondered about the soul of such a city.

Collins liked New York because it made him feel young again, when everything and everyone was new and an adventure. When everything had a new, distinct taste, smell, and feel. He remembered what it was like to smell the hay at the harvest back in County Cork and the excitement he had felt when he had moved to London to work in the post office. Along the way, during his hectic thirty-one years, he had lost his excitement for life. He knew why some people never wanted to grow up. Because everything gets to be stale and repetitive and old. Soon you forget how to feel and your heart goes dead and it's easy to say to Vinny Byrne, "Take him out."

When Collins was young every pretty girl had her own scent. Some wore expensive perfume bought from one of the fancy shops on Grafton Street. You could not miss the aroma, for it filled the RDS in Ballsbridge every August during Horse Show week. This smell was unmistakable. It was the sweet smell of money, old money, well-worn Anglo-Irish money. The servant girls and the scullery maids had a more tentative, mundane smell. Was it powder or shampoo bought in Clery's? Or maybe just the scent of the burst bubble from the bath? And back in Dublin, before he died, Collins couldn't get the smell of girl anymore, not even his fiancée Kitty Kiernan. In the last hectic months before he died, their romance was conducted mostly by letter. Collins remembered holding the letter up against his nose for Kitty's scent, but he could not detect it. Then he couldn't get the taste of the bacon or the aroma of the flowers in spring. But here in New York, in 1992, he could taste the bacon, feel the chill of the autumn air, and begin to wonder what American girls might smell like.

Cities had smells. They came from the clothes drying on tenement lines, food shops like Faicco's and Zito's, and the diesel fuel spewed by trucks as they belched their way by him on Bleecker Street. He even noticed that petrol exhaust smelled different in New York than it did in Dublin. Dublin smelled of coal and peat and stout and Liffey stink. And New York, for Collins, smelled of renewal and hope. But as much as Collins loved New York, he still wondered, where was Sadie's hope? Every person is conceived in passion, but how do some, like Sadie, end up abandoned in indifference? Collins was wise. He knew that the opposite of love was not hate, but indifference. Hate, like love, can stimulate, but indifference deadens the soul. New York had already shown Collins it had a soul, but he wondered if that soul was corrupted, and slowly dying, like his own.

Collins made his way across Abingdon Square and started up Hudson Street. At Jane Street he passed McKenna's Pub, where he could hear music and clanging beer mugs although it was only eight-thirty in the morning. Several doors past McKenna's something caught his eye in the window of Myers of Keswick. It was a British Union Jack, under which a sign proudly proclaimed THE BEST CUMBERLAND SAUSAGE WEST OF ALLONBY. The British and the Irish always had their differences, but, ineluctably, they devoured the same food. As Tom Butler had once proclaimed: "If you like their weather, you'll love their food!"

"Good mornin'," said Peter Myers, the proprietor, in his north England accent.

"How are you?" said Collins, his own accent, part Cork, part London, unconsciously becoming more London than Cork in response to Myers. Collins looked around and was taken back in time. All the comfort foods from his youth were at his fingertips. Inside the front door to his left was a stand of Jacob's Cream Crackers. My God, he thought, poor Seán MacBride. He could not escape that revolution. Jacob's Biscuit Factory on Bishop Street under the command of Thomas MacDonagh, with Seán MacBride tagging along for the joyride. And MacBride, like MacDonagh, would come to his firing-squad end in the yard of Kilmainham. Collins picked up a package of the biscuits for Twomey. Then he scanned the shelves for other dry goods they might allow at the prison. Bovril. God, he loved Bovril. Every tram had a Bovril sign; it was as much a part of Dublin as Nelson's Pillar itself. He picked up a large bottle. He also picked up some marmalade for the Jacob's Biscuits.

"Anything else?" asked Peter Myers. Collins shook his head no. "Well, then, that will be $14.94." Collins looked up behind Myers and on a shelf he saw a teakettle shaped in the head of Winston Churchill. Collins laughed. "Winston would love that," he said to Myers, pointing at the Churchillian teapot.

"*Sir* Winston," Myers corrected.

"Sir Winston, it is," replied Collins. Collins and Churchill had had a rare relationship. Although Collins was a young, hot-to-the-touch revolutionary and Churchill a middle-aged reactionary, they had found a common ground in language. Both had a way with words and loved storytelling. It was easy to dismiss Collins as a wild young terrorist negotiating his country's first great treaty, but

Churchill admired the steadfast young man. It was also easy to dismiss Churchill as the man who thought introducing the Black and Tans into Ireland was the best thing that had happened to Ireland since the Great Hunger, but Collins was wise enough to cut him slack, noting that Churchill had a "more real idea of freedom and care for it than other politicians, and a better understanding of its political framework."

Their friendship had been fueled by Churchill's love of fine cognac, a passion that Collins soon acquired—at the expense of Mr. Churchill's liquor cabinet. Often, after sessions at Number 10 Downing Street had ended, the two of them would steer their way back to Churchill's town house for dinner and more work late into the night. Churchill liked to drink as he worked and insisted that Collins join in the partake. One night it had gotten rough.

"Fuck you," snapped Collins after squabbling for hours over a point of minutiae in the treaty, "I'll never forget you're the one who put that ten-thousand-pound bounty on my head."

"Come now, Michael," Churchill had said, gently laying a hand on Collins's shoulder as the two men had stood face to face, cognacs in hand. Collins pushed Churchill's hand away.

"Wait a minute, my young man," said Churchill, this time taking him by the elbow and tugging him to the far end of the room. "You are not the only one," said Churchill, his voice rising in excitement as he showed Collins a framed wanted poster on the wall, a long-forgotten—except to Winston Churchill—memento of the Boer War. "At any rate," Churchill continued, "I put a hefty price on your bonnet. Look at mine—a miserable twenty-five pounds!" It had broken the ice. Collins laughed as hard as Lloyd George's minister. Another snifter of cognac was presented, and they got back to work.

"Sir Winston," Collins repeated, savoring the memory of his friend, Winston Churchill. Collins handed over another of Butler's twenty-dollar bills, and Myers packed the goods in a plastic shopping bag with a Union Jack on the front. Collins loved it. Bring it in, to get them out, he thought of his prison gifts.

Collins left the food shop, walked across Horatio Street, and entered a playground where kids where scurrying to the ringing bell at St. Bernard's School, located at the intersection of Gansevoort and 13th Streets, near Herman Melville's old hunting grounds. Collins watched them enter the big gray building and sensed there was something amiss here. He thought for a minute and came up with it—there wasn't a black-habited nun in sight! When the door closed behind the last kid, he crossed the street for a closer look at the school. The cornerstone of the building caught his eye: "A.D. 1916." Was it finished before Easter, or after Easter? was the only thing Collins could think. He moved on to the intersection of West 13th Street and West 4th Street. He looked at the lamppost signs and shook his head. "Only in New York," he thought.

He swung east into Eighth Avenue, then around the corner into 14th Street and in the middle of the block found St. Bernard's R.C. Church. St. Bernard's was erected in 1873, when the new steamships from Europe called the Village home on this side of the Atlantic. It was situated in the middle of the old American Ninth Ward, which had existed since the Civil War and was heavily controlled by Tammany Hall's political machine, which meant it was Irish. And out of the Ninth Ward came the stevedores, who docked, unloaded, and fueled the next generation of steamers, the names of which are still legends—*Mauritania, Lusitania, Aquitania, Olympic,* and the one that never saw New York, the *Titanic.* In fact, it was not more than three blocks away at Pier 54, at the foot of West 14th Street, that the *Carpathia* brought *Titanic's* survivors back to New York. Many who had gotten on in Queenstown, County Cork, went straight from the

Carpathia to St. Bernard's to offer thanksgiving for having survived *Titanic's* steerage. Some stayed in the Ninth Ward, making it even more American, and Irish at the same time.

Collins stood in front of Redden's Funeral Home, directly across from St. Bernard's, and shook his head. On this quiet Tuesday morning the New York of 1914 seemed a long way off. The tracks of the Ninth Avenue elevated trains were long gone, as was the Gansevoort Market, and although the meat market and its raw, gamey smell was still going strong, the area was eerily quiet compared to that August day in 1914 when Casement and Collins had arrived in New York. No noisy taxis darting at the occasional horse-drawn hansom cab, no baggage handlers with hand trucks moving millionaires' sea trunks like mini-skyscrapers tilting to a unique New York waltz. No wide-eyed immigrants looking up at the buildings in awe and trepidation. That world of cobblestones, saltsea-meat smells, and elegant steamships was all gone, replaced by 747s almost as high as the steamship funnels themselves.

Collins shook his head. At least St. Bernard's was still there. He scooted across 14th Street and climbed the steps to the old church. Inside there was a quiet and serenity. He blessed himself with holy water and looked around while waiting for nine o'clock mass to begin.

St. Bernard's was a very long church. Golden organ pipes filled its full choir loft, while twin loggias ran the length of the nave. Its most extraordinary feature was its stained-glass windows. Above the altar was a massive depiction of the Crucifixion. Juxtaposed left and right were windows revealing the solemnity of the Annunciation and the triumph of the Resurrection. Collins looked at the deep, arched cathedral ceiling where ten angels prayed, five to a side. He walked down the aisle on the right until he came to a statue of an angel, wings taut in anticipation of evil, with a golden sword in its right hand. There was no placard declaring who it was, so it could be any angel. But maybe it was an archangel. But which archangel? Was it

Michael, his boss? Or Gabriel, or Raphael? Collins thought there were seven archangels, but those were the only three he could ever remember. "So we'll say you're Michael," Collins whispered softly and reached into his pocket for some change.

Collins was an inveterate candle lighter, especially since he had come out of hiding in July 1921, begun negotiations on the treaty, and found peace in the Church. Kitty Kiernan had urged him to take daily mass, confession, and Communion, which he did when he could. Collins smiled at the personal contradictions. He had gone from rabid anticleric to craw-thumping gunman in a matter of years. God was good, but Collins kept his Luger. But you do strange things for the love of a woman—and a country. Because of Kitty he had taken to lighting candles. To remember, protect, and honor her while he was away in London, bickering over minutiae with Lloyd George, Churchill, Birkenhead, and the rest of them. In fact, he lit so many candles that Arthur Griffith had jokingly accused him of "being an arsonist in training." Every time he went to mass Collins lit three candles. It was his trinity. One for Kitty, one for Ireland, and one for Michael Collins. Now Collins dropped the coins in the slot and out of this old habit again lit three candles. And now, again, he thought of Kitty. She couldn't be still alive, he surmised, because she'd be over one hundred years old. Not frail Kitty. Exhausted at a young age. Always taking to bed for sleep, sweet sleep. What had become of her after he had died? She was probably in heaven by now and, maybe, if he got back there, he could see the love of his life again. So this time the three candles would be for Kitty, Martin Twomey, and the one who needed it the most—himself. Then his conscience attacked him as he thought of Sadie. She needed a candle more than the three of them put together. He dropped another coin and lit a fourth. And, for the first time in New York, he felt terribly alone and helpless. "Help me," he softly said to the plaster statue, "help me like you promised."

The bell rang and Collins heard the handful of parishioners stirring as Father Bill O'Donnell came out of the sacristy to say mass, followed by two altar boys. Collins was eagerly waiting for the first sound of Latin so he could dust off his own altar boy Latin: *Ad Deum qui laetificat juventútem meam. Quia tu es, Deus, fortitúdo mea: quare me repulisti, et quare tristis incédo, dum affligit me inimicus?* Then Collins noticed that there was an auxiliary altar in front of the high altar with its massive tabernacle. Father O'Donnell began the mass in English. Collins shook his head. Nothing stays the same, he thought, not even the Holy Mass.

In the middle of mass Father O'Donnell said, "Let's us now extend to each other the sign of peace."

Collins was looking at the other parishioners shaking hands when suddenly there was a tap on his shoulder. Behind him was a young man dressed completely in black leather with Andy Warhol-like bleached-blond hair, a ring stuck in his nose, and another one sticking out of his eyebrow. As Collins turned toward him he physically embraced Collins and bellowed as he hugged him, "Oh, sir, God bless you!" Collins, dumbfounded, tried to pull away, but his newfound friend wouldn't let go of his hand.

"It's all right, lad," said Collins. "God bless you, too." He returned to face the altar, fully aware of two blue eyes burning holes in the back of his head. Now he knew why Sir Roger loved New York.

Collins enjoyed the ritual of the mass until it was time for Holy Communion. He didn't know what to do. Should he receive or not? Exactly what state was his soul in? A state of grace or a state of sin? He didn't have a clue. He looked around, but there was no archangel to guide his decision. He remained seated.

"The mass is ended," said Father O'Donnell. "Go in peace."

"Thanks be to God," said Michael Collins with conviction.

Collins noticed his blond friend waiting for him in the vestibule of the church. "God bless us save us," said Collins under his breath as he scrambled after Father O'Donnell to the sacristy. Collins came upon O'Donnell, startling him and his two altar boys.

"Michael," said O'Donnell, "so nice to see you." He removed his stole and kissed the cross on its back. "Lads," said O'Donnell, "this is my friend Michael." He was going to add "Collins, from Ireland" but thought better about giving out free information, even to two innocent altar boys.

"How are you, boys?" asked Collins.

"Fine," they said in unison as they pulled off their white surplices and began unbuttoning their black cassocks.

"What's your name, son?" Collins asked of the small black boy.

"Abdul," he said, short and sweet.

"And you?"

"Roberto," said the little Latino.

"Do your friends call you Bobby?" asked Collins.

"Yeah," said Roberto abruptly.

Collins reached into his pocket and gave each boy a dollar bill. The boys beamed and then turned to leave. "Hey, not so quick," said Collins. "Who's that on the dollar?" Roberto shook his head.

"I know," said Abdul. "It's George Washington."

"Who was he?"

"He numero uno," said Roberto.

"That's right," said Collins. "He was America's first president. And what's he famous for?"

"He couldn't tell a lie?" said Abdul.

"Not a'tall," said Collins. The boys shook their heads in confusion. "He beat the British!" said Collins with a wink as the boys nodded.

"Okay, boys," said O'Donnell, "time to get back to class." The two boys hung up their vestments and ran out of the sacristy. "I envy their energy," laughed O'Donnell.

"A child is never a tragedy," said Collins. "A wise man once told me that, and he was right. I see you have a school," he continued. "I visited it on my way over here today. The cornerstone says '1916.'"

Father O'Donnell laughed, "1916, eh. Good for us. That's another reason our school is one of the best. If there's one thing Catholic schools do well, it's teaching kids to read and write. If you can read and write you can do anything in life. Most of our students are transients now. Kids whose parents only work in the neighborhood. They drop them off at eight-thirty and pick them up at five. Black, Hispanic. Mostly non-Catholic."

"Non-Catholic?"

"Yes," said O'Donnell, continuing to remove his vestments. "Those two lads are in the minority in that they are Catholics. These are the new Irish of America. Times change. The purpose of Holy Mother Church changes. It's God's will."

"It is, indeed," said Collins.

"I just hope," said O'Donnell wearily, "that after spending my life doing this, there is a God."

"Father," said Collins, "believe me, there is a God, and He's in His Heaven."

"So you believe in God," said O'Donnell.

"That's why I'm here."

"To get Martin Twomey out."

"Both," said Collins.

"Both," said O'Donnell. "One of those revolutionaries with a gun in one hand and a Bible in the other?"

"I never mesh my religion with politics," said Collins, "but my religion guides my politics."

O'Donnell was quiet for a moment. "I'm not sure what that exactly means," he finally said. "You love your country and your religion. I've been in the church for so long I've become numb to it all. And I sometimes doubt my own God. I only hope it's worth it." Collins was silent, almost embarrassed by Father O'Donnell's frankness.

Bill O'Donnell was a bit of a mystery. At fifty-nine he had lived a long, full, yet circuitous, life. Born to working-class Irish in Syracuse, New York, he had wanted to be a priest from the time he had witnessed his first mass as a mere lad. He had been engulfed by the magic of the Church. "Hollywood," Father O'Donnell would often observe, "ain't got nothin' on Rome." Yet his tenure in the Church would be strained. While he away at the seminary at age seventeen, his mother had burned to death in a fire. "It was awful," he told Butler forty years later at the bar and then, uncharacteristically, he didn't say another word for the rest of the night. After he was ordained a Dominican priest, it was off to the missionaries in Latin America for eight years, where he witnessed firsthand how the fruit companies exploited their workers. "There were no happy singing Harry Belafontes down there," said O'Donnell. "No one was singing 'The Banana Boat Song.' No one was singing 'Day-O.' No one rejoiced in the talley-man." He added, "Fuck Chiquita Banana and the corporation she rode in on." He returned home to law school and then moved on to the inner sanctum of Francis Cardinal Spellman up on Madison Avenue. The Cardinal had taken a liking to the young scholar-priest.

"How much of a liking?" Butler had asked.

"Not that much of a liking," replied O'Donnell.

"They say," replied Butler, "that the good Cardinal died of a poisoned altar boy."

"Could be," said O'Donnell. "Only thing he liked more than altar boys was real estate."

"A combustible combination," offered Butler.

The only thing that blew up was Father O'Donnell. Discouraged with the tone of the Church, he left it in 1975. He went from the chancellery office behind St. Patrick's Cathedral to driving a cab at night without a word of complaint. "I saw more holiness in the misery on the streets of the City of New York than I ever saw with all those Roman collars surrounding the Cardinal." He found a walk-up apartment on Downing Street in the Village and soon found the Lion's Head. He became pals with Butler, and pretty soon he was lawyering for the Community Guardian, advocates for the homeless and poor.

After ten years and much satisfaction, his conscience was pricking at him again. He had the same dream at least once a week. It was his mother in flames asking why he had left the priesthood. He had a choice. He could go see a psychiatrist or return to the Church. His call to Madison Avenue was welcomed. The diocese was desperate for priests. They were importing them from everywhere—from Ireland, Mexico, even Nigeria. Would he take St. Bernard's in the Village? But there was a catch. It came along with St. Veronica's on Christopher Street, a dead parish since the Irish stevedores left in the early 1960s and now home to Mother Teresa's AIDS hospice. O'Donnell was delighted. He got to return to his life's work—and keep his saloon.

The sight of the big priest sitting at the end of the bar in a black clerical shirt, *sans* Roman collar, distracted many a horny interlude. But O'Donnell was a street priest who knew just how weak a human being could be, and he knew that a world without sin would merely be Heaven—and he would be unemployed. He never abused his clerical power in The Club, as he referred to the Lion's Head, but he knew how to use his wit like a blunderbuss, if he had to.

There was the case of Jonathan, the film professor, who taught at NYU. He knew everything about everything. If it was sailing, he was Lord Fucking Nelson on the high seas. If it was carpentry, he made

Norm Abram from *This Old House* look like a klutz. On film he could dissect D. W. Griffith, his effects on John Ford, and the tenuous influence of Hitchcock on Scorsese. "Fucking guy thinks he invented celluloid," commented Butler. Then the professor decided to have an affair with busty, lusty Ruby, one of the ladies who frequented the bar. The professor, being discreet, thought no one knew anything about his dalliance. One night the professor sat down next to the priest. He had a smug look on his face. Anticipation, perhaps. If they only knew, the professor thought to himself. He ordered a chablis and readjusted his beret.

"So, Jonathan," said Father O'Donnell, "how's Ruby in the sack?" Jonathan, wannabe auteur, stood up, ignored his chablis, and immediately left the bar, never to return.

"Now there's spiritual counseling the way it should be," declared Butler, to heavy laughter. Pappy O'Donnell stood up and took a bow, then returned to his vodka and soda, still a bit of a wise guy in a cassock.

"Yes," repeated O'Donnell now to Collins, "I only hope it's worth it." O'Donnell cleared his throat, trying to chase the phlegm from his two-Camel-packs-a-day habit. "Mick, we have a great poet in this country," O'Donnell continued. "His name is James Dickey. In one of his poems he wrote:

'Lord, let me die   but not die
Out.'

"There's a message there, somewhere, Michael. I'll have to unearth it some day."

"You will, Father," Collins said evenly. "You will." Then out of nowhere he said, "Pray to St. Michael, the Archangel. He's very good at gathering up expiring souls."

"How do you know, Michael?"

"He helped me find mine," said Collins. O'Donnell shook his

head wearily. "Oh, it must be something to be in Heaven," said O'Donnell. "But what is Heaven?"

"Heaven is the things you love," said Collins. "Like your mother, your father, your friends. Maybe even your pint," he said with a smile.

"Yes," said O'Donnell, "sitting with God watching Babe Ruth swing and sucking on a brew. Geez, it's almost blasphemous."

"Blasphemous or not," said Collins, "that's what it might be. Just as long as people remember you, in some way, there will be a Heaven. Looking at an old photograph and thinking of that individual, saying a prayer for someone dead to get them out of purgatory, appreciating a fine spring day—all these things make a Heaven. It's a good place, a real place, not a place with angels playing harps and strings, but a place of genuine love." Collins thought of Sadie. Simply seeing his picture on that book cover and wondering who in the world was Michael Collins—was that a prayer? Did that help get him sprung from purgatory?

"A place of genuine love," repeated O'Donnell. "I don't think you can paint a better picture of paradise than that." There was something about this fellow Collins, he thought. Spiritual, perhaps.

"I missed the Latin," said Collins.

"Missed it," replied O'Donnell. "Where have you been?" Collins was about to tell him when O'Donnell interrupted. "Another of those cafeteria Catholics who only see the inside of a church for either a wedding or a funeral, eh?" kidded the priest.

"How long has it been now?" asked the coy Collins. "Sure I was only a child."

"Yes, I guess that's right. You must have remembered the Latin mass from your mother's knee." O'Donnell laughed, and Collins nodded. "Angelo Roncalli. Better known as Pope John XXIII. Vatican II in 1962. He said, open the windows and let a little fresh air in. Only problem was, with all the changes happening in the church, the country, and the world, all the Catholics flew out the open windows, never to return." O'Donnell waved his arm in the air. "Look at this place. Big, beautiful nineteenth-century brownstone, and I'm the only one living in it. This used to be a vibrant parish. Can you believe that? They used to have six or seven priests living here, even back in the '60s. It's lonely. That's why I enjoy Sugar and The Club so much." O'Donnell shook his head. "But I guess Holy Mother Church will survive. She's made it this far."

"Can you fill me in on your man Twomey?" asked Collins, changing the subject. O'Donnell nodded. "He's not simple or anything, is he?"

"Why would you think that?"

"Well, he's not in the organization, yet he always ends up in terrible situations, and worst of all he keeps getting caught. He sounds like a dunce."

O'Donnell laughed. "He's just not lucky in the ways of the world, I guess."

"He's not a danger to himself—or to us, is he?" said Collins.

"No," said O'Donnell, "he's bright enough."

"Good," said Collins, "because he's going to have to know what's going on if he wants to get out of that jail. Now, do you have a nice black suit and white Roman collar for me?"

"Do I ever," said O'Donnell. "Was mine before I put on all the weight," he said, cupping his rotund belly.

Collins followed O'Donnell to his bedroom. "Where's the hard dog-collar?" he asked.

"Ah," said O'Donnell, "we only use those on special occasions now. That black shirt you got there. Button it up and stick this yoke in the front." Collins slid the white piece of plastic into the top of the shirt and—presto!—instant Roman collar.

Collins looked at himself in the mirror. "You look as grand as an archbishop," said O'Donnell. Collins smiled. Once head of state, now reduced to an archbishop. "You missed your calling, Michael. You make a grand priest."

"Father," he said. "I made a terrible mistake last night." O'Donnell looked up, concerned. "I let you meet someone who could put you in danger."

"Quinney?"

"Yes," said Collins. "After this morning we'll meet no more. I'll be out of the country in a few days. Just forget you ever met me. If you have trouble, contact Fahey, and the organization will take care of you."

"That won't be necessary. What can they do to me? As far as I'm concerned our meeting last night is protected under the Seal of Confession." Collins smiled and knew he could have used Bill O'Donnell back in Dublin in 1920. "Don't worry about me, Michael. But may I do something for you?"

"Of course."

"May I bless you? And your mission?" Collins immediately fell to his knees, showing no self-consciousness. "Michael," O'Donnell began, placing his hands on Collins's shoulders, "although I have known you such a short time, I have a tremendous feeling of kinship with you. I know you'll do right by the Lord in your mission for justice, and I'll certainly keep you in my heart and in my prayers. We all need the Lord's blessing and protection at all times. Michael, please accept this blessing from a sincere heart, to a sincere heart. And may the blessing of Almighty God, the Father and the Son and the Holy Spirit," said O'Donnell as he raised his right hand, making the Sign of the Cross, "come down upon you this day, guard, guide, and protect you all the days of your life. Go in peace, Michael Collins."

"Amen," said Collins as he stood up and brushed the knees of his black trousers. "Let's get moving, Pappy. I have some Jacob's Biscuits to deliver."

10. |

The two priests hailed a taxi on 14th Street and directed the cabbie to Varick and Houston.

"Father," said Collins, "I have my American passport for I.D. I don't want to spend much time at all. I want to see the layout of the place and talk to Twomey for a minute. A real in-and-out. Alright?"

"You're the boss," said O'Donnell as the cab pulled up in front of the INS Detention Center at 201 Varick.

As they went in the front door and approached the front desk, Collins said out of the side of his mouth, "You do the talking." O'Donnell nodded.

"Good morning," said O'Donnell, "I'm Father O'Donnell. Father Collins and I are here to see Martin Twomey." He was tempted to add, "guest of the nation," but thought better of it. The man behind the desk, wearing an INS uniform, grunted, then punched some information into a computer in front of him.

"How do you spell O'Donnell?" he asked.

"O-D-O-N-N-E-L-L," said the priest.

"Alright," he said. "Proceed left to security, then on to the ninth floor for visitation. You're expected." Collins raised an eyebrow to

O'Donnell as they went into the security station where the first officer waved electronic wands over them. Collins held his breath, but the plastic cell phone did not give him away. The second officer, behind a desk, said: "I.D., please."

O'Donnell offered his New York State driver's license. The officer matched photo and face and duly noted the name in his ledger. "Address?" he said.

"St. Bernard's Church, 328 West 14th Street," replied O'Donnell. "That's for both of us."

"Father?" the officer said to Collins. Collins presented his American passport and was eyeballed. "You were born in Ireland, Father?"

"I was," replied Collins.

"What county?"

"Cork."

"I really loved the Pro-Cathedral there," the officer said.

"The Pro-Cathedral is in Dublin," said Collins, "on Marlborough Street."

"Oh, yes," said the guard.

"You must be thinking of St. Colman's," said Collins. He knew the INS man was playing a game.

"Yes, yes, that's it," he said. "Lovely church. The purpose of your visit with Twomey?"

"Confession," O'Donnell and Collins said in unison.

"You need two priests for confession?" the guard asked.

"Well," said O'Donnell, "actually Father Collins here is a friend of the family from Ireland." Collins looked at O'Donnell like he wanted to kill him.

"Actually," said Collins, "I'm a friend of his wife's family, and they asked me to look in on him."

"Oh," said the INS guard evenly, "I see." They began to turn away when the guard said, "One other thing, Father Collins. What's in the bag?"

Collins held the bag up so the guard could see the red-white-and-blue Union Jack. "Just some food to remind Martin of home," said Collins.

The guard looked in the bag and removed the Jacob's Cream Crackers. He took a letter opener and ripped off the top, removed several crackers, then replaced them. He held the orange marmalade up to the light and saw there was nothing but jelly in the jar. He then opened the jar of Bovril and stuck the letter opener all the way to the bottom of the jar, then tasted it. "I don't know how you people drink this stuff," he said. "Alright, proceed to the ninth floor."

Collins and O'Donnell walked directly to an elevator, punched nine, and stared ahead. Finally Collins spoke, "Friend of the family, eh?"

O'Donnell shook his head. "Mick," he said, "I should have warned you, this place might be bugged."

"Bugged," said Collins, "what's bugged?"

"Recorded. They may be listening to our conversation." Collins nodded his head as the elevator door opened onto the ninth floor. "We're here to see Martin Twomey," O'Donnell told the guard at the desk. They were directed to a side room. There was a table running its length, which was separated in half by a glass partition about a foot and a half high. The two priests sat and waited, not saying a word. Finally a door opened and Martin Twomey was brought in wearing an orange jumpsuit with INS stenciled on the back. Collins smiled; his assignment was an Orangeman. A guard waved Twomey to the table and then sat on the other side of the room.

"Hello, Father O'Donnell, glad to see you," said Twomey. He turned to Collins, surprised. "Father, how are you?"

"Martin," said O'Donnell, "this is Michael Collins from Ireland. He wants to talk to you."

Collins leaned toward the glass. "Martin, I'm not a priest," Collins whispered. "You are being moved to London on the fifteenth. Have they told you that yet?"

"It's news to me," said Twomey.

"I don't want you to say a word about this to anyone," said Collins. "Do you understand?" Twomey nodded. The guard stood up and walked behind Twomey. Collins looked up. "I have a few things to remind you of home, Martin," he said as he handed Twomey the bag.

"Thanks a lot, Father."

"I'll hear your confession now, Martin," he said.

"Bless me, Father," began Twomey. O'Donnell cleared his voice to get Collins's attention, then put his hand into his pocket for his confessional stole. He handed the folded purple stole to Collins who opened it, then kissed the cross on the back of it. O'Donnell nodded.

"Bless me, Father," Twomey began again, "for I have sinned. It's been a week since my last confession. These are my sins." He dropped his voice to a whisper. "What do you want me to do?"

"Be alert," whispered Collins. "I will intercept you sometime before they put you on that plane. You are not going to England!"

"Thanks be to God," said Twomey. Just then there was a beeping coming from Collins's coat.

"Mick," said O'Donnell, "what's that?"

Collins cleared his throat as he retrieved the cell phone from his inside jacket pocket. "Yes," he said.

"One o'clock," said Tom Butler.

"Done," said Collins and snapped shut the cell phone. O'Donnell bit his lip, not knowing if he should laugh or cry. It was the first time he had ever seen a confession interrupted by a cell phone.

"Hey there," said the guard, "you're not allowed to have that in here."

Typically swift screw, thought Collins. They never change. "Oh, sorry about that," said Collins. "I didn't realize."

"I'll hold that for you until you leave, Father," said the guard.

"Thank you," said Michael Collins. He turned to Twomey. "For your penance say five Hail Marys, five Our Fathers, and an Act of Contrition." Collins paused and looked directly at Twomey. For a second he thought he saw Kevin Barry. "On second thought," Collins said, "make that a *Perfect* Act of Contrition."

11. |

Tommy Butler was down at the end of the bar reading the *Daily News* when Collins listlessly walked into the Lion's Head and sat down beside him.

"You see Twomey?" asked Butler, folding up the paper.

"I have," said Collins. His palm swept a space on the bar.

"What do you think?"

"I can't say what I think," said Collins, slowing shaking his head.

"What'll you have?" asked the barman.

"No," said Collins, putting up his right hand, "nothing right now."

Butler could see Collins was down from the visit. "Big joint, isn't it?"

"Jaysus, I've never seen anything like it. Everything's electronic— gates, doors, everything. And everything's on those bloody machines, what do you call them?"

"Computers?"

"Yes, those bloody computers. They know everything about everybody. This eejit included." Collins paused. "If they had those back in Dublin in 1920 I would have been done for."

"No, you wouldn't."

"I would have. Those machines are diabolical."

"Those machines do what humans tell them to do," said Butler. "You would have had your hackers breaking into their system. Instead of getting that extra carbon copy out of Dublin Castle, you would have been reading their e-mail."

"E-mail?" said Collins. "What does that stand for? Eejit-mail?"

"You'd be knowin'," said Butler laughing, sticking his needle into Collins.

"And what's so funny?" said Collins, his ego, even in death, big enough to be bruised.

"Oh," said Butler, master psychologist, "I just thought that perhaps the head eejit had given up on getting Twomey out."

"Not a'tall," said Collins. "We'll get the Orangeman out, yet."

"The Orangeman?" said Butler.

"That's what I call Twomey," said Collins. "They have him dressed up in this orange getup. Where the fuck is your man Earl?" he said as he impatiently looked at his pocket watch.

"It's not one o'clock yet, Mick."

"We have to find out about Quinney or we're done," said Collins, absently swinging the watch on its chain.

With those words a black man with a Mets baseball hat walked into the Lion's Head. He went straight to the end of the bar and stood in front of Collins. "You Collins?" he asked, his head cocked.

"I am," said Collins as he slid the watch into his vest pocket.

"Earl Holder," he said, not bothering to extend his hand. He shot a glance at Butler.

Michael Collins had never spoken to a black person until he met Tommy Flanagan the other night at the Village Vanguard and Sadie earlier in the day.

"You have a problem with me?" asked Holder, looking Collins in the eye.

"No," said Collins. Butler swiveled a bit in his chair to watch the little pissing match unfold.

"You know what I am?"

There was a moment's pause. "You're IAD," said Collins.

Holder laughed. "I thought you were going to say something else."

"Well," said Collins, "you are a Negro."

"Jesus," said Holder, "Negro. I haven't been called a Negro in years. Where you find this wicked mick, Sugar?"

"West Cork, Ireland," replied Butler.

"I ain't a Negro, Collins," said Holder. "I'm black and I'm black through and through and I may be the devil himself. And I ain't lyin'."

"Well, black devil," said Collins, "welcome to hell, because that's what I'm going to put you through."

"Good enough," said Holder, "I can deal with that. Sugar said you got a problem. See if I can solve it."

"Shall we adjourn to the back room?" asked Collins.

"Wait," said Holder, and he ordered a vodka on the rocks. "Lead the way," he said, drink in hand.

The three men sat at the round table in the back. *L'chaim,* toasted Holder as he threw his Mets cap on the table, revealing a full head of hair with streaks of gray just beginning to appear.

"You fellows old mates?" asked Collins.

Holder laughed. "Korea, 1952. What's that, Tom? Forty years? Shit. Yeah, we know each other a long time. Basic training. Fort Fucking Hood, Texas. He was Irish-Catholic and I was black, and those cracker bastards didn't like either of us." Holder laughed.

"We got in trouble everywhere we went," said Butler.

"Remember that time in Georgia," said Earl.

"Shit," said Butler, beaming. "Mick, me and Earl are coming back from leave in New York before they ship our asses over to Korea. We're driving through Georgia, and I'm at the wheel. Earl's sleeping in the back and, of course, I'm speeding because we're late and goin' to be AWOL. Well, here comes the fucking Georgia Highway Patrol. They see our New York license plates, and we know we're dead meat. Luckily, we're both in uniform, there's a war on, so what the hell. He'll probably give us a warning, right?"

"Right, shit," said Holder.

"Guy pulls us over and comes up to me on the driver's side. He says, 'Boy, you were going ninety miles an hour in a sixty-five-mile-an-hour zone. No Yankee goes through Georgia that fast.' And then this motherfucker," said Butler pointing his thumb at Earl, "says 'Yeah, nobody but General Fucking Sherman!'" All three men started to roar.

"Needless to say," said Holder, "we were arrested."

"Arrested!" said Butler. "They almost lynched us. Remember, this is 1952, and they take one look at Earl and you know what they're thinking, U.S. Army uniform or not."

"Uppity nigger, that's what they're thinking," said Holder.

"They locked us up separately," said Butler. "Earl with the blacks and me with the good ol' boys."

"I want to tell you," said Holder, "it was frightening. Never again."

"But we had some good bar brawls, eh, Earl?" suggested Sugar.

"The best," said Holder. "Collins, this man could clear out a bar by himself!"

Butler stood up and grabbed Holder by the jacket, lifting him straight up, then gently reseating him.

"How you do that?" asked Holder. "Man, you look good."

"Collins here," said Butler.

"Collins?" said Holder.

"Collins did it."

"Shit," said Holder. He looked at Butler. "You ain't lyin'!"

"I'm not," said Butler. Holder looked at Collins intently.

Collins finally broke the silence. "You a policeman?"

"Retired. Two years ago," said Holder. "Twenty-eight years on the force. Would have made thirty or thirty-five except for your fucking people."

"What people?" said Collins as Butler suppressed a smile.

"Fucking harps," said Holder. "Made my life miserable."

Collins allowed himself a smile. "Bad, eh?"

"Bad! Motherfuckers drove me into Internal Affairs. Set me up, knocked me down, didn't back me up." Holder looked up to see Collins's reaction. "Graft. Payoffs. Those bums made the professional thieves look like amateurs! And I ain't lyin'."

"Why did you become a policeman?" Collins asked.

"Needed a job. Only have a high school education after coming from the islands."

"Islands?"

"I'm from Jamaica, where the rum come from!"

"No accent, Earl," said Collins.

"Came as a kid to Brooklyn," said Holder. "Anyway, I needed a job, and with Civil Service you get a pension. Why not?"

"You liked the work?"

"Nah," said Holder, shaking his head. "I wanted a job, but I also wanted to help people. Wasn't really cut out to be a cop," he laughed.

"How so?"

"One story tells it all," continued Holder. "I was a transit patrolman. Went to work on a cold winter's night in the early '60s. We used to wear long overcoats then, down to our knees. So I dress in my locker in the Columbus Circle line of the old IRT and head out. *Bingo!*"

"Bingo?" said Collins.

"Bingo," returned Holder. "No fucking gun!"

"Oh, man," said Butler.

"What did you do?" asked Collins.

"What could I do?" said Holder laughing. "I looked fucking mean all night. Couldn't go back and get my gun. Overcoat hid my secret." Both Butler and Collins were shaking their heads. "Should have been a fireman," Holder finally said.

"Why?" asked Collins.

"I've never met an unhappy fireman," said Holder, pausing, "or a happy cop."

"I see," nodded Collins.

"Well, I got a pension and my own detective agency out of it, so everything turned out okay. But I still don't trust your people."

"Alright, Holder. This mick—Mick Collins—will back you up to the death. You understand that?"

Holder looked at Butler and nodded. "Yeah, I understand. What can I do for you?"

Collins lit up a Lucky, blew smoke out of his nose, and began, "We have a problem with a detective named Quentin Quinney."

"Quinney," said Holder. "Doesn't ring a bell."

"Intelligence Division, he claims," said Collins. "Checking on terrorists and subversives."

"Ah," said Holder, "the pussy posse for spics 'n' spades. Keepin' an eye on the brothers." Holder laughed as he rubbed his eyes, and Collins noticed there was hardly a wrinkle on his smooth face. If he didn't know better, he'd swear he was only forty, those extra twenty years somehow disappearing.

"There is such a division, then?" asked Collins.

"Sure, NYPD has a division for everything. That's why there's so much crime, everyone's too busy coverin' each other's ass that nobody catchin' any criminals!" Holder shook his head. "So, what's the problem with Quinney?"

"He's not kosher," said Collins, surprising himself as he used Naomi's terminology.

"How so?"

"I just have a suspicion about him."

"Spit it out," demanded Holder.

"I think he's an informer, but how do I prove it?" asked Collins.

"Money," said Holder immediately.

"Money?" repeated Collins.

"Follow the money." Collins shook his head, and Holder continued. "People in this world do things for only one thing—money. Let's see who our man is getting his money from."

"Well," said Collins, "how do you do that?"

"Check his bank accounts," said Holder.

"He won't let you just check his account," said Collins.

"He won't even know. It's all done with computers."

Computers. Collins smiled. "Can you check right away?"

"I think so. I have this kid at NYU who's a computer expert. He can find out just about anything. Plus I still have pals down at IAD. You grease people in this life and you can find out anything. I'll let you know something by this evening," said Holder.

"Grand," said Collins.

"I may need some cash, if you know what I mean," said Holder, astute businessman that he was.

"Check with Sugar here," said Collins. "He'll get the money from your man in the Bronx for you. Tonight at nine?"

"See you then," said Earl Holder, replacing his Mets cap.

"Oh," said Collins, "one last thing. See if you can find out anything about a girl named Patricia. She was snooping around here last night. They're connected some way."

"You got a last name?" asked Holder.

"That's all I know," said Collins, "but they may work together. I've seen her. She's definitely Irish."

"A broad, eh?" said Holder. "Broads always make my work more interesting. I'll pull his personnel files too. See ya later," and out the door he went.

"So," said Collins across the table from Butler. "How do we get the Orangeman out? Can't be done from the inside."

"Maybe Quinney is right," said Butler. "Ambush the truck outside the prison."

"What if it's a setup?"

"May be a chance we have to take."

"No," said Collins, "I don't like the chance of that chance. But we're going to have to tell something to Quinney tonight, one way or the other."

"You don't think his plan is viable?"

"Oh, it might be. But there's too many loose ends. One, what if it is a setup? They take us all and grab all the headlines."

Butler laughed. "I can just see the *New York Post* headline now: FENIAN SCUM SCAMMED!"

Collins did not laugh. "Two, if we do get Twomey out, what do we do with him? Keep him in a safe house? That won't work. There would be a terrific manhunt, which will be no good for anybody. We really don't want the Americans involved in this. Don't want to get anybody hurt. Let's keep it between the British and ourselves." Butler was quiet, deep in thought. "Remember, Sugar, you're getting in deeper by the hour. If you want out, it's okay with me."

Butler shook his head. "No, I'm in all the way, but how the hell are we going to get Twomey out?"

"I still don't know, but it's not going to be Quinney's way. We're going to tell him how grand we think his plan is, but, let's face it, it's not feasible. Twomey will have to be taken *in* the airport. It's the only solution." Butler looked at Collins, shaking his head, not knowing how they'd take Twomey *anywhere*. "Only one problem, Sugar, is how do we do it and get him on an airplane for Ireland? Where is British Airways located in regards to Aer Lingus? How do we take him *without* the Brits knowing?"

"How are the British not going to know we've taken their prisoner?"

"I don't know," said a pensive Collins. "But what we need is an airport expert."

"Ulysses Morgan," said Butler.

"Ulysses Morgan?" repeated Michael Collins.

"Night manager, WelshDragon Airlines."

"So?"

"WelshDragon is serviced by Aer Lingus."

"I don't get it," said Collins.

"You will."

Collins and Butler emerged from the back room. "Where are you off to?" asked Sugar.

"I have to do a little research by myself for a few hours," said Collins as he looked at a racing bike that had been placed against the wall between the ladies' and men's rooms. Collins loved bicycles, the better to get around busy Dublin town. "Whose bike is that?"

"It belongs to Naomi," said Butler.

"Ah, Naomi," said Collins. "I met her last night."

"Yeah, well, she leaves it here so she doesn't have to haul it up four flights of stairs in her apartment building."

"Do you think she'd mind if I borrowed it for a couple of hours?"

"Nah," said Butler, "bring it back when you're finished with it."

"Grand," said Collins, "I'll bring it back when we meet your man Quinney tonight." With that he swept the bike up with one hand underneath, almost like a waiter, and jaunted out the door.

Outside on Christopher Street he hopped on the bike and started across Seventh Avenue. He flew past the back of the Riviera Restaurant as he picked up speed shooting down West 4th Street. He played with the gears, trying to slow down, but the bike just continued to pick up speed. A car at a stop sign by the Sevilla restaurant at Charles and 4th was beginning to inch out into the street when the driver saw the speeding Collins and jammed on the brakes. "Jaysus," said Collins as he passed Perry Street. He pulled on the brakes and managed to slow the bike just enough to make the left-hand turn at 11th Street. As he approached Bleecker Street he pulled hard on the handbrakes and came to a screeching stop in front of the Biography Bookshop. He was an excellent traffic dodger, but the bike's complicated gear technology clearly had him stumped. He leaned the bicycle against the front pillar of the bookshop and went in.

"Can I help you?" asked the clerk.

"Do you have a biography of Michael Collins, the Irish . . ." Collins stopped because he could not find the adjective to describe himself. Was it statesman, politician, or soldier?

"The Irish terrorist," said the clerk.

"Yes," said Collins in his most even, dead-earnest voice, "terrorist."

The clerk went to the back of the shop and returned with Tim Pat Coogan's biography. She looked at the picture of Collins and then looked at her customer. "How much is that?" asked Collins.

"$16.95 plus tax," said the clerk, now looking at Collins at little harder.

From the street Collins could hear his name. "Yo, Collins," Sadie shouted from the park across the street. "Yo, Collins. Ya bike be goin' down Bleecker without ya!"

"Good Jaysus," said Collins as he rushed out the front door looking for his borrowed bicycle.

"There he goes, Collins," yelled Sadie, pointing toward Perry Street.

Collins pulled his hat over his eyes and took off in a dead run in pursuit of the thief. As the thief approached Perry Street he was cut off by a truck, hit the curb, and went flying in the air. Collins, still an athlete even in a three-piece suit, caught the bike with one hand and grabbed the perpetrator with the other. He placed the bike gently on the sidewalk and in the same motion slammed the thief against the wall.

"You're a right fast gobshite, aren't you now?" he said, squeezing the man's collar.

"Hey, man, you're hurting me," said the thief.

"Am I?" said Collins as he torqued the collar into a tourniquet.

"Shit, man," said the thief, suddenly very afraid because of the look that Collins was giving him.

"Collins," said an out-of-breath Sadie as she ran up, "let that mother go. It's your own fault anyhow, man."

"My fault? He pinched me bloody bike," said Collins.

"Man, Collins, why you leaving a thousand-dollar bike unchained in New York? You crazy?"

Maybe he was. He let go of the kid's shirt. "Get goin' before I kick your arse into your fookin' throat." The thief jumped up, took one look at Collins, and decided to save his arse, whatever that was. He disappeared toward Hudson Street in a flash.

"Collins," said Sadie, "I'm too old to be protectin' your Irish ass. You come to New York, you have to know the protocol," said Sadie, pronouncing it "pro-toe-call." They began walking back, slowly, toward the Biography Bookshop. "Collins, what's an arse?"

He looked at her and smiled. "That's your backside."

"My backside?" she said. "Ah, my booty."

"Yes," said Collins, "your boot."

Outside the bookstore, Collins placed the bicycle where it had been before and turned to Sadie. "Will you keep an eye on that for a moment?"

"Huh," Sadie said, almost in a huff.

After purchasing his biography, he walked across the street with

Sadie, then leaned the bike against a tree. They sat down and Collins thumbed through the book, which quieted him.

"How does it come out?" asked Sadie.

"I die."

Sadie laughed. "We all die in the end."

"Right you are." Up near the children's playground Collins saw a hot-dog cart. "You hungry?"

"I'm always hungry," said Sadie. "Haven't been able to reserve my usual table at the Four Fucking Seasons lately."

Collins got up and walked to the cart. "With everything," the customer in front of him said. When it was his turn, Collins said with confidence, "Three with everything," then watched the ceremony of the dog going into the bun, followed by the mustard, sauerkraut, and red onions. It reminded Collins of the crubeens his mother used to make. Fast food was nothing new. He returned to the bench and presented two dogs to Sadie.

"Thank you," said Sadie. "I am hungry."

"*Tá sinn ocrach,*" said Collins. "We are both hungry." They quietly sat and ate their hot dogs. "How did you become homeless?" he finally asked. Sadie waved at the statue a few feet away called *The Family*.

"It's their fault," she said. Collins looked at the statue, which was a mishmash of mother, father, and three children floating around in a spastic euphoria. Modern art. Collins shook his head. "Check it out," commanded Sadie.

Collins got up and went over to examine the statue. *The Family* was sculpted by Chaim Cross in 1979. Chiseled on the pedestal was DONATED TO THE CITY OF NEW YORK, 1991, IN HONOR OF EDWARD I. KOCH, MAYOR, 1978-1989. Collins came back and sat down. "I take it you don't like this Mayor Koch fellow," he said.

"What's wrong with that statue, Collins?"

Collins shrugged. "Like Koch," said Sadie, her voice rising, "They ain't got no genitalia. Got it? No balls! Just like Koch! Vote for Cuomo. Not the homo!"

Collins was lost. "What did Koch do to you?"

"He took my home away."

"How?"

"Landlords. He made deals with the landlords. He take campaign contributions from the landlords. Campaign contributions, Collins, fancy name for bribes."

"So, how did it affect you?"

"I live in a SRO—that's Single Room Occupancy—and after Koch becomes mayor, they're all gone and I'm on the street. Alone."

Collins shook his head. "You have no family?"

"Had lots of men and one husband. He drank too much Wild Irish Rose, went into decline, and expired."

Collins bit into his hot dog and took a look around the park, which he noticed had an eclectic clientele. At the far end, near where Eighth Avenue began, there was a children's playground where kids, parents, and nannies held forth. The rest of the benches, toward 11th Street, were occupied by retired folks reading newspapers, chess players plotting moves, poets scribbling notes, and the homeless drinking cheap red wine and looking for suckers. Collins watched as the main man set up shop, on top of an old milk carton.

"What's he up to?" Collins asked.

"Three-card monte, Collins."

Monte rang a bell, as in *Monty*—Bernard Law Montgomery. Collins remembered him long before he became Churchill's favorite field marshal—when he was running Black and Tans out of County Cork. And, like another general, George S. Patton, he had little regard for this other Monty.

Monte.

Monty.

Monto.

The life drained from Collins's eyes.

Shankers Ryan.

Collins was back to square one.

It was Bloody Sunday. Again.

Shankers Ryan, British tout. Brother of Becky Cooper, the ring-mistress of Monto's red-light whores.

He could see that dunce of a face of Shankers Ryan now, the dull eyes, the thin, mean line of a mouth.

On the night of Saturday, November 20, 1920, Shankers was sniffing around Vaughan's Hotel. He saw Dick McKee and Peader Clancy leave and head back to their lodging in Monto at 36 Lower Gloucester Street. Ryan followed them, then got in touch with Dublin Castle, and soon the Black and Tans arrived in the night and arrested McKee and Clancy, taking them to Dublin Castle. They beat and tortured McKee and Clancy, but they would not talk. They would not tell them that by this time tomorrow it would be Dublin Castle and its arrogant occupiers who would be terrorized, looking for phantom shooters behind every post box. By the time McKee and Clancy were shot "trying to escape," their faces were unrecognizable. But the operation went on, and the British Secret Service in Dublin would cease to exist before the Angelus would sound that Bloody Sunday at noon.

McKee and Clancy dead. Shankers Ryan still doing his dirty work in Monto.

"Let's take him out," said Vinny Byrne.

"Not yet," said Collins.

"When?" asked Vinny.

"When he thinks he's safe."

Five February 1921. Shankers was feeling safe and sound. Bellying up to the bar at Hynes's Public House on the same Lower Gloucester Street where McKee and Clancy had been abducted. It was ten-thirty in the morning.

Three of the Squad walked in. Not a word was said. Vinny Byrne went right up to him. Shankers knew he was done for and put his hands flat down on the bar. Vinny put the barrel of the gun in Ryan's left ear hole and pulled the trigger. He stepped back and the three of them emptied their guns into Shankers's body.

Bloody Sunday was finally over.

It would become a monument to Collins but an embarrassment to everyone else. Just like Monto. The Legion of Mary would eventually rid it of its whores. The streets would be bulldozed over or, if they still existed, the names would be changed. As if to protect the innocent. There would be no more Monto. Ironically, Lower Gloucester Street, home of spies, touts, and whores, would become Seán MacDiarmada Street, named after Collins's mentor.

Monty of Monto, thought Collins. The whores will be busy.

"You okay, Collins?" asked Sadie. She put her hand on Collins's arm, and the blood returned to his face. His recurring nightmare had passed.

"Three-card monte," said Collins aloud, nodding at Sadie. He got up to take a closer look.

"Bring your bike, Collins," said Sadie.

Collins, bike in hand, walked with Sadie over to the game. "Step right up, my man, and see if you can beat my hand," said the dealer as he deftly flipped and shuffled the cards around. "Pick out the ace of spades," he said with a laugh at his own little joke. Collins inched closer.

"There it is," said another onlooker.

"Right you are, brother," said the dealer, and money exchanged hands.

"Stand right there, Collins," said Sadie. "That man be the fool's stooge."

"Stooge?" said Collins.

"His prop, Collins. They be working together, fool," Sadie said with disgust. "How they ever write a book about you when you be a sucker for three-card monte, Collins?"

Collins shook his head and had to smile. He was used to being treated gingerly by people. Some out of respect; others out of fear. But Sadie treated him like an eejit farm boy in the big city who had "sucker" plastered all over him—and he appreciated it.

"Step up, my man, and win the hand," said the dealer, and a sucker in a suit finally did. Collins kept his eyes on the cards, and the "client" put down ten dollars to match the dealer's. Cards were mixed, shoveled, and jammed. "Where's the ace of spades?" the dealer asked.

"There," said the client.

"Wrong you are," said the dealer as he flipped the next card revealing the ace of spades.

"Jaysus," said Collins, sticking his hand into his pant pocket, "he's good."

"No, you don't," said Sadie.

"But I want to see how it's done," said Collins.

"Collins, it's only the old shell game, but with cards."

"Do you know this lad?"

"Sure," said Sadie.

"Introduce me."

"Yo, Buster."

"Yeah, Sadie," said the dealer.

"This is my friend Collins. Show him how you do it and don't take his money. You understand?"

"Hey, Collins. See if you can find the ace of spades."

Collins stood in front of the dealer, never taking his eyes off his hands. "There," said Collins. "Ace of spades."

"Collins, you be wrong, my man," said Buster the dealer.

"How do you do it?" asked Collins.

"It be sleight of hand, m'man."

"Sleight of hand," said Collins aloud as the bulb went on in his head. "Buster, thank you so much," he said, pushing ten dollars into his hand.

"Why you do that, Collins?" said an annoyed Sadie.

"Because he just made Martin Twomey disappear."

12. |

"How hard is my fortune?" sang Liam Clancy out of the Lion's Head jukebox. *"How vain my repining? The sad rope of death for this young neck is twining . . ."*

Michael Collins was standing at the end of the bar, looking down into his black coffee. "You keep listening to that shit and you'll want to kill yourself," said Tommy Butler as he pulled up a barstool.

Collins looked up. "Too late for that," he said. "But the lad has a lovely voice. Naomi played it for me."

Butler looked at her. She was wearing a short plaid skirt, a white blouse, and knee-high socks. "You look like a Catholic schoolgirl," he said with a well-staged leer. "Want some M&Ms, little girl?"

"Mr. Butler!" she gushed in exaggeration. "What a dirty mind you have!"

"He, he, he," said Tom Butler devilishly. Naomi went down the bar to fill a drink order.

"She's a wonderful girl, Tom," said Collins.

Butler smiled. "You like older women, Mick?"

"Older?"

"How old are you, Mick?"

Collins had to think before answering. "I'm thirty-one," he finally replied.

"Naomi's forty."

"She looks lovely," said Collins.

"Never know she has two kids," replied Butler.

"Kids? She married?"

"Divorced."

"Divorced!" said Collins, alarm in his voice.

"Mick," said Butler, "this is not the old country. People in America get divorced all the time. Besides, she's not a Catholic anyway. A nice Jewish girl."

"Good," said Collins.

"What?" asked Butler.

"Nothing," stammered Collins, averting Butler's stare. "I'm just glad she's not Catholic," he finally said, "because she might still be married."

"I love your Victorian morality," said a bemused Butler.

"What are you talking about?"

"Your Queen Victoria morality."

"I do not have Queen Victoria morality."

"Yes, you do."

"Well," said Collins slyly, "maybe just a little bit." Collins then cleared his throat, and Butler looked at the door to see the arrival of Quentin Quinney. "Let's make this good," said Collins. "Remember, Sugar, always treat your enemies better than you treat your best friends." They both stood up as Quinney approached.

"How are you, Collins, Butler," Quinney said, full of good humor.

"Quentin, let's sit right here," said Collins, gesturing to what the regulars called the "Hy Harris Memorial Table," after the late, hunchbacked manager of the Clancy Brothers who'd slept through most of their concerts at that very small table, wedged between the television stand and the kitchen door. Above the table was an article about the Lion's Head from *GQ* magazine called "The Last Great Saloon" by Fred Exley, who was also known to sleep at this very table. Also on the wall was a framed piece by Joe Flaherty from *The Village Voice* in 1971, "Three Nights Without the Lion's Roar," when the Internal Revenue Service closed the Head for lack of excise. Collins gestured Quinney into the corner table and sat across from him. Sugar grabbed a chair from the back room and sat on it backward, his arms resting on the chair's back. They had Quinney trapped.

"Did you find out that information for me?" asked Collins.

"I did. The man in charge is Charles Hornsmith of the British consulate, up on Third Avenue and 52nd."

"Good job," said Collins. "We'll put a man on him starting tomorrow morning. We also have good news for you—we like your plan for getting your man out of Varick Street."

"Well," said Sugar, "we don't have much choice." Sugar's big lips were turned down, practically imitating a Roman emperor giving the "thumbs down" sign.

"Well, Tom," said Collins, "I think it's a workable plan. What else are we going to do on such short notice?"

"That's the stuff," said Quinney enthusiastically. "This plan will work. We'll make the Brits look like fools!"

A flashbulb from a camera exploded behind Collins's head, literally making him see red. He heard two British accents, a man and a woman. Was it a setup with Quinney? Collins hated cameras, the one tool that would allow the British to identity him. Never was a man photographed at so many weddings with his head turned down or with a friend's hand in front of his face as was Collins. Even in 1992, he still hated cameras. "Excuse me," he said. He stood up and walked over to the man taking a picture of his wife standing in front of the giant, carved lion's head near the end of the bar. "Excuse me," he said again as he took the camera, fiddled with it for a second, and then exposed the film. The stunned man was about to say something when Collins shot him a glare and said, "Don't be impolite. You're not in your own country now." He handed the camera back to the man and returned to his seat. Naomi had been watching the scene, and her eyes began blinking rapidly, a sure sign that she was nervous. The Brit tourist was about to reply to Collins when she said, "Sir, we have a rule in here on photographs," as she made up a new rule. "They are not allowed. However, I should have informed you, so I am in error, and I'll have to buy you a drink on the house." The price being right, the offer was quickly accepted. Collins looked at Naomi, their eyes locking in solidarity and understanding.

Collins resumed his conversation with Quinney as if he had never left. "We'll need your help in the planning only," said Collins. Quinney looked at Collins differently. This man had a mean streak. Cold. Quinney would have to reevaluate Collins.

"Yeah," said Sugar, looking at Collins in near shock. "We couldn't put you out."

"Oh, that's no problem. I'd love to be part of this operation," said Quinney, not so cocky anymore. Collins looked at him and thought, I bet you would.

"We'll meet tomorrow, then, at noon. Is that alright with you?"

"Anything you want, Mick. Anything that is convenient for you."

"Then, we're done," said Collins. "And once again, Detective, thanks for all your help. Fahey was right, we'd be lost without you."

"Yeah, where is Fahey and that priest?"

"Oh, they're out of it now. It's us only. This is going to be some propaganda coup on our part," said Collins.

"You'll make the papers, alright," said Quinney. "Until tomorrow, then." The three of them shook hands, and Quinney headed out the door.

"He may have to go," said Butler icily when Quinney was out of earshot.

"No, need for that, Tom—yet. He's a cute cunt alright, but just trust me."

"I thought you were going to kiss him," said Sugar, the look of disgust still on his face.

Collins laughed as he watched Quinney make his way down the crowded bar and exit just as Holder entered. Quinney bumped Holder as he went up the narrow steps to the street and offered no apology, ignoring Holder's glare. Holder continued into the bar, trailed by Seymour Noz. The two men together were quite a sight.

"Hi, Earl," said Naomi, "the usual?"

"Yeah, thanks, honey." He took the vodka on the rocks, sat down in the seat that Quinney had just vacated, and placed his laptop computer on the table in front of him. "Seymour, you want anything?"

"Shirley Temple. Martini glass. Up. One maraschino cherry," came the reply. Half the bar turned to look at who had made the drink order, and the glances turned to stares when they saw Seymour Noz. The Shirley Temple was delivered and dropped in one gulp. Seymour plucked the cherry from the glass, put it in his mouth, and pulled the stem clear. "Hmmm," he said.

Seymour Noz was Holder's computer geek. He was twenty and doing graduate study at NYU. Tall and skinny, he was dressed in a black suit and white shirt and wore a sporty vinyl black fedora. He took the fedora off, revealing a yarmulke, then fanned himself with the hat.

"Humid," he said. Collins cleared his throat and looked at Holder.

"Mick," said Holder, "this is Seymour Noz. He works for me."

Collins looked at Seymour, his yarmulke, his *payess,* the long unshorn side locks of the Orthodox Jew, the wispy beard, and smiled. It reminded him of some of his meetings with the Chief Rabbi of Ireland, Isaac Herzog, in the old synagogue on the South Circular Road, the area of Dublin that had such a substantial Jewish population then that it was known as "Little Jerusalem." The meetings had been set up by Michael Noyk, Collins's real estate wizard, and Robert Briscoe, who would later become the Lord Mayor of Dublin, both of whom were Jewish.

The Chief Rabbi had been warm to the nationalist cause—sometimes much warmer than the Catholic Church—and he and Collins would often consult on a one-to-one basis. Often the Chief Rabbi would bring along his two-year-old son, Chaim. Years later, the world would be bemused to learn that the sixth President of Israel, this same Chaim Herzog, spoke in an Irish brogue. Collins couldn't care less about religion—all were welcomed in the cause, just as long as the job got done.

"Seymour, lad," said Collins, "nice to meet you."

"Same here, Mr. Collins," he replied.

"Mick."

"Yeah, Mick."

"You want another one of those Shirley things?" asked Collins.

"Sure."

Collins stared at Noz. "How did you meet Earl?"

"He arrested me."

Collins suppressed a laugh and looked at Holder. "For what?"

"Computer fraud."

"I let him walk," Earl said sheepishly.

"Good man," said Collins. "So, Earl, how do you like Quentin Quinney?"

"Haven't met him," replied Holder.

"Yes, you have."

"Where?"

"The man, in the doorway, on your way in."

Holder cocked his head. "That Quinney?"

"Yep," said Butler.

"Shit."

"Should we get down to business?" asked Collins.

"Man, you guys have a problem."

"What?" said Collins.

"Fucker is a double-dipper."

"How so?" asked Butler.

"Besides his NYPD salary, he's been getting twenty-five hundred bucks a month from London—"

"I knew it!" said Collins interrupting.

Holder flipped open the lid of his laptop and plugged it into an extension cord. "Tommy," he said handing Butler a telephone cord, "find me a phone jack." Butler took the wire, ran it along the ceiling A/C ducts, and plugged it into a wall jack behind the bar. Holder hit the on switch, and the silver screen came to life, getting Collins's immediate attention.

"But he's also drawing a check from the Feds for fifteen hundred," added Holder. "I think the Federal money is from the FBI, but I'm still checking."

"He's a double agent," said Collins.

"He's a fucking *triple* agent," said Holder.

"But who's his *real* employer?" asked Butler.

"Doesn't matter," said Collins.

"Here," said Holder to Collins and Butler, "see for yourself. Here's his Chemical Bank account. Seymour hacked in for us. The $1,557 is his NYPD biweekly salary." Butler and Collins leaned over and Holder moved the screen so they could see it. There it was under "Credits":

9/30/92 . . . $1,557.91
10/1/92 . . . $2,500.00
10/1/92 . . . $1,500.00

"Go backward," said Collins. Holder went back to September, then August, then July, and the numbers were repeated over and over.

Collins nodded his head. "You're pretty good with this," he said.

"Seymour here is a good teacher," confessed Holder. "He tells me that in ten years you'll be able to buy anything on a computer, from furniture to pussy." Holder laughed. "This is the intergovernment Internet. Been around since 1969. Better than teletype, fax, anything. You won't know this shit in a couple of years. It'll be all the rage."

"This is grand stuff," said Collins. "What about the e-mails?"

Butler was getting nervous. "Is this legal?" he asked.

"Who cares?" Holder replied.

"I like the way you think, Earl," said Collins as he shot Butler a look of disgust.

"E-mails?" said Holder, surprised. "Who told you about those?"

"Tommy here," answered Collins. "Quinney have e-mail?"

"I don't know," said Holder.

"You have e-mail when you were at IAD?"

"Yeah."

"Well, then, Quinney must have it too," said Collins. "Seymour, can you get us into Quinney's e-mail?"

"Sure," said Seymour, gesturing to Holder to surrender his seat. "What was your log-on at the NYPD?"

"Eholder/iad/nypd."

"What does IAD stand for?" asked Noz.

"Internal Affairs Division,"

"Where does this Quinney work?"

"Intelligence."

"Let's try qquinney/int/nypd and see what happens," said Noz.

"What are you doing, Seymour?" asked Collins.

"Oh, I'm sniffing some data."

"Sniffin'?"

"Yeah," said Noz, "we're going to do a little van Eck phreaking."

"Van Eck whatin'?" said Collins. Holder and Butler had completely blank looks on their faces.

"Yes," said Noz confidently, "I'm going to eavesdrop on his system. I can track anything in an electromagnetic field that is produced by the movement of data."

"You can?" said Collins.

"Yes, I can," said Noz, "You see, when electromagnetic radiation is present, it can be captured from computer displays that use CRTs and other devices."

"It can?" said Collins.

"Yes, it can," said Noz. "And I just did. We're in, gentlemen."

"The Noz knows!" said Holder triumphantly.

"Let's see his e-mail log," said Butler. The log came up with e-mails listed by the latest date and time. "There's an easy one," said Butler, pointing his thick index finger to the screen.

It read: jgarrett@fbi.gov.

"That fifteen hundred is from the FBI," said Collins.

"Look at this," said Holder excitedly, "he's sending a message right now."

The screen told the story: iboxer-clegg@mi5.uk.

Collins's eyes grew large. "MI5," he said, then added, "shite."

"Let's read along," said Holder.

"Sir Ian," the e-mail began, "made contact with IRA boss-man. He plans breakout at INS center on 15th. Suggest you come immediately. QQ."

"Sir Ian Boxer-Clegg," said Collins. "Who's he?" Butler and Holder shrugged their shoulders. "Sugar," Collins finally said, "call

Ernie Fahey and find out who Boxer-Clegg at MI5 is." He shook his head. "I feel sick."

Butler walked away, the cell phone to his ear. Collins blankly watched the Pittsburgh-Atlanta playoff game on television.

"You find out about his lady friend?" asked Collins.

"Yeah," said Holder, "I found her."

"What's Patricia's last name?" Collins suddenly asked.

"O'Malley," said Holder.

"Where does she work?"

"Intelligence also."

"I wonder if there are any e-mails to her?" said Collins. "Seymour," he commanded, "do your thing."

Noz changed screens and there it was: pomalley@nyc.gov/nypd. "Yep."

"I take it Patricia's the girlfriend," said Collins. "Mrs. Quinney?"

"House in Staten Island," said Holder. "Got that from NYPD personnel."

"Only one house?"

"Place in Breezy Point!"

"The Irish Riviera!" laughed Butler, who had returned from his phone call.

"What did Ernie say?" asked Collins, finding no humor in the situation at all.

"He'll have to check," said Butler. "He'll get back to us."

"Quinney's in it up to his neck," said Collins. "And I'm going to snap it off if I have to. What's your take, Earl? You're the Internal Affairs expert."

"He's in Intelligence, right?" said Holder as the other two nod-ded their heads. "The English money is probably coming from MI5, domestic intelligence, who keep their eyes on the Belfast boys. When this fellow of yours got out it must have embarrassed them some-thing fierce. Now they want their payback—and more. With proper intelligence they not only plan to get Twomey back to England, but they might also catch a couple of you guys trying to break him out. Could be embarrassing for a lot of people—the British not being one of them. And since Clinton is for you guys, it would be embarrassing for him, too. Bush could really bash him for catering to terrorists. Nice fishnet they have here, methinks. I think they have you just where they want you."

"How about the Feds?" asked Collins. "Where do they come in?"

Holder laughed. "The Feds and the NYPD hate each other. NYPD thinks the Feds are a bunch of pussies, gathering headlines at press conferences while the New York guys do all the work. My guess is that Quinney is the FBI's snitch inside the NYPD. He's in Intelligence, and he knows what's going on. If NYPD found out about this they would cut Quinney's balls off. Gentlemen, you have a major scandal brewing here."

"Yes, we do," said Michael Collins. "And I have *them* just where I want them."

"You also have a response," said Noz, and Collins peered over his shoulder to see the computer screen.

"QQ, will arrive first BA flight. Boxer-Clegg."

"Boxer-Clegg is your man," said Holder.

"Well, fuck him," spat Collins, clearly annoyed and suddenly combative. "Get up, Seymour," he said to Noz, "and give me that yoke." Collins sat down. "How do I respond to this?"

Seymour leaned over Collins's shoulder and hit the Compose icon, then clicked on Reply. "Type in your response, your message," Noz told Collins, which he began to do.

"You sure you want to do this, Mick?" asked Holder.

"Yes, I do," said a determined Collins. He began to touch-type as Noz, Butler, and Holder looked over his shoulder. "Boxer-Clegg. I know who you are and what you are. You've been warned. Michael Collins, IRB."

Sir Ian Boxer-Clegg, Director of "B" Division of MI5, was almost ready to retire for the night when he heard a "beep" emanating from his laptop indicating he had an e-mail. He saw it was from Quinney. "Boxer-Clegg. I know who you are and what you are. You've been warned. Michael Collins, IRB." The cognac red of his face instantly went white when he read "Michael Collins, IRB."

It must be an IRA hacker, he thought as he finished his drink. They must be catching up on the technology, the Belfast boys. It was after two A.M., but there was something wrong with that message. Terribly wrong. Someone stealing Michael Collins's name. Probably some wise arse. Then he thought back to the history lectures he had sat through at Sandhurst. Collins was the main man. He had written the book about getting rid of the British. There indeed was some-thing wrong here, but what was it? It was "IRB." The Irish Republi-can Brotherhood. There wasn't any IRB anymore, Boxer-Clegg knew, and that was the problem. For it had died that day with Michael Collins at Beal na mBlath.

13. |

At four twenty-eight A.M. the phone rang, waking Tommy Butler out of a fitful sleep. He lifted the receiver. "Yeah. Yeah, Ernie. Okay. Mick, it's for you. Ernie Fahey."

Collins, who had fallen asleep in an armchair, ran his hands over his face and into his hair, trying to bring life back into his fatigued body. "Yes, Ernie. Jaysus, what time is it?"

"It's almost four-thirty, Mick."

"What's up?"

"Sir Ian Boxer-Clegg is the head of 'B' Division, MI5."

"'B' Division," said Collins, still groggy. "He's in charge of the Belfast boys?"

"Correct," said Fahey. "My contact also informs me that Boxer-Clegg is booked on a British Airways jet for New York. He'll be here late this afternoon. This guy is special, Mick. It just can't be a coincidence that he's coming in as Twomey's getting set to go out."

"I agree," said Collins.

Fahey gave Collins the flight number and waited for instructions. "Do you want me to put a tail on him when he arrives?"

"I don't know," said Collins. He stared out the window, unable to think. "Prepare a dossier on him and I'll get back to you, Ernie. I have to think this out." Collins hung up the phone and sat quietly as Butler plopped back onto the couch, staring at the reflection of the streetlights on the ceiling. Angus sat next to Collins and nudged his ankle with his head. Collins reached down and petted the dog. "Good boy, Angus, good boy." Sometimes Collins hated the night, for he knew it was the time when he could too easily pinpoint the coward hiding in his soul.

Collins lit a Lucky, looked at the orange tip in the dark, then snubbed it out in an ashtray. He was lost in self-doubt. He knew the feeling well. It was the same feeling that had struck him just prior to Bloody Sunday, November 21, 1920. The previous months, then, had been hard on him. It had been torture losing friends like Terence MacSwiney, the Lord Mayor of Cork who had starved himself to death in a British prison, and Seán Treacy, shot dead in a blazing gun battle on Talbot Street, just a short walk from Nelson's Pillar and the GPO. That was bad enough. They were men, Fenians. Then Kevin Barry was captured and imprisoned in Mountjoy, scheduled to be hung by the neck. An eighteen-year-old medical student whom the British had captured when a simple ambush went awry. How to get him out? Bring in the Squad. Into Vaughan's Hotel on Parnell Square West. Plans were laid out. They would take down the whole side wall of Mountjoy Gaol and out would come Barry and he'd be off to America, to help churn the propaganda machine. Safe in America with DeValera so Collins could get back to work and dig at the British. But the wall did not come down and the British hung Kevin Barry and Michael Collins sat in his safe house in Phibsborough, lost, just like he was now.

He remembered that day like it was yesterday. He had sat in the kitchen of Dick and Kathleen Bartley at 30 Great Western Square, Phibsborough, not far from Doyle's Corner. He had met Dick through Kathleen, who was a member of the *Cumann na mBan,* the IRA's women's auxiliary. He had come to spend a lot of time with

Dick, an engineer on the Midland Great Western Railway, on his many trips down to Longford to court Kitty Kiernan. That morning Dick had gone off on the early train to Galway from the Broadstone station. Kathleen poured the tea and Collins bounced baby Billy on his lap as Kay, the toddler, pulled on the cuffs of his trousers. A knock had come to the door, and Collins had taken the baby into the front parlor while Kathleen answered the door.

"If it isn't Vinny Byrne," said Kathleen in her County Louth lilt.

"How are you Kathleen?" said Vinny. "Where's the boss?"

Collins came out of parlor with baby Billy flung over his left shoulder and his Luger in his right fist. He looked at Kathleen and Vinny and tried to decide which one was pinker in complexion. They could be brother and sister. Seeing Vinny lifted Collins's spirits. Charles Dalton, one of Collins's daring young men, would later write that "Vinny was an optimist. He was pleased with all the world and everybody in it." Everyone, except the British in Dublin town.

"Any news?" Collins asked, handing the baby to Kathleen, while young Kay tugged again, this time at her mother's dress.

Vinny shook his head. "Your man swung on time."

Collins winced at the bluntness of Byrne's words.

"Ah, sure it was all-a-cod," said Byrne, "thinking we could get the poor lad out of the 'Joy."

Collins looked at Byrne and suddenly became aware of the Pioneer pin in his left lapel. He lowered his eyes and saw the lump of a revolver in the right coat pocket. Vinny was something, thought Collins. He wouldn't touch a drink, but he'd murder in the name of God for Ireland.

Collins grabbed his hat, kissed Kathleen, tousled Kay's mop, then touched his finger to the baby's nose. "Ah, now, that's the good bab-ee," Collins said. "Thanks for the bed and the tay, Kathleen. See you again. Ta."

Collins and Byrne were out the door in a flash, and in long strides they walked around the green that centered the Square, heading for the spire of St. Peter's R.C. Church. Across from St. Peter's they took the first Number 22 tram for Nelson's Pillar.

November 1, 1920. Michael Collins is expected in the south, for it is Terence MacSwiney's funeral day. In Cork City they wait for Collins to appear at the coffin of the late Lord Mayor. The British Army is there. So are the auxiliaries, the Black and Tans, and members of "G" Division of the Dublin Metropolitan Police. All waiting for Collins to show up and give a Fenian eulogy at the coffin of his dead friend. But he is not in Cork City this day. He is in Dublin, failing.

November 1, 1920, and Kevin Barry went to the gibbet as the women in black stood outside Mountjoy on the North Circular Road saying their rosaries for the repose of his immortal soul because Michael Collins was not cunning enough to spring the boy. Collins and Byrne went by Mountjoy on the top of the open tram and the sea of black below began to look like a herd of banshees and the loud hiss of the rosaries became a screeching dirge.

November 1, 1920. All Saints Day. A day of holy obligation. Barry swung, while Collins sat, his Squad impotent, dispersed. Now in New York, Collins sat in a chair and buried his face in his hands. He was dead, but it still haunted him. It was his incubus buried deep in his subconscious, almost forgotten, that invariably leapt out to torment at the worst times. It was Collins's dark secret. And what did he do the last time? He lashed out at the British. He had no choice, for they were there to get him. "We have murder by the throat," Lloyd George smugly said. Collins would show them murder. And fourteen of their secret service agents were plugged. Into bedrooms all around Dublin on that Sunday morning, the Squad went out. Men as different as Vinny Byrne, the cheerful assassin, and the self-effacing and quietly brilliant Seán Lemass, who would be *Taoiseach* when President Kennedy visited Ireland in 1963, went out to do their duty at the behest of Michael Collins. Into bedrooms they went. Sometimes four to a party. Identify your man. Position him. Grab him by the hair and stick the barrel of the gun into the mouth so bullets won't be wasted. "May the Lord have mercy on your soul," Vinny Byrne and the rest of the shooters would sing. A quick bang and brain and bone and hair and blood were all over the walls. A quick recock and another shot for good measure. Let the women scream and cry. Your man was lucky, for he got to die for his country. Like Michael Collins would die for his. Collins's imprint was made. The ruthless terrorist. A secret service cadre no longer existed. David Lloyd George got the message and there would be peace. An Irish peace, which was never very peaceful or quiet. And God would also get the message and Michael Collins would float in the nothingness of purgatory until a bunch of inept revolutionaries and an idealistic Archangel would retrieve him. To make him live again his greatest torment, his own hell.

November 1, 1920.

October 15, 1992. Tomorrow.

What was he to do? There would be no Bloody Sunday this time. Fail, and deserve hell. It ran through Collins's mind, again and again.

A sudden bark came out of Angus.

"Michael," said the Archangel. Collins looked up to see his benefactor standing in front of his own portrait. He could see through the Archangel and still see his own painted image. Collins looked over at Butler, who had fallen back into sleep. *"Mícheál,"* said the Archangel, using the Irish for the first time. *"Me-haul,"* repeated the Archangel smiling, "I like the sound of that." He looked down at Collins. "Do not despair, my son. For you will succeed because of your soul, your conscience. Remember the words of your friend, Terence MacSwiney: 'It is not those who can inflict the most, but those that can suffer the most, who will conquer.'" The Archangel reached

137

down and put his great hand on Collins's head. "You are near the end of your journey now, Michael. I heard your plea as you lit your four candles, and I know you are suffering this very moment because of the task I have assigned you. But believe in the Lord thy God and renounce violence and all will be well. God bless you." The Archangel paused, then added: "Be wise as a serpent and gentle as a dove."

"'Be wise as a serpent and gentle as a dove,'" repeated Collins. "I like that," he said, looking at the Archangel.

"They are the words of Christ our Lord, Jesus," said the Archangel.

"Jesus?" replied Collins, surprised, but when he looked up again the Archangel was gone.

He lit up another Lucky and sucked smoke deep into his lungs in the dark, then exhaling the smoke, like a fierce dragon, through his nose. Was this really happening? Or was it just a bad dream? Was he really dead? And why was he in New York, of all places, in the year 1992, to get some eejit out of jail? This couldn't be happening. He took another drag on the cigarette and stared down at Butler's bare wood floors. Then he saw something. He reached down and picked up a small emerald-green feather. He held the feather in his hand, twirling it in his fingers. Collins smiled, patted the Lucky out, then made the Sign of the Cross. He stood up and walked over to the sleeping Butler, Angus at his heels. "Wake up, Sugar. We have work to do."

14.

It was still dark when a half-asleep Ulysses Morgan arrived. Tommy Butler answered his door, and Morgan said curtly, "Sugar, are you trying to kill me?"

Morgan had sent his last WelshDragon flight off to Cardiff and London at ten forty-five P.M., started drinking at the Lion's Head at midnight, and was home and in bed in his studio apartment on Morton Street by three A.M. He had been awakened by Butler at five-fifteen A.M., had showered and dressed, and had arrived at Butler's home by five-fifty.

"Hughey," said Butler, "a young fellow like you complaining about a lack of sleep. Why, when I was your age, I'd never sleep." Morgan just grunted. "Hughey, this is Michael Collins."

Collins was seated at Butler's kitchen table. The only thing on the table was a single deck of cards. "Ulysses," said Collins in greeting.

"My friends call me Hughey," said the tall, handsome Welshman, who looked down at The Big Fellow.

"Hughey it is, then." Collins gestured toward a chair, and Morgan took a seat. Collins picked up the cards and began shuffling them. Morgan looked at Butler, who shrugged his shoulders.

"Hughey," said Collins, "you look like a man who might enjoy a game of chance."

"My mother told me," said Hughey in his deliberate way of speaking, "never to play a game of chance with an Irishman." He looked Collins right in the eye. "She said—fellow Celts or not—they were far too cunning a people."

Collins, who was spreading the deck in a fan, laughed. "Your mother—like most mothers—is a very perceptive human being. Would you like some of Sugar's coffee, Hughey?"

"Jesus, no," said Morgan. "It was bad enough I had to drink the stuff when I lived here with him."

"Sugar didn't tell me you lived here."

"Oh," said Morgan with a glint in his eye, "Sugar doesn't tell all his secrets to anyone, even Michael Collins." Collins wondered what Morgan meant by that, but he didn't say anything. "Do you know we were bartender partners at the Lion's Head?" Collins shook his head. "I arrive from Wales on a tourist visa, fall in love with New York, end up as a barman working with Sugar, and he ends up saving my ass from the INS."

"INS?" said Collins, raising his eyebrows.

"They find out I don't have a green card and want to deport me."

"And Sugar saves you?"

"Yep," said Morgan, "the Butler did it."

"Ah, shucks," cut in Butler, "it was nothing."

"It was nothing," said Morgan, "if you have a U.S. Congressman in your pocket. Presto! Green card."

"A U.S. Congressman?" said Collins.

Butler smiled. "The good Congressman once had a little problem with drugs and a college coed at the Head. I made it go away. If he didn't help Hughey, I was going to make it reappear—on 'Page 6' of the *New York Post*. And then he was going to go away."

"So you've had your own problems with the INS?" said Collins as he pulled the ace of spades, the queen of hearts, and the king of diamonds from the deck. "I have a problem with them right now that you might be able to solve, Hughey. Can you find the ace of spades?" Collins had the three cards, faceup, in front of him. He flipped them over and started moving them about. He was no Buster the Dealer, but he wasn't bad.

"There," said Morgan as he slammed his hand down.

Collins flipped the card, the queen of hearts. He then gathered the cards again and spread them.

"You didn't show me the other cards," said Morgan.

"You didn't pay," said Collins, "so you don't get to see the lay." Butler laughed at Collins's perfect Buster-the-Dealer inflection. Collins, thought Butler, was a rap artist in training.

Morgan, showing an adept hand of his own, flipped the cards, faceup: the queen of hearts, the king of diamonds, and the jack of clubs. "Where's the ace of spades?"

Collins held up his right hand. He had palmed it.

"You cheated," said Morgan.

"Sleight of hand, m'man," said Collins.

Butler looked at Collins, then Morgan. "Shit," he said, then let out a loud laugh and clapped his hands together.

"What?" said Morgan.

"I want you to help me make the Orangeman disappear from MI5," said Collins. "British Military Intelligence."

Morgan looked at Butler. Butler knew the score and watched as Collins began to woo Morgan. "Where's he going to disappear from?" asked the Welshman.

"A British Airways jet bound for London," said Collins.

"Is he going to reappear?" asked Morgan.

"Perhaps," said Collins.

"Perhaps where?" pressed Morgan.

"Perhaps on Aer Lingus Flight 104 to Shannon."

Morgan nodded. "It can be done," he said.

"Just how?" asked Collins.

"Do you have a pen and paper?" asked Morgan. He began to jot pen to paper, Butler and Collins looking over his shoulder. "Aer Lingus is here," he said, drawing a long box, "at the far end of the International Arrivals building. To the immediate left of Aer Lingus," he said as he drew a circular structure, "you have TWA passenger and cargo. Right next to that," he drew a bold X, "you have British Airways."

"So we're one building off," said Collins.

"You are," said Morgan.

"I'll have to ask Earl," said Collins, "how exactly they transport prisoners around JFK."

"Earl Holder?" said Morgan. Collins gave him a look. "It's okay, Earl and I are old chums. The finest."

"He's sound," said Collins.

"You don't have to be a cop for that. It's done all the time. The U.S. extradited some guy to Cardiff last month on WelshDragon. They take them right to the tarmac and hustle them right on the plane."

"Right on the plane?" said Collins.

"Yes," said Morgan, "they don't even go through the terminal. It's all runway action. They don't want to disturb the other passengers, so the prisoner goes directly from the paddy wagon—"

"Paddy wagon," interrupted Collins, crooking his head to the side in confusion. "Ah," he said brightening, "the Black Maria."

"Yes," continued Morgan with a trace of a smile, "they take the prisoner directly from the Black Maria to the plane."

"How do they actually get them on the plane?" asked Collins.

"You know the umbilical that goes to the plane?" asked Morgan. Collins nodded. "Well, that's called the Jet-Bridge, and it has an outside staircase for access. They pull the car up on the tarmac, your man goes up the stairs, and then they seat him on the plane before the rest of the passengers come on. There is no disturbance. Everything runs very smoothly. Most of the time the other passengers don't know there's a convict on board unless they see the handcuffs."

"How's security?" asked Collins.

"Security," replied Morgan, "is notoriously lax. Most people wouldn't get on an airplane if they knew how bad it is. If you have the right I.D., papers, and an NYPD detective's shield—and balls— you can pull anything off."

Collins pursed his lips. "Hughey, at Shannon, on my way to New York, I saw this big boxlike yoke on a lorry bringing stuff up to the side of the plane. What's that for?"

"That's called a catering truck. They bring the food and beverages up to the galleys."

"Is there room for men in one of them?"

"Sure," said Morgan. "They're extensive, the size of a room. No problem with getting several men on them."

"So that's where we'll do it," said Collins.

"Do what?" asked Morgan.

"Turn the Orangeman into the ace of spades."

Collins washed his hands in the kitchen sink while he listened to WQEW: *"New York, New York . . . it's a wonderful town . . . the Bronx is up, and the Battery's down . . . the people ride in a hole in the ground . . . New York, New York, it's a wonderful town . . ."* He turned the radio off.

"And that's what it is lads, 'a wonderful town.' I love this city," Collins said as he sat down at Butler's kitchen table. Butler was to his left, Fahey to his right, and Holder, laptop open in front of him, sat opposite him.

"Collins," said Holder, "don't you ever sleep? Christ, it's not even seven A.M. yet."

"Earl," replied Collins, ignoring his complaint, "you know why I love this city?"

"No," said Holder sullenly, "please enlighten me."

"Because of three-card monte," said Collins. "I love three-card monte."

"Collins," said Holder, "you're fucking nuts."

"Three-card monte, gentlemen, is a wonderful game."

"Mick," said Ernie Fahey, "what in God's name are you talking about?"

"Three-card monte is going to be Martin Twomey's salvation." Collins was quiet for a moment while all eyes were pulled to him, as if by magnetic force. "It's going to be my salvation also, because that's how we are going to make the Orangeman disappear, just like in three-card monte." Collins abruptly stood up as if suddenly energized. "Are you in, Earl? Will you help us?"

"You know I'm in, man," said Holder. "Christ, whatever you're up to, it's going to be a hoot."

"You have to live here when I'm gone," said Collins. "I don't want you to end up in prison."

"Don't worry about me, Collins. After all, I am being paid. We have a professional relationship." Holder placed his right hand on his heart and solemnly lowered his eyes. "It would be a breach of confidentiality for me to divulge anything to anyone," he said. Spencer Tracy had nothing on Earl Holder.

"Would you like to come to Ireland with me, Earl?"

"Nope. I'm staying right here."

"Good," said Collins. He turned to Fahey. "Whatever this man wants—money or any other kind of support—he gets, got it?" Fahey nodded affirmatively. "Now, Earl, you know who our bagman is."

"Ernie," said Holder, "it's a pleasure to meet you." Fahey smiled and nodded.

Collins turned to Butler. "Sugar, do you have a passport?"

"I do," said Butler. "Why?"

"Because you're coming with me and Twomey."

"Mick, I don't know—"

"No," said Collins, "that's an order. You can come back when things cool down. As for you, Ernie, you're staying here to spin the propaganda machine. I take it you have contacts in Dublin?"

"Very close contacts at the Department of Foreign Affairs," said Fahey.

"Good, because you are going to use them like you never used them before," said Collins. "As soon as that Aer Lingus jet is over Canada, hit the phones and let the world know! I have a meeting with Quinney at noon at the Lion's Head. He's going to be my guest for a while."

"Your guest?" said Holder.

"Yes," said Collins, "we are going to extract Mr. Quinney from the equation for the moment. Quinney is the key, the catalyst. Without Quinney, we have nothing. With Quinney, things move. Do you understand?"

"I don't have a clue what you're talking about, Mick," said Fahey.

"You've lost me, pal," said Holder.

Only Butler nodded.

"Where can we keep him?" Collins wanted to know.

"How about the Lion's Head's office in the basement?" said Butler. "Owner's away, let the Fenians play."

"Private enough?" asked Collins.

"Solid," agreed Holder, nodding his head.

"Hold on," said Fahey. "Why are you kidnapping him? What's he done?"

"Informer," said Collins.

"Informer!" said Fahey. He was stunned by the most notorious word in an Irishman's vocabulary. "You're mad."

"Am I," said Collins. "Earl, enlighten Mr. Fahey."

"Quinney is on the payroll of the NYPD, the FBI . . ."

"God," said Fahey.

". . . and MI5," continued Holder.

Fahey turned ashen. "Jesus, MI5. We're done for."

"I have to know something immediately," said Collins. "When was the last time Boxer-Clegg was in America?"

"Not in three years, at least," said Fahey.

"And how long has Quinney worked for you?"

"Eighteen months."

"He said you two were old friends."

"Not quite," said Fahey. "We were having a fund-raising in the Bronx, and he came up to me and we got to talking."

"Oh, so he came up to you," said Collins. "He volunteered. So he's not such an altruist or old friend, eh?"

"No," said Fahey. "I never met him before that fund-raiser. I thought I did right in trying to get as much intelligence help as I could."

"Ernie," said Collins, "you did do right. Now we're going to do right by Mr. Quinney. Do you pay him for information?"

"I pay him what the information is worth. Since Twomey is so important to the organization, this time he got five thousand dollars. How did you know?"

"I smelled it," said Collins.

"The cocksucker," said Butler. "He's drawing four fucking salaries!"

Collins laughed, and Holder spat. "I'm afraid I'm going to agree with you now, Sugar," said Collins. "I think your man has to go."

"Jesus, Mick," said Fahey, "this is getting sticky."

"Sticky, indeed," said Collins. "Now, the question of the moment is: Has Boxer-Clegg ever met Quinney?"

"Never," said Holder.

"How can you be so sure?" asked Butler.

"Quinney doesn't have a passport. I checked," said Holder.

"Good work, Earl," said Collins, "but does he have an Irish passport?" Holder shrugged his shoulders.

"Let's assume they haven't met," said Holder. "Now what?"

"Now," said Collins, "don't you think I'd make a fine-looking figure as an NYPD detective?"

"You're joking," said Fahey.

"I'm not," said Collins. "If that little weasel has never met Boxer-Clegg—and my guess is he hasn't—I'll meet Sir Ian Boxer-Clegg when he arrives at Kennedy tonight and lead him around New York by the hand."

"How can you be so sure they haven't met?" asked Butler. "This is getting very dangerous."

"It is," said Collins, "but I don't think this is the way these two lads work. Look, Quinney is into everybody. The more inauspicious he is, the better off he is. He was probably recruited by the British Consulate here in New York. Quinney deals directly with Boxer-Clegg, via the telephone, via the e-mail, and the money is wired into his banking account. Boxer-Clegg has his informer in the NYPD, but it's only a voice on the phone, or an e-mail. Their anonymity to each other is important for their own protection. It's perfect for both of them."

"You could be right," said Holder.

"It's our only chance," said Collins. "Ernie, do you have that dossier on Boxer-Clegg?" Fahey handed over the manila folder. Collins flipped through it. "Typical. Sandhurst, all over the Middle East, MI6, MI5 since the '80s." Collins closed the folder and handed it back to Fahey. "Ernie, I haven't looked at a British intelligence agent's dossier in a long time, but they never change. Fancy schooling, police the colonies, then terrorize the colonists. Never changes."

Collins shook his head, pursed his lips, and thought of the Cairo Gang—so-called because they too had been recruited from the Middle East—the British intelligence thugs he had taken out on Bloody Sunday. Somehow it still riled Collins the way the British used the empire to nurture their intelligence agents, then sent them back to their first colony—Ireland—to torment the Irish. He could never forget Tom Clarke's bitter words describing the British as they left the GPO at the end of the Rising: "All they leave behind is their stink."

"I'll meet Tom and Earl in the office of the Lion's Head about eleven forty-five this morning. Earl, bring what you need. You know, handcuffs, whatever, and can you get one of those orange jumpsuits that they seem to love over here so much in a wee size for your man?"

"Sure, that's easy," replied Earl.

"We don't want to mess up Mr. Quinney's sartorial splendor now, do we? And Earl," continued Collins, "don't forget your piece. Quinney is armed, so don't take any chances. Understood?"

"Got it, Mick," said Holder.

Collins got up from the table and began pacing. His intensity was palpable. He swiftly turned to his cohorts. "What are those big black cars called?"

"Limos?" said Butler.

"That's it," said Collins, "the fancy limo." He waved his forefinger in the air at Butler. "Get me one of those for tonight and for all day tomorrow."

"With a driver?" said Butler.

"No, no, no," replied Collins. "We'll supply our own driver. You or Earl."

"Shit," said Holder, "he'll have me shining shoes soon!"

All the men laughed except Collins. "What's the joke?" he said.

"Blacks are frequently shoe shiners or limo drivers," replied Butler simply.

"Bloody marvelous," said Collins. "Both of you better be ready. God knows what will happen." Collins began pacing again, then stopped. "One other thing, Ernie. We'll need another hard man. Do you understand me?"

"I do."

"Not an American, but maybe one of the Belfast boys. Are any available?"

"Ciaran Pike is your man."

"Then Ciaran it is," replied Collins.

"What are you going to do to Quinney?" asked Fahey.

"I don't know. I only hope I don't have to send him to his maker," replied Michael Collins.

15. |

Quentin Quinney walked into the Lion's Head at noon on the dot. The bar was empty, except for Naomi, who was cutting fruit.

Quinney flashed his badge. He always preferred intimidation to finesse. "My name's Quinney, doll," he said to Naomi, "I'm here to see Michael Collins."

Doll, thought Naomi. She took the knife, aimed it at Quinney, and thought how she'd like to give his anatomy the ultimate *bris,* starting with his wise-guy tongue and working her way down. She pointed with the knife to the kitchen door on her right. "Through that door, to the left, down the stairs to the basement, and the office is right in front of you."

Quinney nodded and did what he was told. He rapped on the office door, and Michael Collins said, "Come in."

As Quinney opened the door, Tom Butler grabbed him by the neck and tried to get hold of his right arm. But Quinney was too quick for Butler. He pulled his arm away and reached for his service revolver.

"Weapon!" Holder yelled as Butler tried to squeeze Quinney's head off by the neck. At the sight of Holder, Quinney screamed "Fucking nigger" and leveled the pistol at Collins. Holder grabbed

Quinney's wrist and yanked it up toward the ceiling. Using all his strength, Quinney managed to squeeze off one round. The sound of the explosion filled the tiny office as the bullet tore into Michael Collins's forehead, lifting him off the ground. In the air he listed, then hit the floor facedown like a deadweight.

Butler slammed Quinney's head against the desk as Holder snapped his elbow and the gun rattled to the floor. "Motherfucker," said Holder.

Tom Butler rammed his fist into Quinney's eye, putting his lights out. As Quinney hit the floor, Holder kicked him in the ribs, then handcuffed his hands behind his back as he kneed him in the lower spine.

Facedown on the cold concrete floor, Michael Collins opened his eyes.

"Mick, Mick, oh my God, Mick," said Butler, almost in a hush, as he fell to his knees and pulled Collins by the shoulder, gently cupping his injured head in his arm. "Call 911," he barked at Holder.

"What for?" said Collins, pulling himself into a sitting position. There wasn't a mark on him. "Nice job, men, but I see the both of you are a wee bit rusty," he said as he rubbed his forehead with the back of his right hand. "If we have to do this again, let's put your man down before he gets his gun out."

"Are you okay?" asked Butler incredulously.

"Man," said Holder, snatching the .38 off the floor, "I saw that shell go into your head. What's going on?"

Collins stood up and smiled at Butler and Holder. "Let's wake up our friend," he said. Butler looked on the desk where a pint glass was still filled to the top with beer from the night before. The beer was as flat as piss and smelled worse. He took the glass and poured it onto Quentin Quinney, who awoke with a groan. Butler grabbed Quinney by the collar and flung him against the wall. "Do your stuff," Collins said to Holder, making sure not to mention any names.

Holder went to his knapsack and pulled out the cotton wool and duct tape. Quinney was still groggy as Holder told him, "Keep your fucking eyes shut." Holder placed the cotton over Quinney's eyes, then held it in place with a six-inch piece of duct tape. He unlocked the handcuffs. "Okay, strip."

Butler pulled his jacket off as Quinney slowly undid his tie. He tossed the jacket to Collins, who took out Quinney's gold detective shield and admired it. Quinney took off his shirt and then slowly undid his belt and started to slide his pants down, feeling for his escape. He was so close when he heard the hammer of the .38 click, and Holder shoved the revolver into his ear.

"Death wish, detective?" said Collins, and Butler pulled Quinney's .22 backup pistol out of his ankle holster. Quinney sighed, and Holder undid the hammer.

"Almost," whispered Quinney.

"Yeah," replied Collins, "you were almost dead."

Off came the shoes. All Quinney was wearing now was his underwear and socks. Holder recuffed him and pushed him into a chair.

"You scream," said Holder, "and I'll cut your fucking tongue out, you understand, pally?" Quinney sat silent. Butler, in a move he learned from the Christian Brothers, gave him a cuff at the base of his skull. "Understand?" Holder repeated, and Quinney grunted his acknowledgment.

"Collins," said Quinney quietly, cocking his head to the right, like a blind man. "I hit you square. You should be dead."

Collins grunted. Holder took out the electric razor and started giving Quinney a buzz cut.

"You hear me, Collins?" said Quinney again. "You should be dead."

Holder hit him with his knuckles. "Shut the fuck up," he said to Quinney.

Collins laughed. "Maybe, Detective, you got lucky and didn't end up killing anyone this time. Maybe God was looking out for you."

"God?" said Quinney. "Shit."

Holder finished Quinney's hair. "Stand up and turn around," said Holder. He unlocked the handcuffs once again and handed Quinney a Department of Corrections orange jumpsuit with DOC stenciled on the back. "Get into these," Holder commanded.

Quinney felt the jumpsuit and stumbled to get into it.

"Hurry up," said Butler.

"I can't see," said Quinney.

Butler put his mouth to Quinney's ear and said evenly, "Shut the fuck up or you won't be hearing anything soon, either. You understand?" Quinney nodded. When Quinney finally got the jumpsuit on, Holder cuffed him behind his back and then pushed him back into the chair. Butler applied leg shackles, then pulled off one of Quinney's socks, rolled it into a ball, and stuffed it into Quinney's mouth. Holder sealed Quinney's lips with more duct tape. Quinney gulped for air. "Breathe through your nose, asshole," said Butler.

Holder handed Quinney's .38 to Collins. "Here's the biscuit," he said.

"Biscuit?" said Collins, surprised.

"Street slang," replied Holder, "for a piece."

"Biscuit," repeated Collins as he placed Quinney's service revolver in the belt holster. "A Jacob's Biscuit," smiled Collins. "Come on, lads. Let's go upstairs for a while."

"Wet the tay," said Collins to Naomi as he sat down at the bar. Naomi returned from the back room with a cup of boiling water and a tea bag. She held the tea bag in front of Collins, as if trying to hypnotize him. "What in the name of God is that?" he said.

"A tea bag," said Naomi.

"God bless the Americans," said Collins, "they invented a bag to make tea with. How does it work?"

"Try inserting it into your cup of water," said Naomi coyly.

Collins did what he was told, and the water turned into tea. It was an Irish feast of Cana. "Milk and sugar, please," he said.

"For what?" asked Naomi.

"Sweet tea, my dear," said Collins. "Irish sweet tea."

"No lemon?"

"Do I look like I have scurvy?" asked Collins. Naomi grunted and did what she was told. "The only problem with this," continued Collins, "is that you can't read the tea leaves." Butler had a Coca-Cola, and Holder a vodka on the rocks. "So much for nonviolence," Collins finally said, putting out a Lucky in the plastic ashtray.

"He started it," said Holder.

"Just what I'd expect an ex-policeman to say," said Collins, grinning. Holder nodded his head and shrugged his shoulders.

"It's the only thing this type of guy understands," added Butler.

Collins nodded his head in agreement. "You're right, unfortunately."

"What if someone's looking for him?" asked Naomi.

"You know nothing," said Butler. Naomi nodded.

"Welcome to the *Cumann na mBan*," said Collins, laughing.

"The what?" said Naomi.

"The IRA's women's auxiliary."

"So I'm only good enough for the auxiliary," said Naomi. "I don't even get into the regular IRA?"

American women, thought Collins. "Oh, yes," he said. "Everyone is equal in America. In that case," Collins said as he placed Quinney's biscuit on the bar, "You go downstairs and—"

"No, thank you," said Naomi, and Collins placed the gun back in the belt holster. "What are you doing with him down there?" she asked.

"I'm letting him think," replied Collins.

"About what?"

"About if he's going to be killed."

"You're not, are you?" asked Naomi alarmed.

"No," said Collins, "but I've learned over the years that the careful application of terror is also an excellent form of total communication. I'm not going to manhandle him more than I have to. But I've found thinking of death is good for the soul."

"How's the head, Collins?" asked Holder.

"What happened?" Naomi interjected, concerned.

"Quinney shot Mick in the head," replied Butler.

"Straight through the forehead," added Holder for emphasis.

Naomi looked at Collins. In profile he had a classic Celtic forehead, jutting out just above the eyebrows—almost Neanderthal in a way. "I thought I heard something downstairs, but I don't see any wound," she finally said.

"God is good," replied Collins.

"But—" she began.

Collins placed one hand on Naomi's wrist and put the other to her lips. "No more about this," he said looking Naomi intently in the eyes. "Do you all understand?"

A chill ran down Holder's back. "Yeah, Collins," he said. "Yeah, now I understand."

"Fuck, fuck, fuck, fuck," Quentin Quinney growled into the sock in his mouth as the office door was slammed.

He listened as the three men climbed the creaking stairs above the office. As soon as the footsteps disappeared he flipped his body over onto the floor, hoping that they didn't hear him as he hit the deck. The exertion of falling over left him out of breath. He gulped for air but only succeeded in swallowing a little piece of his sock. Be calm, he told himself. Quiet. Breathe through your nose. He began to take regular full breaths through his nostrils. He was okay. But how was he going to get himself out of this mess?

The phone. Where's the phone? He was blind and gagged. Collins had turned him into fucking Helen Keller. "Oh, shit," he thought. He tried to reconstruct the basement in his mind's eye to find the telephone. He inched around on the ground, very gingerly because it was hard to breathe, hoping to find a telephone wire. All he succeeded in doing was getting his cuffed hands scraped. He tried to pull his wrists and hands under his ass and to the front, but he couldn't. Exhausted, he rolled over into the fetal position.

That fucking Collins, he thought. Who was setting up who? He couldn't believe what they had done to him. He always thought Ernie Fahey was a lightweight. Ernie was a fund-raiser and a PR man, basically. Good in front of a TV camera explaining away the latest IRA atrocity. He had never held a gun in his life. Where did Collins, the fat man, and the nigger come from? He wanted to roar in anger, but he knew he'd better relax—anger would only choke him to death.

Quentin Quinney had always been the runt. All his brothers were bigger than he was. Christ, even his sister outweighed him. But he made up for his smallness with energy and grit. He always came at you. And he was tough. He learned at an early age of the shit-pecking order. Someone shat on the guy above you, who shat on you, so you better have someone below you to shit on, too. It was a poor philosophy of life, he knew, but so far it had worked for him.

He had worked for every single thing he had ever gotten out of life. He had worked for his badge. He had worked for the affections of his wife. He had worked for that house on Staten Island where his wife and two boys lived. And to Quinney, work equaled money. You needed money for a wife, a house, and tuition to send your kids to private Catholic schools. His children would not be going to public school with the spooks. He would not have his kids imitating them by wearing pants that were four sizes too big for them, constructed to reveal the crack of their asses. He had no intention of hearing rap shit music coming out of his sons' bedroom, either.

He had fought for everything he got. He did four years at the John Jay College of Criminal Law for his degree and then joined the force. He ended up walking a beat in the Thirtieth Precinct in Harlem. They called it the "Dirty Thirty" because of the corruption going on up there. When he was new he had noticed a lot of cops with envelopes bulging with greenbacks. He soon learned that the money had been coming from drug dealers. Not arrested drug dealers, but ripped-off drug dealers. He kept his mouth shut and his eyes open. As one of the newer members of the precinct he was presumed clean and was eventually given a call by the brass in One Police Plaza downtown. You want a detective's shield? Then help us out. Which he did. Got the goods on four of his fellow officers. "Ratfink scumbag," the Police Benevolent Association delegate had labeled him. But Quinney didn't care. He was out for himself. On the force less than eighteen months, and he had made detective. As soon as the indictments went down, he was out of the Three-Oh and into intelligence—where he found the real money was. Soon he knew everyone who was anyone in the intelligence establishment and he was willing—for a fee—to help them solve their own intelligence "problems."

And he needed the money because he had met Officer Patricia O'Malley, who also worked in intelligence. She was something, alright. The first time he saw her his dick had almost burst through his zipper. She was instant erection material. A few drinks, a pat on the ass, and one thing had led to another, which led to their little bungalow on Breezy Point. Their "honey nest," she had called it. It was their little secret, and like everything else in life, secrets demanded money. Money for him had become an elixir. It gave him power. Wife and kids in one life, Patricia in the other. It was kind of exciting in its own way. But it was also a lie. And he was living a giant lie. He could lie with the best of them. He could look his wife in the eye and lie so convincingly that she actually believed him. He was working undercover. He was working a stakeout. He was working on a special intelligence project for the commissioner. He was so good at it that he began to believe it himself.

But the lies and the absences had eventually taken their toll. His wife had grown cold. His kids, now in high school, were distant, more interested in girls and cars than in their father the cop. Maybe it was the residual Catholic guilt of his childhood. He often thought of an annulment as a solution. Catholic divorce. Good Catholics got annulments. He had researched it. Lucille Ball had gotten an annulment from Desi Arnaz—two kids and all—and had gotten remarried by the fucking Cardinal in St. Patrick's Cathedral. Even Giuliani, the guy Dinkins had beaten to become mayor, had gotten an annulment because he had married his cousin. Rudy claimed ignorance, which was a neat trick. Quinney heard that it had only cost Giuliani ten grand. But Quinney wasn't married to his cousin or a movie star. He was just a cop who knew that this part of his life was over. But he didn't know how to let it go.

Let go and go to O'Malley.

He knew his life was a deceit—to both his family and his job—but he was trapped in it, and he couldn't let go because one duplicity fed the other. But he thought he had everything under control. Nobody knew. Except Collins.

That fucking Collins, he thought again. Fuck, how did he do it? He had hit him straight through the forehead at close range. Pop! But there had been no blood splatter. The force of the shot had driven Collins to the floor. And no blood. He couldn't have missed him, but apparently he had. Michael Collins. He knew that name. His father was a great one for Irish history, which he had gotten from his own father, who had fought in the War of Independence. Family history had it that grandfather Quinney was in the GPO.

Even if it was not true, it was a great legend. Quinney thought the old man had probably made it up. What was the harm? A real cock-and-bull story, but colorful.

Yet Collins knew his family boast was a fraud. But how?

"I know because *I* was there!" Collins had said the other night. "There were no Quinneys in the GPO in 1916."

He was adamant about it. He couldn't forget how intense Collins's blue eyes were as he destroyed the Quinney family myth. Said it right out. Said he was *there,* in the fucking GPO of all places.

Could it be true?

Here was a man he could not lie to or deceive. Or, apparently, shoot. It was almost as if Collins were a spirit. "A fucking ghost," he thought. "A fucking *Fenian* ghost."

When the three men got back to the office Quinney was on the floor, inching his way like a snake for the telephone on the desk.

"Baaad detective," said Holder as if talking to a recalcitrant puppy. Butler reached down for Quinney, picked him up like a bag of dirty laundry, and placed him back in his chair.

"Now, where the fuck did you think you were going?" asked Collins. Quinney tried to talk with the sock in his mouth but was only making gurgling sounds. "Take that yoke off his mouth," commanded Collins. Holder ripped the duct tape from his mouth and pulled out the sock. Quinney gulped for oxygen like a fish out of water.

"You murdering cocksuckers!" he screamed.

Holder crammed his hand around Quinney's neck, gripping his Adam's apple in a choke hold between his thumb and his forefinger. Collins put his mouth right to Quinney's ear. "Don't give me any of that sanctimonious cowshite," he said, "I know your filthy record and I wouldn't touch it with a rubbishman's gloves."

"Next time I'll dial 911," said Quinney.

"There won't be any next time," said Collins. "Anyway, why would you want to do that? If the police come, we'd have to turn over your bank records to them. There would be a lot of questions about why the FBI and MI5 have you on their payrolls. Wouldn't there?"

"You can't intimidate me," said Quinney. "Fuck you, Collins."

"I don't have to intimidate you," said Collins. "After all, I only have you in a basement, in an orange getup, your head shaved, your eyes covered with duct tape, and your hands cuffed behind your back. Why would I want to intimidate your after all that?"

"Wait till NYPD Intelligence gets here," retorted Quinney.

"Wait till IAD gets here," said Holder. "How will you be explaining Breezy Point to Internal Affairs?"

That shut Quinney up. "Detective," began Collins, "do you want to tell me about Sir Ian Boxer-Clegg?" Quinney let out with a chunk of spit that flew past Collins's head. Tommy Butler rammed his fist into the side of Quinney's head, knocking him off the chair. "Enough," said Collins quietly. "Put him back in the chair." Collins took a long breath. "I see that you don't want to talk about Boxer-Clegg, Detective, so we won't. Let's get back to Breezy Point."

Once again Quinney grew silent, which impressed Holder. He stuck his index finger in the air to get Collins's attention. Holder knew that Collins had pushed Quinney's button.

Holder knew these people—the Irish in the police. He had worked among them for nearly thirty years, and he knew what an isolated group they were. They were like an Irish clan—they talked only to cops, they drank only with cops, and they didn't trust any-one who wasn't an Irish cop just like themselves.

"Breezy Point," began Holder, letting the letters roll off his tongue. Holder had figured out that Breezy Point to Quentin Quinney was what Monte Carlo was to Prince Rainier. Holder had been there once, back in the late '60s. He had driven out there with his friend and cop partner Freddy Walsh and Freddy's parents. As they approached the security station, which looked just like Checkpoint Charlie in Berlin in 1961, Earl asked Walsh what all the security was for.

"Oh," said Freddy's mother in the backseat of the car, "that's to keep the niggers out."

Earl couldn't believe what he'd just heard and turned to see a very purple Mrs. Walsh suddenly realize that there was a nigger sitting in the front seat of her son's car. It was after this that the casual bigotry of the American Irish never failed to surprise Holder. "That's all right, Mrs. Walsh," Holder had calmly said, "but why, in God's name, would *they* want to get in?" Holder could never figure out the Irish attraction to Breezy Point. All it had was a bunch of old huts on concrete blocks stuck in the sand. Holder knew of the Irish and their relationship to the land, but it seemed that in America they had traded earth for sand.

"Ah, yes," continued Holder, "the gentle Atlantic waves hitting the shoals of Queens. The sun, the waves, the Budweiser . . ."

"Aren't you forgetting something?" Butler cut in.

"Ah, yes," picked up Holder, "what's a house without a woman in it?"

"Yes," continued Butler, "what's a house without a woman?"

"But not just any woman," said Holder.

The three of them just looked at each other. Collins stepped forward. "Not just any woman, Detective." Collins paused for effect. "Certainly not Mrs. Quinney." First Quinney turned pink. In a few seconds he was brilliant crimson.

"And what's a house without a woman," Holder said again, then paused. "The missus doesn't know about the bungalow, does she?"

Quinney bit down on his lip, not knowing what to say.

"And Mrs. Quinney doesn't know about Patricia O'Malley either," finished Collins. There was total silence as Collins let it sink in. Collins finally realized what Holder already knew: that Quinney was afraid of only one person in this world—his wife. They had Quinney, and Quinney knew it.

"Let's make a deal," Collins finally said.

"A deal," said Quinney. "Why should I make a deal with you guys? You're going to kill me one way or another."

"I'm not going to kill you," said Collins. "But let's face facts— you're going to do what I want you to do. Why take your whole family—and the girlfriend—with you? We'll not release any of the"— Collins searched for the right word—"eh, *unsavory* details to the press. That's a promise. You have my word. Make it easy on yourself—and them."

"I don't want my wife to know about Patricia," Quinney said quietly.

"You put yourself in this fix," said Collins, "but we certainly won't be the ones to inform on you."

"How can I trust you?"

"Look," said Collins, "I don't give a fuck about where you make your money. After we bag Twomey and are gone, you can steal the Crown Jewels for all I care."

"I still think you'll kill me," said Quinney.

"Why?" said Collins.

"Because I know who's in the organization."

"Look," said Collins, "if any of my people get hurt all I have to do is make one phone call, and your life will be worth nothing. Do you understand?"

"I do."

"Besides," added Collins, "you may be worth more to the organization working on the inside for us."

Dollar signs, Fenian dollar signs, danced in Quinney's mind.

"Do you think?" said Quinney.

Collins smiled. It wouldn't be the first time he had turned a cop.

"We'll see," he said, then paused. "Do we have a deal?"

Quinney finally nodded his head. "Deal," he said.

"You are, indeed, a double agent for the FBI and MI5, is that not true?"

"I am."

"Have you ever met Sir Ian Boxer-Clegg of MI5?"

"Not yet."

"Yet?" said Collins.

"I'm supposed to pick him up at JFK tonight."

"I have to ask you about Charles Hornsmith of the British Consulate. He is your contact and you do meet face to face, is that not true?"

"It's true," said Quinney. "He's the one who made the original deal with me. He's my bagman."

"Is he in on this operation?" asked Collins.

"Not really," said Quinney. "He's basically a paper pusher, not an enforcer. I think he can be scared off."

"What did you tell them about the operation to free Twomey?"

"I didn't tell anyone anything," said Quinney. Collins looked dubious. "This means a lot to Boxer-Clegg. I was going to let him get all the glory. I figured you would opt to hijack the van as it was leaving Varick Street. I was going to get the details from you at our meeting today and relay them to Boxer-Clegg."

"So Boxer-Clegg wanted all the glory for himself, is that it?" asked Collins.

"He's really psyched out over Twomey. He takes it as a personal affront that he escaped in the first place," said Quinney.

"Good enough," said Collins, gesturing toward Quinney. Butler retrieved the sock and was about to stuff it into Quinney's mouth when the detective spoke again. "One more thing. Do I have your word of honor, Collins, that you'll do right by my wife, my kids, and Patricia?"

"You have my word," said Collins.

"Then there's something you should know about Boxer-Clegg—he's a fucking faggot."

"You mean he's gay?" said a surprised Collins.

"Yeah," said Quinney, "just like the rest of them in MI5 and MI6. As queer as Philby's whole gang. A real flamer."

"How do you know?" said Collins.

"I'm in intelligence, remember?"

Collins gestured to Butler and the gag was stuffed back into Quinney's mouth. Collins had only one thought: *The ghost of Roger Casement / Is beating on the door.*

"What are you going to do?" asked Butler.

"The bastards did it to Casement," said Collins, his lips hardly moving. "Now I'm going to do it to *them*."

London's Heathrow Airport was fogged in so severely that it was impossible to see past the wings of the parked jets.

Sir Ian Boxer-Clegg was incensed by the delay as he reached the head of the priority check-in line.

"How long?" he snapped as he handed his ticket and passport to the clerk.

"Excuse me, sir?" said the clerk.

"How long before we can take off?"

"Best estimates, sir, are between two and three hours."

"My God," said Boxer-Clegg.

"That's the best we can do, sir."

"That's the problem with having a subsidized national airline," muttered Boxer-Clegg.

"Pardon?"

"It's run by peasants."

The clerk wanted to grab Boxer-Clegg by the ascot, but he needed the job. "Yes, sir," was all he said.

Boxer-Clegg took his boarding pass and headed for the British Airways VIP lounge. Inside the lounge was a barbershop. "Sir Ian," said the aged barber.

"Bobby," said Boxer-Clegg, "it's been a while."

"Last summer, I believe," said the Bobby the barber. "Your holiday in Spain."

"Holiday?" snickered Boxer-Clegg. "Some holiday, looking for Basque terrorists."

"Important stuff?"

"Top priority," said Boxer-Clegg. "You still give the best shave in London?"

"I do, indeed, sir."

"Then let's get on with it. I only ran the electric razor over it this morning. Going to be stuck here for hours. Might as well have it done."

"Good decision, sir," said Bobby as he helped Boxer-Clegg off with his jacket. "Would you like a shoe shine also?"

"Why not," said Boxer-Clegg, removing his ascot, and Bobby waved over the West Indian shoe shine man. Boxer-Clegg put his foot on the shine box as Bobby began wrapping steaming towels around his face. Boxer-Clegg felt the prick of the shoe shine brush through his sock and said through the towel, "Don't be so bloody clumsy!" in a voice that could chill. The shoe shine man meticulously finished his job.

"I hope you didn't get any polish on my socks," he said to the shine. "Thank you so much," he added as he coolly handed a fifty-pence piece to the man.

The man looked at the tip and wanted to tell Boxer-Clegg that he could shove his fifty pence where Jack stuck the rusty shilling, but this was not the kind of man you said this to. A simple "Thank you" followed, and Boxer-Clegg knew he still had the power to keep people in their place.

"Where are you going today?" asked Bobby the barber.

"America. New York."

"Big business?"

"Remember that breakout the IRA pulled in a Belfast courthouse several years ago?"

"Several of your men were shot, weren't they?" inquired Bobby.

"Two killed," said Boxer-Clegg. "Well, one of these patriots"—he pronounced *patriots* like it was a synonym for *shit*—"is coming home with me tomorrow."

"Good show," said Bobby.

"Good show, indeed," agreed Boxer-Clegg with some hubris. "We'll give him a good show. There's won't be any more coddling by the American authorities and politicians. And I'll be the one bringing him back to London," he said, imagining the "perp-walk" from the plane in front of the TV cameras. "Then we'll see how tough that IRA thug Martin Twomey really is," his voice beginning to build up volume in anticipation of having Twomey to himself, "when he's alone with me in the interrogation room." He caught himself. "But I shouldn't be telling you this."

"Your secret couldn't be safer," said Bobby as he began shaving Boxer-Clegg's neck.

"I appreciate that, Bobby."

"Yes," said Bobby, "you're safe as safe can be. Safe all the way."

Bobby splashed Boxer-Clegg's face with lime-scented English Leather aftershave. The MI5 sector chief shook his head at the sting. "Bobby," he said, "will you hand me my laptop?" Boxer-Clegg removed the computer from its carrying bag and attached the electrical plug and the phone jack. "Here," he said, handing them to Bobby, "plug these in." Bobby did as he was told. It was not common to see a customer use a laptop, but it had been done before. "Let's see what the world has for us today," said Boxer-Clegg as he checked his e-mail. There were two e-mails from Quinney. The first, sent before he was taken prisoner, confirmed his flight number and arrival time in New York. The other was from the hacker, Michael Collins.

"Why don't you reply to me?" Collins had written, clearly trying to bait Boxer-Clegg. "Like the rest of MI5 scum, you are a coward hiding behind the power of the Crown. Come to New York at your own risk. Michael Collins, IRB."

"That fucking Michael Collins again," said Boxer-Clegg.

"Sir?"

"That fucking Collins keeps hacking into the system. He even knows I'm coming to New York." But he had no intention of answering Collins's e-mail. "Fuck Collins," said Boxer-Clegg as he created a new document and e-mailed Quinney, warning him that someone was hacking into his computer.

But it was no use, because Earl Holder was monitoring Quinney's e-mail traffic. "Mick," said Holder, laughing, "he's complaining to Quinney that you're hacking into the system." Collins looked at the e-mail and smiled. "Quinney will never see it," said Collins.

Boxer-Clegg sighed, then stood up and reknotted his red ascot. Bobby helped him into his jacket, brushing his shoulders clean of any short hairs. "Have a safe trip to America, Sir Ian," Bobby said as he accepted Boxer-Clegg's one-pound gratuity.

"Thank you, Bobby, I will."

Boxer-Clegg zipped his laptop back into its case and headed for the bar in another room off the barbershop. Bobby the barber went into his small cubicle and called his wife. "Sir Ian's flight to New York is delayed, but he's definitely going to collect our friend Martin. He's very annoyed at Michael Collins and his computer games. Give my regards to Ernie Fahey." He hung up the phone.

At the bar, Sir Ian Boxer-Clegg had his first Beefeater's of the day. It was nine A.M., London time.

—

The three men and Naomi were at the point end of the Lion's Head bar. "Who's this Philby fellow Quinney mentioned?" asked Collins.

"MI6 master spy," said Butler. "Had a whole bunch of British homosexuals working for him and the Russians back in the '40s and '50s. A notorious bunch, but they were good, and they basically got away with it."

"Traitors," said Collins.

"In that case, yes," said Butler, "and also the best."

"What are we going to do with the homosexual information on Boxer-Clegg?" asked Holder.

"Find a way to put him in a vulnerable position," replied Collins.

"And the best way to put him in a vulnerable position," said Butler, "is to make him feel right at home."

"In a gay bar," said Holder.

"Exactly," said Butler.

"Do we have any men who can infiltrate?" asked Collins.

"What are you looking for," asked Holder, "someone to volunteer to suck cock?" The thought stunned Collins, but then he heard the two men laughing. "Are you volunteering, Mick?" Earl added the zinger.

"Mick," said Butler, "just close your eyes and think of Ireland!"

Butler and Holder laughed harder. "You buggers," added Collins with a grin. He knew he'd been taken.

"But Earl," said Butler, "it wouldn't be the first time in Irish history that there have been gays in the movement. Just the other morning Mick and I were chatting about Sir Roger Casement."

"Will you leave Sir Roger alone?" insisted Collins.

"There's also been rumors about schoolmaster Pearse," added Butler as Collins shook his head. "And how about MacDiarmada, Mick, do you think he was gay?"

"Not a'tall," said Collins earnestly, "he was a Belfast man!"

"I guess that settles that," said Butler, laughing, "but there's a better way of infiltrating besides boyfriends."

"How?" asked Collins.

"Bartenders in gay bars," said Earl.

"Aren't they gay, too?" queried Collins.

"Not necessarily," said Butler. "A lot of gay joints are owned by straights and they want their own behind the bar. That way they know the bartenders aren't giving the place away in free drinks to their boy-toys."

"Do you have a gay bar for me?" asked Collins.

"How about Julius's over on 10th Street?" said Holder.

"Neil Granger's the barman there," added Butler. "Couldn't be a better situation."

Just then the front door opened, and the afternoon conversation was stopped dead as a young man approached the bar.

"Can I help you?" asked Naomi.

"Excuse me," he said in a hard Belfast accent, "I'm looking for a Mick Collins. I was told I could meet him here."

Naomi didn't blink. "And what's your name?"

"Ciaran Pike."

"There's another Belfast man, Collins," said Holder.

Collins gave Holder a look that could kill and then said, "Ciaran, lad, Mick Collins here."

Pike came down the bar and shook Collins's hand. "Ernie Fahey sent me, Mr. Collins."

"Mick will suffice," said Collins. "Can I get you a drink?"

"Don't drink," said Pike. "Pioneer."

"Good man, yourself," said Collins, reminded of Vinny Byrne. "This is Tom Butler, Earl Holder, and the beauty is Naomi Ottinger."

"How do," said Pike to one and all, his lips hardly moving. Collins shook his head. It reminded him of the Northern Irish, both Catholic and Protestant. Dealing with Edward Carson on the treaty he had first noticed the tight-lipped reluctance to spill words. Unlike their Southern counterparts, they seemed to feel that the pissing of vowels, like wasting food, was a sin. Collins wondered, Were all Belfast men born ventriloquists?

"Earl," said Collins, "will you take Ciaran downstairs and show him the ropes?"

"Will do, Mick,"

"I think me and Thompson here—"

Butler interrupted him. "How do you know my first name is Thompson?"

"It's on your American Express card," said Collins.

"Oh," said Butler.

"As I was saying," continued Collins. "I think me and Mr. Butler will take a walk over to Julius's. Is your man Granger working yet?"

"Should just be coming on," said Butler.

"Grand," said Collins. "Earl, after you show Ciaran around, why don't you pick up the limo and meet us at Julius's."

"Yes, sir," said Holder, and Butler and Collins left the Lion's Head.

The short walk from the Lion's Head to Julius's at the corner of 10th Street and Waverly Place took but a few minutes. Butler pulled the front door open for Collins and followed him in. "It's Raining Men" was playing on the jukebox, and two middle-aged queens in the center of the bar turned to give Collins an approving once-over, saw Butler behind him, then returned to the bar. "All the good ones are taken," one said to the other in a huff. Collins and Butler jammed into the Waverly Place window seat by the curl of the bar.

"Sugar," said the barman, extending his hand.

"I always knew you'd end up in a wrinkle bar," said Butler as he shook Neil Granger's hand hard.

Granger gave a smirk and then his expression changed because of the strength of Butler's handshake. "Your arm, Sugar," said the barman, "has a powerful shake."

"It does," said Butler, not wanting to get into the whole thing.

"This is my friend Michael Collins from Ireland. Mick, Neil Granger." Granger stuck out his mitt, which was almost as big as Butler's, to shake hands, and Collins noticed a blue-and-red tattoo on Granger's right forearm. It was the eagle, globe, and anchor of the Marine Corps, with USMC on the top and SEMPER FIDELIS on the bottom. Collins, an astute military historian, immediately thought of Belleau Wood. It was big news in 1918. The Germans were only fifty miles from Paris, and the French army was in retreat, advising the Marines to do the same. But the Marines stayed and, taking tremendous casualties, stopped the Germans in their path. Collins liked the Marines. They fought.

"From Ireland," one of the old queens whispered to the other in a giggle. "I wonder if he speaks Erse!"

Granger turned from Butler and Collins. "Ladies," said Granger, "are you trying to commit suicide . . . again?" The snickering stopped, and Granger turned back to Collins and Butler. "Something to drink?"

"No," said Collins, "I think we'll pass this time." Collins looked around the place, which almost reminded him of a country pub. Dark walls and little nooks and crannies. On the wall were pictures of old prizefighters from the days when it was a straight neighborhood joint. There were also newer, more outrageous photos of its present-day clientele. So this is what a faerie fort looks like, thought Collins.

"To what do I attribute the pleasure of your company?" asked Granger.

Collins looked at Butler and nodded. "Neil," said Butler, "we need your help."

Neil Granger was six feet two inches tall and weighed over 250 pounds. His clothes were a throwback to the New York days when all men wore shirts and ties to the ballpark and removed their hats inside churches and bars. He wore a white shirt with a black necktie and a butcher's white apron, its strings double-strung around his wide middle and tied in the front. A Vietnam vet, he looked like a refrigerator with a crew cut.

"How can I be of service?"

"How're your ears?" asked Butler.

"They work," said Granger.

"Would they work for me?" asked Collins.

"Depends on what they hear."

"How about a British accent?" said Butler.

"How bad is it?"

"Pretty bad," said Collins.

"How will I know?"

"Earl will be with him," said Butler.

"Let's see how it develops," said Granger noncommittally as he turned and walked down the bar to fill a drink order. Butler and Collins looked at each other and Collins shook his head.

The limo pulled up, and Holder got out and headed for the bar. As he opened the front door he heard the bar go silent. Collins had made Holder dress up in a black suit with a matching chauffeur's cap. He looked like a surly mortician.

"You guys ready?" asked Holder.

"Neil will be looking for you later," said Collins.

"Got it," said Holder, and the three of them headed for the limo.

Suddenly Collins stopped in his tracks as if he had forgotten something. *"Semper Fi,"* he said as he threw off a quick, sharp salute.

"Semper Fi," said Granger as he returned the salute, then watched Collins walk out the door.

16. |

"The L.I.E. is murder this time of day," said Tom Butler from behind the wheel of the limo. "I betcha that the Van Wyck is all fucked up, too."

Michael Collins already knew that New Yorkers loved to bitch about their traffic. Also their subways, taxicabs, and weather. On the radio that's all they ever talked about—over and over again. WINS Radio's famous twenty minutes. How many times, Collins wondered, do New Yorkers have to be told that it's going to rain before the clouds shed their water?

Butler was driving because Holder hated driving. A real New Yorker, Holder didn't learn to drive until he was twenty-nine. "I'll take the subway, thank you," was his retort when stunned adults learned of his malady. He had learned to drive because he needed it in his police job; he couldn't expect to be chauffeured around like an Inspector. Collins and Holder sat opposite each other in the back, while Butler cursed the very potholes that he was driving straight through.

"Alright now," said Collins. "We'll stop in to see Hughey Morgan at WelshDragon first, then we'll traffic over to British Airways to pick up your man Boxer-Clegg." He paused before asking, "Sugar, you sure your man Hughey will help us?"

"Hughey's the best," said Butler. "Besides, he thinks he owes me for that green card—which he doesn't. Don't forget he's a Celt too. He's not all that fond of the Brits either. Actually," continued Butler, "I'm more concerned about Granger."

"He'll be fine," said Collins.

"What makes you so sure?" asked Holder.

"I know his type." Butler and Holder exchanged doubtful glances in the rearview mirror. "Do you remember down at the Vanguard when I asked Tom Dillon where his people were from?"

"Sure," said Butler.

"And what did he say?" asked Collins.

"He said he didn't know, didn't care, and that anyway he was an American."

"Exactly," said Collins. "Dillon was an American until that British drunk started complaining about how Americans didn't know how to make a martini. Dillon went up one side of that fellow and down the other. One sound of that Brit accent can turn any Irish-American into a Fenian."

"You sound awful positive about the whole thing," said Butler.

"I am," said Collins. "Give me that cell phone. I want to call your man Hornsmith from the British Consulate."

"No, you don't," said Holder.

"Why not?"

"They can trace it, that's why," replied Holder. "You'll use a public phone. Tom, pull over when you can."

Butler did just that, pulling the car over in Jamaica, Queens, not far from Kennedy Airport. "Back home in Jamaica, maaan," said Butler with an ersatz West Indian accent. Ignoring him, Holder and Collins got out of the limo. Holder dropped the quarter and got the Consulate's number from information. He dialed the number and handed the phone to Collins. "Good afternoon," said a female voice, "British Consulate, may I help you?"

"Charles Hornsmith," said Collins.

Collins heard his line ring. "Charles Hornsmith," the voice said.

"I'll say this only once. If you are seen anywhere near Martin Twomey tomorrow, you will be shot on sight," said Collins. "This is not a threat. This is a warning."

"Who is this?" asked Hornsmith.

"The Irish Republican Brotherhood," Collins said and then slammed the receiver into its cradle.

Holder and Collins got back in the limo. "How did it go?" asked Butler.

"It should hold him for a while," said Collins.

As the limo entered Kennedy Airport, Charles Hornsmith was in a panic. He couldn't tell the Consulate's security detail because it involved a clandestine operation. Nothing worse than a clandestine operation, he thought, that everyone knows about. He was going to call Quinney, but he didn't know how Boxer-Clegg would react to the breach of secrecy. Finally, he picked up the phone, called 911, and reported the threat. Two detectives from the Seventeenth Precinct on East 51st Street walked across the street to the office of the British Consulate on Third Avenue between 51st and 52nd Streets and then discreetly escorted Hornsmith in an unmarked police car to his home on the Upper West Side. The police assured Charles Hornsmith that it was probably just another Irish crank call. Hornsmith did not tell them of Sir Ian Boxer-Clegg's imminent arrival. They stationed a patrol car outside his apartment on Riverside Drive. With one phone call Collins had subtracted Hornsmith from the equation, for Charles Hornsmith was a man who had no intention of dying for his country.

"Not bad for an old Lion's Head bartender," said Butler as he looked out of Hughey Morgan's office window at WelshDragon Airlines. He was looking down on two Boeing-747s. The one on the left was Aer

Lingus's *St. Patrick,* just in from Shannon, and the other was WelshDragon's, getting ready to make its way back to Cardiff later that evening.

"What a fucked-up day," said Morgan. "Everything coming out of the British Isles—" he stopped for a moment and looked at Collins before adding, "—and Ireland is totally fucked up because of the weather. First storms, now fog."

"How about Boxer-Clegg's flight?" asked Collins. "He was due in around half past three or so."

"What's the flight number?" asked Morgan.

"British Airways 306 from London," said Butler.

Hughey Morgan punched the information into his computer and looked up. "Your man's still in the air," he said. "They were three and a half hours late getting out because of the fog. Won't be here till near seven P.M."

"What kind of airplane is he flying?" asked Collins.

"British uses almost all 747s on the North Atlantic runs," replied Morgan.

"Good enough," said Collins. "At least it gives us some time to reconnoiter the aerodrome."

"Aerodrome?" said Morgan.

"You know what I mean," said Collins.

Morgan nodded. "Would you guys like a tour?"

Collins smiled. "Hughey, you're a mind reader."

"You got your shields?" asked Morgan.

Holder pulled his out and put it in the pocket of his chauffeur's coat. Collins pulled Quinney's shield out and tried folding it into place without success. "How does this yoke work?" he asked Holder. Holder turned the gold shield around and placed it in Collins's breast pocket. It glistened in the afternoon sun.

Morgan went into his desk and produced three I.D. tags. Each man clipped one to his lapel. "Well," said Morgan, "at least two out of three have police badges. Gentlemen, let's look like we're on an official police walk-through for the extradition of a prisoner."

Morgan took them down by a back elevator to the tarmac. It was windy and loud and the air smelled of aviation fuel. They were standing under the nose of *St. Patrick,* Aer Lingus's lead jet that matriculated the daily New York–Shannon-Dublin run on Flight 104. "Want to take a drive?" asked Morgan.

"Where to?" shouted Collins over the engine noise.

"Eventually, British Airways?"

"Perfect," replied Collins.

"Follow me," said Morgan, directing them to a catering truck. The truck was painted with palm trees that surrounded the dark blue lettering: OASIS AIRLINE CATERING. Morgan had a quick discussion with the driver of the truck, then invited his three friends to climb in back. Shortly, they were all crammed into what was basically a small room containing the precooked flight dinners.

"What's on the menu tonight?" asked Butler.

"Looks like baked ziti for the poor Aer Lingus folks," said Morgan.

"Affggh," said Holder, "I'd rather eat hospital food."

"I didn't think the meal was that bad coming over on Aer Lingus," said Collins, defending his national carrier.

"Oh," said Butler, "listen to the Irish Gourmet here!" All of them laughed except Collins.

"I know my food," said Collins seriously, "and I know what I like."

"Yeah," said Holder, "did you know Butler had a cookbook on *The New York Times* best seller list a couple of years ago?"

"Go 'way," said Collins.

"Yeah," said Morgan, *"The Joy of Boiling."* Now even Collins laughed. It was obvious that it was a barroom routine they had been working on for a long time.

"The secret to fine Irish q-zine," said Butler as the truck lurched into gear, "is if you think it might be ready, boil it for another hour!"

"Oasis handles the catering for a lot of the airlines here at Kennedy, including WelshDragon, Aer Lingus, and British Airways," said Morgan, serious again.

Collins nodded his head affirmatively. "So there are plenty of these lorries around, then?"

"Yes, there are," replied Morgan.

The catering truck parked under the port side of the Aer Lingus 747. Using hand controls, Morgan began raising the catering box, with a thud, to height of the cockpit, about three stories above the ground. When he had the box where he wanted it, he manipulated the door on the side of the jet. He turned a handle and pushed the door up, in, and out. "Okay, men, you can at least help me," he said as he started pushing the food carts into the galley. Used carts were pushed out in return, and Morgan passed them to Collins, who pushed them to Holder, who slid them to Butler. Next, bags full of garbage and empty soda and beer cans came out. "Use the hand truck on the beer," said Morgan to Butler, who did just that, gathering a huge stack of beer and soda and rolling it by hand truck onto the 747.

"Everyone on vacation today?" asked a huffing Butler.

"I thought you might like to have a little contemplative quiet today," replied Hughey Morgan, and Collins nodded his head. As food and beverages were hauled on board, Collins walked around the first-class cabin. Collins stared straight ahead, his arms folded across his chest, in silent contemplation. "How do you know he won't be flying tourist?" Morgan asked.

"I know my man Boxer-Clegg from his dossier," replied Collins. "He doesn't fly steerage"—a term Hughey Morgan had never heard applied to air travel. "If he has to pay himself, he'll be sitting up here." Collins took one more walk around the cabin before getting back into the catering box. Morgan pulled the door of the jet closed and manipulated the gears, lowering the catering box back onto the bed of the truck.

"I take it," said Collins, "that this Aer Lingus 747 is about the same as a British Airways one?"

"They're almost identical," said Morgan. He picked up the interior telephone and told the driver, "Okay, Jack, let's go for a ride." The truck proceeded under the tail of the Aer Lingus 747 and headed toward the TWA terminal.

"How long's the ride?" asked Collins.

"Oh, about five minutes," said Morgan.

"Any ground rules?" asked Collins.

"Just watch what you're doing. You can't be drifting out on the runway and running into planes." The driver of the catering truck stuck close to the parked airliners as he circled the TWA fleet being stocked and unloaded. As they turned past the TWA terminal they saw the British Airways terminal. "If you're lucky, Mick," continued Morgan over the din of the jet engines, "they'll have the jet parked here at the far end of the terminal. Quicker drive back to Aer Lingus." The truck pulled up to the first gate, which was empty. "Not so complicated, is it?" said Morgan, smiling.

"How did you know?" asked a surprised Collins.

"How else would you turn the Orangeman into the ace of spades?"

Earl Holder drove the limo up to British Airways arrivals and parked it right in front. As soon as he turned off the ignition there was a fist pounding on the glass of the driver's-side window. "Hey, you, what's the matter with you? You can't park here." It was Kennedy Airport Traffic Enforcement Control. "Metermaids disguised as pricks," Holder said to Collins and Butler in the back of the limo.

Holder rolled down the electric window and flashed his gold detective's shield. "Hey, asshole, you got a problem?" he shouted. The Traffic Enforcement Control officer, suddenly very quiet, shook his head no. "Good," said Holder, "because this is official business." Holder rolled up his window, and the three men got out. As they entered the British Airways terminal, Holder said, "Collins, always remember—there's power in that shield."

Holder had come prepared. He had a sign with SIR IAN on it, which gave out just enough information while at the same time protecting privacy. The three men huddled together at the exit gate. "Alright, lads," said Collins. "Sugar, you stand to the side while Earl and I pick up your man. Take a taxi. I'll see you back at the Lion's Head." Collins looked at the overhead television monitor and saw that BA306 had already landed. "He should be out any minute," he said to Holder. Collins scanned the group coming out from Customs and brightened when he saw the red ascot. "There's your man, I bet," he said to Holder.

Holder agreed. "I think you're right," he said as he held up the sign, making it easier to see. Boxer-Clegg saw the black chauffeur and the white Irish cop and made a beeline for them.

"Sir Ian?" asked Collins.

"Dreadful flight, Quinney," he said as he handed his bag to Holder.

"Good to meet you," said Collins as he tried to sharpen his Cork-London-Dublin accent into a Brooklyn twang. "I'm sorry about the flight," he said, shooting a few syllables through his nose for effect. Collins had decided that Quinney's Brooklyn accent bore some resemblance to the Southside Dublin Liberties accent of the Coombe. The rebel Liberties. Marrowbone Lane was never far away, it seemed. Collins had stuck his hand out to shake hands, but Boxer-Clegg had walked right by him. Collins felt like an eejit with his hand extended into the open air. He rushed after Boxer-Clegg and Holder and caught up with them as they were exiting the terminal. Holder opened the back door of the limo for Boxer-Clegg, and Collins climbed in after him. Holder then got in and gunned the engine, pulling the car away from the curb with a jolt. Sir Ian was rocked to his side and had trouble righting himself.

"Goddamn it, man!" he screeched at Holder. "Are you bloody mad, or just incompetent?" Holder did not even turn around as the limo picked up speed. "Close that bloody partition," Boxer-Clegg snapped at Holder, who did as he was told. Holder had already bugged the back of the car and was listening as he rolled. "Bloody Gurkha!" said Boxer-Clegg as Collins thought he detected a slur in his voice. "What I need is a bloody drink. Any gin, Quinney?"

"Yes, sir," said Collins. He opened a panel and displayed a full bar, including a bottle of imported Bombay gin, appropriately adorned with a portrait of Queen Victoria on its label.

Boxer-Clegg dropped a gin and tonic in a second and poured himself another. "God save the Queen!" he said.

"You'd be knowin'," replied Collins tersely.

"Do you know what they did to me on that bloody plane?" Boxer-Clegg asked. Collins shook his head no. "They cut me off. Forbade me another drink. In first class, no less."

"Hard to believe," said Collins. The second drink seemed to calm Boxer-Clegg. "Where to?"

"What?"

"Where are you staying?"

"The Plaza, of course," said Boxer-Clegg. Collins didn't even bother telling Holder where to go, because he knew Holder was listening to his conversation via a tiny earphone.

Boxer-Clegg sat facing the front of the limo while Collins sat on a side seat to his right. Collins eyed Boxer-Clegg as he visually savored his drink, staring at it with an alcoholic lust. Finally, Boxer-Clegg gulped his drink, then leaned over to the wet bar and poured himself another Queen-ful. Gin, thought Collins, God help us. Collins assiduously avoided gin because it made him crazy. When he drank the stuff he could feel the bolts that held the top of his head on coming loose. Collins was beginning to get a headache just watching Boxer-Clegg drop gin after gin.

"Well, Quinney," Boxer-Clegg finally said, his thirst seemingly quenched, "is he or isn't he?"

Collins looked blankly at Boxer-Clegg. "Is he or isn't he what?"

"Going to escape, Detective," said Boxer-Clegg.

"He might," said Collins with a pause, "or he might not."

"I've come three thousand miles to hear you tell me that?"

"You've come three thousand miles, Sir Ian," said Collins evenly, "because you want to play the hero on the television. Isn't that true?"

Collins eyes were bolted on Boxer-Clegg, and the Englishman hedged in his seat. Ignoring Collins's question, he said, "I have extradition authority. I have the papers from the foreign office." Collins was quiet. "Do you want to see them?"

Collins could not have cared less about his papers, but he said, "Let me take a look." With a swift perusal he returned the papers to Boxer-Clegg. "They seem to be in order," said Collins.

"And yours?" said Boxer-Clegg smugly in a seemingly new rendition of I've-shown-you-mine-now-you-show-me-yours.

Collins would not play Boxer-Clegg's little game. He pulled out Quinney's detective shield and held it up to Boxer-Clegg's face, almost pushing it into his nose. "Is everything alright, Sir Ian?" Collins said with a curtness that got Boxer-Clegg's attention. Holder was right, thought Collins, there was power in the shield. He waited a second for emphasis. "There's talk they may try and take him at the airport, here, tomorrow afternoon," said Collins. "But I think it's a red herring. They'll try and take him—if they try at all—as he leaves the Federal lockup at 201 Varick Street."

"Did you get my e-mail about Michael Collins?" asked Boxer-Clegg.

"Yes," said Collins, "I did. You sounded upset."

"Upset," snapped Boxer-Clegg. "Of course I'm upset. How in God's name did he manage to hack in? We're supposed to be secure.

He's trying to intimidate me. Stop me from taking Twomey back to London. Michael Collins. Same fucking name as the terrorist."

Collins decided to humor him. "Collins? What's so special about Collins? I've never heard of him."

"You never heard of Michael Collins?"

"Oh," said Collins, "the fellow who went to the moon?"

"Jesus," said Boxer-Clegg. "Collins, the Irish revolutionary."

"He's still alive and hacking in?" asked Collins.

"It's not that Collins, obviously," said Boxer-Clegg, exasperation in his voice. "But his namesake, the famous wee Fenian scum."

Wee Fenian, thought Collins, he picked up that phrasing in Belfast from the police. He's a beauty. Collins shook his head blankly.

"You've never heard of Michael Collins, Quinney? For God's sake, man, he's the terrorist's terrorist."

"He is?" said Collins innocently.

"Not only did he free Ireland back in the 1920s, but he's been an inspiration to terrorists all over the world."

"He has?"

"The Red Chinese"—he pronounced it *Chine-ee*—"Mao used his methods in his revolution in China. Yitzhak Shamir of Israel used his terror tactics against us—the British—in Palestine in the '30s and '40s when he was in the *Irgun* and *Lehi*."

"The *Irgun* and *Lehi*? What are they?"

"The Jew IRA," said Boxer-Clegg, eliciting a smile of satisfaction from Collins. "Shamir even lifted his secret code name from Collins—'Michael.'" Collins nodded, this time with only the slightest hint of a smile. "Shamir," continued Boxer-Clegg, "would go on to become Prime Minister of Israel. Not bad for an old terrorist."

"Not bad at all," agreed Collins.

"What exactly do you have on this Michael Collins?" Boxer-Clegg asked.

"Not much," said Collins. "I know he's in the country, but I don't know where's he's staying."

"Do you have a photograph?"

"No," said Collins, "apparently he doesn't like being photographed." Boxer-Clegg nodded. "Maybe you could run his name through your computer system in Belfast," Collins helpfully suggested.

"A waste of time," said Boxer-Clegg.

"Why?"

"Do you know how many Michael Collinses we have on that computer system since it was started in the early '80s?" Collins shook his head no. "One hundred and thirty-four Michael Collinses! It's a bloody joke. Every Collins family in Ireland must name their first son Michael."

"Talk about your needle in the haystack," said Collins coyly, and Boxer-Clegg nodded.

Boxer-Clegg finally chuckled. "The Irish do love their terrorists. I know you're Irish-American, Quinney, but you have to admit the problem with the Irish," said Boxer-Clegg with just the hint of a slur in his voice, "is that they tend to romanticize their terrorists."

Collins smiled and couldn't restrain himself from saying: "But, Sir Ian, hasn't it been said that one man's terrorist is another man's patriot? Look at your own examples, Mao and Shamir."

"Well, yes," Boxer-Clegg stuttered in an almost Nixonian way, "but, you know, a terrorist is, ah, a terrorist." He paused to take another sip of gin, then remained silent for a good five minutes. "Quinney," Boxer-Clegg finally said absently, "I'll need a gun and I'll need this limo for the duration."

"The car is yours," said Collins, "and I'll have a weapon for you tomorrow."

"Good," said Boxer-Clegg.

"When will you coordinate with the American and British authorities?" asked Collins.

"At the last possible moment," said Boxer-Clegg. "They won't know anything until tomorrow afternoon at the airport. They don't even know I'm here. This way there is no interagency rivalry or any of that rubbish. I will present the papers before takeoff and be on my way with Twomey." Boxer-Clegg looked up and smiled at Collins. "I've waited three long years for this opportunity. They made my men in Belfast look like amateurs. And what are they? Why, they're just plain—"

"Terrorists," interrupted Collins.

"Yes, Quinney," said Boxer-Clegg, "plain terrorists."

"There's a lot of talk," said Collins, "that Twomey is innocent. Even the Irish government has lobbied for his freedom."

"Ireland," said Boxer-Clegg, shaking his head sadly, "is an illegitimate state. It still should be part of the United Kingdom." He looked straight at Collins. "These IRA madmen force you to take steps that are drastic. Did you hear about that SAS job down in Gibraltar?"

"SAS?" said Collins.

"Special Air Services," said Boxer-Clegg, "when we preempted those IRA men who were up to no good. I was the architect of that one."

Collins raised his eyebrows. "Preempted?"

"Assassinated."

"You're a bit of a terrorist yourself, then, Sir Ian."

Boxer-Clegg poured himself another drink, then raised it to Collins in salute. "Touché, Detective."

They were driving across the Queensborough Bridge, and the United Nations Building was aglow in the early-autumn evening. "It's a beautiful sight," said Collins.

"It's shit," said Boxer-Clegg. "It's all shit. Look, you're dealing with animals in Africa or the Middle East or wherever and you have to meet these savages in that building. They understand one thing."

"Indeed," said Collins.

"The boot on their neck."

"And you apply that boot well, I understand," said Collins.

Because of the alcohol Boxer-Clegg didn't know if he had detected a certain mocking in Collins's voice. "And the Irish," he continued, "are no different from the rest of them."

"If the boot is so powerful, Sir Ian, how come it hasn't worked in eight hundred years in Ireland?"

Boxer-Clegg was silent for a moment then said, "What are they all anyway? But bomb-throwing cowards."

"*The man who throws a bomb is an artist,*" replied Collins quietly, "*because he prefers a great moment to everything.*"

"Who are you quoting?" asked Boxer-Clegg, "The latter-day Collins, Gerry Adams?"

"G. K. Chesterton," said Collins simply.

Boxer-Clegg did a double take. He was impressed. *The Man Who Was Thursday,*" he said to Collins shaking his head. "You think like a terrorist."

"How else would I catch them?" said Collins.

Holder pulled the limo up in front of the Plaza Hotel. "The car is at your disposal for the rest of the evening, Sir Ian," said Collins.

"Yes, yes," said Boxer-Clegg, "I may need it in an hour or so. I may want to relax later with a drink or two downtown."

Earl Holder took Boxer-Clegg's carry-on bag into the Plaza, and Michael Collins hailed a cab and headed for Greenwich Village.

Collins walked into the Lion's Head on a high. Naomi and Butler looked at him expectantly. "I think we can do it," he said.

Naomi placed a shot glass in front of him and poured the Black Bush. "Congratulations," she said.

"How did it go?" asked Butler.

"He's a fookin' drunk," said Collins. "He'll be seeing double tomorrow with that gin hangover and won't know what's happening to him. Eejits," said Collins as he shook his head.

"What?" said Sugar.

"I can't believe these eejits. They never change. They still hate the colonists. Do you know what he called Earl? A Gurkha!" Butler gave a belly laugh.

"What's a Gurkha?" asked Naomi.

Collins smiled. "A Gurkha is a hard-fighting Nepalese soldier in the British army. They were the Brits' first blacks, you could say." Naomi nodded her head.

Butler then went over to the jukebox and played "The Rocky Road to Dublin," sung by Liam Clancy. Soon the chorus was upon them: "*One, two, three, four, five, hunt the hare and turn them down the Rocky Road, all the way to Dublin, whack fol-la-de-lar.*"

Suddenly a song of the blight became a chant of celebration. In one gulp, Collins swallowed the whiskey, then slammed his hand on the bar. "Fill 'em up!" he said, high on the moment.

Naomi was doing just that when a Generation-X type on in-line skates struggled to get down the steps of The Head. He opened the door and wheeled himself into the room. He stopped at the bar next to Collins. "Hey, babe," he said to Naomi, turning his baseball cap backward. Collins looked at him sideways and decided he wasn't going to let this eejit upset his day. "Hey, babe," he said again, "how about a Black and Tan?"

Collins snapped his head around. "A what?" he demanded of the stranger.

"A Black and Tan, dude."

Collins pivoted at the bar and hit the Gen-Xer with an upper-cutting left just under the chin, sending his hat flying and landing him on his rump. "How dare you?" said Collins advancing on the fallen skater. "How dare you," he repeated, murder in his eyes.

Then the light went on in Tommy Butler's brain—Dublin 1920.

"Jesus, Mick! It's not that. It's not what you think." Collins wasn't finished. He advanced on the young man, who sat stunned, his skate wheels spinning forsakenly. "Mick, it's not that kind of Black and Tan. It's a drink. Stout and beer."

Collins stopped cold in his tracks.

"Naomi," said Butler, "get him out of here. I'll cover the rest of your shift." Naomi picked up her pocketbook, flipped up the bridge of the bar, took Collins in hand, and they exited together, leaving the skater stupefied on the floor.

As they crossed Seventh Avenue, Naomi took Collins's arm and said, "I can't believe you hit that man because he just wanted a Black and Tan."

"Do you know what a Black and Tan is?"

"It's a drink."

"It's a murdering British thug," said Collins, stopping. Behind the Riviera Bar on West 4th Street he took her in his arms and kissed her.

"A thug," she said.

"A murdering thug," he said as Naomi surprised him, sliding her tongue into his mouth.

"Murdering," Naomi said as she pulled away and caught her breath. She was ready. "Let's go to my place."

Naomi Ottinger lived in a large two-bedroom rent-controlled apartment on West 11th Street, between West 4th Street and Waverly Place. "No elevator. You'll have to walk up," she said as she began to climb the four flights.

"Elevator?" questioned Collins.

Naomi smiled. "Lift, to you."

"Ah, the lift." Naomi smiled. She was going to give him lift very soon. "Your kids?" Collins said, puffing, as he followed her up the stairs, eyes firmly on her exquisite backside.

"It's okay," she assured, throwing her voice over her left shoulder, "they're with their father for the night. He lives uptown." She flipped the key in the lock, and they entered the apartment. Once inside she threw her arms around him, backing him against a wall. Collins had a look of near terror in his eyes. "Don't be shy, Mickey. It's alright," she said, running her hands through his dark brown hair.

"How old are they?" he asked, halfheartedly trying to change the subject.

"Ashley's eleven, and Josh is seven," she said. "They're great kids."

"Why the divorce?"

"Didn't work out."

"Everybody seems to be divorced over here, even the Catholics," said Collins.

"Times change," said Naomi.

"Perhaps," said Collins, "it is a mistake to love anyone too much."

"No," said Naomi, "you can't live like that. You have to give your heart."

"And soul?" added Collins.

"Yes," she agreed, "heart and soul." Naomi grabbed Collins by his necktie and led him to her bedroom. Before he knew it she was unbuttoning his vest while he was undoing his tie. She kissed him flush on the lips. "You're my love lamb, you know."

Now it was "love lamb." With Kitty it had been "Ducky." She used it all the time. Ducky this and Ducky that. What was it with women and their pet names? And Kitty would sometimes let it slip out in public. How was he to run a state and be known as Ducky? General Ducky.

Kitty didn't really care about politics, and it was hopeless trying to get her to understand it. It had made Collins cross. But he could not stay cross for long. For Kitty knew his "soft corner," the place where there was no politics, no "G" Division detectives to frighten, no posing for the camera at Number 10 Downing Street. Only Collins the man, the lonely man.

He leaned down to Naomi and kissed her neck, then stopped in surprise. "I can smell you," he said.

"Jeez," said Naomi, "what a romantic. He can smell me!" She pulled her shirt over her head, then unhooked her bra in the back, letting it slide down her arms and drop to the floor.

"You don't understand," said Collins as he eyed her small, perky breasts and her round, brown, erect nipples.

"Oh, I understand," she said unbuckling his belt, "you silver-tongued Irish Romeo."

"I must sound like an eejit to you."

Naomi turned serious. "I do understand, believe me."

"No, you don't," said Collins. He stepped out of his pants, and Naomi grabbed his boxer shorts by the waistband. "It's a sign," said Collins awkwardly. "It shows my heart is alive."

Naomi laughed as she slid his boxers to the floor. "I bet it's a sign," she said with a laugh as she placed her hands under his balls and gently squeezed, "and I bet your heart isn't the only place you're alive."

"Naomi," he whispered as she gently pulled him by the penis close to her.

"My goodness, Mr. Collins," she said in mock shock, "you're not Jewish!"

"You make a joke out of everything," Collins said, but Naomi put her index finger to his mouth, pushed him back on the bed, then stripped off her jeans. "Okay, Big Fellow, you're mine, all mine!" she said, falling on top of him.

The lovemaking had gone on for hours. After the last orgasm Naomi had kissed Collins and he fell off to the side, deep in a satisfied sleep. What was it with orgasm and sleep in men? she thought, and smiled. She lit a cigarette and watched the slow, almost imperceptible rise and fall of Collins's chest. He was truly beautiful, she thought. Irish white skin, different from any other white skin on earth, so translucent that the blue veins looked like they were almost bursting through fine, white marble. He was almost hairless, except for his underarms and pubic area. His hands were extraordinary, long and willowy like a woman's and without a sign of a callus. Delicate, yet at the same time dangerous. His nipples were dark pink and taut, with but a few dark hairs surrounding them. Without thought Naomi put the cigarette out and put her mouth to his chest, suckling at his dry breast. She awoke Collins.

"Naomi."

"Yes, honey," she replied, and still in sleep he wrapped his arms around her. He kept his eyes closed and there were no other words spoken. Together, they lapsed into deep sleep.

"He seemed like a walking blasphemy," Collins's favorite writer, G. K. Chesterton, had once written about another fictitious revolutionary, "a blend of the angel and the ape." Naomi didn't know Chesterton's work, but she would have agreed that these words suited Collins well.

There was something about Collins that made women want to mother him. To men he was direct, demanding, often curt. With women, he seemed to find laughter easier and his good looks—often hidden in scowls while at his brutal business—attracted them. The little cowlick at the back of his head made him even more boyish and enchanting, adjectives that men—whether friend or foe—had never used to describe him.

While Collins consciously manipulated men to get them to do unpleasant things for him, there was no manipulation of women, for he loved them for what they were. While men had to be motivated by Collins, women were motivated because of him. Even from his earliest childhood women had loved him. His mother, granny, and sisters doted on him and treated him as if he were a plaything, a living doll, dressing him up and playing house with him. While men could be put off by his boisterousness, women were enchanted by the shyness he showed around them. Kitty Kiernan, the moody fiancée he would not live to marry, was adept at seeing both the ape and the angel in Collins, and she had tried to blot out the ape. Lady Lavery had loved the angel, but it was an admiration stimulated by the danger that was enveloped by the revolutionary ape. Naomi loved the contradiction—a dangerous man with a refreshing shyness toward women. The shyness was a mask for his raw sexuality, a sexuality that Naomi had craved and finally conquered. Like Kitty Kiernan and Lady Lavery before her, she had to have him.

Their sleep would not last long. It started with a howl that slowly brought both of them out of their daze. It sounded like a cross between a runaway ambulance and a cat being castrated with a chain saw. Collins opened his eyes.

"Good Jaysus," he said. "What in the name of God is that?"

"It's only a car alarm," Naomi replied. "It'll go off in a minute." They did not move and kept their eyes closed waiting for the alarm to stop. Five minutes, seven minutes. After ten minutes Collins ripped the sheet off them, jumped up, and headed for his clothes, piled on a chair across the room.

"Mick, Mick," she said, "what are you doing?"

"I don't know how you people put up with this shite," he said as he pulled Quinney's snub-nosed .38 Colt Police Special out of his hip holster. "What is wrong with these people?" he said as he headed for the window.

Collins opened the window that looked down on West 11th Street and began aiming the revolver. The sound of the window opening brought Naomi to full attention, and she screamed, "Mick, don't, don't," as she leapt from the bed. Collins pulled the hammer back on the gun and took aim, but before he could fire the alarm went silent.

Naomi pulled his arm back into the window. "Are you insane?" she asked him. "What's wrong with you? You're so careful in all your planning and you do a stupid thing like this, shooting a fucking car!"

Insane, thought Collins. He was insane. He was subject to these "queer fits," as he called them. Just like that day at Beal na mBlath. He put the gun back into the holster and slid back into bed. Naomi followed him.

"Are you alright?" she finally asked.

Collins grunted. "I'm a fookin' eejit." He paused. "*Insane* is too nice a word." He lit a Lucky Strike hurriedly and blew the smoke out of his mouth in disgust. "I am insane," he said. "I *must* be insane to be doing what I'm doing here." Naomi took his other hand and held it. "Do you know the last time I acted like that?" Collins asked her.

"No, I don't," she replied.

"Twenty-two August 1922. Beal na mBlath, County Cork."

"1922?" said Naomi. She didn't have a clue what Collins was talking about.

There was a stone silence between them. "I feel terribly guilty about us," he finally said to Naomi.

"Why?"

"Because," stammered Collins, not knowing what to say.

"Don't you believe in love at first sight?"

"Don't you mean lust?" He was sorry the moment the words left his lips.

"Mick," Naomi said, "what we just had was more than lust. That was love—at least on my part."

Collins was tongue-tied. He didn't know what to say. "But you don't understand," he finally uttered as he thought of Kitty and all the explaining and overexplaining he was always forced to do with women.

"Oh, I understand," said Naomi. "You think this is a one-night stand."

Collins had never heard the term before, but he quickly caught on.

"It may have to be a one-night stand, sweetie."

"Why?"

"Because I'll be out of here tomorrow, and I will never return."

"Then I'll visit you in Dublin."

"I won't be in Dublin."

"Well, where will you be?"

"I don't know," said Collins. "I truly don't know."

"Mick," she said, putting her hand on the back of Collins's head, then kissing him on the forehead, "what is it? You can tell me. Do you have a girlfriend, or a wife?"

Collins laughed. "No, I don't have a wife or a girlfriend." He paused, then tried the truth. "What if I told you I didn't exist? That I'm mere vapor?"

"Well," Naomi said, reverting to her wise-guy facade, "that was a pretty good facsimile of a real man before."

"Oh, Naomi," said Collins, "I don't exist. I haven't existed since 22 August 1922."

"August 1922?" she said.

"1922," he continued, clearly in distress, "and I got out of that car to shoot at some eejit rebel on the hill."

"What happened?"

"He hit me."

"Where?"

"With a bullet in the back of my head," said Collins. "In the back of my eejit head." Her reaction to the terrible truth was as if Collins had slapped her across the face; she was stunned. Then, she began to cry and Collins held her in his arms and she knew he was telling the truth. This man of thirty-one lying in bed next to her had, indeed, been hit in the back of his head with the bullet on the deadly palindrome of 22/8/22. And he had died.

"Mickey," she said taking his head in her hands, "I'm sorry. I'm so, so sorry." She took his head, braced it in both her hands, and kissed his forehead. "1922?"

"You don't believe me?"

"I do now," she said. "I truly do. But . . ."

"But what," he said.

"But what are you doing here?"

"You wouldn't understand," said Collins. "It's a Catholic thing."

"Try me."

"I'm on a mission for salvation. Twomey is my ticket home."

"Ireland?"

Collins smiled. "No, my beautiful Jewish colleen, not Ireland."

"Where then?" she persisted. "Can I visit someday?"

"Someday you will, Naomi, someday you will," said Collins as he wiped a tear away from her cheek. "Someday you'll understand all of this, and you'll be amazed, and you'll want to tell the world, but you won't."

"I won't."

"No," said Collins, "because they wouldn't believe the fantastic story you'll tell of ancient Irish revolutionaries and mad archangels, all having queer fits as they search for a truth. My story is at the very frozen limit."

"How will I know it's all true, then?" she asked.

"I'll send you a symbol," said Collins not knowing what he was talking about, "to prove my love and truthfulness."

"Promise?"

"I promise," he said, and he pulled the sheet up over them, held Naomi in his arms, and prayed they would both find sleep.

Collins awoke and lit another Lucky Strike. One hand rested on Naomi's pubic hair, while the other was cocked in the air, smoke lazily floating skyward.

"Did you enjoy yourself?" asked the Archangel.

Collins with guilt and ginger removed his hand from Naomi's pubic region and sat up in the bed. He looked like he had been caught with his hand in the cookie jar. Naturally, he tried to turn the onus onto the Archangel. "I see you've been keeping a pretty close eye on me lately," Collins said curtly.

"Not really," said the Archangel absently. "I just happened to be in the neighborhood. I was working an exorcism over in Jersey." Even Collins had no retort to that. "Is everything fine, my son?"

"Now you've caught me at another mortal sin," said Collins.

"Mortal or venal, or a sin not at all," said the Archangel. "Remember what St. John said: 'For if sin be natural, it is not sin at all.' That's up to you to decide."

"Me?" said Collins. "But the Church says that sex outside of marriage is a sin."

"So be it," said the Archangel. "Or you can decide."

"I can decide?"

"You have free will, my son. You can decide what is right and what is wrong. That's why they call it a conscience."

"Indeed," said Collins, "and you know the state of my conscience."

"Michael," said the Archangel, "your conscience is your most exquisite gift."

"A gift? I'm afraid I haven't used the gift very well."

"You have used the gift perfectly," said the Archangel.

"Perfectly?"

"Perfectly," reiterated the Archangel, "because you think about right and wrong. Then you use your free will."

"To murder people." This time the Archangel was silent. "Is that a proper use of free will?"

"What do you think?"

"I don't think it is."

"Then," said the Archangel, "you have used your conscience superbly."

"Superbly?" said Collins. "Then I don't get it."

"And that's what purgatory is for, Michael," said the Archangel. "And that's why we're here together in this room tonight." And together they were. Collins, naked, in bed and the Archangel stuck up in the corner of the room near the ceiling.

"Thank you for this morning," said Collins. The Archangel shook his head in confusion. "The shooting," added Collins.

"Ah," said the Archangel, "the shooting."

"I didn't feel a thing," said Collins.

"And why should you?" Now Collins shook his head in confusion. "You've used up your limit."

"My limit?"

"Yes," said the Archangel, "only one death per human being." Collins smiled and shook his head in acknowledgment. "It's been quite a violent day," the Archangel said quietly.

"I know," Collins said softly. "I didn't want it to go that way, but we had no choice."

"I wasn't talking about Quinney," said the Archangel. "In the bar, later."

"I'm sorry," said Collins. "I lost it. He said Black and Tan and I saw red. How was I to know it was a bloody drink?"

"And you were going to shoot that car before," said the Archangel.

"I don't know what came over me," said Collins. "I would have shot it, too—"

"Only I turned the alarm off," interrupted the Archangel.

Collins shook his head in remorse. The Archangel smiled. "So you're sorry?"

"I am," said Collins, "and I'm also sorry about what we did to Quinney today."

"Perhaps tomorrow will be better," said the Archangel, not too concerned.

"I hope so," said Collins, covering himself up as he became aware of his nakedness. Naomi turned in her sleep, pointing her bare bottom toward Collins and the Archangel. Collins took note of what might have been an editorial comment and covered Naomi's rump with the sheet. The Archangel suppressed a smile, and the silence between them grew.

"Why did you pick me?" Collins suddenly asked.

"I've already told you that," said the Archangel.

"No, you haven't," insisted Collins. "There's more to it than that." There was an awkward silence. Then Collins said, "What exactly does an archangel do?"

The Archangel smiled. "That's a hard question, Michael. An archangel does many things. Foremostly, I act as a messenger between God and humankind."

"So," said Collins, "you're God's personal messenger to me?"

"You could say that."

"God takes that much interest in one simple human being?"

"Michael, no one has ever called you simple, ever."

Collins laughed and didn't know what to make of it. "Are you my guardian angel?"

"I never really thought of it like that, Michael."

"But you're keeping a close eye on me, aren't you?"

"I try to screen you from evil. I watch and help when I can."

"Like you helped Tommy Butler?" There was silence from the Archangel. "Did you do that?"

"No," said the Archangel, "I didn't do that."

"Did the Lord?'

"No," was the Archangel's reply.

"Then who?"

"You."

"Me?" said Collins. "You're daft!"

The Archangel smiled. "Why not you? You are one of God's spirits, and God resides in you. You have the love of God in you. Maybe your love of your friend brought about a cure. Did you ever think of that?"

"No," said Collins. "Never."

"Did you ever think that it was God's way of saying He trusts you? That you are someone special to Him?"

"Have you ever seen something like this before?" asked Collins.

"Michael, I've been here before there was an Earth. Of course I've seen it before. I've seen it with Moses. I've seen it even with Joan of Arc."

"But how can that be?" said Collins. "I'm so full of evil. No wonder my enemies called me the devil incarnate."

"Evil," said the Archangel, "has no positive nature. And you were not made with the sinful nature of the devil, Michael, for there is purity in your wickedness. You seek the positive in your life, in your friends and your causes. Therefore, you cannot be evil. Your quests are never mundane. You never seek the folly of earthly belongings. You seek only great things, like the freedom of a nation, the dignity of a people, the right of a nation of people to demonstrate its free will."

"So I cured Tommy Butler?"

"In a way," said the Archangel.

"Through God's love?"

"And through your acceptance of that love."

"I'm confused."

"You should be," laughed the Archangel.

"How did I end up with you and not some of the other Archangels?"

"Because we are alike," said the Archangel.

"I'm not like you at all," said Collins.

"Oh, you are," said the Archangel. "Remember, first and foremost, we are both children of God. I, like you, was a commander of an army and I, like you, was forced to drive evil from my Kingdom."

"Heaven?" said Collins.

"There was no place for Satan in Heaven and in the name of the Lord thy God I drove him ruthlessly from the sight of God to the eternal perdition of hell."

"So we both led a great fight," said Collins.

"I won mine, Michael, and you did well in yours."

"Most say I lost."

"You won more than you think you did."

"Are there any other reasons you were assigned to me?" asked Collins.

"Well," said the Archangel, "I am the Patron Angel of entities that embody your nature."

"Such as?"

"Chaos." Collins laughed. "Insomnia. Truth. Righteousness. War."

"Is that all?" asked Collins.

"Repentance."

"Repentance," repeated Collins. "I will never have enough repentance for all the death I caused."

"Perhaps not," said the Archangel, "but at least you think about your actions and the repercussions they had on your soul."

"I hope that's enough," said Collins.

"Michael," said the Archangel, "you are brought near to me by your faith. You have a special gift, for there is no misery in your soul." Collins seemed despondent. "Do you remember what your Kitty wrote to you in her last letter?"

"I do," said Collins, "because I could not believe it."

"What did she say?" asked the Archangel.

"She said, 'But God is very good to you.' I thought she was making a joke."

"It is no joke, Michael," said the Archangel. "God is very good to you. He took you in your prime because of your extraordinary gifts, He assuaged your soul in purgatory, basically letting it rest after a tumultuous life. And He gave you a second chance, to see if you learned anything."

"It is sheer torment," said Collins, again despondent.

The Archangel was silent. Finally, he said, "I know your secret, Michael."

"My secret?"

"You know," said the Archangel quietly.

"What?"

"You are the terrorist who has never murdered anyone."

"They still died."

"But not by the hand of Michael Collins."

"Does it make any difference?" asked Collins.

"Some," said the Archangel.

"Those fourteen British Secret Service agents from Bloody Sunday are still dead. I didn't kill them, but I caused their deaths. All the others, too."

"Like Sir Henry Wilson," said the Archangel.

"Wilson was running a pogrom in the North."

"Like—"

Collins cut the Archangel off. "Like that bastard Captain Lee-Wilson who beat Tom Clarke and stripped him naked after the Rising. It took six years, but the lads on my orders finally got him down in County Wexford. Like Alan Bell, that shite of a bank examiner from Belfast who was getting close to the national loan money and was hammered by the Squad on the top of a tram in Sandymount. All of them and more I've forgotten." The Archangel was silent. Finally, Collins said, "It's even worse than if I had actually killed them myself, because I have destroyed other men's souls when I asked them to kill for me."

"That may be true, but who can really say what's in a man's soul—or his heart?" said the Archangel.

"Not even an Archangel?"

"Especially an Archangel. Michael," said the Archangel, "you have matured."

"How so?"

"I remember when you liked to get 'a piece of ear'; when you liked to wrestle with your men."

"I didn't know you always kept that close an eye on me," said Collins. "Anyway, the only wrestling I do nowadays is with my conscience." The Archangel smiled. "Bloody Sunday," continued Collins, "changed everything."

The two of them were silent until the Archangel asked, "What are you thinking, my son?"

Collins smiled. "I was just thinking about Vinny Byrne," said Collins. "How is Vinny?"

"Vinny is fine," said the Archangel. "He should be out of purgatory any decade now. He's not very repentant, you know, but Vinny has a special gift that cannot be faulted. He's a true believer."

"The best," said Collins. "Fearless. And what a shot!"

"Michael," said the Archangel in a voice full of sanction.

"I'm sorry," said Collins. "I just wish to God this was all over."

"And, God willing, it will soon be over," replied the Archangel.

"Will you give me your blessing?" asked Collins.

The Archangel smiled. "*Mícheál,* you have *always* had my blessing."

"But—" Collins cut in. But when he looked up, the Archangel was gone.

—

Naomi awoke in the morning and, with her eyes still closed, turned her arm toward Collins to pull him closer to her. Her hand found nothing but sheet, which brought her fully awake instantly. Maybe he had gone to the bathroom. But there wasn't a sound in the house. She looked to the chair, but there were no clothes. He was gone. She stood up and stretched, feeling sexy in her nakedness, and a smile crossed her face as she thought about the night before. Then the smile turned to a frown when she thought of his confession of his own death. How could it be? Was he real, or not? Then, looking at his side of the bed, she saw something. It was a lone emerald-green feather.

By nine forty-five P.M. Holder had been sitting in the limousine for an hour and a half waiting for Boxer-Clegg to reappear. He was beginning to get concerned that the MI5 chief had snuck off by himself when he came out the front door of the Plaza, resplendent in fresh clothes. This time he wore a blue ascot.

Holder got out of the car and ran around to open the door for Boxer-Clegg. He was surprised when Sir Ian offered a cheerful "Thank you."

Holder noticed that Boxer-Clegg now had an earring in his left earlobe. Must think he's a fucking pirate, thought Holder. After closing the back door, he returned to the driver's seat and asked, "Where to?"

"Oh," said Sir Ian, "go downtown and I'll decide along the way." Holder slid the limo out onto Fifth Avenue and headed south. As they crossed 57th Street Boxer-Clegg asked pleasantly, "Could you close the partition?"

"Sure," said Holder. He closed the partition and placed his earphone in his left ear. Boxer-Clegg was using the limo phone, and Holder could hear the individual beeps as he dialed his number.

"Shit," said Holder quietly. He had forgotten to bug the phone. Now he would hear only one side of the conversation.

"Hello, Lock&Chain," said Boxer-Clegg, "is Josie there?"

Holder could hear the striking of a match and the deep inhaling of smoke. Within seconds, smoke was seeping into the driver's section. Holder started sniffing, and then it became obvious. Boxer-Clegg had lit a joint.

"Josie?" said Boxer-Clegg. "It's Ian from London. My friend Lyle was supposed to tell you I'd be calling." Holder drove as slowly as he could so he could carefully monitor the one-sided conversation. Again he cursed his stupidity for not tapping the phone. "Are you available tonight, Josie? You are! Well, then I'd be delighted to pick you up. Exactly where?" As soon as he hung up the phone, the partition between driver and passenger began to come down. Apparently, Boxer-Clegg had found the right button in the ceiling control-console of the limo. "Driver," he said, "I'd like to pick up a friend downtown."

"Yes, sir," said Holder.

"He's at a club called the Lock&Chain down on Ninth Avenue off 14th Street. Do you know it?"

"Yes, sir, I do," said Holder. The partition again went up and more marijuana smoke infiltrated his space.

Holder went down Fifth Avenue to 14th Street, made a right, and drove west. He passed St. Bernard's Church and made a wide left into the meat-market section of the Village. There was a young, slim, blond male standing in front of the Lock&Chain. Boxer-Clegg's window came down and he called out, "Josie?"

"Ian?"

"Yes, love," said Boxer-Clegg. He opened the door and Josie climbed in. Holder waited for his command. The partition finally came down, and Boxer-Clegg said, "Just drive. We don't know where we're going yet."

"Jesus," said Holder to nobody. Making an illegal turn, he pulled the car around and into Hudson Street, up past Abingdon Square, and into Bleecker Street. It was time to make a command decision. He turned left at Bleecker and 10th Street and gunned the car, making sure he'd make the light at Seventh Avenue. He brought the limo to a stop in front of the Three Lives Bookshop, across the street from Julius's. He hoped they'd get the hint. Holder could hear them in back, smoking grass and talking lovers' talk, Boxer-Clegg calling Josie "Bitch," and Josie calling Boxer-Clegg "Mammy." Holder wondered how Collins had managed to talk him into this situation.

The partition came down again. "What a brilliant idea!" exclaimed Boxer-Clegg. "I haven't been to Julius's in years. Let's go in." It was Holder's first break of the day. He hustled out of the car to open the back door, then scrambled across the street to open the front door of Julius's. As they went in, Holder was sure to catch the eye of Neil Granger.

Two spaces at the bar were open, and Sir Ian and Josie sat down. "What'll it be?" said Granger.

"I'll have a Bombay and tonic," said Boxer-Clegg. He turned to Josie. "What would you like, love?"

Granger looked at Josie, and alarm bells began to go off. He looked like he was about sixteen. "Sir," he said to Josie, "I'll have to see some I.D."

"Why?" said Boxer-Clegg.

"Because, my friend," said Granger, "he doesn't look like he's twenty-one, and that's the drinking age in this state." Granger made Boxer-Clegg's drink as Josie rooted in his wallet for I.D. Granger put the gin and tonic down in front of Boxer-Clegg who downed it in one swallow. Finally Josie pulled out a driver's license. Granger put on his glasses and held the license at arm's length, his eyes coming up a bit short, so he could see the fine printing on the DOB. "July 4, 1970," Granger finally said. "You're a Yankee Doodle Dandy," he added.. "What'll it be?"

"A Baileys on the rocks," said Josie. A Yoo-hoo chocolate soda drink with chemicals. Granger knew he had an amateur in front of him. The two of them cuddled and talked for an hour, and Granger wondered why Collins wanted these guys watched. It wasn't anything that he hadn't seen before.

As the hour grew late, the gin and tonics became Bombays on the rocks. As Josie sipped a Baileys, Boxer-Clegg would drop three gins. The more Josie drank, the more reticent he became. Alternately, the more gin Boxer-Clegg drank, the more amorous he became. The bar was getting busy, but Granger hovered near the couple. He could see Holder through the 10th Street window, leaning on the hood of the limo.

"Another Bombay," said Boxer-Clegg. He watched as Granger poured the drink and then replaced the bottle on the shelf next to the cash register. Suddenly Sir Ian was mesmerized. He couldn't take his eye off the bottle of Bombay and the portrait on its label of the old queen, Victoria. Here he was in a gay bar in Greenwich Village and there was the queen, like a mother hen, watching over him. It seemed he couldn't escape the reach of the empire.

And that was all he had after all these years, a job doing the dirty work of the shrinking empire. He'd been around. He started his career in MI6 and did a lot of work in South Africa in the '70s. In the early 1980s he found himself in the Middle East, where he held various assignments in Egypt, Lebanon, and Saudi Arabia. His specialty was intelligence, and he was good at it. He knew people, and he knew what people wanted. It was amazing what he could learn from the Egyptians or the Saudis by offering a week in London complete with hotel, theater tickets, and sex. All on the cuff. The Arabs were devout Muslims, but they were not fools. They knew how to separate the temporal from divine—especially when they were freed from the region. They all had their price—and remarkably, it was never steep.

It had all started to fall apart in Saudi Arabia. The problem with being stuck in the Saudi Kingdom was that it was dry. Muslim Prohibition, they used to call it. Of course, although it was never admitted, there was booze at the British Embassy, but strict rules applied. Drinking was confined to the Embassy and only the Embassy. Never with the Arabs. If the Americans or the French or the Australians came over, that was permissible. The whole thing still made him mad as hell. He should have shown more self-control.

It was the same old story. The drink and the loneliness of his staccato life made him do stupid things. He had no real friends, no close family. His job was his life. And that was fine. But he had never overcome his drive for "the pretty things in life," as he described his need for boys. Black boys, white boys, bronzed Arab boys, even the occasional Irish boy. There was something about boys that made them wonderfully nubile to Boxer-Clegg. The softness of the young teenager, the eager, embarrassed erection of bursting hormones, the precocious small bottoms, that said it all for Sir Ian Boxer-Clegg. If he could not love, at least he could lust. Boys made his life worth living. None of the politics of the crafty Arabs or the politically insane Irish. Lust was above mere politics and mundanity; thus, in its own way, there was a strange purity attached to it for Boxer-Clegg.

There had been a reception for the Italians, and the champagne and cognac had flowed liberally. Near midnight Boxer-Clegg had gone outside the Embassy compound for a breath of air and a cigarette, also verboten in Riyadh. When a car had pulled up he went over. "Want a cigarette?" he asked the handsome young Arab, who nodded yes. "You suck cock?" was his next query. The response was the car being put into gear and pulling away at a high speed. He had read the situation wrong. Guess he doesn't want to suck cock, thought the polluted Boxer-Clegg.

Ten minutes later the Saudi moral police pulled up. Boxer-Clegg had seen what was coming and had retreated into the safety of the Embassy compound. But it was too late. Late the next day he was on a plane for London. There would be no international incident over the likes of Boxer-Clegg. The British ambassador told him to shut up and accept his transfer into MI5. And that's how he had gotten to Belfast, because he could not control himself, or his demons, in Saudi Arabia.

He would prove them wrong. He had thrown himself headlong into his work. Weekdays in Belfast, always home for the weekend in London. The old, gray, industrial Victorian city of Edward Carson and James Craig was his workplace, not his home. He had, in his methodical way, become a master at rooting out the plans of the Provisional IRA. He had become a fixture at the Maze prison. He knew every prisoner, his strengths, and his weaknesses. And he knew how to exploit them because he had a gift—Republicans sang for Sir Ian Boxer-Clegg. Tricks he had learned in South Africa and Beirut worked just swell in Belfast City. The more the rebels talked, the more he moved up the MI5 chain of command. When he broke the high-publicity Castlelye bombing case in County Tyrone, he had gone to the top of the MI5 class in Belfast and found himself knighted for his work with the "wee Fenians," as he liked to call his opponents.

But even the Order of the Garter didn't give him true satisfaction. For he was not liked by the men he worked with. No matter how meticulous an intelligence officer he was, his compatriots—all fine Belfast Protestants—knew of his weakness and of course did not approve. He had heard the snickers about his knighthood, and they had stung. "He only accepted the Garter because he thought it would supplement his wardrobe nicely," they had said, well behind his back. But damn them, he had gone to Windsor Castle and knelt before the Queen, and they hadn't.

Boxer-Clegg pounded his fist on the bar, making Josie jump in the seat next to him and gaining the attention of Neil Granger from the end of the bar. "Fucking Saudis," he said, wondering why he was still stuck in the godforsaken Belfast backwater and not in the sexy, tumultuous intrigue of the Middle East where the real action was.

It was Wednesday, Robin Byrd night, a tradition at Julius's. Toward midnight the crowd became thick and a raucous cheer of "Put it on, put it on," went up. Granger took the TV remote from the top of the cash register and put on the local smut station, Channel 35. It was almost time for the *Robin Byrd Show,* a public access strip show featuring naked dancers joyfully displaying their swinging willies and gyrating coochies.

"Josie," said Boxer-Clegg in a definite slur, "I'd love to work ya." Josie looked away. "We can go back to the Plaza," continued Boxer-Clegg, "and then I'll work ya, Josie, I'll work ya." Granger noticed Josie's body language, which told him Josie was trying to extradite himself from Boxer-Clegg's company. The more Boxer-Clegg put his hand on Josie's arm and shoulder, the more Josie turned his head away from Sir Ian.

"No," snapped Josie in response to something Boxer-Clegg whispered in his ear. Boxer-Clegg waved Granger for another round. Boxer-Clegg again whispered in Josie's ear, and the response was the same, "I said no!"

"No?" said Boxer-Clegg. Josie had turned his body away from Boxer-Clegg. He was looking out the Waverly Place window. Boxer-Clegg put his hand on Josie's shoulder again, but it was brushed away. "Josie, bitch," he said quietly.

"The answer is no," was the reply.

Boxer-Clegg took his cigarette out of the ashtray in front of him, took a drag, and then, as if it was the most natural thing in the world, stuck the burning ember into Josie's neck, just below his left earlobe.

"Good Jesus!" screamed Josie. "Are you mad? You've burned me!"

Patrons backed away from the two, and Granger, realizing what had just happened, barked at Boxer-Clegg, "Hey, you. What the hell's the matter with you? Get the fuck out of here!"

Granger saw the burn—almost the size of a dime—and began throwing ice cubes in a bar towel. "Here," he said, handing the towel to Josie. "Hold that there." As Granger reached out over the bar to Josie he noticed that Boxer-Clegg hadn't moved. "I told you to get the fuck out of here, mister."

It was midnight and the clapping began as Robin Byrd began to sing *"Baby, Let Me Bang Your Box."* In the immediate vicinity of Boxer-Clegg and Josie chaos reigned as patrons realized what Boxer-Clegg had just done. They were trying to get away and out the door as more customers were entering, turning the end of the bar into a phalanx.

Boxer-Clegg was oblivious. He didn't say a word. He was in his tough-guy, MI5 mode. He just reached out to Granger and grabbed him by the necktie. Neil Granger's father was a retired Jersey City cop, and the two often commiserated about the similarities and the dangers their jobs held. "Son," the senior Granger had once said, "never let them strangle you, if you know what I mean."

"Do you know who I am?" said Boxer-Clegg as Granger's neck-tie, a snap-on, pulled away in his hand.

"Yes, I do," said Granger. "You're the asshole holding my fucking necktie!" Granger rushed from behind the bar, and Boxer-Clegg, finally realizing in his drunken stupor that he looked like a fool holding Granger's tie in midair, reached for the gun that Collins hadn't given him yet. With his hand empty, the next thing Boxer-Clegg knew was that Granger's huge arm, the one with SEMPER FIDELIS tattooed on it, had him by the ascot.

"Baby let me bang your box," sang Robin Byrd as the Julius crowd joined her in song. Granger *"Semper Fi-ed* Boxer-Clegg as he lifted

him by his ascot and the back of his belt. Patrons situated by the door were amazed to see Boxer-Clegg take flight as Granger launched him out the door. Within seconds Boxer-Clegg was lying facedown in the gutter at the corner of Waverly and 10th.

"And stay out," said Neil Granger. He turned, gave Earl Holder a short, snappy salute, then reentered Julius's to a standing ovation and a chorus of *"Neil can really bang my box! Neil can really bang my box!"* Neil Granger smiled shyly, then went behind the bar and once again began pouring drinks.

17. |

Butler was awakened at six-thirty A.M. by the sound of water hitting the bathroom sink. From the couch, where he had fallen asleep, he could look down the hall and see Collins, wearing only his shorts, shaving. Collins loved gadgets, Butler had noticed, but he could not get used to the electric razor Butler used. All it seemed to do was batter his white Irish skin red and fail to cut those little hairs in the valleys of his neck. He had gone out to the "chemist," as he called it, to Bigelow's on Sixth Avenue, and bought a straight razor, cup and brush, and a bar of shaving soap. That Bigelow's was still there across the street from the Jefferson Market Courthouse surprised Collins. He had shopped there for perfume for his sister Hannie in 1914. Bigelow's, Collins noticed, had changed and was now well lit since the dark, noisy, and frankly sinister Sixth Avenue el was gone.

"Haven't sold one of these straight razors since old man Boyle died last summer," said the pharmacist to Collins. "They must have went out of style by 1910," he added.

"1922," deadpanned Collins, and the pharmacist nodded.

Butler could see Collins conjuring up the concoction in the cup, and then, like a priest at High Mass, begin the ceremony with the brush, rubbing the foam on his face and neck. Father Collins at the holy sacrifice of the chin hair, thought Butler.

Collins liked shaving with a straight razor because he could hear his beard being cut off at the skin. He puffed out his cheek and went at it. There was nothing like the clean scrape of a good straight-razor shave.

"Jaysus," said Collins as the steaming water accidentally hit his hand. He took a towel and dried his hands, then turned on the radio on a shelf to the right of the medicine cabinet mirror.

Butler always kept his bathroom radio on WCBS-FM for the oldies. His kitchen radio, which Collins had become adept at playing with, was usually left on WFAN so he could listen to the Mets. Butler hated the Yankees and considered American League baseball inferior. To Butler, the Yankees were racist fascists, owned by a convicted felon—which he never failed to point out. There was also a stinking hubris emitted by Yankee fans; they actually thought that God owed them a yearly championship. When Billy Martin died on Christmas Day 1989, a distraught Yankee fan had commiserated with Butler at the Lion's Head, "Well, Tom, Billy's now up there with the Babe, Lou Gehrig, and the others."

"He's in the hot-stove league!" replied Butler, with a scowl on his face, putting a proper perspective on it.

Even as Jackie Robinson and Willie Mays were redefining the New York game by their power, speed, and defense, the Yankees enforced their own apartheid. After the New York Giants left for San Francisco in 1957, Butler would never go to Yankee Stadium. As a child living in Washington Heights, at night he could see that magic aureole of light emanating from the Polo Grounds—that old maiden aunt of a ballpark, big and busty with a huge centerfield of a backside—from his bedroom window, which was in the tenement over his father's bar, The River Shannon. When the old man had immigrated to America he had, like so many of the traveling Irish, become a Giants fan because of the manager, John J. McGraw. If it was good enough for Mr. McGraw, it was good enough for Mr. Butler, Senior and Junior. What was love, Butler often thought, but Willie Mays shagging fly balls in the Polo Grounds on a New York summer's afternoon?

"WCBS-FM," the station jingle intoned as Collins continued scraping his face with the straight razor. "This is the morning mayor," said the DJ, Harry Harrison, "and remember that every brand-new day should be unwrapped like a precious gift. Now here's a song from the Divine Miss M, 'From a Distance.'"

Collins wasn't really paying attention as the tune began to play. He was thinking of Naomi and her body and how he could actually smell her beautiful sexual fragrance right now. He didn't want to think of Quinney, Boxer-Clegg, or the Archangel anymore. Just the scent of Naomi and the feel of their coupling bodies.

"From a distance the world looks blue and green and the snowcapped mountains white. From a distance the ocean meets the stream and the eagle takes to flight," sang Bette Midler, and Collins stopped shaving, having completed only one cheek, captured by the song.

"From a distance we all have a love and no one is in need," sang Midler beautifully, and Collins thought of Naomi, his love, and Sadie, a friend who was in need. *"And there are no guns, no bombs, no disease, no hungry mouths to feed,"* continued the song.

Was it the Archangel challenging him again? Collins began to shave his other cheek when Midler went into the chorus: *"And God is watching us, God is watching us, God is watching us . . . from a distance."*

Collins stopped, looked in the mirror, then began working on his sideburns, which he cut straight and high just where his ear sprang from his head. *"From a distance you look like my friend, even though we are at war."* Collins thought of Quinney, whose life was firmly in his hands—as if he were a god. *"From a distance I just cannot comprehend what all this fighting's for."* Neither could Collins. His whole life was a fight, and where had it gotten him? *"And God is watching us, God is watching us, God is watching us . . . from a distance."*

It was as if he was trapped. There would be no escape until his mission was completed. Collins snapped off the radio and hurriedly began shaving his neck.

"The curse of God on ya, ya 'hoor," spat Collins.

Butler got up and went to the bathroom. "What's the matter?"

"Fookin' eejit razor," said Collins. He looked like he was about to have a stroke. Blood was running down his chest and onto the floor. Butler took a piece of toilet paper and stuck it to the nick.

"Didn't they have toilet paper back in Dublin in 1922?" Butler said, and then he began to laugh.

"What's so fookin' funny?" Collins wanted to know.

"Quinney hits you with a bullet between the eyes, and there's not a drop of blood," said Butler in a belly laugh. "You nick yourself shaving, and it makes the place look like an abattoir."

"That bloody Archangel," said Collins, beginning to laugh himself. Soon they were both doubled up in laughter.

Butler cleared his voice. "Where were you last night?" he said, as if he didn't know the answer.

Collins looked at the floor. "I was with Naomi," he finally said, looking up.

Butler was quiet for a second. "Does she know the truth?"

"I told her," said Collins, "but I don't know if she believes me. You know how women are."

"Mick," said Butler, "no one knows how women are." Collins smiled. Finally, Butler said, "Mick, I'm going to miss you."

"Yes," said Collins, suddenly quiet, "it's our big day. One way or another, it will soon be over."

"Well," said Butler, "it certainly isn't starting off very well."

"How so?"

"Holder and Granger reported to me about Boxer-Clegg late last night."

"What happened?"

"Sir Ian," said Butler, "seems to have a problem with alcohol, young boys, and cigarettes."

"Cigarettes?"

"Yes," said Butler, "he likes to put them out on his boyfriend's neck."

Collins turned pale. "Christ," he said. "I don't like this."

"What did you expect of the guy?" asked Butler.

"I expected I could trick him," said Collins. "Now I'm afraid that my trick will turn him into a crazed sadist."

"What should you care?"

"I care," snapped Collins. "I want to do this as painlessly and quietly as possible. Enough is enough." Collins began pacing. He had been warned. "Sir Roger knows," he said, shaking his head in belief.

"Sir Roger knows what?" asked Butler.

"Nothing, nothing," replied Collins. "Call a Fenian quorum for eight A.M. Hughey, Earl, Ernie, and yourself. Let's go over the final plan."

"Will do," said Butler.

Collins thought of the Archangel once again and had a call of conscience. "I'll tell you something, Sugar, if it's the last thing I do on this earth, I will help one human being." He went to the telephone and dialed St. Bernard's. "Father Bill? Mick Collins here. Can I see you right away? I'll come by the rectory. I have a favor to ask of you." Collins turned his back to Butler and spoke so softly into the telephone that Butler could not make out what he was saying. "Thanks, Pappy, see you then," said Collins, and he hung up the phone.

Collins began putting on his clothes. Even in a hurry, he could make a perfect Windsor knot, Butler noticed. "Where are you going?" asked Butler as Collins buttoned his vest.

"I'm going over to St. Bernard's to see Father Bill," said Collins over his shoulder as he went back to the bathroom. He took the straight razor and put it in his coat pocket.

"Will you be back in time for the meeting?"

Collins threw on his suit jacket and headed for the hall door. "I will," he said. "But I have to do a favor for a friend who once helped an Irishman who was new in town."

"Hey, Sadie," said Collins.

In the doorway of the Biography Bookshop a body under torn blankets moved, slowly.

"Rise and shine," said Collins.

"That you, Collins?" she finally said, hearing the unique Cork accent.

"Yes, Sadie. It's time to get up."

"I don't feel so good, Collins," she said looking up at Collins, splendid in three-piece suit and homburg.

"You'll be feeling better when I get finished with you. Come on now." He helped her to her feet. "Come on now, you've got to pack up."

"Pack up?" said Sadie. "You gettin' like the cops, always harassin' decent folk."

"Come on now, Sadie," said Collins as he threw her belongings into the A&P shopping cart.

"What's the rush, Collins?"

"I'm leaving for Ireland tonight, and we have to get you taken care of first," said Collins.

"Taken care of," protested Sadie. "Ain't nothin' wrong with me."

"You said you didn't feel so good," said Collins as he began to push the A&P cart up Bleecker Street.

"Too much bad wine last night," Sadie offered.

"Well, I'm not going home to Ireland and leaving one of my best agents out on the street."

"What you talkin' about, Collins?"

"I have a place for you to stay," he replied.

"No, you don't," she said authoritatively. "I know about them homeless shelters. They steal anything, and you got to watch out because they'll steal your booty and your booty."

Collins didn't have a clue what she was talking about. "I'm not taking you to a homeless shelter," he said as they wound their way up Hudson Street on the opposite side of the Village Nursing Home at West 12th Street.

"I'm better off on the street," Sadie said finally.

"I have a priest friend up on 14th Street," said Collins as they passed Myers of Keswick.

"A priest," said Sadie. "I'm a Baptist!"

"I don't care what you are, Sadie, my friend needs someone to clean up after him."

"Clean up! What you think I am, Collins, a goddamn maid?"

Collins laughed. "Sadie," he said, "what would you rather do. Cook and clean up after one lone priest or sit in that bookshop doorway in January with snow up to your arse?"

"Frozen booty," she finally said quietly. "Collins, you have a point."

Collins rang the bell on the rectory. Bill O'Donnell answered the door wearing a cassock that made him look pregnant. "Hello, Sadie," said O'Donnell, "Mick just told me a lot about you over the phone. Won't you come in?"

"Geez, Collins," said Sadie as she came in and sized up O'Donnell, "he's a big one."

Taking it in his stride, O'Donnell laughed, then said to Collins, "I thought I wasn't going to see you again." Collins struggled to get Sadie's A&P shopping cart in the narrow door.

"Huh," said Sadie, "you lucky, Reverend. I can't get him out of my hair." O'Donnell instantly knew why Collins loved this woman.

"Sadie," said Collins, "tell Father O'Donnell here how you became homeless."

"They closed my SRO," she said. "Mayor Koch and all those other real estate thieves. Put me out on the street."

"Did you try to get welfare or food stamps?" asked O'Donnell.

"Wouldn't give it to me," said Sadie, "said I wasn't qualified, then they shuffle me off to other offices all over the city. I told them I needed a place to sleep and they send me to a homeless shelter, which is worse than livin' in the gutter. Tell them I was hungry and they gave me peanut-butter-and-jelly sandwiches. Breakfast, lunch, and dinner, peanut-butter-and-jelly sandwiches. Meanwhile, Mayor Koch and his rich friends are at the Tavern on the Green drinking some nice bow-joe-lay!"

O'Donnell smiled, but Collins wasn't amused. "Some fucking government you have here," he said to O'Donnell.

"Now Mick," said O'Donnell.

"Don't 'now Mick' me," said Collins. "These frauds, these politicians like Koch work for the people—not the other way around."

"They say you can't beat City Hall," said O'Donnell.

"Father," said Collins, "contrary to popular opinion, the law is not a sacred thing. Laws are made up by men with prejudices, hatreds, and petty envies. Very few laws are touched by the deity." Collins was almost in O'Donnell's face. "Remember, if you can't manipulate it, change it. If you can't change it, destroy it. Then start again."

"Pretty radical," said O'Donnell.

"Fenian Rules," spat Collins. If only he had the time, Collins thought. "Look," said Collins to O'Donnell, "see what you can do for Sadie. Manipulate the system. Don't let the system manipulate you."

"It's so big. They can make you feel impotent," said O'Donnell. "Powerless."

"There's plenty of power in that collar of yours, Father," said Collins. "And who better to defend than the powerless?" O'Donnell did not respond. "I'll tell you a little secret, Father," said Collins. "I've seen it from both sides—I toppled a government with revolution and I built one with resolution. There's a simple trick politicians have that they use against their foes. You deny your enemy their humanity. In the Great War the British were not fighting the Germans; they were fighting the Huns. I never fought the Crown Forces. I fought a bunch of jailbirds called the Black and Tans. Take away people's humanity and you reduce them to mere tools, ripe for manipulation. But it's up to you to manipulate them and their system."

"You're right," said O'Donnell. "I'll make a few calls after all this is over."

"Be sure you do," said Collins.

"But now I have to go over to the prison to give Twomey Holy Communion."

"Don't," said Collins.

"Why?"

"Just don't," said Collins again. "I want them to think Twomey is on his own."

"Deserted?"

"By even his own priest," added Collins.

O'Donnell nodded knowingly. "I see," he said.

"Well, Sadie, Pappy," Collins finally said. "I'm off now. This time tomorrow I'll be back in Ireland." Collins smiled. "I think you make a nice couple," he said as he headed toward the door.

"Collins," said Sadie as Collins opened the rectory door. "Be sharp." She turned to the wooden door that led to the next room and knocked deliberately on it three times. "Collins, you understand?"

The blood drained out of Collins's face as he stopped, looked at Sadie intently, then nodded. He walked out onto West 14th Street, a curse from the old country following him.

Days started early at 201 Varick Street. Martin Twomey knew something was up when he wasn't allowed out of his cell for breakfast. His breakfast of concentrated orange juice, cornflakes, milk, and coffee came on a tray without an explanation. Twomey loved fruit, but today there wasn't any. "I'd rather have a yellow banana," he whispered, "than a red bandanna." Today, he would have to do without.

Soon two guards took him to shower and shave by himself. Collins was right, Twomey thought, something is up. When he returned to his cell a cheap, government-issued suit was waiting for him. He decided to sit on his cot and wait for the inevitable. It wasn't long in coming.

"Mr. Twomey," said Assistant Warden Hitchens, "you're going home to London this afternoon."

"England," said Twomey, "is not my home. I'm from Ireland."

"For the rest of your natural life, Mr. Twomey," said Hitchens, "England will be your home." *Natural,* the way Hitchens pronounced it, sounded ominous.

"Where's the extradition papers?" demanded Twomey. "I want to see my lawyer, Abe Goldstein from the O'Dwyer firm."

"Mr. Goldstein will be informed after the fact," said Hitchens. "The Brits are running this show. He can blame the President, Mr. Bush. This comes from the top."

"This is illegal," said Twomey. "My rights have been violated."

"Mr. Twomey," said Hitchens, "you don't have any rights right now."

"Can I make a phone call?"

"Forbidden," said Hitchens.

"I want to see my priest, Father O'Donnell."

"Even your priest has deserted you today, Mr. Twomey," said Hitchens. "O'Donnell just called. He can't make it today." Hitchens laughed and then walked away, leaving Twomey thinking of the other priest, Father Collins. Collins had warned him to be ready and, unlike his two previous encounters with the British authorities, this time he would not be a hapless spectator.

In her heart Patricia O'Malley knew something was wrong. It wasn't that Quentin Quinney hadn't called her—Mrs. Quinney often interfered with their plans—but there was something gnawing at her gut. She had not heard from Quinney in twenty-four hours, and she could not locate him. No one else seemed to miss him; they just assumed he was in the field doing his job.

She couldn't take it anymore. She picked up the phone and called Charles Hornsmith at the British Consulate.

"Mr. Hornsmith called in sick this morning," said the receptionist. "Can I direct you to someone else?" O'Malley hung up the phone.

She tried information, but the number was not listed. For Christsakes, she finally said to herself, you work in police intelligence, use your head. With that she logged in to her specially equipped home computer and pulled up NYNEX's unlisted directory for Manhattan. She dialed Charles Hornsmith's unlisted number.

"Mr. Hornsmith," she began.

"Yes."

"This is Patricia O'Malley. I'm a friend of Quentin Quinney." Hornsmith's heart sank.

"What do you want?"

"I'm looking for Detective Quinney."

"How should I know where he is?"

"You are extraditing Martin Twomey today, are you not?"

"I have nothing to do with that," said Hornsmith. "Are you trying to provoke me? Are you with the IRA?"

"IRA?" said O'Malley. "Mr. Hornsmith, I'm with NYPD Intelligence."

"Don't you people talk to each other?"

"About what?"

"About the threat I received yesterday."

"About what?"

"About staying away from Twomey. They said they'd shoot me on sight. I'm not leaving the house today."

O'Malley thought for a second. "Okay" she said. "I'm calling because I can't locate Detective Quinney."

"Maybe they got him."

"Who?"

"The IRA, or the Irish Republican Brotherhood, whatever they're calling themselves these days."

O'Malley was quiet for a second. "Maybe Collins has something to do with this."

"Collins?" said Hornsmith.

"Yes," said O'Malley. "Quentin was on to a Michael Collins from Ireland who he thought was sent over here to spring Twomey."

"Tell me no more," said Hornsmith.

"Knowledge is important."

"It can also be a killer," reminded Hornsmith.

O'Malley could tell that Hornsmith was genuinely frightened. "Sit tight," she said, "I'll get back to you." Hornsmith hung up the phone, hoping never to hear from her again.

After Collins left the rectory he headed toward the river. He turned left at the corner of 14th Street and swung into where Hudson Street

begins its trek south. Bobbing like a fighter, he ducked animal car-
casses as they were taken out of refrigeration trucks, slung on hooks,
and rolled into the meat butchering plants. He crossed Hudson
Street at Gansevoort and entered a tiny square bordered by Greenwich, Gansevoort, Little West 12th Street, and Ninth Avenue. The
square had no name; it was still paved with its original cobblestones
and looked like it was a part of a Hollywood set for a Belgian village.
Collins liked this part of the Village the most, for it was the least
changed, looked a little like Dublin, and reminded him of his time
here in 1914. He continued down Gansevoort Street, turned left on
Washington Street, then walked down Horatio Street. A block away
from the Hudson he could finally smell the river. It was not the
pungent smell of 1914, a smell thick with the coal exhaust from the
many liners, but an earthier, almost fishy smell of a river recovering
from a century of pollution. He saw a huge black ship steaming
upriver to its terminal in Midtown. Right in front of him, rising
over ten stories, it blotted out New Jersey on the opposite shore. On
the bow could be clearly seen: *Queen Elizabeth 2*. One look and
Collins knew it was sixty-six thousand tons of prefabricated junk. It
didn't have the class of the *Lusitania* or the *Mauritania,* not to mention the soul. Collins looked toward 12th Street where the last
Cunard pier stood, ready to collapse. All the other piers had been
cleared away in anticipation of a park, a highway, or just the scrub-
bing away of history. Collins walked right up to the front of Pier 52
and looked hard. Stepping back, through the muck, grime, and in-
stitutional green paint, he could see it through the decades of city
smut: CUNARD LINE. He had gone back to England from this pier
on the brand-new *Aquitania* in September 1914. Most of the time
at sea was spent either at the bar or looking for the periscopes of
imaginary German U-boats. But it would be eight months until
the U-20 would find and ambush the *Lusitania* off the Old Head
at Kinsale, County Cork.

New York to Cork. It was a small world.

Collins was agitated. As he watched the *QE2*'s casual wake as she steamed upriver, the SOUTHAMPTON painted on the stern getting smaller by the second, Sadie's ominous warning kept coming back to him. He knew he would have to be very careful today. Precision was the rule of the day. One misstep, and people were going to die. He didn't care about himself, but he cared for his men, Twomey—and, oddly enough, even Quinney. Pull the cute trick, Collins thought, and let everyone live.

Collins continued south on West Street, turned left at Christopher Street, and walked the three blocks back to Butler's apartment. He opened Butler's door with his own key, then walked in and was surprised to see that the entire group was there waiting for him. There was tension in the air. He took off his homburg and threw it in the middle of the kitchen table. "A prompt group I have here," said Collins. They all sat down at the table, and Collins asked, "Are we ready?"

There was nothing but silence. Then Holder piped up, "I fucking well am!"

"Me too," said Butler.

"Ditto," said Fahey.

And Hughey Morgan slammed his hand on the table. "Let's give them," the Welshman said, "a day the English will remember for a long time."

"Fuckin'-A," said Holder, and Collins knew they were ready.

"You're first, Hughey," said Collins. "Is the catering lorry ready?"

"An empty truck will be waiting for you near the employee parking lot at the far end of the International Arrivals Building," said Morgan. "I'll leave all that you'll need on the seat—I.D., work clothes, and the like. From there, it's all up to you."

"Good enough, Hughey," said Collins. "Earl, do you know this area?"

"Yeah," said Holder, "we've used it before on extraditions. We'll park the car there and move right along to British Airways."

"Hughey," said Collins, "you've taken care of our Aer Lingus tickets?"

"Three first-class to Shannon," said Morgan. "I'll be waiting for you on the plane."

"Grand," said Collins. "Mr. Butler."

"Yes, sir."

"You play chauffeur today."

"Yes, sir," said Butler as Holder flipped his chauffeur's cap across to Butler, who tried it on. It looked like a beanie on Butler's immense bald head. All it needed was a propeller. "You can keep the hat for a souvenir," said Butler, flipping it back at Holder.

"Fuck you," said Holder, and everyone at the table laughed.

"As soon as you get to the airport with Boxer-Clegg, Sugar," said Collins, "go to Hughey and we'll meet you on the plane. When we're finished here you can drive me up to the Plaza to give Sir Ian his gun."

"Gun?" said Holder, concerned. "You want to give a gun to that fucking psycho?"

"I'm giving him Quinney's," said Collins. "It makes the package tighter."

"I see," said Holder.

Collins looked at Fahey and Morgan. He decided he should let them in on the secret, too. "Gentlemen," he said, "we learned something about your man Boxer-Clegg last evening."

"Yes?" said Fahey, all ears.

"Sir Ian," said Collins, "delights in torture."

Fahey laughed. "Tell me something I don't know." Collins raised his eyebrows. "I just found out that Sir Ian is a Picasso with a pair of pliers," said Fahey. "A lot of our lads in Belfast are one testicle down, one testicle to go." There was silence around the table. "What did he do now?" asked Fahey.

"Stuck his cigarette out on his boyfriend's neck," said Holder. "Tried to pull some shit on Neil Granger, and the old Marine used a little hand-to-hand on him at Julius's last night. I had to pick him up out of his own blood and puke, take him back to the Plaza, and tuck him in."

"Good man yourself there, Earl," said Collins, "but I want to impress upon all of you how dangerous this man is. He's a drunk who delights in sadism. Let's handle him very gingerly during this day. I want this operation to go smoothly, without a hitch. I don't want anyone—and I mean anyone—to get hurt. This is one twisted sonofabitch."

"And you, Ernie," said Collins, "I'll admit I had my doubts about you, but you're the best. After the three of us take off, how long before we're over Canada?"

"Approximately an hour and a half out of JFK," said Fahey. "About eight-thirty P.M. New York time, one-thirty A.M. Dublin time."

"As soon as we clear American airspace," said Collins, "wake up your people at the Irish Foreign Ministry and your contacts in the Irish, American, and British presses. I want to see fireworks!"

"You can depend on me, General," said Fahey. Collins looked at Butler, and Butler nodded. Fahey knew.

"One other thing, Earl," said Collins. "Look out for the unexpected. If something happens you have the contacts with the police. Use them." Holder nodded. "Let's be smart and do this right."

Collins pulled Holder's laptop in front of him. "One last message for Sir Ian," said Collins as he began to touch-type: "You are a lucky man, for you know the date of your death: October 15, 1992. Michael Collins, IRB." All three men were peering at the computer screen as Collins hit the Send icon. Holder laughed. Morgan blew a low whistle, while Fahey and Butler were stunned into silence.

Thump. Thump. Thump.

They all heard the thuds on the door. As distinct and clear as One, Two, Three. No one had buzzed from downstairs.

"I wonder who that is?" said Holder as he stood up.

"Don't bother," said Collins casually, "there's no one there."

"Oh yeah?" said Holder cautiously as he drew his gun, hid it on the side of his pant leg, and advanced on the door. "We'll see." Holder looked through the peek hole. He didn't see anything. He opened the door, stepped into the vestibule, and looked both ways. The hall was empty. "Nobody there," he said.

"I told you so," said Collins.

"What does it mean?" said Butler.

"It means someone is going to die," said Collins quietly.

"How do you know?" asked Holder as he returned to the table.

"Because the Three Knocks follows my family."

The first time he had experienced it was in 1907 when he was living with his sister Hannie in London. No one was at the door after the three knocks. "There's been a death," said Hannie. Four days later the telegram came from Cork telling of their mother's demise.

"Jesus, Mick," said Butler laughing, "like my old man used to say, 'You're full of *pishogue!*'"

"Sugar," replied Collins, "this is no laughing matter."

"How can you be so sure?"

"It only happened twice to me," said Collins. "When my mother died."

"And . . . ?" said Butler.

"In the Imperial Hotel in Cork City . . ."

"Yes?" said Butler.

". . . on the morning of the day I died," said Michael Collins.

18. |

Tom Butler parked the limo in front of the Plaza Hotel, and Michael Collins jumped out of the front passenger's seat, then bounded up the steps of the hotel. He looked around the sumptuous lobby of the Plaza and thought, Well, this must be how the other half lives. It certainly wasn't Vaughan's Hotel on Parnell Square West, and it would even make the Shelbourne of his day look a bit shabby.

Collins lifted up the phone and asked the hotel operator for Boxer-Clegg. The phone rang five times before it was picked up. "Yes," said Boxer-Clegg.

"Sir Ian?"

"Yes, yes," said Boxer-Clegg, "who is this?"

"It's . . . ," Collins paused to get it right, "Detective Quinney."

"Quinney!" said Boxer-Clegg, "come right on up. Suite 14A."

In minutes Collins was knocking on Boxer-Clegg's door. "Did you have to rap so hard?" said a pained Boxer-Clegg, dressed in pajamas and robe. He immediately pulled Collins by the wrist over to a table where his laptop sat. "Look at that," he said, gesturing at the open e-mail on the screen. Collins read his own words: "You are a lucky man, for you know the date of your death: October 15, 1992. Michael Collins, IRB."

"Collins again," said Collins.

"Is that all you have to say?" Boxer-Clegg said, clearly agitated and just a bit frightened.

Collins thought Boxer-Clegg looked like the owl of death. He was suffering from jet lag, a gin hangover, and the missing hours from the end of the previous night. His eyes, bloodshot, were sunk in deep, dark circles. His hair was mussed, and a day's worth of beard covered the sagging turkey skin of his neck. At least now Collins knew why Boxer-Clegg always wore an ascot. Another rap came at the door: "Room service," the voice called out. Boxer-Clegg opened the door, and a waiter wheeled in his breakfast—a pitcher of Bloody Marys. Glasses filled with ice and celery stalks were set up on the food cart. Boxer-Clegg signed the bill and as soon as the waiter left poured his first drink of the day. "Will you join me, Quinney?"

"No, thank you," said Collins, shaking his head.

"I've got to go on the wagon, Quinney," said Boxer-Clegg, "but not just today."

"I understand," said Collins, delighted that Boxer-Clegg was in the state he was in. "I've come with my delivery."

"Delivery?" said Boxer-Clegg, apparently not remembering his requests of the night before.

"Your biscuit and your limo," said Collins.

"Biscuit?" repeated Boxer-Clegg.

Collins opened his belt buckle and removed Quinney's .38 Special, with its ammunition pouch, and handed them to Boxer-Clegg. "Of course," said Boxer-Clegg. "A biscuit," he laughed. "Oh, this is grand, grand." He paused for a second, his confidence fully recovered. "Just let that fucking Collins try something," he said, leveling the pistol.

Collins smiled. Yeah, he thought, grand.

Boxer-Clegg put down his Bloody Mary and went to the window overlooking Central Park for the light of the morning.

Collins followed him. Boxer-Clegg snapped open the cylinder of the .38 and spun it, making sure it was loaded. "Haven't used one of these in quite a while. What will you do for a gun?"

"I have one," lied Collins, pointing to his ankle.

"An ankle holster," said Boxer-Clegg. "You New York Police are precious." His hangover seemed to be leaving him.

"How did it go last night?" asked Collins with just a hint that he knew something that Boxer-Clegg didn't.

"Fine, very fine," said Boxer-Clegg, who couldn't remember anything after he picked up young Josie in the meat-market district and had the first of his gins at Julius's. "Delightful time," he said as he poured himself another Bloody Mary.

"What are your plans for the day?" asked Collins.

"Depends on your intelligence," said Boxer-Clegg. "Could you run it by me again?"

Collins knew he didn't remember much of their conversation of the previous evening. "My theory is that if they try to take Twomey, they will try to take him as he leaves 201 Varick Street."

"You're not sure this will happen?"

"Being led by Michael Collins or not—"

"Collins again," said Boxer-Clegg.

"Collins or no Collins," said Collins, "this is one highly inept group. Don't expect much."

"But if they do try," said Boxer-Clegg, "I want to be there."

"Then," said Collins, "you should park right near the truck bays on Houston Street."

"That's right," said Boxer-Clegg. "I want to be right on top of them—just in case."

"Just in case," repeated Collins.

"Just in case," Boxer-Clegg absently repeated himself. "What time is the prisoner scheduled to be moved?"

"Four-fifteen."

"The height of rush hour?"

"Purposely," said Collins truthfully. "There's protection in numbers, especially when the numbers are innocent commuters in their cars."

"I see," said Boxer-Clegg.

"How about the extradition papers?" asked Collins.

"How so?"

"You said your own people didn't even know you were in the country," said Collins. "Won't there be problems about who has the authority in this case?"

"My contact at the British Consulate is the only one who knows I'm here," said Boxer-Clegg. "I better call him." Collins nodded his head as Boxer-Clegg dialed the British Consulate only to be told that Charles Hornsmith had called in sick. Boxer-Clegg opened a small appointment book on the telephone table and dialed Hornsmith's home phone. "Hornsmith?" Boxer-Clegg barked into the phone.

Hornsmith, thought Collins, this is just bloody great.

"Sir Ian?"

"How can you call in sick on a day like this?" asked Boxer-Clegg.

"You haven't heard?"

"Heard what?"

"That the IRA has planned my assassination, and Detective Quinney has been abducted!" said Charles Hornsmith, his voice rising.

"Man," said Boxer-Clegg, "what in the devil's name are you talking about?"

"The IRA," said Hornsmith, "says it will shoot me on sight if I'm seen near Twomey today. And they've already kidnapped Quinney."

"Kidnapped Quinney," said Boxer-Clegg, getting Collins's rapt attention. "What rubbish!"

"Rubbish?" repeated Hornsmith.

"Quinney's right here with me at the Plaza," said Boxer-Clegg. "Hold on. I'll put him on the line." He handed the phone to Collins.

"Hornsmith?" said Collins in his best Brooklyn-Liberties accent, "it's Quinney. What's all this about my being abducted?"

"Your friend, Patricia, says—"

"Patricia," said Collins irritably, "is a stupid bitch." Boxer-Clegg nodded his head in agreement; he knew a lot about bitches.

"But she said—" continued Hornsmith.

"I don't care what she said," continued Collins, "she's wrong. I've been in the field for the last twenty-four hours getting this extradition ready and looking out for terrorists."

"Of course," said Hornsmith, "she was just so convincing about you." Hornsmith felt something was wrong. "Is that really you, Quinney?"

"Of course it's me," said Collins, trying to shoot a little more Brooklyn into his newfound accent. "If she calls back, tell her I'll see her tonight. Here's Sir Ian."

Boxer-Clegg took the phone. "Feel better, Hornsmith?"

"Yes, Sir Ian," said Hornsmith, not at all sure he felt better.

"Quinney's a fine man," said Boxer-Clegg. "Stop worrying." Michael Collins let out his breath in relief. "Now about these extradition papers. I want you to meet me at the airport tonight to make sure the transition goes smoothly."

Hornsmith bit his lip, then finally said, "I'll see you at JFK."

Boxer-Clegg hung up the phone. "He's a bit of a hysteric," he said. Collins nodded. "All because of one little threat on the telephone. If I believed all the threats the IRA has made against me I'd never get out of bed in the morning."

"I'll see you at the airport tonight," said Collins, then added for good measure, "I hope you don't have any more annoying e-mails."

Boxer-Clegg ignored the dig. "You won't be at the prison this afternoon?"

"That's INS territory," said Collins. "I'll handle the transition at the airport. I have a full day ahead of me, but feel free to use the limousine for whatever your needs are."

"I will," said Boxer-Clegg as he shook Collins's hand. Just then, three quick knocks came to the door. "That must be housekeeping," said Boxer-Clegg.

He opened the door, but there was no one there. Michael Collins was not surprised.

Patricia O'Malley was at a dead end. No one she had spoken to in the department had shown any concern over the missing Quinney or that afternoon's extradition of Twomey. No one except her had ever heard of an IRA agent named Michael Collins. She decided to call Charles Hornsmith again.

"Hello," said Hornsmith.

"Mr. Hornsmith, this is Officer O'Malley again."

"You can rest easy, Officer," said Hornsmith, "I just spoke to your Detective Quinney within the hour."

"You did?"

"Yes," said Hornsmith, "he sends his regards and says he'll see you tonight."

"You're sure it was him?"

"Of course," replied Hornsmith. "He was with Boxer-Clegg at the Plaza. Boxer-Clegg can vouch for him."

O'Malley thought for a second. "How can he do that?" she finally said. "Boxer-Clegg has never met Detective Quinney." There was silence at the end of the phone line. "Isn't that correct?" she asked.

"Yes, it is," admitted Hornsmith.

"Are you sure it was Quinney?"

"I'm eighty percent sure," said Hornsmith.

"Only eighty percent?"

Hornsmith hesitated. "I'm *pretty* sure it was him." He paused again. "Anyway, I'll be seeing him and Boxer-Clegg at Kennedy tonight. I'm the referee if there's a fight over the jurisdiction in this case."

"What time."

"About six o'clock."

Hornsmith heard the click of the phone. He didn't even get a "good-bye." O'Malley got the Plaza Hotel's phone number from information. "Sir Ian Boxer-Clegg," she said to the hotel operator.

"Sir Boxer-Clegg has already checked out."

Patricia O'Malley knew she was behind, but she felt she was gaining on Michael Collins.

Quinney's ears pricked up when he heard the door to the office being opened. Collins gestured to Ciaran Pike to step outside. "Go upstairs and get something to eat," Collins told him. "When you're finished come back down and we'll get Mr. Quinney here ready for his trip." Collins went inside the office and closed the door.

Quinney sat in his chair, quietly resigned. Collins went over and pulled the duct tape off his mouth and removed the sock. Quinney coughed as air filled his lungs. "We'll have to let this dry out," said Collins as he slung the sock over an overhead pipe. Quinney was a mess. He was black and blue from the pummeling that Butler and Holder had given him, and all he had been given to eat was a hamburger without the bun and a tumbler of juice. Worse still, he stank of the dead beer Butler had poured over him.

"I have to go to the bathroom," he said to Collins.

Collins stood Quinney up by grabbing him by the front of his orange jumpsuit. He took the keys to the handcuffs from a hook near the ceiling and undid one of the bracelets. He led Quinney out of the office to the back of the basement, behind the walk-in box, and recuffed him to a pipe, allowing him a free hand. "Do your stuff," said Collins. He returned to the office, sat down, and lit himself a Lucky Strike. He had left the door to the office ajar, and he could hear Quinney unzipping his jumpsuit. Collins put his feet to the edge of the desk, pushed back in the chair, then blew blue smoke to the ceiling. He could hear Quinney's piss hitting the basement wall. When he heard the zipper going back up he threw the cigarette to the ground and stamped it out. He went out and saw Quinney standing in the piss-fog created when his hot urine had hit the cold, damp wall. He looked like an orange ghost. Collins retrieved Quinney from his improvised latrine. Inside the office he recuffed Quinney behind the back and quietly set him into his chair. Quinney cowered before him. But Collins just pulled the duct tape off his eyes, and the cotton coverings fell to the floor. "It'll be over in a few hours," Collins said to Quinney.

Quinney had been in the dark for the last twenty-four hours, and the sudden light had stunned him into another kind of blindness. He looked up, and it seemed like the sun was rising from behind Collins's head. The huge shoulders, covered in the dark blue suit, with the light just peeping out from the sixty-watt bulb behind him reminded Quinney of an eclipse. He had a feeling he was about to be eclipsed himself.

Collins lit another Lucky Strike and took a deep drag. "Would you like a fag?" he asked Quinney.

"A fag," thought Quinney. He couldn't help but smile. Two doors down from the Stonewall, and he was being offered a fag. "Yeah," said Quinney, "I would." Collins took the cigarette out of his own mouth and placed it in Quinney's. Quinney sucked in as hard as he could, and the smoke seemed to fill every crevice in his body. His vision blurred; he felt like he was getting high. He tilted his head toward Collins and out the side of his mouth said, "Take it out." Collins removed the cigarette, and Quinney blew out the last of the smoke, coughing as he did. He looked at Collins and said, "How did you do it?"

"Do what?"

"That trick before, when I shot you."

"There's an old saying where I come from," said Collins. "You can't kill a good man twice."

"I never heard it," said Quinney.

"That's because I just made it up," replied Collins.

"They should have carted you out of here in a body bag," said Quinney.

Collins was quiet as he intently looked at Quinney. "Years from now," he finally said, "you'll tell your grandchildren this fantastic ghost story about this fabulous phantom who defied the rules of nature and physics."

"Then," said Quinney, "it won't be a Holy Ghost story."

Collins nodded. "That it won't," he agreed.

"So, what's the trick?"

"The trick," replied Collins, "is that I don't exist."

"They'll find you," insisted Quinney.

"You don't understand," said Collins. "I don't exist. I am a figment—whatever that is. I haven't existed since 1922."

Quinney was quiet. "Give me another drag," he said. Collins put the cigarette back in his mouth, let Quinney suck on it, then removed it. Quinney was really getting high now, and with the blue smoke in front of him, Collins almost looked like an apparition. Quinney laughed. "That's how you knew that was a cock-'n'-bull story, right?"

"About your grandfather in the GPO in 1916? Yeah, that's how I knew."

"You were really there?"

"I was," said Collins.

"Only I could be caught by a fucking ghost," he said, and he began to laugh. Quinney shook his head. "Everything was going so smoothly. I'm making money hand over fist, then you, the fat man, and the nigger show up and I'm cooked."

"Maybe if you respected people more you wouldn't be in this state."

"Yes," said Quinney, "I'm in a terrible state."

"You're in the Free State," said Collins, but Quinney didn't get his joke.

"What are you going to do with me?"

"I can't tell you that," said Collins, "but you'll soon see."

"Not even terrorist to policeman?"

"Not even freedom fighter to corrupt cop," replied Collins in exasperation. "What, in God's name, makes you tick?"

"Money."

"Money? Money's not worth shite in this world. Only a fool pursues money for the sake of money."

"Then what are you?" shot back Quinney. "Some kind of fucking philanthropist?"

"I believe in something," said Collins. "Money has no conscience."

"Conscience! So that makes you better than me?" replied Quinney. "Sure, pal." He grunted. "Caught by the fucking Three Stooges—Collins, the fat man, and the nigger."

"Will you stop using that filthy word?"

Quinney shrugged. "If you like. Just 'cause I stop using the word doesn't stop him from being a nigger, you know."

"You're a cute 'hoor," said Collins as he stood over Quinney and looked down. Quinney expected to be belted out of the chair any second, but Collins let his urge pass, and Quinney was grateful. Nothing more was said for a few moments as Collins and Quinney alternatively took drags on the smoke.

"What was it like?" asked Quinney when Collins pulled the Lucky from his lips.

"What?"

"The GPO in 1916."

"You know about that?"

"My old man was a student," said Quinney, "and he made sure I was, too."

Collins was silent for a moment. "Then you know who I am?"

Quinney didn't answer right away because he was thinking about yesterday's gunplay. Finally, he said, "Yes, I do." Collins just stared at him. "You know," Quinney added without attitude, "when I was a kid, you were always a hero in the Quinney household." Collins didn't say a word but turned his head away from Quinney. "So," said Quinney, "how was the GPO in 1916?"

Collins wiped his eye and turned back to Quinney. "Well, it was a fookin' disaster," he said with bluster and they both broke out in laughter, but for different reasons. "It was an education in how not to run a revolution. I had to deal with the British, looters, and then the cheerin', jeerin' 'hoors throwing scorched, still-hot bricks at us when we came out and they marched us up to Rutland Square. Someone once said the only difference between the Irish in Dublin and Belfast is that in Belfast they have the decency to stab you in the front." Collins laughed. "It was the most exhilarating week of the my life—and also the worst. And somehow I hoped it would never end."

Quinney was looking at Collins intently, genuinely interested on Collins's take on one of the great dramas of the twentieth century. "You wasted your time as a revolutionary," Quinney finally said.

"How so?"

"DeValera got all the glory."

"And all the subsequent grief," replied Collins. "I've been read-ing that I was lucky to be relieved when I was. The future, the historians say, would have crushed me." He laughed. "I guess I'll never know."

"Relieved?"

Collins pointed his index finger to his head and used his cocked thumb to simulate the hammer on a gun. "Relieved," he said.

"You know the thing that bothers you about me, Collins? We're not that much different. Different agendas; same methods."

"Maybe," said Collins, "but I don't hate like you do. That's the difference between us—you take it personally. If I took things personally how would I have ever negotiated the treaty?" For once, Quinney didn't have a ready response. "Don't dwell in hate," warned Collins, "because you may find you've lost the ability to love."

"Say what you want," said Quinney after a long pause, "but from now on whenever you shave you will see my face in the mirror." Quinney was still combative, and in a strange way Collins admired the little git for it. He could have used Quinney back in 1920. He wouldn't put him on the Squad, but he'd have used him in an emergency—like Bloody Sunday. Collins placed the duct tape back over Quinney's eyes and was about to do the same with his mouth when Quinney said, "I guess I'll see you in hell, Collins."

"Perhaps you will," said Michael Collins in a whisper. "Perhaps you will."

19.

Tom Butler was standing in front of the limousine taking the morning sun. As soon as Boxer-Clegg emerged from the Plaza—splendid in blue blazer and a lime-green ascot, *sans* earring—Butler walked around to the passenger's side and opened the door. "Sir Ian?"

"Yes," said Boxer-Clegg. "What happened to the colored chauffeur?" he asked as he handed his bag to Butler.

Butler wished Holder were here to hear this. "He said he had enough of you last night, and they sent me instead," Butler fibbed, wanting to let Boxer-Clegg know that he knew the score. Boxer-Clegg's memory of the previous night was slowly coming back, and he didn't want to think about it. "Where to?"

"Let's head for the Village," said Boxer-Clegg almost as if he couldn't help himself from repeating the stupidities of the night before.

Collins, Angus in tow, stopped at the corner of Christopher Street and Sheridan Square, across the street from Village Cigars. He looked downtown and saw nothing but the twin towers of the World Trade Center, which looked to him like a couple of steel cereal boxes. He stood up on his toes, but he could not see the

Woolworth Building from where he stood. When he was here in 1914 he could see the Woolworth Building from everywhere in New York. Then it was the tallest building in the world, at a mere sixty stories. Now, although still an architectural gem, it was a dwarf.

It was still one of things about 1914 New York that stuck in his mind. He remembered the Woolworth Building lobby because of its extraordinary beauty. Marble staircases so shiny you could see your reflection on the steps. The ceilings had taken his breath away with their birds, interlocking Celtic-like circles, and wonderful blinking stars. There were choirlike lofts, wonderful gargoyles hidden in the most unlikely places, and lifts that made him feel like he was going into a confessional when he entered them. He had gone to the observation floor and was amazed at the immense traffic in the Port of New York. He could see the ship quarantine at the Narrows between Brooklyn and Staten Island to his south, and he could see Bronx farmland to his north. It was fun watching the el trains run below, so tiny they looked like toys. When he returned to the main floor he envied the lift operator because laboring in this building must be like working in a great cathedral.

And he had talked about the Woolworth Building with Naomi. Both had been entranced by its beauty and it became an easy way to talk to a beautiful woman. He had always had trouble talking to beautiful women because of his shyness. Much of his phony bluster hid this shyness. Big, rough, and tough, most thought—and frightened by the ladies. Some men drank to give them courage; Collins blustered. It was that way with Kitty, too. But now Naomi was his Kitty, and in a few hours he would never see her again. Maybe a picture of the Woolworth Building would help her remember him and that first night at the Lion's Head. Naomi was the only reason he wanted to stay in New York, which was impossible. He somehow felt his life was being orchestrated by the Archangel—he could understand that—but why introduce a woman into the equation? The Archangel had given him a handful of days, an impossible task, and had overwhelmed him emotionally. Collins—just like a man—didn't know if his love of Naomi had helped or hindered him. But she was now a part of him, and he couldn't go without leaving her a memento of their time together.

Collins walked up Seventh Avenue South until he reached the Art Sanctuary, next door to the Village Vanguard. The small frame shop was run by Artie Scott, known around the Village as the man with the good heart and the bad left ventricle. To keep the heart pumping, Artie—a dead ringer for the late actor Jeff Chandler—firmly believed in the medicinal and recuperative powers of red wine, two glasses a day, depending on the size of the goblet and the bottle.

The tiny Art Sanctuary had everything from Picasso and Matisse prints to photographs of the Village and Old New York. The frames were mounted outside on chicken wire, and Artie had strategically rigged mirrors so he could work in his little shop and still keep an eye out for roaming art predators. Even with a bad ticker, at six feet five inches, his face beet red and his hair steel gray, he could make a very worthy adversary.

Collins stuck his head inside the minuscule shop. "You Artie?"

"I am."

"Tom Butler said you could help me out?"

"Tom Butler? Be glad to. What are you looking for?"

"Do you have any pictures of the Woolworth Building?" asked Collins.

"I have a picture of the Woolworth Building that could have been taken by Charles Lindbergh himself," said Artie.

"That's nice," said Michael Collins, who had no idea who Charles Lindbergh was. "I'll take it."

"I'm so depressed," said Naomi to Ciaran Pike as she cleaned a glass behind the bar at the Lion's Head.

"Understand," said Pike, a man with a seeming aversion to the personal pronoun.

"And what are you depressed about?" asked Collins as he burst through the open door with a picture frame under one arm and Angus under the other.

Naomi looked at him sadly. "You know what I'm depressed about."

"Me leaving?" said Collins as he gently placed Angus on the bar.

"Something like that," she said, and Angus gave her a lick of a kiss, making Naomi laugh.

"There," said Collins to Angus, "you'll make me jealous. Come here," said Collins to Naomi, trying to lift her spirits. Naomi leaned over the bar and Collins kissed her flush on the lips. He took off his homburg and placed it on her head. "Here. I won't be needing this anymore." Naomi pulled on the brim of the hat and made a funny face for Collins, mugging like a child. "I also have another gift for you."

"What?"

"Angus. Butler wanted to know if you'd take care of him while he's in Ireland."

"Of course," said Naomi.

"And now," said Collins, "the final prize. Do you know what that is?" he asked as he handed the frame to her. She was quiet for a second as she looked at the photograph, which was a puzzle in itself. It was a picture, obviously photographed from an airplane, of the tower of a building shooting up from and out of a heavily clouded sky. It almost looked like a castle from a spooky fairy tale. Naomi shook her head. "Artie Scott says a fellow by the name of Charles Lindbergh could have taken that."

"Lindbergh?" said Naomi.

"Yes, Lindbergh," said Collins. He paused. "Who the hell is Charles Lindbergh? I don't have a clue."

That elicited a laugh out of both Naomi and Pike, and Naomi solved both mysteries. "Charles Lindbergh was an American who became the first man to fly the Atlantic, New York to Paris, solo. I think around 1927. Also a big fan of Hitler and a virulent anti-Semite."

"Ah," said Collins, "Herr Hitler again."

"Anyway," said Naomi, "Lindbergh had an airplane, and he could have taken this picture of the Woolworth Building."

"That's the girl!" said Collins, "you got it," as he added another kiss for good measure. Collins then turned to Pike and was all business again. "How's your man down below?"

"Fine," Pike said. "Just waiting for Earl. Says he wants to dress your man up grand."

"Good," said Collins. "I want to leave at four o'clock sharp."

"No problem," said Pike.

"You can drive, right?" asked Collins.

"Have to," said Pike. "Can't be waiting for the buses in Belfast." Pike paused. "Someone might blow them up." Collins didn't know if Pike was putting him on or not. Just then, Holder walked into the Head, carrying Quinney's newly dry-cleaned suit.

"He'll smell like an angel," said Holder, "when I get through with him."

"He's going in style," said Collins.

"These are Mr. Q's traveling clothes," said Holder. "Wouldn't want our boy to look like a bum."

"Earl, you think of everything," said Collins.

"I have to," replied Holder. "Worked with you fucking donkeys for thirty years and you guys think of nothing!"

Collins held up his hands in mock surrender, and both Holder and Pike disappeared behind the giant kitchen doors. Naomi still held the picture of the Woolworth Building in the clouds. "I guess we'll always have the Woolworth Building," said Naomi. It was too bad, she thought, that they didn't even have time to watch *Casablanca* or *Laura,* her favorite movies, together. "Up in the clouds," she said softly, looking at the picture.

"Please God," said Collins as he started to follow his men downstairs.

"Go dTéghe Tu, Mo Mhuirnín, Slán," Naomi blurted out. Her eyebrows rose in shock at what she had just said to Collins in Irish: "May you go well, my love, safely."

Collins smiled and nodded. *"A chroi,"* he said, for he knew his magic had indeed touched her heart and her soul.

Boxer-Clegg directed Butler to the same route he had followed the night before. Soon they were breezing down 14th Street, cutting into Hudson Street, and approaching Abingdon Square. At the corner of Bank and Bleecker Streets he got out of the limousine. "You can follow me from here," said Boxer-Clegg.

"What?" said Butler.

"Follow me."

"Why?"

"Because," said Boxer-Clegg, "I want to go antiquing."

"Oh," said Butler, "I see." And follow him Butler did, a few yards behind as Boxer-Clegg rubbed his nose up against the windows of antiques shops, occasionally going in to browse. He's turned me into the Geisha Chauffeur, thought Butler as he slowly inched his way up Bleecker Street, discreetly trailing Sir Ian Boxer-Clegg.

Down below in the Lion's Head basement Earl Holder was preparing Quentin Quinney for his trip. Quinney stood against the wall he had previously used for a urinal. All he was wearing was the duct tape over his eyes.

"The water is going to be cold," said Holder, turning onto Quinney the hose that the bar regularly used to clean the sidewalk.

"Good Jesus!" said Quinney as the spray hit him.

"Shut up and move that soap, Detective," said Holder. "All over now, all over." Five minutes later Holder threw Quinney a towel. "Dry off," Holder said. Holder then presented Quinney with new underwear, socks, shirt, and tie. Next Quinney put on his newly dry-cleaned suit, which looked good considering the beer drenching Tom Butler had given it. Quinney was given back his belt and shoes. "Are we ready to go?" asked Collins.

"Not quite yet," said Holder. "Detective," said Holder to Quinney, "I have to change your eye coverings. If you open your eyes and see me I am going to have to kill you. Do you understand?" Quinney, defiant as ever, did not answer. "Do you understand?" said Holder as Pike cuffed Quinney in the back of the head.

"Yes!" said Quinney. "I understand."

"Then keep your fucking eyes shut," admonished Holder as he roughly ripped the duct tape from Quinney's eyes.

"Jesus Christ," Quinney screamed, but he did not open his eyes.

"Shad-up," said Holder as he applied a specially cut piece of silver-colored duct tape that fit perfectly around Quinney's eyebrows and nose. Holder pulled a pair of black wraparound sunglasses out of his pocket and put them on Quinney.

"Perfect," said Collins. Holder nodded, and Pike pulled Quinney out of his chair, marched him upstairs, and headed for the car that would take them to Kennedy Airport.

Sir Ian Boxer-Clegg continued to jauntily promenade down Bleecker Street as if he didn't have a care in the world. As he approached Perry Street, Butler saw him return to the car and open the passenger's-side door, but he did not get in. In his side-view mirror Butler could see Boxer-Clegg take a long quenching drink of a clear liquid on the rocks. He knew it wasn't water. Boxer-Clegg replaced the glass and closed the back door. The block between Perry and Charles Streets on Bleecker was one of the best blocks for antiques stores in the Village. Boxer-Clegg went a few doors down, popped into the Pierre Deux antiques shop, exited, and came back to the car. Butler finally figured it out. He was driving a bar car. This kept on for a good half hour until Boxer-Clegg stumbled across CONDOMania near the corner of West 10th Street. He went into the store and didn't come out for a good twenty-five minutes. The old queen, thought Butler, has found his element—antiques and prophylactics. Butler shook his head as Boxer-Clegg finally emerged and got into the back of the limo. "Where to now?" he asked.

"Just go along 10th Street until you come to Waverly Place," Boxer-Clegg responded. Returning to the scene of the crime, thought Butler. He slowly inched the limousine along 10th Street until Boxer-Clegg said, "Pull up by that bookstore." The partition was down, and Butler could see Boxer-Clegg longingly check out what was going on in the window of Julius's. Will he or won't he? "Driver," he finally said, "make a right here and at the corner." He's a bit of a coward, thought Butler, as he followed his orders perfectly. "Slow down," was the command as they approached the Stonewall. Boxer-Clegg saw it was still closed then said, "Across Seventh Avenue to the left." The limo passed the Lion's Head and crossed the avenue. "Up here to the left." Butler pulled up in front of Boots & Saddles, reputed to be Rock Hudson's favorite hangout in New York. You had to hand it to gay bars, Butler thought, they were the only businesses in the city that adhered to truth in advertising. Whether it be Rawhide, the Ramrod, the Anvil, or the Badlands, the name of the bar always told you that what you see is what you get. "I think it's time for the first of the day," lied Boxer-Clegg, and Butler suppressed a laugh.

Patricia O'Malley got out of the cab on Sheridan Square and walked to the Lion's Head. Naomi was glumly standing behind the beer pumps, shaping and reshaping Collins's hat. She was shocked to see O'Malley. The sartorial contrast between the two women was remarkable and revealed much about their attitudes. O'Malley was dressed to the nines, while Naomi was comfortable in tight jeans and a T-shirt. O'Malley wore a black suit, her mini-skirt riding well up her thigh. She had a white blouse with a wide jabot that failed to hide her full bosom. Her ensemble was completed with dark stockings, four-inch heels and a small black pocketbook that hung from her shoulder on what must have been a three-foot leather strap.

"Can I help you?" asked Naomi.

"Oh," said O'Malley, "I was supposed to meet Michael Collins here," she said, looking at the homburg in Naomi's hands. Although she had never seen Collins wearing a hat, O'Malley had a feeling. Women knew these things. O'Malley could almost catch Collins's scent off Naomi.

Angus, behind the bar with Naomi, growled.

"Haven't seen him for days," said Naomi, her stare making O'Malley uncomfortable. "He must have forgotten."

"Maybe he did," said O'Malley, who turned and started walking out. Suddenly she stopped. "You haven't seen Detective Quinney lately, have you?"

"No," lied Naomi, "don't know the man."

"Thank you," said O'Malley who was now positive there was something drastically wrong. Outside the Lion's Head she hailed a cab. "JFK, British Airways," O'Malley said, and the term *hat trick* flashed through her mind.

Naomi knew she had to reach Collins immediately. But how? Hughey Morgan? Maybe. Then it hit her. Collins's favorite toy—the cell phone. She picked up the Head's phone and dialed Tom Butler's number. She prayed Collins had the phone and not Butler. "Hello," Michael Collins said.

"Mick? It's me, Naomi."

"Hi dear, miss me already?"

Naomi thought she was going to cry, but then pulled herself together. "You have some nerve—" Then she heard Collins's heavy laugh, and she had to smile herself. "Mick, this is serious. Patricia O'Malley was just here looking for you. She was also asking about Quinney."

"Good Jaysus," said Collins. "Thank you. I'll always love you."

The phone line went dead before Naomi could say the same. She put his homburg on the back of her head and knew she would never feel this way about a man again.

Down at 201 Varick Street they brought Martin Twomey's lunch to his cell. Watery broth, American cheese on white, an apple, and a cup of tea.

"When you're finished with that," said Assistant Warden Hitchens, "get dressed in that suit." He began to walk away, then turned. "You wouldn't want to miss your flight to London now, would you?"

Twomey nodded and smiled at the slick Hitchens, who was filled with hubris. Hubris can evaporate rapidly, Twomey knew. In Hitchens's case, Twomey thought, it would take only another twelve hours.

The procession continued down Christopher Street. First it was twenty minutes in Ty's, right next door to Li-Lac Chocolates. Looking in Li-Lac's window, Butler was getting distressed and his willpower was about to collapse when Boxer-Clegg rescued him by climbing back in the limo. They continued down Christopher Street, past the Federal Archives Building on the left and St.

Veronica's R.C. Church on the right. They passed Mother Teresa's AIDS hospice on Washington Street and ended up in front of The Spartacus Suppository Bar, a foreboding structure at the foot of West Street. Butler was beginning to feel like a pimp. Boxer-Clegg was in the bar—which boasted in its front window THE BEST GRECIAN FEAST IN THE VILLAGE—for less than a minute. Butler, always the fanatical ball fan, surmised he was a pitcher, not a catcher.

"Take me to Varick and Houston," Boxer-Clegg said when he had seated himself. In the rearview mirror Butler could see his passenger with a gin in one hand and Quinney's .38 Police Special in his other. "I may get lucky today, after all," said Boxer-Clegg in a voice that chilled even Butler.

20. |

When Twomey finished his lunch he dressed in his government-issue brown suit. While waiting for the warden he had gathered together all his worldly goods: letters from his wife and children and his toiletries. He had left what remained of the Bovril and Jacob's Biscuits Collins had brought him. Then he sat on his bunk and waited some more. Prison was like the army, Twomey thought, hurry up and wait.

Finally Hitchens reappeared with two INS officers. "It's time, Twomey," he said as the officers entered his cell and handcuffed him in the front. Then they attached manacles to his legs. Twomey picked up the brown bag that he had put his possessions in, and Hitchens snatched it out of his hands. "No cargo, Twomey." Twomey looked hard at Hitchens and wished he was the murderer the British made him out to be.

As he was led down the hall past the other cells, a commotion began as inmates started stamping their feet, whistling, and banging anything available on jailbars. Hispanics, Russians, Haitians, Nigerians, Senegalese, Cambodians, and Chinese—all of whom had come to America in search of a dream that had been put on hold by the

INS. As he was about to leave the cell block, Ming-Lin, a brave man who had fled a Red Chinese prison in exchange for Varick Street and to whom Twomey had tried teaching English, reached out and touched Twomey as he went by. "Up the Republic!" Ming-Lin cried out in heavily accented English as Martin Twomey exited the cell block to thunderous applause.

Earl Holder was about to pull up to the parking gate adjacent to the International Arrivals building. "Collins," he said, "put your shield on." Collins took the shield and slid it into his breast pocket. "I'll do all the talking," Holder said as car came to a halt in front of the checkpoint, manned by a Port Authority policeman.

Holder handed papers he had forged to the black PA cop. "How's it going?" the cop said. "You still doing this shit?"

"What?" said Holder.

"I remember you from LaGuardia doing this extradition shit. Why they got a NYPD detective doing this shit?"

"Important cargo," said Holder, nodding to the back of the car.

"I catch your meaning," said the cop as he waved them through.

The catering truck was exactly where Hughey Morgan had said it would be. The key was in the ignition, and on the seat were I.D. badges and rolled-up overalls from the Oasis Airline Catering firm. Collins motioned Pike to the overalls. "Put that on," he said, "and for God's sake don't talk unless you have to." Pike pulled the white work overalls with the blue OAC on the back over his own clothes. He then got behind the wheel while Collins, Holder, and Quinney climbed into the back. Pike turned the ignition key and gingerly started on his trip to British Airways.

—

It was early rush hour, and Varick Street was already jammed with heavy traffic. From West Street Butler cut through Morton Street and then swung the limo down Seventh Avenue South. At Houston and Varick he pulled to a stop.

"Can't you get any closer to those lorry bays?" Boxer-Clegg asked, pointing at 201 Varick Street.

"Sure," said Butler, "why didn't you say so?" Butler drove on to King Street, made a right into Hudson, then slid the limo back into Houston Street and parked the limo, part in the street and part on the sidewalk, in the middle of the block. Boxer-Clegg had his perfect view of the truck bays.

"There it is," said Boxer-Clegg absently as he looked at an INS mini-van.

"What's that?" said Butler, playing the dummy.

"Nothing, absolutely nothing" said Boxer-Clegg as he poured himself another drink. They sat and waited. Boxer-Clegg put the still-full drink down. "I have to pay attention," he said aloud to himself.

"What are you looking for?" asked Butler.

"Wee Fenians," said Boxer-Clegg as Martin Twomey was brought onto the loading dock by two INS officers. "Wee Fenians." He laughed, and Butler felt very uncomfortable. Two other INS officers with pump shotguns were at their side. "Here it is," said Boxer-Clegg as Twomey was uneventfully put into the mini-van. The four officers also got in and the van pulled out, making a right at Hudson Street and heading uptown to the Queens-Midtown Tunnel. "Bloody Quinney!" spat Boxer-Clegg as he put Quinney's .38 back in its hip holster.

"What?" said Butler.

"Nothing. Nothing at all." The lack of deadly action had upset Boxer-Clegg. "Blast them," he said. Butler thought he was having either a sissy-fit or he was mentally disturbed. Maybe both. "This traffic is maddening," he finally said to Butler. "I want to beat that van to JFK."

"No problem," said Butler, and he went off in search of the Williamsburg Bridge, the fast route to Kennedy.

The Oasis catering truck pulled up near Gate 6 of British Airlines. The British Airways Boeing-747 just in from London was in turn-around and was being serviced. Collins called for a quick meeting. Holder turned Quinney toward a corner of the catering truck box and handcuffed him to a metal bar. Quinney was going nowhere. Collins, Pike, and Holder stood on the tarmac.

"I want to case this place out," said Collins.

"Be careful," said Holder.

Collins nodded. "Ciaran," he said, "as soon as you see the INS arrive, bring your lorry up to the plane. Be there, or everything will be hashed up."

"Will do," said the Belfast man, and Collins made his way toward Gate 6.

Butler pulled the limo up to British Airways departures. He had made the drive from the city in rush hour in less than forty-five minutes. It had to be some kind of world record. Boxer-Clegg got out with his single carry-on bag.

"Thank you, my man," he said to Butler. "Do I have to sign for anything?"

"No," said Butler, "it's all on Detective Quinney."

"Good-bye, then," said Boxer-Clegg, and he headed for the terminal.

"Good-bye," said Butler. He locked the doors of the limousine and dropped the keys into a nearby sewer before walking over to Aer Lingus to meet Hughey Morgan.

—

Inside the terminal Boxer-Clegg met up with Charles Hornsmith and Inspector James Noel of the London Police. "I have jurisdiction," said Boxer-Clegg.

"But—" began Inspector Noel.

"I'm sorry, Inspector," said Hornsmith, "but I must agree with Sir Ian. In this case he has jurisdiction. His papers are in order. He'll be taking your seat on the jet."

"Alright," said Noel, hardly upset that he would get to spend at least another day in New York.

21. |

Patricia O'Malley jumped out of the taxicab in front of British Airways and ran like a halfback in high heels, turning heads as she flew by. If O'Malley was anything, she was a stunner with impeccable taste.

O'Malley ran up to the information desk and flashed her badge. "I need to see someone from security," she said. "It's a matter of extreme urgency."

After conferring with the British Airways security chief, O'Malley was directed to the elevators and the third-floor administrative offices where she could meet with Port Authority police. Collins was coming down the stairs when the elevator doors opened, and O'Malley practically ran into him. They were alone. They both backed off in surprise, like gunfighters sizing each other up. They drew the line at four feet. O'Malley eyed the gold-and-blue detective shield Collins was wearing in his breast pocket. Shield 534. She knew.

"Fancy meeting you here," said O'Malley.

Collins eyed her. Her mini-skirt was so short he surmised that the back of her arse was probably falling out of it. She was something, Collins thought, half Irish and half fox. "Yes," he finally said, "fancy meeting you here, Officer O'Malley."

That cat was also out of the bag. She knew he knew. And he knew she knew. She began backing farther away, but there was no place to go. Just a single elevator, which was stopped at another floor, and the staircase, which Collins was blocking. She was getting nervous because he was so big. Collins could see her apprehension. "I'm clean," he said, holding his jacket open, showing no gun, and slowly advancing on her. She turned into the corner and pulled the strap of her pocketbook into her, trying to get her gun. It was obvious she was searching for her gun, because she certainly wasn't wearing a piece anywhere under those clothes. "Officer," said Collins as he tried to wrest her arm clear of the pocketbook. Here he was, minutes away from succeeding, and O'Malley had to show up. "Give me that," he said. But O'Malley was in a box, in a crouch, and he could not get at her. She was well trained, Collins could see. She relied on her center of gravity to thwart Collins. Maybe he should just knock her out, but the closer he got to Twomey the more he thought of Tom Clarke's admonition: "No violence. No killing. No maiming." Suddenly she swung around and hit Collins a vicious shot in the cheekbone with her elbow. So much for Tom Clarke, thought Collins, and where's the bloody Archangel when you really need him? Momentarily stunned, Collins stepped back as she swirled the pocketbook around, now trying to get control of it. Collins went to his jacket pocket, pulled out his Bigelow straight razor, and in one motion flipped it open and sliced the strap on the handbag just as O'Malley opened it. The bag hit the deck, followed immediately by her small snub-nosed .38. She dove toward the floor, but Collins's hand snatched the gun away from her.

"You fucking terrorist!" O'Malley said, out of breath.

"You're not hurting my feelings, miss," said Collins quietly, his hand rubbing his bruised cheekbone. "On the floor, straight down," he said to her, the gun against the back of her head, and she came to rest prostrate on the floor. "Keep your nose glued to that floor and put your hands behind your head. Don't move." She did what she was told.

"Where's Quinney?" she finally said. "I know you've got him. You're wearing his fucking shield."

"He's fine," said Collins. "No need to worry."

"Where is he?" O'Malley demanded.

"All I can say," said Collins, "is that I've hidden your man in plain sight. Now shut your gob." He pressed the gun against her head. "Interlock your fingers." O'Malley felt the cold metal of her handcuffs snap around her wrists. Then there was quiet. O'Malley did not move for several minutes. Then she turned slowly around to find that Collins was gone. Her gun and the handcuff keys were resting on top of her pocketbook, which was neatly tucked into a corner of the hallway.

The INS van drove across the tarmac and pulled up to the stairs of the Jet-Bridge that led into the British Airways Boeing-747 parked at Gate 6. Four officers got out; they opened the door of the van and then surrounded and escorted the handcuffed and shackled Twomey to the outside stairs. Collins and Holder were waiting for them. "There's the Orangeman," said Collins. "Lots of firepower, too," he added.

Collins and Holder approached the INS officers. "We'll take it from here," said Holder. "Take the cuffs off him. The shackles too."

"This is irregular," said one of the INS officers. Holder's stomach flip-flopped with nerves.

"Sonny," said Holder putting on his game face, "I've been doing this since before you were born." Collins thought the whole operation was going down the drain.

"Hey, Earl," said another INS officer, "how's it hangin'?" It was Petey Boyle, retired NYPD detective, working on his second pension at the INS. "You still doing this shit? I thought you hung 'em up a couple of years ago."

"Shit," said Holder as his heart started beating again. "You know I'm going out with my boots on."

"And your drawers around your knees," said Petey, who used to be known around the department as "Prankster" Boyle because of his penchant for practical jokes. "What's the problem here?"

"Don't know," said Holder, offering his forged papers. "We're here under special orders to take the prisoner and make sure he gets on that London flight. Apparently a lot of people in Washington have the shits about Twomey here."

"Yeah," said Boyle, "Washington always has the shits about something." Boyle looked at the papers. "They look good to me," he said to the INS officer who had originally confronted Holder.

"The cuffs, officer," said Holder.

The other officer scrutinized the papers and turned to Boyle with an uneasy look on his face. "I'll vouch for Holder," Boyle said. "Worked on the Force with him."

"You'll have to sign for him," the first INS officer said to Holder, still unconvinced.

"No problem," said Holder. Holder signed, the handcuffs and ankle shackles were removed, and the three men started walking up the stairs, Holder first, followed by Twomey, then Collins.

"Earl," yelled out Boyle, "one more thing." The three men stopped in their tracks and turned gingerly back toward Boyle.

"Yes?" said Holder.

"You want to have a drink sometime?" said Boyle. "So we can lie about old times to each other?"

"I *love* to do that," said Holder with relief. "You know where you can reach me."

The three men entered the tube of the Jet-Bridge and walked into the 747's port side, just aft of the first-class compartment. They continued across the plane by walking straight through the galley. The starboard door was ajar, and Collins pulled it in, then pushed it out. Holder leaped over the air gutter between the plane and the catering box. He immediately uncuffed Quinney from his pole, pulled the duct tape from his mouth, and pushed him toward the 747.

"Mr. Collins," said Twomey, "thank you."

"Later, lad, later."

Twomey leaped into the catering truck and Holder, in turn, handed Quinney to Collins. Here was the moment Collins had waited seventy years for—vindication for his failure to save Kevin Barry from the hangman. It was Collins and Quinney, with Boxer-Clegg waiting for them in the first-class compartment. Boxer-Clegg heard them and called out, "Is that you, Quinney?"

"You open your fucking mouth," said Collins sticking the straight-edged razor in Quinney's back like the barrel of a gun, "and you're dead."

Collins steered Quinney toward first class, where Boxer-Clegg was already seated, a drink in his hand.

"Sir Ian," said Collins, smiling as he saw the lime-green ascot.

"Quinney," said Boxer-Clegg as he stood up out of his seat.

"I'm Quinney," said the real Quentin Quinney, and Boxer-Clegg smiled.

"Sure you are," said Boxer-Clegg as Collins held up the keys to Quinney's handcuffs.

"Do you want me to take the cuffs off?" asked Collins.

"Not quite yet," said Boxer-Clegg. "Not quite yet."

Collins gave the handcuff keys to Boxer-Clegg, then stuck his hand out. "Sir Ian, it was a pleasure working with you."

"Same here, Quinney," said Boxer-Clegg. "I'm sure we will be seeing each other in the future as long as this Belfast thing keeps going on."

"Boxer-Clegg," said Quinney, "you stupid Limey. It's me— Quinney."

Collins turned around and walked out the way he had come in. He jumped the two feet into the waiting catering truck as Holder brought the truck extension down to the ground, and the three men squeezed into the cab alongside Pike. "Let's go, Ciaran," said Collins. "We got your man." Ciaran Pike gunned the catering truck and headed for Aer Lingus, five minutes away.

Patricia O'Malley was huddled with Immigration, NYPD, the Port Authority, and officials from the British Consulate, including Charles Hornsmith. "He's here," she said. "I know Collins is in this airport, because I've just been held up by him."

"Why did you let him go?" asked Hornsmith.

"I didn't let him go," she said gruffly. "He let me go."

"He let *you* go?"

"Yes," said O'Malley, slightly flustered. "He did."

"Doesn't seem to be such a dangerous guy," said the man from the INS.

"Oh," said O'Malley tartly, "he's a real sweetheart. All he's done is kidnap an NYPD detective. Yeah, a real sweetheart."

"Are you sure Quinney's been kidnapped?" said Captain Haynes of the NYPD.

"For God's sake," said O'Malley, "Collins is wearing his fucking shield! He's pulling a scam right under our noses."

"Where's Collins now?" asked Haynes.

"I don't know, and I don't care," O'Malley responded. "I'm more concerned about the safety of Quinney. He's in the airport."

"How do you know?" asked Hornsmith.

"Because Collins told me so."

"What exactly did he tell you?"

"He said," said O'Malley, "and these are his precise words, 'He's hidden in plain sight.'"

"What the hell does that mean?" asked Captain Haynes. "Plain sight."

O'Malley pursed her lips, then brightened. "Not *plain* sight. *Plane* sight! Collins told us! I can't believe it. Quinney's on that British Airways jet." The room emptied in less than fifteen seconds.

The British Airways crew was in the cockpit of the 747, just beginning their preliminary checklist. Down below, the flight attendants were shifting food and drink around the galleys, and those working in first class were preparing their pretakeoff drinks and hors d'oeuvres.

"I'm telling you, Boxer-Clegg, I'm Quinney." Boxer-Clegg took another sip of his drink as Quinney stood before him, still handcuffed in back. "You're a fucking asshole," said Quinney. "Your career is over when they find out how you fucked this whole thing up. What a fucking asshole!"

Boxer-Clegg gulped the last of his gin and tonic, put the empty glass down, and stood looking at Quinney, with his cropped hair and wraparound sunglasses. Boxer-Clegg, full of gin, never even gave it a second thought that this might *not* be Martin Twomey. In fact, right now, he didn't care.

"So the wee Fenian thinks I'm an arsehole, eh? Well, we'll see who's the arsehole here, me boyo," Boxer-Clegg said as he pushed Quinney to the back of the first-class section. "I'm an arsehole, eh." He took out Quinney's own revolver and slammed it against Quinney's forehead, knocking him to the ground. With his hands cuffed behind his back, Quinney had no balance, and he couldn't right himself. "So I'm a fucking arsehole, you murdering Fenian scum," Boxer-Clegg said as he kicked Quinney in the ribs. Quinney wailed from the pain. Terrified, he inched on the floor trying to get away from the man he could not see. "If I'm an arsehole," said Boxer-

Clegg, "then you're a dead man!" Boxer-Clegg picked Quinney up and slammed him against the starboard door that Collins had left ajar.

Patricia O'Malley and her entourage came running up the Jet-Bridge as Boxer-Clegg took one more step toward Quinney, grabbed him with two hands, and once again slammed him against the door, which opened as Quentin Quinney sailed through, twisting like a handcuffed missile, to the tarmac below.

"Freeze!" cried O'Malley, snub-nosed .38 in hand, as she saw Boxer-Clegg shove Quinney through the door. She ran past Boxer-Clegg to the door of the plane and saw Quentin Quinney lying front-down under engine Number 3, his neck and head twisted at a horrible angle. One of the British Airways ground crew who was putting passengers' bags into the plane's hold ran over and moved him by the shoulder, his head wobbling like a rag doll. He removed Quinney's sunglasses and for a moment thought that Quinney had no eyes, but it was only the carefully manicured duct tape that Holder had fashioned for the job. Quentin Quinney was dead. His hands were still handcuffed behind his back. O'Malley was half hanging out of the 747 and she could see it was definitely her lover on the ground below. "How is he?" she yelled above the din of the airport. The man on the ground shook his head. O'Malley wanted to cry, but that could wait. O'Malley was a pro—there was work to be done; there was plenty of time for crying later. "Somebody call for an ambulance," said O'Malley, and Captain Haynes quickly snapped the orders into his police walkie-talkie.

"Freeze?" said Boxer-Clegg, oblivious. "Freeze? My dear, why all the dramatics over a wee terrorist?"

"That was no 'wee terrorist' as you put it, mister," replied O'Malley, "that was a New York City Police officer." O'Malley spun Boxer-Clegg around and was about to disarm him when she was intercepted by Charles Hornsmith.

"Don't interfere with me," warned O'Malley, "I'm placing this man under arrest."

"You don't have the authority," said Hornsmith.

"Yes, I do," replied O'Malley looking to Captain Haynes, who was surveying the scene intently.

"No, you don't," said Hornsmith. "Sir Ian has full diplomatic immunity."

"No, he doesn't," replied O'Malley. "He's a cop, not a diplomat. We're going to the stationhouse."

"Sir Ian is not going to any stationhouse," replied Hornsmith. "He's flying back to London on this airplane."

"And this airplane is not going anyplace," said O'Malley testily, "until Sir Ian gets his ass off it."

Another officer from the British Consulate tried to shield O'Malley from Boxer-Clegg. He gave her a shove toward the door that Quinney had just traveled through. "Hey," said O'Malley, her voice rising, "you have some kind of problem?"

"Yeah," said Ronnie Dryer, who ran the Irish Desk at the Consulate, "yeah, pet, maybe I do."

"Pet my Irish ass," said O'Malley to Haynes. "Did you see what he did to me?"

"Yes, I did," said Haynes. He turned to Hornsmith. "Is Sir Ian going to leave this plane voluntarily?"

"He's not leaving," replied Hornsmith smugly, "either voluntarily or involuntarily. Diplomatic immunity. Plain and simple." Boxer-Clegg, in a gin daze, nodded serenely.

"Is that so?" said Captain Haynes, and he put his walkie-talkie back to his mouth. "This is Captain Haynes," he barked through the intermittent static, "10-13, 10-13, British Airways, Gate 6."

"10-13, British Airways, Gate 6," said the voice at the other end of the walkie-talkie, "10-4."

"What's a 10-13?" asked Boxer-Clegg of Hornsmith.

"Officer in distress, asshole," replied Officer Patricia O'Malley.

Ciaran Pike carefully made the five-minute trek around the TWA terminal and brought the catering truck to the side of *St. Colmcille,* Aer Lingus Flight 104 to Shannon and Dublin.

"Where's *St. Patrick?*" asked Collins, his heart sinking as he stepped back into the catering truck. Collins was a believer in omens, and he didn't like the change of planes to *Colmcille.* Holder brought the catering box up to the starboard door. Hughey Morgan and Tom Butler were standing in the doorway of the 747, waiting for them. Holder turned to Collins. "Hang in there, man," he said. "Have a good flight."

Collins nodded and placed his hand on Holder's shoulder. "Earl, you make a hell of a Fenian. I'll never forget you."

"Shit," said Holder, embarrassed. He shouted to Butler aboard the 747, "Pardner, you're finally getting that vacation in Ireland you always wanted."

"I'll be back soon, Earl," said Butler.

"Maybe we'll catch a Mets game in the spring," said Holder as he waved to his friend of forty years. "And I ain't lyin', you fat Irish fuck."

Twomey and Collins hopped onto the Aer Lingus 747, and Hughey Morgan closed the door. Twomey took a window seat, Butler the aisle seat next to him, and Collins the opposite aisle seat.

"Sheila," said Morgan to the flight attendant, "I think these men deserve a drink."

"Three Irish," said Collins.

"Make that four," said Morgan as the passengers began to file on board. "A toast?" asked Morgan.

"To Martin Twomey," said Collins. "A free Irishman."

"A free man," echoed Butler and Morgan.

"Thank God," said Twomey, and Collins thought that Twomey was more right than he knew.

"Where's *St. Patrick*?" asked Collins.

"Probably being serviced in Dublin," said Morgan. "Nothing unusual here." Collins shook his head, his agitation clearly showing.

"Time to go, Hughey," said Sheila the flight attendant.

"I'm going to miss you guys," Morgan said.

"And you will be missed," said Collins as he shook Morgan's hand.

"You owe me a bottle of Irish whiskey," said Morgan to Butler. He rubbed Butler's bald head in affection, gave a short wave to Twomey, and stepped off the jet.

A tug tractor pushed the 747 away from the gate and turned it toward the runways. *St. Colmcille* taxied out and joined a short queue. Just after seven P.M. the jet turned left onto runway 31-L and accelerated, hurtling down the bumpy runway and finally lifting its precious cargo high over Jamaica Bay and the Rockaways on its way home to Ireland.

Aer Lingus Flight 104 was the last plane to leave John F. Kennedy International Airport for nearly two hours. NYPD and Port Authority police descended on British Airways, responding first to a call of an officer in distress and later to a call of an officer down on the job—Detective Quentin Quinney, dead on the tarmac.

22. |

"Do you know what day this is?" a relaxed Collins asked Butler as his drink was replenished by a flight attendant.

"Let's see," said Butler looking at his watch. "It's nine P.M. New York time, which would make it two A.M. local Irish time. It's a new day—October 16."

"Do you know what famous event happened on October 16?"

"I do," said Butler.

"What?"

"The miracle New York Mets won the fourth game of the World Series over the heavily favored Baltimore Orioles on October 16, 1969. J. C. Martin ran in the baseline and got hit in the ass with the ball, and Rod Gaspar scored the winning run."

"You and your baseball again," replied Collins, shaking his head. "But that's not what I was thinking of."

"Oh?"

"I was thinking of a very special birthday."

"You're right. A very famous Irishman," teased Butler.

"Yes," said Collins, "that's it."

"Oscar Wilde!"

"Ah, Oscar," said Collins. "Another victim of the twisted morality of Edward Carson. First they persecuted Oscar, then Sir Roger. Do you see a pattern here? But no, I wasn't talking about Oscar Wilde."

"Eugene O'Neill?"

"Jaysus," said Collins, "who's Eugene O'Neill?"

"Playwright of the century," replied Butler.

"Really," said Collins. "I'm so ignorant of the last three-quarters of this century. I picked up as much as I could about Hitler, Lindbergh, World War II, and now Mr. O'Neill. What county was he from?"

"American born. Father was a Kilkenny man," said Butler. "You had great parallel careers—he as a writer, you as a Fenian."

"I see," said Collins.

"I'm still looking for your famous Irishman." Butler paused for effect. "It wouldn't be Michael Collins, by any chance?" he finally said.

Collins looked Butler in the eye and smiled. "You knew all along, didn't you?"

"I did indeed," said the Sugarman. "I've been researching you. Happy birthday, Mick."

Collins nodded. "It took me a long time. At least someone remembered this time." His last birthday had been forgotten. Kitty had forgotten. The staff had forgotten. So it was a lonely birthday in London as the work on the treaty went on. Only his sister Helen the nun, Sister Celestine, had remembered.

"You sound hurt," said Butler.

"I'm only human," replied Collins.

"No, you're not," Butler shot back, suppressing a smile that made Collins grin broadly, showing the gap between his front teeth.

They were served their dinners. Collins wasn't hungry, so

Butler devoured his filet mignon for him. "I guess your three-knock theory doesn't hold up after all," said Butler between bites.

Collins looked at him ominously. "We're not home yet," he said.

"Mr. Collins?" said the flight attendant. Collins nodded. "The captain would like to see you in the cockpit." Collins unbuckled his seat belt and followed the flight attendant up the winding stairs to the upper level lounge and then into the cockpit of the 747.

"Captain Quinn," she said, "this is passenger Michael Collins."

The captain turned around and waved Collins to the jump seat behind him. "Dick Quinn," he said and then introduced Collins to his copilot, First Officer Johnny Holland, and the flight engineer, Paddy Farrell. "I didn't know we had a VIP onboard, Mr. Collins," said the captain.

"VIP?"

"Very Important Person," said Quinn.

"I'm not," said Collins. "Martin Twomey is the important person here."

"Tell that to the *Taoiseach*," said Captain Quinn. Collins nodded blankly. "The *Taoiseach*," said Quinn. "Mr. Reynolds." None of it meant anything to him. "The Prime Minister of Ireland is going to meet you at Shannon," said Quinn.

"*An Taoiseach*," said Collins. He couldn't help but smile. I was *An Taoiseach*, thought Collins, before there was a *Taoiseach*.

"Yes, Mr. Reynolds," replied Quinn. "He'll be meeting you and your party."

Collins smiled. "Ernie did his job."

"Ernie?" asked Quinn.

"It's not important," replied Collins, delighted. "How much longer?"

"We'll be in County Clare and on the ground within an hour."

"Thank you, Captain," said Collins. "Thanks for the news. It takes a lot off my mind." Collins began to get out of the jump seat.

"One other thing, Mr. Collins," the captain said. "I have a message for you from Hughey Morgan of WelshDragon."

"Hughey?"

"Yes," said Quinn. "Hughey wants you to know that Quinney is dead."

The news stunned Collins so, he looked as if he had been hit on the side of the head with a shovel. "Dead!" he nearly shouted. "Oh, my God," he said, beginning to cry. "Oh, my God," he said in quieter voice. He stood up out of the jump seat and dropped to his knees on the flight deck, a few feet in front of the throttles. His move startled First Officer Holland, who instinctively protected the running throttles with his left hand. Then Collins did the only thing he could for his dead adversary. He said a Perfect Act of Contrition. "Oh, my God," he began as tears poured from his eyes. "I am heartily sorry for having offended Thee, and I detest all my sins, because I dread the loss of heaven and the pains of hell, but most of all because they offend Thee, my God, Who art all-good, and deserving of all my love," spoke Michael Collins. "I firmly resolve, with the help of Thy grace to confess my sins, to do penance, and to amend my life. Amen."

"Amen," added Captain Dick Quinn, senior pilot of Aer Lingus.

Collins returned to his seat on the aisle, the tears still moist on his cheeks. "You look like you've just seen a ghost," said Butler.

"I think I have." He paused. "Quentin Quinney is dead."

"Dead!" said Butler. "My God, what happened?"

"Boxer-Clegg. He apparently killed him in a rage. Beat him, then threw him, still handcuffed, off the airplane, onto the tarmac. What's that on a 747? Three, four stories? He was dead as soon he hit the ground."

"Can I get you anything?" the flight attendant asked, the flickering of the in-flight movie illuminating, then eerily blackening, her features.

"Irish," replied Collins. "Neat." Collins and Butler sat in their opposite aisle seats, both silent. The flight attendant put Collins's whiskey in front of him. He began talking, looking straight ahead. "I still have that great Collins touch," he said bitterly. "Whatever I touch dies. Nothing survives the great Collins touch. I touch an idea, a movement, a crooked little eejit policeman, and they all die."

Butler reached across the aisle and touched Collins's arm. "It's alright, Mick. You did your best. They weren't supposed to kill him. They never figured out what you did."

"I killed him as if I'd shot him myself. I knew what I was dealing with in Boxer-Clegg, a drunken sadist. I should have seen it coming. God help Quinney, and God help my soul." Butler reached across the aisle and again patted Collins's arm. Collins wouldn't look at him or the sleeping Twomey. "What gives me the right to do this to men?" he finally said. "Who the fuck made me God?"

"You did it for Ireland," Butler said.

"I did it for myself. My Big Fellow ego. I always had to be the big man, the pusher, when I was always nothing more than the head guttersnipe." He finished his whiskey. "And now I'll be going wherever they send failures. I couldn't free Kevin Barry. I couldn't free Ireland. And when I freed Martin Twomey some unfortunate, petty eejit of a policeman had to die." Collins stared straight ahead, looking at an in-flight movie he could not comprehend, all his thoughts centered on Quentin Quinney. Then all of a sudden, the shade across Collins's soul lifted. "St. Colmcille," he said.

"What?" asked Butler.

"This airplane is named for St. Colmcille."

"So?"

"Do you know what that means?"

"I haven't a clue," said Butler.

"Dove of the Church," replied Collins as he felt the knot in the middle of his chest dissolve. Butler shrugged his shoulders. "He was a great scholar, defender of poets, who was banned from Ireland because of his love of books."

"Where'd you learn all this stuff?" asked Butler.

"As a child, from my mentor, Denis Lyons, in the National School at home," replied Collins, savoring one last time his happy childhood. "Colmcille was something," continued Collins. "Once he prophesied to one of his acolytes, 'In three days, go early in the morning to the western shore of this island. At the ninth hour, a crane, weary and driven before the wind, will descend to our beach. Lift it tenderly and carry it to some neighboring cottage where, for three days, it shall be nursed to health.'" Collins paused for effect. "'Then will it wing its way back to Ireland.'"

"That's lovely," said Butler.

"I feel like that crane," said Collins, "winging my way back to Ireland."

Airboats, archangels, doves, and cranes, thought Collins. All winged creatures. And for the first time since he had returned to Earth, he felt at peace.

"This is Captain Quinn," said the voice on the intercom. "We'll be landing at Shannon shortly. Thank you for flying Aer Lingus, and we look forward to seeing you in your future travels. *Slán leat.*"

Collins could hear the landing gear groan as it was lowered over the Cliffs of Moher. As the plane banked, he looked out at the gray Irish dawn and the rain splattered across the window. The wing tipped again, and he could see the green fields and the gray roads and multicolored houses of County Clare. The plane leveled out, and the wheels of the 747 hit the ground. Michael Collins was home.

As the door of the plane next to first class was being opened, Collins, Twomey, and Butler prepared to depart.

"Martin," said Collins, "the *Taoiseach* is here to see you."

"My God," said Twomey.

"Ernie hit the jackpot," said Butler.

"The two of you will be fine," Collins said, "and I'll be leaving you soon."

"After you meet the *Taoiseach*, right?" asked Twomey.

"If it's God's will," said Collins. "In case we get separated, Martin, always remember Ireland. And always do the right thing for her—no matter what the consequences."

"I will, Mick," said Twomey. "I will."

"And Sugar," said Collins as he embraced him, "don't forget to pray for me."

"I will not pray for you," said Butler, still holding Collins's shoulder.

"Why not?" demanded Collins, agitated.

"Because where you're going you won't be needing my prayers anymore. *You pray for me.*"

Collins looked Butler in the eyes for several moments, then undid the fob and took the watch from his vest pocket. "I want you to have this, Tommy."

"Why?"

"Just say," said Collins with a sad smile, "that my time's up." Butler took the watch and chain, and Collins said, "Let's go meet the *Taoiseach*."

As they departed the plane Collins got a whiff of the cool, damp Clare air of early morning, and he knew he was finally home. The three men began making their way down the Jet-Bridge. As they came to the end they were blinded by the television lights.

"Martin, oh Martin," said Twomey's wife as she hugged her husband.

"Maura, Maura," Twomey said, surprised to see his wife.

"Mr. Twomey," said the Prime Minister of Ireland as he squeezed into the television picture with all the skill and conceit of the politician, "Albert Reynolds."

"*Taoiseach*," said Twomey. "You must meet my friends." He turned around, and the first he saw was Butler. "This is Tommy Butler, who helped get me away, and," he said looking around for Collins. "And this is Michael Collins. He must be here somewhere. Only I can't find him."

And with that there was a thunderbolt from the sky—like artillery from heaven—and heavy rains flooded Shannon Airport and the whole of County Clare. The banks of the River Shannon exploded in overflow, tossing fish—flipping but not dying—onto grass a mile away. A second thunderbolt hit the nose of *St. Colmcille* and shorted out all the power in the 747 as it blew away the Jet-Bridge, exposing all to the elements. The *Taoiseach* was drenched and blown to the ground. Television lights burst, and cameras halted. Martin Twomey held onto his wife for dear life as Tommy Butler looked up wild eyed, the rain soaking him. He glowed as beads of water rolled off his bald head. Butler extended his arms, stood firm at the onslaught, his belly exposed, and exulted in a bath of purity, like a child in cool water on a hot summer's day.

Then, as quick as it had come, the rain stopped. It was replaced by a blistering sun, the brightest that had ever been seen in County Clare. So bright that flowers bloomed as far north as Connemara, as far south as the Ring of Kerry, and as far east as Beal na mBlath in West Cork. Dispersed fish took flight and flew back to the Shannon. Buds appeared on trees, even as their orange autumn leaves still clung to the branches.

It reminded Michael Collins of Beal na mBlath as he was stunned by the light and felt himself being hurled through the atmosphere—like a reentry astronaut in reverse—propelled into outer space, toward the scorching brightness of the sun, now naked in beauty to reveal the genius of the Almighty. Adrenaline flowed, shooting him even faster like a finely crafted aerodynamic projectile. He began to spin tight like a missile and, through his brilliant blue eyes, he could finally see the prize. He accelerated toward it. Up, up, up, as if being guided by the wild, but steady, hand of an old friend.

And on October 16, 1992, his thirty-second birthday on this Earth—and the Celtic Normandy feast day of St. Michael, the Archangel—Michael Collins, on the emerald green wings of an Archangel, ascended into heaven for all eternity.

Earl Holder's contacts at IAD were very interested in the financial gyrations of the late Quentin Quinney's bank accounts. This information, in part, and the eyewitness account of Officer Patricia O'Malley made sure that Sir Ian Boxer-Clegg was arrested before he fled the country. Despite the initial claims of diplomatic immunity by the British Embassy in Washington, Luigi Baroni, the District Attorney of Queens County—fully aware of the large contingent of Irish voters in Woodside and other areas of the borough—vigorously brought second-degree murder charges with depraved indifference against Boxer-Clegg. Sir Ian, arrogantly refusing a plea bargain, was convicted of the crime in July 1993, although not by a jury of his peers by any means. He is presently serving twenty-five years to life in the Clinton Correctional Facility in Dannemora, New York, where he is known as "the Ascot" to his fellow inmates and where all his sexual fantasies have been fulfilled.

Tommy Butler returned to New York at Christmas 1992, a hero, and was given the Key to the City by Mayor David Dinkins. Sadie Robinson became Father Bill O'Donnell's live-in cook and housekeeper at St. Bernard's, and Father O'Donnell gained another twenty-five pounds. Pappy O'Donnell dusted off the law books and became an advocate for the homeless and the poor and a frequent target for the tirades of Mayor Rudolph Giuliani. O'Donnell, however, had the last laugh when the courts upheld a class-action suit he brought on behalf of the poor and the homeless that alleged that they had been illegally denied food stamps and welfare benefits by the City of New York.

In November 1992 Naomi Ottinger discovered she was pregnant. The only man she had slept with in the previous year was Michael Collins. With two young children and an ex-husband full of questions, Naomi thought about an abortion. It was in this period of torment that she would dream of Collins, who would always reassure her that "a child is never a tragedy." At the age of forty she knew it was her last chance to be a mother again. Then she remembered what Collins had told her: "I'll send you a symbol to prove my love and truthfulness." She decided to have the child, and when she did, her dreams about Michael Collins ceased, as if both their minds were at ease. On July 14, 1993, a boy with the dark chestnut hair and the blue eyes of his father was born. People on the street would often comment on his beautiful skin. "He's so beautifully white," they would say. "You should have seen his father," Naomi would reply. Although Naomi was a nonreligious Jew, she decided to have the child baptized in the Catholic faith. Michael Collins III was baptized by Father Bill O'Donnell at St. Bernard's Church. His sponsors were Tom Butler, Earl Holder, and Sadie Robinson. Young Mickey, as he was called, was a happy little boy with a great curiosity who, like his father's friend Vinny Byrne, took great joy in the world and everything and everyone in it. He was a magical child whose presence could soothe the angry and bring a smile to the unhappy and tormented. Bullies, after one stern glance from young Mickey, looked for prey elsewhere. "This child is marked for greatness," said Father O'Donnell on the day Mickey was baptized, and there was no disagreement from the people who knew and loved his father. When he was growing up Mickey would often ask about his father. "Would you like to visit him?" Naomi would ask and she would take him to the lobby of the Woolworth Building. "Where is he?" he would ask. "He's up there in those stars," Naomi would say as she pointed to the ceiling. "He is, indeed," young Mickey would say with an inflection that could only be from County Cork.

Angus, the feisty cairn terrier, although still Butler's dog at heart, moved into the Ottinger household and became Mickey Collins's constant companion.

Ernie Fahey went back to his job on Wall Street, and Earl Holder continued to work as a PI. The Lion's Head closed on October 12, 1996 ("Columbus Day, not St. Patrick's Day," Butler sagely observed), and Naomi Ottinger and Tommy Butler continued to work at various watering holes around the Village. Butler, who loves to bet on the ponies, refers to them as entry 1 and 1A in the Saloon Sweepstakes.

Bill Clinton was elected President of the United States in November 1992 and immediately broke Britain's hegemony on the State Department's biased policy toward Ireland by appointing Jean Kennedy Smith, JFK's sister, United States Ambassador to Ireland. For the first time, the voice coming out of Dublin held more weight with the President than that of the London ambassador. This was followed in 1994 by granting a visa to *Sinn Fein* "terrorist" Gerry Adams, allowing him to enter the United States for the first time. This set the ball rolling for peace talks, which were birthed by Senator George Mitchell in the historic Good Friday Agreement of 1998.

Martin Twomey returned to his home in County Kerry, where he enjoyed some celebrity. At the urging of Gerry Adams, he stood for TD in the Tralee constituency in 1996 and was elected to the *Dail* in Dublin as a member of the *Sinn Fein* party. In the spring of 1998, remembering Collins's parting words about Ireland: "Always do the right thing for her—no matter what the consequences," he campaigned hard for a "Yes" vote on the Referendum on Northern Ireland amending Articles 2, 3, and 29 of the Irish Constitution.

On May 22, 1998, the people of Northern Ireland voted by seventy-one percent to find a way to peace—without violence. In the Irish Republic a whopping ninety-four percent of the Irish people voted to amend the Constitution, basically removing the last vestiges of Eamon DeValera's legacy—and firmly reestablishing and reaffirming the constitutional sagacity of Michael Collins.

POSTSCRIPT

On October 16, 1998—the 108th anniversary of Michael Collins's birth—John Hume, a Catholic from Derry, and David Trimble, a Protestant from Belfast, were awarded the Nobel Peace Prize for their heroic work on the Northern Ireland peace process.

BIBLIOGRAPHY

Many of these books contain nuggets of information about Michael Collins, his methods, and his personality. Perhaps the best book on Collins the man is *Enchanted by Dreams* by Joe Good. Good knew Collins in London before the Rising, in prison in Wales, and then back in Dublin. It is here that I found the invaluable piece of information that Collins, Ireland's first Finance Minister, had attended an economic conference in 1913 at which Vladimir Lenin was a lecturer. Another book with a telling portrait of Collins the leader is Charles Dalton's *With the Dublin Brigade,* which is long out of print. Dalton details the Collins management style—get responsible people and delegate—and gives a thrilling and chilling view of Dublin during the War for Independence. Of course, Tim Pat Coogan's biography of Collins is filled with gems (such as, was Tim Healy a British intelligence mole?). And I am indebted to Coogan for giving me the idea of sending Collins with Casement to New York. According to Coogan, a telegram from the German Imperial Embassy in Washington to the Foreign Office in Berlin, dated September 1, 1914, read: "An Irish priest [sic] named Michael Collins and Sir Roger Casement are going to Germany in order to visit the Irish prisoners." All I did was turn them in the opposite direction, speeding toward New York on the *Lusitania*. The best way to research Collins is to pick up a book of any contemporary of his and look in the index. You'd be surprised how many people Michael Collins knew!

Augustine, Saint, *The City of God* (New York: Modern Library, 2000)

Bunson, Matthew, *Angels A to Z: A Who's Who of the Heavenly Host* (New York: Crown, 1996)

Clarke, Kathleen, *Revolutionary Woman: Kathleen Clarke 1878–1972, An Autobiography* (Dublin: O'Brien Press, 1991)

Coogan, Tim Pat, *Michael Collins: The Man Who Made Ireland* (New York: Palgrave/St. Martin's, 2002)

Chesterton, G. K., *The Man Who Was Thursday* (London: Penguin, 1986)

Dalton, Charles, *With the Dublin Brigade (1917-1921)* (London: Peter Davies, Ltd., 1929)

Dwyer, T. Ryle, *Big Fellow, Long Fellow: A Joint Biography of Collins & DeValera* (New York: St. Martin's Press, 1999)

Ellmann, Richard, *James Joyce* (New York: Oxford University Press, 1983)

Fagan, Terry, and the North Inner City Folklore Project, *Monto: Madams, Murder and Black Coddle*

Golway, Terry, *Irish Rebel: John Devoy and America's Fight for Ireland's Freedom* (New York: St. Martin's Press, 1998)

Good, Joe, *Enchanted by Dreams: The Journal of a Revolutionary* (Dingle, Co. Kerry: Brandon, 1996)

Holroyd, Michael, *Bernard Shaw: The One-Volume Definitive Edition* (New York: Random House, 1997)

Horgan, John, *Seán Lemass: The Enigmatic Patriot* (Dublin: Gill & Macmillan, 1997)

Inglis, Brian, *Roger Casement: The Biography of a Patriot Who Lived for England, Died for Ireland* (New York: Harcourt Brace Jovanovich, 1973)

Kearns, Kevin C., *Dublin Pub Life and Lore: An Oral History* (Niwot, Colorado: Roberts Rinehart Publishers, 1997)

Keogh, Dermot, *Jews in Twentieth-Century Ireland: Refugees, Anti-Semitism and the Holocaust* (Cork: Cork University Press, 1998)

Lieberson, Goddard (producer), *The Irish Uprising 1916-1922* (New York: A CBS Legacy Collection Book/Macmillan, 1966)

Mackay, James, *Michael Collins: A Life* (Edinburgh: Mainstream Publishing Company, 1996)

Neligan, David: *The Spy in the Castle* (London: Prendeville Publishing Ltd., 1999)

O'Connor, Ulick, *The Times I've Seen: Oliver St. John Gogarty, A Biography* (New York: Ivan Obolensky, Inc., 1963)

O'Connor, Frank, *The Big Fellow* (New York: Palgrave USA, 1997)

Ó Broin, León (editor), *In Great Haste: The Letters of Michael Collins and Kitty Kiernan* (Dublin: Gill & Macmillan, 1983 and 1996)

Reilly, Robert T., *Irish Saints* (New York: Avenel Books, 1981)

Simpson, Colin, *The* Lusitania (New York: Ballantine Books, 1972)

Stafford, David, *Churchill and Secret Service* (New York: Overlook Press, 1997)

Stewart, A. T. Q. (editor), *Michael Collins: The Secret File* (Belfast: Blackstaff Press, 1997)

Wilkinson, Burke, *The Zeal of the Convert: The Life of Erskine Childers* (Sag Harbor, New York: Second Chance Press, 1985)

mG 9/03

M

16/02